J. Huff Jones

# MIRIAM MONFORT:

## *A NOVEL.*

BY THE AUTHOR OF

"THE HOUSEHOLD OF BOUVERIE."

"Fancy, *with* fact, is just one fact the more."

"Let this old woe step on the stage again,
Act itself o'er anew for men to judge;
Not by the very sense and sight indeed,
Which take at best imperfect cognizance.
Since, how heart moves brain, and how both move hand,
What mortal ever in entirety saw?
Yet helping us to all we seem to hear,
For, how else know we save by worth of word?"
BROWNING, "*The Ring and the Book.*"

NEW YORK:
D. APPLETON AND COMPANY,
549 & 551 BROADWAY.
1873.

## DEDICATION.

---

*This book is dedicated to the memory of one most dear, who saw it grow to completion with pleasure and approbation, during the last happy summer of a life since darkened by misfortune. Peace be his!*

*MONFORT HALL.*

"Not one friend have we here, not one true heart;
We've nothing but ourselves."

"There's a dark spirit walking in our house,
And swiftly will the destiny close on us.
It drove me hither from my calm asylum;
It lures me forward—in a seraph's shape
I see it near, I see it nearer floating—
It draws, it pulls me with a godlike power,
And, lo, the abyss! and thither am I moving;
I have no power within me—but to move."

"He is the only one we have to fear, he and his father."

COLERIDGE'S *Translation of Schiller's "Wallenstein."*

# MIRIAM MONFORT.

## PART I.

## *MONFORT HALL.*

### CHAPTER I.

My father, Reginald Monfort, was an English gentleman of good family, who, on his marriage with a Jewish lady of wealth and refinement, emigrated to America, rather than subject her and himself to the commentaries of his own fastidious relatives, and the incivilities of a clique to which by allegiance of birth and breeding he unfortunately belonged.

Her own family had not been less averse to this union than the aristocratic house of Monfort, and, had she not been the mistress of her own acts and fortune, would, no doubt, have absolutely prevented it. As it was, a wild wail went up from the synagogue at the loss of one of its brightest ornaments, and the name of "Miriam Harz" was consigned to silence forever.

Orphaned and independent, this obloquy and oblivion made little difference to its object, especially when the broad Atlantic was placed, as it soon was, between her and her people, and new ties and duties arose in a strange land to bind and interest her feelings.

During her six years of married life, I have every reason to believe that she was, as it is termed, "perfectly happy," although a mysterious disease of the nervous centres, that baffled medical skill either to cure or to name, early laid its grasp upon her, and brought her by slow degrees to the grave, when her only child had just completed her fifth year.

My father, the younger son of a nobleman who traced his lineage from Simon de Montfort, had been married in his own estate and among his peers before he met my mother. Poor himself (his commission in the army constituting his sole livelihood), he had espoused the young and beautiful widow of a brother officer, who, in dying, had committed his wife and her orphan child to his care and good offices, on a battle-field in Spain, and with her hand he had received but little of this world's lucre. The very pension, to which she would have been entitled living singly, was cut off by her second marriage, and with habits of luxury and indolence, such as too often appertain to the high-born, and cling fatally to the physically delicate, the burden of her expenses was more than her husband could well sustain.

Her parents and his own were dead, and there were no relatives on either side who could be called upon for aid, without a sacrifice of pride, which my father would have died rather than have made. He was nearly reduced to desperation by the circumstances of the case, when, fortunately perhaps for both, she suddenly sickened, drooped, and died, in his absence, during her brief sojourn at a watering-place, and all considerations were lost sight of at the time, in view of this unexpected and stunning blow—for

Reginald Monfort was devoted, in his chivalric way, to his beautiful and fragile wife, as it was, indeed, his nature to be to every thing that was his own. Her very dependence had endeared her to him, nor had she known probably to what straits her exactions had driven him, nor what were his exigencies. Perhaps (let me strive to do her this justice, at least), had he been more open on these subjects, matters might have gone better. Yet he found consolation in the reflection that she had been happy in her ignorance of his affairs, and had experienced no strict privation during their short union, inevitably as this must later have been her portion, and certainly as, in her case, misery must have accompanied it.

Her child, in the absence of all near relatives, became his charge, and the little three-year-old girl, her mother's image, grew into his closest affections by reason of this likeness and her very helplessness. Two years after the death of his wife, he espoused my mother, a bright and beautiful woman of his own age, with whom he met casually at a banker's dinner in London, and who, fascinated by his Christian graces, reached her fair Judaic hand over all lines of Purim prejudice, and placed it confidingly in his own for life, thereby, as I have said, relinquishing home and kindred forever.

A hundred thousand pounds was a great fortune in those days and in our then modest republic, and this was the sum my parents brought with them from England—a heritage sufficiently large to have enriched a numerous family in America, but which was chiefly centred on one alone, as will be shown.

My father, a proud, shy, fastidious man, had always been galled by the consciousness of my mother's Israelitish descent, which she never attempted to conceal or deny, although, to please his sensitive requisitions, she dispensed with most of its open observances. That she clung to it with unfailing tenacity to the last I cannot doubt, however, from memorials written in her own hand —a very characteristic one—and from the testimony of Mrs. Austin, her faithful friend and attendant—the nurse, let me mention here, of my father's little step-daughter during her mother's lifetime, and her brief orphanage, as well as of his succeeding children.

Stanch in his love of church and country, we, his daughters, were all three christened, and "brought up," as it is termed, in the Episcopal Church, and early taught devotion to its rites and ceremonies. Yet, had we chosen for ourselves, perhaps our different temperaments might, even in this thing, have asserted themselves, and we might have embraced sects as diverse as our tastes were several. I shall come to this third sister presently, of whom I make but passing mention here. She was our flower, our pearl, our little ewe-lamb—the loveliest and the last—and I must not trust myself to linger with her memory now, or I shall lose the thread of my story, and tangle it with digression.

With my Oriental blood there came strange, passionate affection for all things sharing it, unknown to colder organizations—an affection in whose very vitality were the seeds of suffering, in whose very strength was weakness, perhaps in whose very enjoyment, sorrow. I have said my mother died of an insidious and inscrutable malady, which baffled friend and physician, when I was five years old. She had been so long ill, so often alienated from her household for days together, that her death was a less terrible evil, less suddenly so, at least, than if each morning had found her at her board, each evening at the family hearth, and every hour, as would have been the case in health, occupied with her children.

My father's grief was stern, quiet, solitary; ours, unreasonable and noisy, but soon over as to manifestation. Yet I must have suffered more than I knew of, I think, for then occurred the first of those strange lethargies or seizures that afterward returned at very unequal intervals during my childhood and early youth, and which roused my father's fears about my life and intellect itself, and gave me into the hands of a physician for many years thereof, vigorous, and healthy, and intelligent otherwise as I felt, and seemed, and *was*.

It was soon after the first settling down of tribulation in our household to that flat and almost unendurable calm or level that succeeds affliction, when a void is felt rather than expressed, and when all outward observances return to their olden habit, as a car backs slowly from a switch to its accustomed grooves, that a new face appeared among us, destined to influence, in no slight degree, the happiness of all who composed the family of Reginald Monfort.

It was summer. The house in which we lived was partly finished in the rear by wide and extensive galleries above and below, shaded by movable *jalousies;* and, on the upper one of these, that on which our apartments opened, my father had caused a hammock to be swung, for the comfort and pleasure of his children. With one foot listlessly dragging on the floor of the portico so as to propel the hammock, and lying partly on my face while I soothed my wide-eyed doll to sleep, I lay swaying in childish fashion when I heard Evelyn's soft step beside me, accompanied by another, firmer, slower, but as gentle if not as light. I looked up: a sweet face was bending over me, framed in a simple cottage bonnet of white straw, and braids of shining brown hair.

The eyes, large, lustrous, tender, of deepest blue, with their black dilated pupils, I shall never forget as they first met my own, nor the slow, sad smile that seemed to entreat my affectionate acquaintance. The effect was immediate and electric. I sat up in the hammock, I stretched out my hands to receive the proffered greeting, and then remained silently, child-fashion, surveying the new-comer.

"Kiss me," she said, "little Miriam. Have they not told you of me? I am Constance Glen—soon to be your teacher."

"Then I think I shall learn," I made grave reply, putting away the thick curls from my eyes and fixing them once more steadily on the face of the new-comer. "Yes, I *will* kiss you, for you look good and pretty. Did my mother send you here?"

"She is a strange child, Miss Glen," I heard Evelyn whisper. "Don't mind her—she often asks such questions."

"Very natural and affecting ones," Miss Glen observed, quietly, and the tears sprang to her violet eyes, at which I wondered. Yet, understanding not her words, I remembered them for later comprehension; a habit of childhood too little appreciated or considered, I think, by older people.

She had not replied to my question, so I repeated it eagerly. "Did my dear mother send you to me?" I said. "And where is she now?

"No, tender child! I have not seen your mother. She is in heaven, I trust; where I hope we shall all be some day—with God. *He* sent me to you, probably—I fancy so, at least.

"Then God has got good again. He was very bad last week—very wicked; he killed our mother," whispering mysteriously.

"He is never bad, Miriam, never wicked; you must not say such things—no Christian would."

"But I am *not* a Christian, Mrs. Austin says; only a Jew. Did you ever hear of the Jews?"

Evelyn laughed, Mrs. Austin frowned, but Miss Glen was intensely grave, as she rejoined:

"A Jew may be very good and love God. That is all a little child can know of religion. Yet we must all believe God and His Son were one." The last words were murmured rather than spoken—almost self-directed.

"Is His Son a little boy, and will he be fond of my mother?" I asked. "Will she love him too? Oh, she loved me so much, so much!" and, in an agony of grief, I caught Miss Glen around the neck, and sobbed convulsively on her sympathetic breast. Again Evelyn smiled, I suppose, for I heard Miss Glen say, rebukingly:

"My dear Miss Erle, you must not make light of your little sister's sufferings. They are very severe, I doubt not, young as she is. All the more so that she does not know how to express them."

Revolving these words, I came later to know their import. They seemed unmeaning to me at the time, but the kind and deprecating tone of voice in which they were conveyed was unmistakable, and that sufficed to reassure me.

"And now, Miriam, let me go to my room and take off my bonnet and shawl, for I am going to stay with you. Perhaps you will show me the way yourself," she said, pausing. "Bring Dolly, too;" and we walked off hand-in-hand together to the large, commodious chamber

Mrs. Austin pointed out as that prepared for our governess. I recognized my affinity from that hour.

There, sitting on her knee, with her gentle hand on my hair, and her sweet eyes fixed on mine, I learned at once to love Miss Glen, or "Constance," as she made us call her, because her surname seemed over-formal. She wished us to regard her as an elder sister, she said, rather than mere instructress, deeming rightly that the law of love would prove the stronger and better guidance in our case, and understanding well, and by some fine magnetic sympathy as it appeared, my own peculiar nature, to which affection was a necessity.

Ours was a peaceful and happy childhood under her gentle and fostering rule; and, when it ceased, all the wires of life seemed jangled and discordant again.

She lived with us three years as friend and teacher. At the end of that time her vocation and sphere of action were enlarged, not changed, for she married my father, and thus our future welfare seemed secured.

Alas for human foresight! Alas for affection powerless to save! Alas for the vanity of mortal effort to contend with Fate!

Our home was in one of the chief Northern cities of that great republic which has for so many years commanded the admiration, respect, and wonder, of the whole world. The house we occupied was situated in the old and fashion-forsaken portion of the city. From its upper windows a view of the majestic Delaware and its opposite shores was afforded to the spectator; and the grounds surrounding the mansion were spacious for those of a city-house, and deeply shaded by elms that had been lofty trees in the time of General Washington.

Four squares farther on, the roar of commerce swelled

and surged, in storehouse and counting-room, on mart and shipboard and quay; but here all was quiet, calm, secluded, as in the country, miles beyond.

Two houses besides our own shared the whole square between them, though ours, the central one, possessed the largest inclosure, and was the finest residence of the three, architecturally speaking; and the inmates of these dwellings, with very few exceptions, constituted for years our whole circle of friends and visitors.

So it will be seen how secluded was the life we led, how narrow the sphere we moved in, despite our acknowledged wealth, which, with some other attributes we possessed, had not failed, if desired, to confer on us both power and position in the society we shunned rather than shared.

To my father's nature, however, retirement was as essential as routine. He was one of those outwardly calm and inwardly excitable and nervous people we sometimes encounter without detecting the fire beneath the marble, the ever-burning lamp in the sarcophagus, unless we lift the lid of rock to find it—an effort scarcely worth the making in any case, for at best it lights only a tomb.

Extremely mild and self-contained in manner, and chary of opinion and expression, he was at the same time a man of strong and implacable prejudices and even bitter animosities when once engendered. I do not think his affections kept pace with these. He loved what belonged to him, it is true, in a quiet, consistent way, and his good breeding and practised equanimity were alone sufficient to secure the peace, and even happiness, of a household; but of much effort or self-sacrifice I judge him to have been incapable.

He was a handsome man in his stiff and military way

—well made, tall, commanding in figure and in demeanor, stately in movement. His features were regular, his teeth and hair well preserved, especially the first, his hands and feet aristocratically small and shapely, his manner vaguely courteous. He was a shy rather than reserved person, for, when once the ice was broken, his nature bubbled over very boyishly at times, and his confidence, once bestowed, was irrevocable. Like most men of his temperament, he was keenly susceptible to deferential flattery, and impatient of the slightest infraction of his dignity, which he guarded punctiliously at all points. It was more this disposition always to wait for overtures from others, and to slightly repel their first manifestations, from his inveterate shyness, than any settled determination on his part, that made him such an alien from general association. Nervous, fastidious, exacting—what had he in common with the texture of the new society in which he found himself, and what right had he to fancy himself neglected where the "go-ahead" principle alone was recognized, and time was esteemed too precious to waste in ceremony?

Yet this injured feeling pursued him through life and made one of his peculiarities, so that he drew more and more closely, as years passed on, into his own shell, which may be said to have comprised his household, his comforts, his hobbies, and his narrow neighborhood, in which he was idolized, and the sympathy of which was very soothing to his fastidious pride.

Nothing so fosters haughtiness and egotism as a sphere like this, and it may be doubted whether the crowned heads of the world receive more adulation from their households than men so situated.

From the moment he set his foot on the threshold of

his own house, nay, on the broad, quiet pavement of his own street, with its stately row of ancient Lombardy poplars on one side, and blank, high-walled lumber-yard on the other, he felt himself a sovereign—king of a principality! king of a neighborhood!—what great difference is there, after all?

It was only the hypochondriacal character of his mind that shielded him from that chief human absurdity, pomposity. He needed all the praise and consolation his friends could bestow simply to sustain him—no danger of inflation in his case! He was shut away from self-complacency (the only vice to which virtue is subjected) by the melancholy that permeated his being, and which was probably in his case an inheritance—constitutional, as it is said to be with things.

Perhaps it will be well to give, in this place, some more vivid idea of our home, which, after all, like the shell of the sea-fish, most frequently shapes itself to fit the necessities and habits of its occupants.

Our house had been built in early times, and was essentially old-fashioned, like the part of the city in which it was situated. My father, soon after his arrival in America, had fancied and purchased this gloomy-looking gray stone edifice, with its massive granite steps (imported at great cost, before the beautiful white-marble quarries had been developed which abound in the vicinity of, and characterize the dwellings of, that rare and perfect city), and remodelled its interior, leaving the outside front of the building, with its screens of ancient ivy, untouched and venerable, and changing only the exterior aspect of the back of the mansion. Very striking was the contrast between the rear and front and exterior and interior of "Monfort Hall," as it was universally called.

The dark panel-work within had all been rent away, to give place to plaster glossy as marble, or fine French papers, gilded and painted, or fresco-paintings done with great cost and labor, and indifferent success. The lofty ceilings and massive walls formed outlines of strength and beauty to the large and well-ventilated apartments, which made it easy to render them almost palatial by the means of such accessories and appliances as wealth commands, and which were lavished in this instance.

The back of the house was, however, truly picturesque. Here a bay window was judiciously thrown out; there a portico appended or hanging balcony added to break the gray expanse of wall or sullen glare of windows; and a small gray tower or belfry, containing a clock that chimed the hours, and a fine telescope, rose from the octagon library which my father had built for his own peculiar sanctum after my mother's death, and which formed an ell to the building. The green, grassy, deeply-shadowed lawn lay behind the mansion, sloping down into a dark, deep dell, across which brawled a tiny brook long since absorbed by the thirsty earth thrown out from many foundations of stores and tenements and great warehouses hard by; a dell where once roses, lilacs, guelder-globes, and calacanthus-bushes, grew with a vigor that I have nowhere seen surpassed.

It was not much the fashion then to have rare garden-flowers. Our conservatory contained a fair array of these, but we had beds of tulips, hyacinths, and crocuses, basking in the sunshine, and violets and lilies lying in the shadow such as I see rarely now, and which cost us as little thought or trouble in their perennial permanence, whereas the conservatory was an endless grief and care, although superintended by a thoroughly-taught English gardener, and kept up at unlimited expense.

My sister—for so I was taught to call Evelyn Erle—revelled in this floral exclusiveness, but to me the dear old garden was far more delightful and life-giving. I loved our sweet home-flowers better than those foreign blossoms which lived in an artificial climate, and answered no thrilling voice of Nature, no internal impulse in their hot-house growth and development. What stirred me so deeply in April, stirred also the hyacinth-bulb and the lily of the valley deep in the earth—warmth, moisture, sunshine and shadow, and sweet spring rain—and the same fullness of life that throbbed in my veins in June called forth the rose. There was vivid sympathy here, and I gave my heart to the garden-flowers as I never could do to the frailer children of the hot-house, beautiful as they undeniably are.

"Miriam has really a *vulgar* taste for Nature, as Miss Glen calls it," Evelyn said one day, with a curl of her slight, exquisite lip as she shook away from her painted muslin robe, the butter-cups, heavy with moisture and radiant with sunshine, which I had laid upon her knee. "She ought to have been an Irish child and born in a hovel, don't you think so, papa?" and she put me aside superciliously. Dirt and Nature were synonymous terms with her.

My father smiled and laid down his newspaper, then looked at me a little gravely as I stood downcast by Evelyn.

"You *are* getting very much sunburnt, Miriam, there is no doubt of that. A complexion like yours needs greater care for its preservation than if ten shades fairer. Little daughter, you must wear your bonnet, or give up running in the garden in the heat of the day."

"I try to impress this on Miriam all the time," said Mrs. Austin, coming as usual to aid in the assault, "but she is so hard-headed, it is next to impossible to make her mindful of what I tell her. Miss Glen is the only one that seems to have any influence over her nowadays." She said this with a slight, impatient toss of the head, as she paused in her progress through the room with a huge jar of currant-jelly, she had been sunning in the dining-room window, poised on the palm of either hand, jelly that looked like melted rubies, now to be consigned to the store-room.

"Well, well, we must have patience," was the rejoinder. "She is young—impulsive (I wish she were more like you, Evelyn, my dear!), her mother over again in temperament, without the saving clauses of beauty and refinement; these she will never attain, I fear, and with much of the characteristic persistence of that singular race, which in my wife, however, I never detected, though so much nearer the fountain-head!" This was said half in soliloquy, but Evelyn replied to it as if it had been addressed to her—replied, as she often did, by an interrogatory.

"What tribe did her mother belong to, papa?"

"The tribe of Judah, I believe, my love, was that her family traced their lineage from; but you question as if it were Pocahontas there was reference to instead of a high-bred Jewish lady!" speaking with asperity.

"I meant no offence, papa, I assure you," said Evelyn, quietly; "I only asked for information. Certainly there *is* something very grand in being related to King David."

"There is, indeed," said a gentle voice close at hand. Miss Glen had entered silently as they were speaking.

"There was genius in that strain of blood, Evelyn, nay, more, divinity. Christ claimed such descent. Let us never forget that! He, the universal brother." She spoke with feeling and dignity, and led me away, lecturing me greatly as she did so for not obeying Mrs. Austin as to the sun-bonnet bondage, which she promised to make as light as possible by purchasing for me a new French contrivance called a *calèche*, light and airy and sheltering all at once.

I was seven years old then, and the understanding was complete between us that endured to the end, but as yet there was no foreshadowing of her marriage with my father.

She had been engaged, when she came to us, to a gentleman, who must have perished at sea soon afterward—a young naval officer who had gone out on board of the United States sloop-of-war Hornet, the fate of which vessel is still wrapped in mystery, though that it foundered suddenly seemed then, as now, the universal opinion. Miss Glen some time before had made up her mind to this, and was stemming a tide of grief with great fortitude and resolution, while she was laying the foundations of character and education in her two very opposite pupils, both of whom she guided with equal ability.

My father was not unaware of her sufferings. I think, indeed, this community of sorrow first attracted him toward her, and later he was confirmed in his admiration of her womanly self-control and beauty of character, by the development he saw in his children, the work of her hand. That he was ever profoundly in love with her I do not believe, nor did she pretend to any passionate regard for him. Respect, friendship, confidence, mutual esteem, were the foundations of their union, which certainly promised enduring happiness to all concerned, and which was looked on with favor by the whole household, not excepting Mrs. Austin herself.

"If any successor of your dear mother *must* come, Evelyn," I heard her say one day to my sister, "we had better have her we know, to be sure, than a mere stranger, but I *must* say I can't see why your papa does not content himself as he is. I am sure he seems very happy in his library and his greenhouse, and driving out in his Tilbury, or with you two young ladies in the coach of afternoons, and chatting and smoking of evenings with Mr. Bainrothe or old Mr. Stanbury. I should think he might have had enough of marrying by this time, and funerals and all that. Your own precious mamma first, an earl's own daughter (Evelyn Erle, never forget that, if your father *was* a poor soldier! you have grand relations in England, child, if you are not as rich as some others I could name), and then your mother and Miriam's, Miss Harz that was, such an excellent woman for all her persuasion, to be sure; better than some Christians, I must say; and she just three years and a half laid in her grave!" A doleful sigh gave emphasis to this remark. "I was never more surprised, I must confess, than when he sent for me last night to tell me he was to marry Miss Glen next week! Who is she, I wonder, Evelyn; did you ever hear her speak of her kinfolks? Not a soul except two or three of her church-people has been near her since she has been here, and Franklin says she very seldom gets letters." A pinch of snuff emphasized this remark.

"I heard her say she had only one brother, Mrs. Austin, and that he was in some distant part of the world, in India, or New Orleans, or some such place, she does not know herself exactly where. He is a young lad, and she grieves about him; his picture is most beautiful, I think. He ran off and went to sea, and it almost killed her. That was some years ago, and since then she has been teaching in a great school until she came to us, and was never so peaceful before, she says, as she is now. I think she will make papa happy too, and keep him in his own family, since she has none of her own. I was so afraid it was Mrs. Stanbury at one time."

"I never thought of that," said Mrs. Austin, starting. "What put it into your head, Evelyn, and what made you so close-mouthed about it? Child, you have an old head on young shoulders—I always said so; as like your own precious mother as two peas. Yes, that would have been a nice connection truly! The two young Stanburys forsooth, to divide every thing with you and Miriam, and her rigid economy the rule in the house, and Norman riding over every one on a high horse, and that lame brat to be nursed and waited on! Any thing better than that, Evelyn. You are right, my dear." And she tapped her suggestive snuffbox.

My elder sister was about thirteen years old when she uttered those oracular sentences which elicited Mrs. Austin's commendations, and her own clear-sighted *prévoyance;* and I, at eight, whose mind was turned to any subject save that of marrying and giving in marriage, stood confounded by her superior wisdom and discretion. I gazed upon her open-mouthed and wide-eyed as she spoke, drinking in every word, yet very little enlightened, after all, by her remarks. She turned suddenly upon me, and tapped my cheek slightly with her fan. It was a way she had of manifesting contempt.

"Now run and tell Mrs. Stanbury every word I have spoken, just as soon as you can, Miriam, do you hear?

Don't forget one syllable, that's a darling. Come, rehearse!"

"Won't it do after dinner, sister Evelyn?" I asked, gravely and literally. "I want to go and see about my mole, now—my poor mole that Hodges wounded with his spade this morning. It suffers so dreadfully!"—clasping my hands in a tragic manner, not unusual with me when excited.

"There! what did I tell you, Mrs. Austin? You will believe my report of Miriam another time—little blab! There is nothing safe where she is, and as to keeping a secret, she could not do it if her own life were at stake, I verily believe."

"I *can* keep a secret," I said, fiercely, "you know I can! You burnt my finger in the candle to make me tell you where the squirrel was, and I would not do it. Now, miss, remember that, and tell the truth next time!"

"What a little spit-fire," said Evelyn, derisively.—"You see for yourself, Mrs. Austin."

"O Evelyn, Evelyn, did you do that?" moaned the good woman. "Your little sister's hand! To burn it so cruelly, and in cold blood. I would not have believed it of you, my Evelyn—that was not like your mamma at all," and she shook her head dolefully. "Miriam is a brave child, after all." A wonderful admission for her to make.

"If you believe every thing that limb of the synagogue tells you, Mrs. Austin, you will have a great deal to swallow, that is all I shall say on the subject," and she turned away derisively.

"Do you mean to deny it, then, Evelyn Erle?" asked Mrs. Austin, earnestly, laying her hand on her arm, and shaking her slightly as she was about to leave the room.

"Come back and answer me. I hope Miriam is only angry—I hope you did *not* do this thing."

"I will not be forcibly detained by any old woman in America," said Evelyn, struggling stoutly, "nor questioned either about a pack of fibs. Miriam knows better than to tell such stories—or ought to be taught better."

"It was no story," I said, solemnly. "It was true. You did burn my finger, and begged me not to tell Constance or papa afterward, and I never told them, because I never break my word if I can help it, and I wouldn't have told Mrs. Austin (but I didn't *promise* about her, you know), only you twitted me so meanly, and made me so mad—and it all came out. For I can keep a secret! I know where that squirrel is now, Evelyn Erle, but I will never tell any one—never—not even Constance Glen. I promised myself that, and crossed my heart about it when you tried to cut off its tail—its pretty, bushy tail that God gave it to keep the flies off with."

Mrs. Austin was shedding tears by this time; Evelyn's insolence and duplicity had stung her to the quick, and she saw, with real concern, that I had justice on my side. She had relinquished her hold on Evelyn, who stood now sullenly glaring at me, pale as a sheet, her eyes white with rage, looking like heated steel, her lips trembling with passion.

"You *shall* tell me where that squirrel is, or I will appeal to papa," she said, sharply. "It was mine. Norman Stanbury said so when he brought it here and gave it to me. You heard him, little cheat!"

"He told me to feed it, and take care of it, and not let it get hurt, if he did give it to you," I replied, doggedly, "and I did what he told me. You are a born tyrant, Evelyn. Constance told you so a month ago,

2

when you twisted Laura Stanbury's arm for not teaching you that puzzle; and there is a wicked word I know that suits you to-day, only I am afraid to say it—Constance would be angry—but it begins with an L and ends with an R, and has only four letters in it. There, now!"

I well deserved the slap, no doubt, that rang down with such lightning speed and force on my cheek, and, fortunately, Mrs. Austin arrested my panther-like spring toward Evelyn, or the nails I held in rest might have brought blood from her waxen face, and marred its symmetry for a season. As it was, I screamed wildly, until Miss Glen came in, attracted by my cries, and, receiving no satisfactory explanation as to their cause, led me to her own apartment to compose, question, and rebuke me in that firm but gentle manner that ever calmed my spirit like oil poured upon troubled waters. The end of the matter was that, when I met Evelyn again, I went up to her in a spirit of conciliation, and mutely kissed her as a sign of peace and penitence.

It was a matter of indifference to me that this advance was carelessly received, since it satisfied my conscience and her who stirred its depths—nor did my cheek flush at the derisive taunt that followed me from the room after this obligation to self was discharged—"Now tattle again, little prophetess," for thus she often alluded to my Hebrew name and its signification, "and produce my squirrel, or look well to your wounded mole!"

This threat was not without its effect. In a deep, leafy covert I concealed my poor dying patient, "earthy, and of the earth"—literally, in every sense—but the squirrel still enjoyed its sequestered home on the topmost branch of an English walnut-tree, from which it cheerfully, but cautiously, descended at my call when I went out to carry it almonds or filberts from the dessert (invariably served with wine to my father, who, in observance of his English custom, sat alone some moments after the ladies of his household had withdrawn from table), nor did Evelyn have the despotic pleasure of abbreviating his right of tail.

## CHAPTER II.

My father's marriage was solemnized very quietly in that old gray church with its fairy chime of bells, all alive on that occasion, which stood in the busy street not far from our quiet house. An aged and reverend bishop, who had administered the sacred communion to Washington and his wife when the city we dwelt in had been the temporary residence of that chief, performed the ceremony, which, with the exception of my father's immediate household and neighbors, none were invited to witness. When the solemn rite was ended, I made my way to Constance, so fair that day in her pearl-gray robes and simple white bonnet, and clasped her hand. She stooped down and kissed me many times, to conceal her tears, probably.

"Call me mamma now, dearest," she said, at last; "and let the name be as a new compact between us. Now let Evelyn come to me, my love, she, too, is my daughter; and go with Mrs. Austin."

I did as she directed, grasping Mrs. Austin's hand tightly as we walked home, and proceeding at so brisk a pace that she was often obliged to check me.

"Poor child, why should you rejoice so?" she said, mournfully. "Don't you know you have lost your father from this hour? Do you suppose he will ever love you as well again—you or Evelyn? Poor, ignorant, sacrificed babes in the woods!"

"I don't care," I said. "I have got my new mamma to love me, even if he does not. 'Mamma—mamma Constance!' how pretty that sounds. Oh, that is what I shall always call her from this time—'Constance,' as usual, you know, with 'mamma' before it." And I kept repeating "mamma Constance," childishly.

"Foolish thing," she rejoined. "I wish you had your sister Evelyn's consideration; but at any rate," she murmured, "the money will be all yours. He cannot alienate that; yours by marriage contract, not even to divide with Evelyn, and" (elevating her voice) "that you will surely do hereafter, will you not, Miriam?"

"I don't know," I replied; "not unless she is good to me and stops calling me 'little Jew,' and other mean, disagreeable names. But I always thought Evelyn was the rich one until now. She has so many fine clothes, and such great relations, you say, in England."

"True, true, gentle blood is a fine heritage; but your mother had great store of gold, and, when your papa dies, all this will belong to you (it is time you should know this, Miriam), and you will have us all to take care of and support; so you must be very good, indeed."

"I am so sorry," I said, with a deep sigh and a feeling that a heavy burden had been thrown suddenly on my shoulders; "but I tell you what I will do" (brightening up), "I will give it every bit to mamma, and she will support us all. She will live much longer than papa, because she is so much younger—twenty years, I believe. Isn't that a great difference?

"Your father will outlive me, child, I trust, should such a state of things ever come to pass; but I am old, and shall not cumber the earth long," and a groan burst from her lips.

"How old *are* you, Mrs. Austin?" I asked, with a feeling of awe creeping over me, as though I had been talking to the widow of Methuselah, and I looked up into her face, pityingly.

"Fifty-five years old, child, come next Michaelmas, and a miserable sinner still, in the eyes of my Lord! I was a widow when I went to hire with Mrs. Erle, Evelyn's lady mother—that was soon after she married the captain, who had only his sword—and I have lived with her and hers ever since, and served them faithfully, I trust, and I hope I do not deserve to be cast on strangers and upstarts in my old age, even if one of them happens to marry your father. Constance Glen, forsooth!" and she drew up her stiff figure.

"To be wicked and old must be *so* dreadful," I said, thoughtfully shaking my head and casting my eyes to heaven.

"What are you thinking about, child?" she asked, jerking my hand sharply. "Who is it that you call such hard names—'wicked and old' forsooth? Answer me directly!"

"It was what you said a while ago about yourself I was thinking of, Mrs. Austin," I replied. "To be more than half a hundred years old! It is so many years to live; and then to be such a sinner, too—how hard it must be! I always thought you were very good before; and I am sure you are not gray and wrinkled and blear-eyed, like Granny Simpson!"

"Granny Simpson, indeed! You must be crazy, Miriam Monfort! Why, she is eighty if she is an hour, and hobbles on a cane! I flatter myself I am not infirm yet;

and, if you call a well-preserved, middle-aged, English woman, like me, *old*, your brains must be addled. Look at my hair, my teeth, my complexion "—pausing suddenly before me and confronting me fiercely. "See my step, my figure, and have more sense, if you *are* a little foreign Jewish child. As to sinfulness, we are all *sinful* beings, more or less. To be *wicked* is a very different thing from sinful. I never told you I was wicked, child. What put that into your head?"

"Oh, I thought they were the same thing. Which is the worst, Mrs. Austin?" I asked, with unfeigned simplicity.

"There, Miriam, step on before! you walk too fast anyhow for me to-day. Besides, your tongue wags too limberly by half. You always did ask queer questions, and will to your dying day. No help for it, I suppose, but patience; but it is all of that Gipsy blood! Now, Evelyn's line of people was altogether different. She has what they used to call in England 'blue blood in her veins;' do you understand, Miriam? Blue blood! Catch her asking indiscreet questions! Take pattern by your elder sister, Miss Miriam Monfort, and you will do well."

Not knowing what evil I had done, or how I had offended, or how blood could be *blue*, yet sorry for having erred, I made my way as I was told to do, speedily and silently homeward, and was glad to find shelter from all misunderstanding and persecution in the arms and shadow of my "mamma Constance," as I called her from that hour.

But, to Evelyn she was "Mistress Monfort," from the time she espoused my father; and the coldness between them (they were never very congenial) was apparent from that time, in spite of every effort on the part of my sweet mamma to surmount and throw it aside.

It is time I should speak of those few neighbors who composed our society at this period, and to whom some allusion has already been made—the occupants of those two houses which, as I have said, divided with ours the square we lived in, with their grounds. These green-shaded yards were divided one from the other by slender iron railings, which formed a line of boundary, no more, and presented no obstacle to the exploring eye. Graceful gates of the same material opened from the pavement, common to all, and presented a symmetrical and uniform appearance to the passer-by. Stone lions guarded ours, but Etruscan vases crowned the portals of Mrs. Stanbury and Mr. Bainrothe, filled with blooming plants in the summer season, but bare and desolate and gray enough in winter.

Mrs. Stanbury, our right-hand neighbor (ay, in every way right-handed), was a widow lady of about thirty-five years of age. Her husband had been a sea-captain, and, being cut off suddenly, had, with the exception of the house she lived in, left her no estate. She owed her maintenance chiefly to the liberality of his uncle, a gruff old bachelor of sixty or more, who lived with and took care of her and her children in a way that was both kindly and disagreeable. He was a bald-headed man (who flourished a stout, gold-headed cane, I remember), with a florid, healthy, and honest face and burly figure, engaged in some lucrative city business, and entirely devoted to his nephew and niece, Mrs. Stanbury's only children, the one fifteen and the other about twelve years old at the time of my father's marriage.

Strangely enough, her own deepest interest, if not affection, seemed centred at this period in her little orphan ward and nephew, George Gaston, a child of nine years old, who had recently come into her hands; singularly gifted and beautiful, but lamed for life, it was feared, and a great sufferer physically from the effects of the fatal hip-disease that had destroyed the strength and usefulness of one limb, and impaired his constitution.

Mrs. Stanbury herself was a lady-like and pretty woman, fair and graceful, and her daughter Laura closely resembled her; both sweet specimens of unpretending womanhood; both devoted to the discharge of their simple duties and to one another; both entirely estimable.

Norman Stanbury was of a different type. He had probably inherited from his father his manly and robust person, his open, dauntless, dark, and handsome face, in which there was so much character that you hardly looked for intellect, or perhaps at a brief glance confounded one with the other. He was the avowed and devoted swain of my sister Evelyn, from the time when they first chased fireflies together, up to their dancing-school adolescence, and for me maintained a disinterested, brotherly regard that was never slow to manifest itself in any time of need, or even in the furtherance of my childish whims. Our relations with this family were most friendly and agreeable. There never was any undue familiarity; my father's reserve, and their own dignity, would of themselves have precluded that certain precursor to the decline of superficial friendship; but a consistent and somewhat ceremonious intercourse was preserved from first to last, that could scarcely be called intimacy.

Between George Gaston and myself alone existed that perfect freedom of speech and intuitive understanding that lie at the root of all true and deep affection. His delicacy of appearance, his stunted stature, his invalid requisitions, nay, his very deformity, for his twisted limb amounted to this, put aside all thought of infantile flirtation (for we know that, strange as it may seem, such a thing does exist) from the first hour of our acquaintance. He always seemed to me much younger than he was, or than I was—as boys, even under ordinary circumstances, are apt to appear to girls of their own age, from their slower development of mind and manner, if not of body.

But this lovely waxen boy, so frail and spiritual as to look almost angelic, and certainly very far my superior intellectually, seemed from his helplessness peculiarly infantile in comparison with my robust energy, and became consequently, in my eyes, an object of tenderest commiseration. From the first he clung to me with strange tenacity, for our tastes were congenial. He brought with him from his Southern home stores of books and shells and curious playthings and mechanical toys, such as I had never seen before, and to spread these out and explain them for my amusement was his chief delight.

My memory in turn was richly stored with poetry, some of it far above my own comprehension, but clinging irresistibly to my mind through the music of the metre. I had revelled in old ballads until I could recite nearly all of these precious relics of heroic times, or rather chant them forth monotonously enough in all probability, yet in a way that riveted his attention forcibly, and roused his high-strung poetic temperament to enthusiasm.

When ill or suffering, if asked what he needed for relief, he would say "Miriam," as naturally as a thirsty man would call for a glass of clear cold water. For his amusement I converted myself into a mime, a mountebank. When I went to the theatre, the performance must be repeated for his benefit, and many characters centred in one.

For him I danced the "Gavotte," the "shawl-dance," as taught to do by Monsieur Mallet, at the great dancing-school on Chestnut Street, or jumped Jim Crow to his infinite amusement and the unmitigated disgust of Evelyn, to whom his physical infirmity made him any thing but attractive. Such personal perfection as she possessed is, I am afraid, apt to make us cold-hearted and exacting as to externals in others. Evelyn could endure commonplace, but could not forgive a blemish. Once Norman Stanbury came very near losing her favor for having a wart on his finger; another time, she banished him from her presence for weeks, for having stained his hands, beyond the power of soap-and-water or vinegar to efface, in gathering walnuts. Certainly no despot ever governed more entirely through the medium of fear than did she through the tyranny of a fastidious caprice united to a form and face of surpassing beauty and high-bred grace.

Even my father fell under this requisitive influence of hers. Propriety, the quality he worshipped, stood forth enshrined in her, and, from the lifting of her fan to the laying down of her knife and fork, all was faultless. The prestige, too, of birth, his special weakness, lingered about her, and elevated her to a pedestal above any other inmate of his household.

Her mother, who married him for convenience, and whose selfish requisitions had almost driven him mad, was the honorable Mrs. Erle, and an earl's daughter. He had loved my mother twice as well, found her ten times more attractive and interesting, devoted and congenial; admired her grace, recognized all her worth, not only in deed but in word, and with a fidelity of heart that never wavered even when he married again. Yet the prestige of descent was wanting in her and hers, or rather, such as it was, brought with it ignoble and repulsive associations *only*. He was not the man to reach a hand across Shylock and the old-clothes man, to grasp that of the poet-king of Israel; or Esther, the avenging queen of a down-trodden nation; or Joab, strong in valor and fidelity; or Deborah, inspired to rule a people from beneath the shelter of her palm-tree in the wilderness.

The grandeur of the past, in his estimation, was eclipsed by the ignominy of the present; but with me it was otherwise, and, as I grew old enough to recognize the peculiar traits of that ancient people from which I sprung, it pleased me to imagine that whatever there was about me of fiery persistency, of fearless faith, of unshrinking devotion, nay, of bitter remembrance of injuries, and power to avenge or forgive them, as the case might be, sprang from that remarkable race who called themselves at one time, with His permission, the chosen children of God.

I think these very characteristics of mine repelled my father and jarred on his nervous temperament, endangering that outward calm which it was his pride and care to preserve as necessary to high-bred demeanor, and thus intrenching on his ideas of personal dignity. Yet, with strange inconsistency, it was her very indulgence of these peculiarities that inclined him most strongly to Constance Glen, and finally, I am well convinced, determined him on making her his wife, as one well suited to secure the welfare of his turbulent and incomprehensible child, his "rebellious Miriam," as he sometimes called me when milder words availed not.

He had, as I have said, an "English" horror of scenes and excitement of any kind. He was conservative in every way. He believed in the British classics, and would not admit that any thing could ever equal, far less surpass them (dreary bores that many of them are to me!). Walter Scott's novels were the only ones of later days he ever allowed himself to read approvingly; for, once being beguiled, against his will almost, into sitting up late at night to finish a new work called "Pelham," he frowned down all allusion to the book or its author ever afterward, as derogatory to his dignity.

"Bulwer and Disraeli are literary coxcombs," he said, "who ought not to be encouraged, and who are trying to undermine wholesome English literature."

"O father," I ventured to observe on one occasion, "'Vivian Grey' is splendid. It is a delightful dream, more vivid than life itself; it is like drinking champagne, smelling tuberoses, inhaling laughing-gas, going to the opera, all at one time, and, if you once take it in your hand, nothing short of a stroke of lightning could rend it away, I am convinced. Do read it, sir, to please me, and retract your denunciation."

"Never," he said firmly, solemnly even, "and I counsel you, Miriam, in turn, to seek your draughts of soul from our pure 'wells of English undefiled,' rather than such high-flown fancies and maudlin streams as flow from the pen of this accomplished Hebrew. There is a little too much of the Jeremiah and Isaiah style about such extracts as I have seen, to suit my taste."

"The idea of a Jew writing novels!" said Evelyn, derisively as she sipped her wine.

"Or the grandest poem in the world!" added Mr. Bainrothe, who was dining with us that day, coming to the rescue quite magnanimously as it seemed, and for once receiving as his recompense a grateful look from the stray lamb of the tribe of Judah, reposing quietly in a Christian fold.

"What poem do you allude to?" said Evelyn, superciliously. 'Paradise Lost?'—Oh, I thought Milton was a Unitarian, not quite a Jew; almost as bad though!"

"No, the book of Job," replied Mr. Bainrothe. "It was that I alluded to."

"And the Psalms," I added, breathlessly.

"Dear me," said Evelyn, "what an array of learning we have all at once! Why, every Sunday-school child knows about the Psalms. David and Solomon did nothing else but sing and dance, I believe."

"Irreverent, very, Evelyn," said my father, looking at her a little severely, in spite of his own "Jeremiah" and "Isaiah" allusions. I had never heard him check her so openly before, and enjoyed it thoroughly. My smile of approbation provoked her, I suppose, for she pursued:

"I am so tired of having the Bible thrown at my head; you must excuse me, papa. For my part, I find the New Testament all-sufficient. I weary of the horrors of those Jews; worse than our Choctaw Indians, I verily believe."

"So they were, so they were, my dear," said my father, complacently, "but for some reasons we must always treat their memory with a certain respect. They were God's people, remember, in the absence of a better, and their history is written in this book, which we must all revere."

"A very great people, surely," said Mr. Bainrothe, "and destined to be so again. Don't you think so, Miriam?"

"I don't know," I said; "I have never thought of such a possibility before, I acknowledge, yet it is natural

I should incline to my mother's people, and I can say heartily, *I hope so*, Mr. Bainrothe."

"Then you want to see the Christian religion trampled under foot," said Evelyn, spitefully, fixing her eyes on mine.

The blood rose hotly to my temples. "No, no, indeed! You know I do not, Evelyn, for it is mine; but Christ died for all, Jew as well as Gentile. Through him let us hope for change and mercy and peace on earth. When infinite harmony prevails, the Hebrew race will find its appointed place and level again, through one great principle."

"My idea is, that it has found its appointed place and level, and will abide there.—But to digress, when do you expect your son, Mr. Bainrothe?"

I have anticipated by many years in giving this snatch of conversation here. Let us go back to the time of my father's marriage, and to affairs as they stood then, for precious are the unities.

I need not drop Mr. Bainrothe, however, and it was of him, our left-hand neighbor, so intimately connected with our destiny, one and all, that I was about to speak when the digression occurred which led me from the high-road of my story.

Our "sinister neighbor," as my father laughingly called him sometimes with unconscious truth, in reference to his *left-hand* adjacency, was a handsome and gentlemanly-looking man of no very particular age, or rather in his appearance there was no criterion for decision on this subject. His form was as slender and elastic, his step as light, his teeth, hair, and complexion, as unexceptionable as though he had been twenty-five; nor were there any of those signs and symptoms about him by which the weather-wise usually measure experience and length of days.

If care had come nigh him at all, it had swept as lightly past him as time itself. His address was invariably urbane, self-possessed, well-bred; his voice was pleasant, his smile rather brilliant, though it never reached his eyes, except when he sneered, which was rarely and terribly.

They glittered then with a strange cold light, those variegated orbs, but their ordinary expression was earnest and investigatory. They were well-cut eyes, moreover, of a yellowish-brown color, and I used to remark as a little child—for children observe the minutiæ of personal peculiarities much more closely than their elders—that the iris of both orbs was speckled with green and golden spots, which seemed to mix and dilate occasionally, and gave them a decidedly kaleidoscopic effect.

His skin was clear and even florid, and his lips had the peculiarity of turning suddenly white, or rather livid, without any evident cause. This my father thought betokened disease of the heart, but I learned later to know it was the only manifestation of suppressed feeling which the habit of his life could not overcome, and that proved him still mortal and fallible.

He had bought and moved into the house he occupied, in his single estate, with a few efficient servants, soon after my father had taken possession of his own larger mansion, and it was not long before the best understanding existed between these two. My father's *hauteur* was no safeguard against the steady and self-poised approaches—his shyness found relief in the calm self-reliance of his "left-hand" neighbor; and, as they were both lovers of books, rather than students thereof, a congeniality of tastes on literary subjects drew them together in those hours of leisure which Mr. Bainrothe usually passed in his own or my father's library, in the cultivation of the *dolce far niente* —I beg pardon—his mind.

What his occupation was, if indeed he had any worthy of a definite name, I never knew. That he was a kind of intermediate agent or broker I have since suspected. His leisure seemed infinite. He came and went to and from the business part of the city several times a day, and often in the elegant barouche he kept, with its span of highly-groomed horses and respectable-looking negro driver in simple livery—an old retainer of his house, as he informed my father, faithful still, though freed in the time of universal emancipation.

His association was undoubtedly, to some extent, with the best men of the town—bankers and merchants chiefly; and once, when my father had called in a considerable sum of money which he had loaned out at interest on good mortgages, for a term of years, he was so obliging as to interest the most notable bankers of the city in its safe and prompt reinvestment.

This gentleman dined with us on one occasion at this period, when his conference with my father intrenched on our late dinner-hour, and I shall never forget the singular beauty of his face and expression, nor the charm of his manner, as he sat at our board discoursing, with an *abandon* and witchery I have observed in no one else, on subjects of art and letters, on men and manners, of nations past and present, until hours fled like moments, and time seemed utterly forgotten in the presence of geniality and genius. Then, starting gayly and suddenly to his feet, he remembered an engagement, and sped away so abruptly that his visit seemed to me but a vision breaking in on the monotony of our lives, too bright to have been lasting.

Afterward, invitations came repeatedly to my father, for his grand dinners and *levées*, from this potentate, for he *was* a prince and a leader in those days of a society that, more than any other I have known, requires such leadership to make its conventionalities available; but these were not accepted, though appreciated and gratefully acknowledged. Nor could Mr. Bainrothe, with all his influence over him (that rare influence that a worldly and efficient man wields over a shy and retiring one unacquainted with the detail of affairs, and dependent upon active assistance in their management), prevail upon him to break through the monotonous routine of his life so far as to accept any one of them. His church, the theatre, when a British star appeared, his hearth and home—these were my father's hobbies and resources. Travel and society abroad he equally shrank from and abjured, or the presence of strange guests in his household circle.

"I will change all this, when I grow up, Mrs. Austin," I heard Evelyn say, one day. "We shall have parties and pleasures then, like other people, and, instead of masters and tedious old church humdrums, Mr. Lodore and the like, you shall see beaux and belles dashing up to this out-of-the-way place; and I will make papa build a ballroom, and we shall have a band and supper once a month. You know he can afford any thing he likes of that sort, and as for me—"

"Child, it will never be," she interrupted, shaking her head gravely. "Mr. and Mrs. Monfort" (my father was again married then) "are too much wedded to their own ways for that, and, besides, you and Miriam will not be ready to go out together, and the money is all hers—

don't forget that, my dear Evelyn, and *you* must go back to England to your own, and I—"

"That I will never do," she in turn interrupted haughtily. "Play second fiddle, indeed, to mamma's grand relations, mean, and proud, and presumptuous, I dare say, and full of scorn for me (a poor army-captain's daughter), as they were for my father? No, I shall stay here and shine to the best of my ability. The money is all papa's while he lives, and he is still a young man, you know, and Miriam's turn will come when mine is over. One at a time, you see. Good gracious! it would seem like throwing away money, though, to dress up that little dingy thing in pearls and laces. Ten to one but what she will marry that lame imp next door as soon as she is grown, and endow him with the whole of it—that 'little devil on two sticks,' and I must have my run before then, of course." She laughed merrily at the conceit.

"I hear you, Evelyn Erle," I exclaimed tragically from the balcony on which I sat, engaged, on this occasion, in illuminating, with the most brilliant colors my paint-box afforded, a book of engravings for the especial benefit of George Gaston. It was his private opinion that Titian himself never painted with more skill, or gorgeous effect, than the youthful artist in his particular employ. "I hear you, miss, and you ought to be ashamed of yourself to talk so behind his back, of a poor, afflicted boy like George, too good, a thousand times too good, to marry any one, even Cinderella herself. 'The devil on two sticks,' indeed!"

"Don't preach, I pray, Miriam. You have quite a dispensation in that way lately, I perceive. If you *must* eavesdrop, keep quiet about it now and hereafter, I beg."

"I was not eavesdropping," I screamed. "I have

been painting out here all the afternoon, and Mrs. Austin knows it, and so might you. You are always accusing me of doing wrong and mean things that I would cut off my"—hesitating for a comparison—"my curls rather than do. Let me alone!"

"Your curls, indeed!" and she came out of the window and stood on the balcony beside me. "Do you call those tufts your curls?" taking one of them disdainfully with the tips of her dainty fingers, then pulling it sharply. "They make you look like a little water-dog, that's what they do, and I am going to cut them off at once. —Bring me the scissors, Mrs. Austin, and let me begin."

In the struggle that ensued my paints were upset, my pallet broken, and my book drenched with the water from the glass in which I dipped my brushes, but, as usual, Evelyn gained the victory which her superior strength insured from the beginning, and fled from my wrath, after holding my hands awhile, laughingly entreating mercy.

"I will kill her some day, Mrs. Austin, if she persecutes me so," I cried, as I lay sobbing on the bed after the conflict was over. "I am afraid of myself sometimes when she tantalizes me so dreadfully. I am glad you held me when I got hold of the scissors; I am glad she held me afterward. I might—I might"—I hesitated —"have stabbed her to the heart," was in my mind, but the tragic threat faltered upon my lips.

"Pray to God, Miriam Monfort, to subdue your temper," said the well-meaning but injudicious nurse, solemnly. "Your sister is old enough to make sport with you whenever she likes, without such returns."

"I wish mamma was at home," I said, still sobbing. "She would not allow me to be so treated; but it is always the way—as soon as she turns her back, Evelyn besets me, and you look on and encourage her."

"I do no such thing," said Mrs. Austin, sharply. "You have no business to take up cudgels for every outsider that your sister mentions, as you do. She is afraid to speak her mind before you, for fear of a fuss."

"I hate deceit," I said, wiping my eyes; "and deceitful people, too. I love my friends behind their backs the same as to their faces—just the same."

"What makes you mock Mr. Bainrothe then, and show how he minces at table, and uses his rattan?" she asked.

"Mr. Bainrothe is not my friend; besides, I said no harm of him. I don't love him, and never will, and he knows it."

"Were you rude enough to tell him so, Miriam?"

"No, but he understands very well. I never mimic any one I love."

"Yet you love that rough, old Mr. Gerald Stanbury, as cross as a cur. What taste!"

"Yes, from my heart I love him. He is good, he is true, he is noble; that is what he is. He has no specks in his eyes. He does not say, 'Just so,' whenever papa opens his lips."

"O Miriam! not to like him for that!"

"No; that is just why I *don't* like him. He has no mind of his own—or maybe he has two minds. Mamma thinks so, I know."

"She has told you so, I suppose?"

"If she had, I would not talk about it. No, she never told me so. I found it out myself. I know what she thinks, though, of every one, just by looking at her."

"Then what does she think of me?" asked Mrs. Austin, sharply.

"That you are a good, dear old nurse," I said, with a sudden revulsion of feeling, jumping up and throwing my arms about her; "only a little, very little, bit fonder of Evelyn than me. But that is natural. She is so much prettier and older than I am, and takes better care of her clothes. Besides, I am cross about dressing, I know I am; and afterward I am always so sorry."

"My Miriam always had a good heart," said Mrs. Austin, quite subdued, and returning my embraces. "And now let me call Charity to wash and comb and dress you before your mamma comes home. You know she always likes to see you looking nicely. But soon you must learn to do this for yourself; Charity will be wanted for other uses."

"I know, I know," I cried, jumping up and down; "Evelyn told me all about it yesterday," and the flush of joy mounted to my brow. "Won't we be too happy, Mrs. Austin, when our own dear little brother or sister comes?" And I clasped my hands across my bare neck, hugging myself in ecstasy.

"I don't know, child; there's no telling. What fingers" (holding them up wofully to the light); "every color of the rainbow! That green stain will be very hard to get out of your nails. How careless you are, Miriam! But, as I was saying, there's no telling what to expect from an unborn infant. It's wrong to speculate on such uncertainties; it's tempting Providence, Miriam. In the first place, it may be deformed, I shouldn't wonder—that lame boy about so much—short of one leg, at least."

"Deformed! O Mrs. Austin! how dreadful! I never thought of that." And I began to shiver before her mysterious suggestions.

"Or it may be a poor, senseless idiot like Johnny

Gibson. *He* comes here for broken victuals constantly, you know, and your mamma sees him."

"Mrs. Austin, don't talk so, for pity's sake," catching at her gown wildly; "don't! you frighten me to death."

"Or it may be (stand still directly, Miriam, and let met get this paint off your ear)—or it may be, for aught we know or can help, born with a hard, proud, wicked heart, that may show itself in bad actions—cruelty, deceit, or even—" she hesitated, drearily.

"Mrs. Austin, you *sha'n't* say such things about that poor, innocent little thing," I cried out, stamping my foot impatiently, "that isn't even born."

"Well, well; there's no use rejoicing too soon, that's all I mean to say. And why *you* should be glad, child, to have your own nose broken, is more than I can see," with a deep and awful groan.

"For pity's sake, stop! I *am* glad, I *will* be glad, there now! as glad as I please, just because I know mamma will be glad, and papa will be glad, and George Gaston will be glad, and because I do so adore babies, sin or no sin; I can't help what you think; I say it again, I *do* adore them. No, I ain't afraid of 'God's eternal anger' at all for saying so; not a bit afraid. What does He make them so sweet for if He does not expect us to love them dearly—His little angels on earth? Whenever a baby passes here with its nurse, I run after it and stop it and play with it as long as I can; and oh, I wish so often we had one of our own here at home!" embracing myself again with enthusiasm.

"Evelyn is right; you are a very absurd child, Miriam," she said, smiling, in spite of her efforts to keep grave; "very silly, even."

"And you are a very foolish, dear old nurse, and you

*will* love our baby, too, won't you now?" clasping her also, zealously.

"Be still, child—here comes Charity. She will think you crazy to be rumpling my cap in that way, and talking about such matters. You are getting to be a perfect tomboy, Miriam! What would your papa say if he could see you now, so dirty and disorderly—your papa, as neat as a pink always?—Charity, what kept you so long to-day? Be quick and get Miss Miriam's new cambric dress, and her blue sash, and her new, long, gray kid gloves, and her leghorn hat, and white zephyr scarf. She is going to drive out presently with her mamma and papa, and must look decent for once in a while." After a pause she continued: "Miss Evelyn was dressed an hour ago, and is ready at the gate now, with her leghorn flat on and her parasol in her hand, I'll be bound," looking from the window. "There comes Norman Stanbury home from school. That's the idea, is it?" and the good nurse looked grave. "It will never do, it will never do in the world," she said, as she glanced at them, then turned away, shaking her head dolefully. "My child, my pretty piece of wax-work, must do better than that comes to. Her blood must never mix with such as runs in the veins of the Stanbury clan."

About a month later the feeble wail of my little sister greeted my ear as I entered my mamma's room one morning, in obedience to her summons, and my heart was filled with a rapture almost as great as hers who owned this priceless treasure.

Three weeks later, very suddenly and most unexpectedly, my dear mamma was stricken mortally as she sat, apparently quite convalescent, in her deep chair by the cradle, smiling at and caressing her infant. Mrs. Austin and I were alone in the room with her; papa and Evelyn had gone out for a walk. I had just been thinking how very pretty she looked that day in her white wrapper, with a pink ribbon at the throat, and her little, closely-fitting lace cap, through which her rich brown hair was distinctly visible. She had a fine oval face, clear, pallid skin, and regular though not perfect features, and never appeared so interesting or beautiful as now, in the joy and pride of her new maternity. Suddenly she grew strikingly pale, gasped, stretched out her hands, fixed her imploring eyes on me, and fell back, half fainting, in her chair.

By the time we had placed her on her bed she was insensible, breathing hard, though with a low fluttering pulse, that kept hope alive until the doctor came. The moment he beheld her he knew that all was over; remedies were tried in vain. She never spoke again, and, when my father returned an hour later, a senseless mass of snow replaced the young wife he had left, happy and hopeful.

I was spared the first manifestations of his agony, in which disappointment and the idea of being pursued by a relentless fate bore so great a part, by my own condition, which rendered me insensible for nearly thirty hours, to all that passed around me. It was afternoon when I awoke, as if from a deep sleep, to find myself alone with Mrs. Austin in my chamber.

Except from a sense of lassitude I experienced no unpleasant sensations, and I found myself marveling at the causes that could have consigned me in health to my bed and bed-gown, to my shadowed chamber and the supervision of my faithful nurse, when the sound of suppressed yet numerous footsteps in the hall below met my ear, and the consciousness that something unusual was going on took possession of and quickened my still lethargic faculties.

"What does all this mean, Mrs. Austin?" I asked at last, in a voice feeble as an infant's, "and what are those steps below? Why am I so weak, and what are you doing here? Answer me, I beseech you," and I clasped my hands piteously.

"Eat your panada, Miriam, and ask no questions," she said, lifting a bowl from above a spirit-lamp on the chimney-piece, and bearing it toward me. "Here it is, nice and hot. The doctor said you were to take it as soon as you awoke."

I received eagerly the nourishment of which I stood so greatly in need, spiced and seasoned as it was with nutmegs and Madeira wine, and, as I felt new strength return to me with the warmth that coursed through my veins, the memory of all that had passed surged rapidly back, as a suspended wave breaks on the strand, and with the shock I was restored to perfect consciousness.

"I know what it all means now," I cried. "Mamma! mamma! Let me go to my poor mamma!" and before she could arrest my steps I flew to the head of the stairway, dressed as I was in my white bed-gown, and was about to descend, when Dr. Pemberton stopped my progress.

"Go back, Miriam; I must see you a moment before you can go down-stairs," he said, calmly, and with authority in his voice. "Nay, believe me, I will not restrain you a moment longer than necessary, if you are obedient now."

"Do you promise this?" I cried, sobbing bitterly.

"I do," and he led me gently back to Mrs. Austin,

then examined my pulse, my countenance carefully, inquired if I had taken nourishment, gave me a few drops from a vial he afterward left on the table for use, and, signifying his will to Mrs. Austin, went calmly but sorrowfully from the room.

My simple toilet was speedily made. My dress consisted of a white-cambric gown, I remember, over which Mrs. Austin bound, with some fantastic notion of impromptu mourning, a little scarf of black *crèpe*, passing over one shoulder and below the other, like those worn by the pall-bearers; and, so attired, she took me by the hand and led me, dumb with amazement and grief, through the crowd that surged up the stairs and in the hall and parlors below, into the drawing-room, where, on its tressels, the velvet-covered coffin stood alone and still open, its occupant waiting in marble peace and dumb patience for the last rites of religion and affection to sanctify her repose, ere darkness and solitude should close around her forever.

The spell that had controlled me was rent away, when I saw that sweet and well-beloved aspect once again fixed in a stillness and composure that I knew must be eternal, the tender eyes sealed away from mine forever, the fine sensitive ear dull, expression obliterated! I flung myself in a passion of grief across the coffin. I kissed the waxen face and hands a thousand times and bathed them with scalding tears, then stooping down to the dulled ear I whispered:

"Mamma! mamma! hear me, if your soul is still in your breast, as I believe it is; I want to say something that will comfort you: I want to promise you to take care of your little baby all my days and hers, to divide all I have with her—to live for her, to die for her if such need comes—never to leave her if I can help it, or to let any one oppress her. Do you hear me, Mamma Constance?"

"What are you whispering about, Miriam?" said Mrs. Austin, drawing me away grimly.

"There, did you see her smile?" I asked, as in my childish imagination that sweet expression, that comes with the relaxation of the muscles to some dead faces toward the last of earth, seemed to transfigure hers as with an angel grace. "Her soul has not gone away yet," I murmured, "she heard me, *she believed me*," and I clasped my hands tightly and sank on my knees beside the coffin, devoutly thanking God for this great consolation.

"Child, child, you are mad," she said, drawing me suddenly to my feet. "Come away, Miriam, this is no place for you; I wonder at Dr. Pemberton! That coffin ought to be closed at once, for decay has set in; and there is no sense in supposing the spirit in the poor, crumbling body, when such signs as these exist," and she pointed to two blue spots on the throat and chin.

I did not understand her then—I thought they were bruises received in life—and wondered what she meant as well as I could conjecture at such a time of bewilderment; but still I resolutely refused to leave my dear one's side, sobbing passionately when Mr. Lodore came in to take me away at last, in obedience to Dr. Pemberton's orders.

"Come, Miriam, this will never do," he said. "Grief must have its way, but reason must be listened to as well. You have been ill yourself, and your friends are anxious about you; if your mamma could speak to you, she would ask you to go to your chamber and seek repose.

Nay, more, she would tell you that, for all the thrones of the earth, she would not come back if she could, and forsake her angel estate."

"Not even to see her baby?" I asked, through my blinding tears. "O Mr. Lodore, you must be mistaken about that; you are wrong, if you are a preacher, for she told me lately she valued her life chiefly for its sake; and I heard her praying one night to be spared to raise it up to womanhood.—Mamma! mamma! you would come back to us I know, if God would let you, but you cannot, you cannot; He is so strong, so cruel! and He holds you fast." And I sobbed afresh, covering up my face.

"Miriam, what words are these?—Mr. Monfort, I am pleased that you have come. It is best for your little daughter to retire; she is greatly moved and excited;" and, yielding to my father's guidance and persuasion, I went passively from the presence of the dead, into which came, a moment later, the hushed crowd of her church-people and our few private friends, assembled to witness her obsequies.

Evelyn Erle accompanied my father to the grave as one of the chief mourners, and at my entreaty Mrs. Austin laid my little sister on the bed by my side, and I was soothed and strengthened by the sight of her baby loveliness as nothing else could have soothed and strengthened me.

Then, solemnly and in my own heart, I renewed the promise I had made the dead, and as far as in me lay have I kept it, Mabel, through thy life and mine!

I roused from an uneasy sleep an hour later, to find George Gaston at my side.

"I have brought you this, Miriam," he said, "because

I thought it might help you to bear up. It is a little book my mother loved; perhaps you can read it and understand it when you are older even if you cannot now. See, there is a cross on the back, and such a pretty picture of Jesus in the front. It is for you to *keep* forever, Miriam. It is called Keble's 'Christian Year.'"

"Thank you, George," and I kissed him, murmuring, "But I do not think I shall ever read any more," tearfully.

He, too, begged to see the baby for all recompense—his darling as well as mine thenceforth; and I recall to this hour the lovely face of the boy, with all his clustering, nut-brown curls damp with the clammy perspiration incident to his debility, bending above the tiny infant as it lay in sweet repose, with words of pity and tenderness, and tearful, steadfast eyes that seemed filled with almost angelic solicitude and solemn blessing.

Two guardians of ten years old then clasped hands above its downy head, and in childish earnestness vowed to one another to protect, to cherish, to defend it as long as life was spared to either. Hannibal was not older than we were when he swore his famous oath at Carthage, kneeling at the feet of Hamilcar before the altar, to hate the Romans. How was our oath of love less solemn or impressive than his of hatred?—pledged as it was, too, in the presence of an angel too lately freed from earth's bondage not to hover still around her prison-house and above the sleeping cherub she left so lately!

Such resolutions, however carried out, react on the character that conceives them. I felt from that time strengthened, uplifted, calmed, as I had never felt before. I learned the precious secret of patience in watching over that baby head, and for its sake grew forbearing to all around; toward Evelyn, even, whose taunts were so hard to bear, so unendurable on occasions.

"There is a great change in Miriam," she said one day to Norman Stanbury. "I believe she is getting religion, or perhaps she and George Gaston are training themselves to go forth as married missionaries, after a while, to the heathen. They are studying parental responsibility already, one at the head and the other at the foot of the baby's cradle-carriage, but I am afraid it will be but a *lame* concern, after all."

We both heard this cruel speech and the laugh that succeeded it, in passing by, as it was intended we should do, probably—heard it in silence, and perhaps it may be said in dignity, not even a remark being interchanged between us concerning it; but I saw George Gaston flush to the roots of his hair.

A few minutes later we were ourselves laughing merrily over the baby's ineffectual efforts to catch a bunch of scarlet roses which George dangled above her head, and, altogether forgetful of Evelyn's sneer, bumped our heads together in trying to kiss her.

In truth, my superb sense of womanhood lifted me quite above all frivolous suggestions; thenceforth George seemed to me physically almost as much of a baby as Mabel, and was nearly as dependent on my aid. In his sudden fits of exhaustion and agony of such uncertain recurrence as to render it dangerous for him to venture forth alone, he always turned with confidence to my supporting and guiding hand.

I taught him his lessons in the intervals of my own studies, which he recited when he could to a private teacher, the same who gave me lessons.

Evelyn preferred a public school, and was sent, at her

own request, to a fashionable establishment in the city attended by the *élite* alone, as the enormous prices charged for tuition indicated, as a day-boarder. There she became proficient in mere mechanical music—her ear being a poor one naturally—and learned to speak two languages, dance to perfection, and conduct herself like a high-bred woman of fashion on all occasions and in all emergencies—each and all necessities for a belle, which, it may be remembered, she had aspired to be, and announced her intention of becoming.

The fame of my father's wealth, her own beauty, tact, and grace, and elegant attire, rendered her conspicuous among her school-mates, and from among these she selected as friends such as appeared to her most desirable as bearing on her future plans of life. So that already Evelyn had made for herself a sphere outside and beyond any thing known in "Monfort Hall" or its vicinity.

My father, who, like all shy persons, admired cool self-possession and the leading hand in others, looked on with quiet approbation and some diversion at these proceedings. He gave her the use of his equipage, his house, his grounds, reserving to himself only intact the refuge of his library, from which ark of safety he surveyed at leisure, with quiet, curious, and amused scrutiny, the gay young forms that on holiday occasions glided through his garden and conservatory, and filled his drawing-room and halls with laughter and revelry.

On such occasions I was permitted, on certain conditions, to appear as a spectator. One of the most imperative of these was, that I was never to reveal to any one that Evelyn was not my own half-sister.

"You are not called upon to tell a story, Miriam, only to give them no satisfaction. You see they might as well think part of all this wealth, which came from your mother, is mine. It will in no way affect the reality —only their demeanor—for they every one worship money."

"I would not care for such girls, sister Evelyn, nor what they thought," I rejoined. "Besides, are you not an earl's granddaughter; why not boast of that instead, which would be the truth?"

"An earl's fiddlestick! What do you suppose American girls would care for that? Nor would they believe it, even, unless I had diamonds and coronet and every thing to match. Your mother had diamonds, I know, but mine had not. By-the-by, where are they, Miriam? I have never seen them."

"I do not know, Evelyn," I replied, gravely. "I have never thought about them until now. I am so sorry your heart is set upon such things. You know what Mamma Constance used to tell us."

"Oh, yes, I remember she croaked continually, as all delicate, doomed people do, I believe. It was well enough in her case, as she *had* to die; but, as for me—look at me, Miriam Monfort! Do I look like death? No; victory, rather!" and she straightened her elastic form exultingly. "And you, too, little one, are growing up strong and tall and better-looking than you used to be," she continued, patting my cheek carelessly. "The Jewish gaberdine is gradually dropping off; I mean the dinginess of your early complexion. By the time I have had my successful career, and am settled in life, yours will begin. Help me now, and I will help you then."

"You are only a school-girl," I said, sententiously. "You had better be thinking of your lessons, and let beaux and diamonds alone. I would be ashamed to keep a key to my exercises and sums, as you do. I would blush in the dark to do such a thing."

"I am not preparing myself for a governess, that I should make a point of honor of such things, little pragmatical prig that you are; nor are you, that I know of. You will always have plenty of money. 'Rich as a Jew' is a proverb, you know, all the world over."

The taunt had long since lost its sting; so I replied, meekly:

"We none of us know what may happen. I should like to be able to support myself and Mabel, if the worst came. Old Mr. Stanbury says all property is uncertain nowadays, especially in this country."

"Oh, don't repeat what that old croaking vulgarian and general leveller and democrat says, to me! A democrat is my aversion, anyhow. I wonder papa can tolerate that coarse old Jackson man in his sight. 'Adams and the Federal cause forever,' say I; and all aristocratic people are on that side. I never enjoyed any thing so much as our illumination when Mr. Clay gave his casting vote, and carried Congress. The Stanbury house was as dark as a grave that night; but Norman was in our interest, and I made him halloo 'Hurrah for Adams!' That was a triumph, at all events. It nearly killed the old gentleman, though."

"If I were a man, *I*, too, would vote for General Jackson," I said, defiantly. "He was such a brave soldier; he could defend our country if it was attacked again. Besides, I like his face better than old moon-faced Adams; and I despise Norman for his time-serving."

"Miriam, I shall tell papa if you utter such sentiments again; you know how devoted he is to the Federal party, and you ought to be ashamed of yourself."

"That is just because Mr. Bainrothe over-persuaded him. He used to admire General Jackson. I heard him say once, myself, he would be the people's choice, next time."

"I thought you accused Mr. Bainrothe of toadying papa. Where, now, is your boasted consistency?"

"Evelyn, you know very well that is the way to rule and toady papa. Yield to him apparently, and he will let you lead him and have your own way pretty much. You have found that out long ago, Evelyn." And I looked at her sharply, I confess. She colored, but did not reply. "There is more," I said. "A girl who would be ashamed of her own mother, and afraid to acknowledge her poverty, would not scruple to do this. I believe you are almost as great a humbug at heart as Mr. Bainrothe himself," and I smiled scornfully. "That is what *some* people call him."

She turned on me with cold, white eyes and quivering lips; she shook me by the shoulder until my teeth chattered and my hair tossed up and down like a pony's mane blown by the winds, with her long, nervous fingers.

"Inform on me if you dare," she said, "or utter such an opinion to papa, and I will make you and your baby both suffer for it, and that lame hop-toad too, who follows you everywhere like your shadow! Moreover, if you do breathe a syllable of this slander, I shall tell Mr. Bainrothe your opinion of him, and make *him* your enemy. And mark me, Miriam Monfort, precious Hebrew imp that you are, you could not have a direr one, not even if you searched your old Jewish Bible through and through for a parallel, or called up Satan himself. I shall tell papa, too, that you are a story-teller, so that he will never again believe one word that you say, miss!"

"You could not convince him of that," I said, disengaging myself from her grasp, "if you were to try, for I have honest eyes in my head, not speckled like a toad's back, nor turning white with rage like a tree-frog laid on a window-sill; but, if you ever dare to lay your hand on me again, Evelyn Erle, I will tell papa *every thing*—there, now! This is the last time, remember."

"I did not hurt you, and you know it, Miriam; I only shook you to settle your brains," and she laughed a ghastly laugh, "and to make you a little bit afraid of me."

"I am not afraid of you," I said, "that is one comfort; and you can never make me so again; and I am not a mischief-maker, that is another; so rest in peace. *Pass* for my sister if you choose, and are proud of the title; I shall not say yes or no, but of this be certain, you are no sister of mine, though I call you such, either in heart or blood. I do not love you, Evelyn Erle; and, if I were not afraid of the anger of God and my own heart, I would *let* myself hate you, and strike you. But I always try and remember what mamma said, and what Mr. Lodore tells us every Sunday. Yet I find it hard."

"Little hypocrite! little Jew!" burst from her angry lips, and she left the room in a whirl of rage, not forgetting, however, to write me a very smooth note before she went to school next morning, which was, with her usual tact, slipped under my pillow before I awoke; and, after that, all was outward peace between us for a season.

Evelyn was about sixteen when this occurred, I nearly twelve. The next year she left school and made her *début* in society, and, through her machinations, no doubt, I was sent away to a distant boarding-school for two years, coming home only at holiday intervals thereafter to my dearest baby, my home, my parent, and narrow circle of friends, and finding Miss Erle more and more in possession of my father's confidence, even to the arrangement of his papers and participation in the knowledge of his business transactions, and entirely installed as the head of the house, which post she maintained ever afterward indomitably.

Singularly enough, however, Mr. Bainrothe seemed secretly to prefer me at this period, however much he openly inclined to her, and he lost no occasion of privately speaking to me in rapturous terms (such as I never heard him employ in the presence of Evelyn and my father) of his only son, then absent in Germany engaged in the prosecution of his studies, but to return home, he told me, to remain, as soon as he had completed his majority.

It was only through our knowledge of his son's age, and his admissions as to the time of his own early marriage, that we arrived at any estimate of Mr. Bainrothe's years; for, as I have said, Time, in his case, had omitted what he so rarely forgets to imprint—his sign manual on his exterior.

## CHAPTER III.

The school to which I was sent was half a day's journey from the city of our residence, situated in a small but ancient town of Revolutionary notoriety. The river, very wide at that point, was shaded by willow-trees to some extent along its banks, immediately in front of the Academy of St. Mark's, and beyond it to a considerable distance on either hand. The town itself was an old-fashioned, primitive village rather than burgh, quaintly built, and little adorned by modern taste or improvement; but the air was fine and elastic, the water unexceptionable, and bathing and boating were among our privileged amusements. Among other less useful accomplishments, I there acquired that of swimming expertly; and, as a place of exile, this quaint town answered as well as any other for the intended purpose.

For, notwithstanding my father's assurances that Dr. Pemberton had recommended change of air—to some degree true, of course—and that he himself believed a public course of study would exhaust me less than my solitary lessons, to which I gave such undivided attention, and notwithstanding Evelyn's professions of regret at the necessity of parting with me, and Mrs. Austin's belief that the "baby was killing me by inches," since she took it into her head to sleep with no one else, and to play half the night, and to stay with me all day besides, I felt myself "ostracized."

The whole matter was so sudden that I scarcely knew what to make of it. Mr. Bainrothe alone let in a little light upon the subject by one remark, unintentionally, no doubt:

"The fact is, Miriam, you are getting too much wound up with that Stanbury family, and you would be perfectly entangled there in another year. The idea of putting the whole hardship of George Gaston's education on your shoulders was worthy of diplomatic brains, and something I should scarcely have suspected that calm, quiet little woman to have been capable of conceiving. There is an old, worn-out plantation in the Gaston family, that your money would set going again, no doubt, with accelerated velocity. Did you never suspect any thing of that sort?" he asked, carelessly.

"Never; nor did I suppose any one else was stupid or wicked enough to entertain such an idea. I, being tolerably acute, *knew* better, fortunately."

"My dear little girl, you are entirely too chivalrous and confiding where your feelings are engaged. What if I were to assure that this plan had been agitated?"

"I should think you had been deceived, or that you were deceiving me, one or the other. I should not *believe* you, that would be all. You understand me now, Mr. Bainrothe; there are no purer people than the Stanburys—I wish every one was half as good and true."

"Old Gerald at the head of them, I suppose?" with a sneer and a kaleidoscopic glance.

"Mr. Gerald Stanbury at the head of them," I reiterated firmly, adding: "These are friends of mine, Mr.

Bainrothe; it hurts and offends me to hear them lightly discussed. If I am sent away from home to break off my affection for them, the measure is a vain one, for I shall returned unchanged."

"Yes, but with enlarged views, I trust, Miriam," he rejoined, pertinaciously. "See how Evelyn was improved by her two years at school; besides, how would you ever increase your circle of acquaintances here, studying alone, or even with your shy disposition, at a day-school?"

"I am sent from home, then, to make acquaintances it seems, and to prepare for my *début* into society? Very well, I shall not forget that; but pray, what particular advantage in this respect does a country-school present?"

"Oh, the very first people send their daughters to St. Mark's. If I were training a wife for my son, I should educate her there. What higher eulogium could I bestow, or"—dropping his voice—"what higher compliment pay you, Miriam?"

"If he were a king's son, you could not speak more confidently," I rejoined, with inexcusable rudeness. "Remember, too, you are *not* training a wife for your prince in disguise." But I was annoyed and irritated by his patronizing manner, and the suspicion that took possession of me from that time, that he had aided Evelyn in this conspiracy against my peace for selfish views.

He laughed carelessly and turned away, but I saw triumph in his variegated eye; yet was I powerless to resent it.

"I am leaving my poor papa bound hand and foot," I thought, "in designing hands, but I cannot help it. He has chosen for himself, I will not entreat his affection, his confidence, misplaced as they surely are. I *cannot* do this if I would; something stronger than myself binds me to silence. But O papa, papa! if you only knew how I loved you, you would not suffer these strangers to take my place, or banish your poor Miriam so cruelly!"

"Don't let Mabel forget me," were the last words I spoke to Mrs. Austin, as with a bursting heart I turned from the lovely child I had made perhaps too much an idol; "and George, let her see George Gaston every day; it will be a comfort to both." So, choking, I went my way.

I bade Evelyn "good-by" gayly, Mr. Bainrothe superciliously, my father bitterly, for I felt his ingratitude to my heart's core; and, under dear old Mr. Stanbury's escort, went to the steamboat, there to find one of the lady principals of the academy ready to take charge of me on our brief voyage. It was not in my nature to cherish depression or to make complaints and sudden confidences, and we chatted very cheerfully all the way up the river on indifferent subjects chiefly; sharing fruit and flowers, and general observations and opinions, so that I felt quite inspirited on my arrival, and made, I have reason to believe, no unfavorable impression.

My school-girl experiences I shall not record here. They were pleasant and profitable on the whole, and I earned the esteem of my teachers, by my zeal and diligence in my studies, and made some few valued friends more or less permanent, but none so dear as those I left behind.

Laura Stanbury, quiet and uninteresting as she seemed to many, had a hold on my heart that no newer acquaintance could boast, and for dear George Gaston, where was there another like him? I have known no one so gifted, so spiritual, so simply affectionate, as this child of genius and physical misfortune, whose short but brilliant career is engraven on the annals of his country, I well believe, indelibly.

When I was fifteen years old, I was recalled suddenly and in the middle of a busy session to my home, by the severe and almost fatal illness of my father. He rallied, however, soon after my return, and I had the inexpressible satisfaction of hearing Dr. Pemberton, our good and skillful family physician, pronounce him out of danger a week later, but he would suffer me to go from him no more. The voice of Nature asserted her claim at last, and, feeling within himself that indescribable failure of vitality in which no one is ever deceived, and which can never be explained to or wholly understood by another, he desired me to remain with him through the remainder of a life which he foresaw would not be long.

It was in vain that Dr. Pemberton tried to rally him on the score of his old hypochondriacal tendencies, or that Evelyn quietly remarked: "I am sure, papa, I never saw you looking better! It is a pity to interrupt dear Miriam now in the full tide of her studies. I am sure that *I* am willing to devote every moment of my time to you if needful;" or that Mrs. Austin added: "Miriam is so well, and growing so fast, that I am afraid to see her take on care again, for fear of a check; and now that Mabel is partly weaned from her they are both happy to be separated;" or that Mr. Bainrothe carelessly interpolated: "Let the child go back, my dear Monfort, or you will spoil her again among you. She is developing splendidly at St. Mark's, and you have twenty good years before you yet, with your unbroken English constitution."

Not even the joy manifested by George Gaston and

Mrs. and Miss Stanbury, or bluff old Mr. Gerald, at the good news of my return, could shake his resolution.

"Miriam shall leave me no more while life is mine," he said, "be it long or short. When she marries, I will surrender every thing I possess, save a stipend, into her hands, and Evelyn and Mabel and I to some extent will be her pensioners thereafter. Until that time, matters will stand as they do now."

"Folly, folly, Colonel Monfort! You talk like a dotard of eighty; you, a superb-looking man yet, younger than I am, no doubt; young enough to marry again, if the fancy took you, and head a second family."

"Why not say a third?" asked my father, sadly. "Don't you know, Bainrothe, I am a fatal upas-tree to the wives of my bosom? See how it has been already."

"Better luck next time. Now, there is the Widow Stanbury, willing and waiting, you know, and a dozen others."

I turned a flashing eye upon him that silenced him.

"You know better than that," I said, in suppressed tones, hoarse with anger. "Better let that subject rest hereafter, unless, indeed, your object is feud with me. You shall not slander my friends with impunity, nor must you come any longer between me and them and my father."

I spoke for his ear alone, and waited for no reply. I understood his game by this time, as he did mine.

"His son, indeed!" I murmured, with a scornful lip, as I found myself alone. "I would cut off my right hand before I would give it to a Bainrothe," and I scoffed at him bitterly in the depths of my resentful Judaic heart.

About this time I passed through a painful trial. It was autumn, and early fires of wood had been kindled in the chambers; more, so far, for the sake of cheerfulness than warmth. Mabel was playing on the hearth of her nursery preparatory to going to bed, and I was in the adjoining room, my own chamber, making an evening toilet, for Evelyn expected a party of young visitors that night, and my presence had been requested.

Mrs. Austin, it seemed, had left the room for one moment, when a cry from Mabel brought me to her side. She had fanned the fire with her little cambric night-dress, and was already in a blaze. I caught Mrs. Austin's heavy shawl from the bed, and promptly extinguished the flames, but not without receiving serious injury myself. The child, with the exception of a slight but painful burn on her ankle, was unhurt, but my left arm and shoulder and bosom were fearfully burned, and for some days my life hung on a thread.

Months passed before I was able to leave my own chamber, and the blow to my health was so severe as to induce a return of those lethargic attacks from which I had been entirely free for the last two years. It is true they were brief in duration compared to those of old, but that they should exist at all was a cause of anxiety and disquietude both to my father and physician.

By the first of March, however, I was again in glowing health, and no trace remained, except those carefully-concealed scars on my shoulder, of my fearful injury.

Soon after this accident had occurred, two circumstances of interest had taken place in our household and vicinity. One of these was the return of Claude Bainrothe from abroad, and the other the rather mysterious visit of a gentleman, young and handsome, but poorly clad, who had inquired for my step-mother, Mrs. Constance Monfort, and on hearing, to his surprise and grief, apparently, that she was dead, had gone away again without requesting an interview with any other member of the family.

He had met Evelyn at the door just as she was about to step into the carriage, dressed for visiting, and had said to her, merely (as she asserted), as he turned away, evidently in sorrow:

"I am the brother of Mrs. Monfort, once Constance Glen—now, as you tell me, no more. What children did she leave?"

"One only—a daughter," was Evelyn's reply. "Not visible to-day, however, since she was severely burned a few days since, and is still confined to her bed; not dangerously ill, though."

"I passed on then, as quickly as I could," said Evelyn, "for I saw no end to questioning, and had an appointment to keep. I said, however, civilly, 'Suppose you call another time, when papa is disengaged. To-day he could not possibly receive you,' pausing on the steps for a reply. This was of course all that was required of me, but he merely lifted his hat with a cool 'Thank you, Miss Monfort,' and went his way silently. He evidently mistook me for you, Miriam, and I did not undeceive him. My greatest oversight was in forgetting to ask for his card; but his name was Glen, of course, as hers was, so it would have been a mere form."

"The whole transaction seems to have been inconsiderate on your part, Evelyn," I remarked, as mildly as I could. "Mamma's brother! Oh, what would I not have given to have seen him! Did he never return, and where is he now?"

"No, never that I know of, and he has disappeared. He walked by here a few days later, Franklin says, when he was standing at the door with papa's tilbury, still very poorly dressed, but neither stopped nor spoke. You could not have seen him in your condition, at any rate, Miriam, so you need not look so vexed; and I had no idea of having papa annoyed so soon after his severe attack. Besides, I want no such claims established over Mabel. She is ours, and need desire no other relations. The next thing would have been an application for money, or board and lodging, or some such thing, no doubt."

"How old did he seem to be, Evelyn?" I asked, conquering a qualm of feeling at these words, and inexpressibly interested in her relation.

"I'm sure I can't tell, Miriam; about twenty-five or six, I suppose; the usual age of all such bores. You know mamma was seven or eight and twenty when she died, and she said he was much younger than herself, you may remember."

"Oh, yes, I recollect perfectly. Did he resemble mamma, Evelyn? Was he tall or short, fair or dark? Had he her lovely eyes? Do tell me about him."

"None of these things. A sort of medium man; not at all like mamma, however, as far as I could see on such brief scrutiny, and as well as I remember; with fine eyes, however. Not as good-looking as Claude Bainrothe, by any means. Commonplace, very, with a seedy coat. By-the-way, Miriam, *he* will be back next week, I believe, and then you will see this phenomenon. You know Mr. Bainrothe and papa design you for one another."

"Papa, indeed! I suppose you mean Claude Bainrothe," and I laughed disdainfully, I fear. "Nay, it is you rather, Evelyn, who have captivated this piece of perfection, as far as I can learn. At least, this is the report that—" I hesitated—colored.

"Finish your sentence, Miriam. The report that your faithful spies, Laura Stanbury and George Gaston, have brought to you in your solitude. They are very observing, truly," she pursued. "Creatures that never penetrate beneath the surface, though. Self-deluders, I fancy, however, rather than story-tellers."

"Do you pretend to deny it, Evelyn? Now, look me in the eyes and say 'No' if you dare," and I grasped her slender wrists playfully. She opened her large, blue eyes and fixed them full on mine, responsively.

"*No!* Now you have the unmitigated truth. Ah, Miriam, I have no wish to interfere with you," and she leaned forward and kissed my cheek tenderly, disengaging her hands as she did so. Her manner had so changed to me of late that she was growing rapidly into my affections, and I returned her embrace cordially.

In the next moment we were laughing merrily together over the ridiculous schemes of the elder Bainrothe, so transparent that every one understood them perfectly, motive and all, and which my father winked at evidently, rather than favored or encouraged, as our charlatan thought he did—"Cagliostro," as we habitually called him.

"The fact is, prophetess, the person in question would not suit you at all, with your grand ways and notions and prospects. I have fathomed his depth pretty successfully, and I find him full of shoals and shallows. Pretty well for a flirtation, though, and to keep one's hand in, but unavailable any further."

"Having brought him to his knees, you are perfectly willing to pass him over to me as a bond-slave. Is that the idea, Evelyn?"

"Exactly, Miriam; you are always so penetrating! But don't tell, for the world. Old Bainrothe would never forgive me; and, as I once before told you in one of my savage moods, his enmity is dire—satanic!"

"I am not afraid of Cagliostro, or his animosity," I answered; "never was, Evelyn, as you know. The best way to disarm him is to confront him boldly. He is like a lion in that alone. I wish, though, he would give me a little of his elixir of life, for dear papa; he has never looked himself since that attack, though better, certainly. —oh, decidedly better, of course, than I dared to hope at one time ever to see him again. Yet I am very anxious."

"Papa is well enough, Miriam; you only imagine these things. At fifty, you know, most men begin to break a little; then they rally again and look almost as well as ever in a few years, up to sixty or seventy. Look at Mr. Lodore! He looked older when we first knew him than he does now; and so did Dr. Pemberton."

"That is because they have both filled out and grown more florid and healthy; but papa is withering away, Evelyn; shrinking day by day—his very step has changed recently. Oh, I hope, I hope I may be deceived!" And I covered my face with my hands, praying aloud, as I did sometimes irresistibly when greatly excited. "God grant, God grant us his precious life!" I murmured. "Spare him to his children!"

"Amen!" said Evelyn Erle, solemnly.

A few evenings after this conversation I went to see and hear the opera of "Masaniello," then all the rage, and at the zenith of its popularity, with Mrs. Stanbury, Laura, and George Gaston—Norman had been recently placed in the navy and he was absent now, and Mr. Gerald Stanbury obstinately refused to accompany us to that "monkey-and-parrot show," as he deliberately dubbed the Italian opera.

"When men and women who are in love or grief, or who are telling each other the news, or secrets, stop to set their words to music, and roar and howl in each other's ears, the world will be mad, and the opera natural," he said. "I will not lend my countenance before them to such a villainous travesty."

As "Masaniello" had nearly had its run, and Evelyn was disinclined to see it again, having attended during the winter about twenty representations of this great musical spectacle, I was fain to go with our neighbors and their very youthful escort, or forego my opera.

As we entered the crowded lobby, Laura and I walked together behind George Gaston and Mrs. Stanbury, dropping later into Indian file as the crowd increased, in which order I was the last. I wore a rich India shawl, that had been my mother's, caught by a cameo clasp across the bosom. Suddenly I felt the pin wrenched away and the shawl torn from my shoulders. In another moment there was a cry—a scuffle—a fall—and a prostrate form was borne away between two policemen, while a gentleman, with his cravat hanging loose and his hair in wild confusion, came toward me eagerly, extending the shawl and clasp.

"These are yours, I believe, young lady," he remarked, breathlessly, throwing the shawl about my shoulders as he spoke, and laying the broken clasp in my hand. "I am happy to restore them to you."

The whole transaction had been so sudden and so public, that there had been neither time nor room for trepidation on my part. My own party, pressing steadily on, had not yet missed me, so that, even in that moment of excitement, I surveyed my champion with an eye capable of future recognition.

"Thank you," I said. "I hope you are not hurt in my service?"

"No, no; not at all—that is, very slightly, indeed. Pass on, I will attend you safely to your seat," and, obeying the wave of his hand, I followed the direction of Mrs. Stanbury's white plume as observingly as did the followers of Henry of Navarre, without turning again until I reached the box she had entered. I was shocked then, as I bowed my thanks, at the ghastly whiteness and expression of my escort's face, but he vanished too quickly to permit of inquiry or remark at that season.

I had still time before the curtain rose to relate my adventure, which brought the blood hotly to George Gaston's brow as he listened to it.

"There it is!" he muttered. "It is all very well with me in peaceful times, but, when it comes to battle, a poor, lame wretch is of little account. I might as well be a woman;" and the tears flowed down his quivering cheeks. "It was shameful, disgraceful, that any other man should have defended you, Miriam," he added, in a broken voice, clinching his hands, "than I, your escort."

"You did not even see the affair, George," I remonstrated. "Had you been as strong as Samson, and I know you are just as brave, you could not have helped me, for there I was lagging away behind, through my own fault, and how could you, in front, between your aunt and Laura, possibly know what danger was in store for me? Now, I shall feel provoked if you show so much morbid feeling; besides, reflect, you are but a boy, dear George. No youth of your age is ever very strong."

"A boy! and what are you, Miriam Monfort, that you taunt me with youth! a woman, I suppose—a heroine!" with bitter sarcasm in his voice and eye, for the first time in his life so directed to me. I gazed at him in mute surprise.

"My dear George, you are very unreasonable, indeed," said Mrs. Stanbury. "What has Miriam done to deserve such a taunt? I never knew you to behave in such an uncourteous way before."

"You must be crazy, George Gaston," added Laura Stanbury, sharply. "Don't you know you are attracting attention toward our box. Be still directly!"

"Oh no, it is only the magnificent Miss Monfort that every one is staring at," he sneered. "The grown-up lady, the heroine, the heiress, who lingers behind in the lobby, in order to get up little melodramas of her own at the opera where such things are admissible, at the expense of her lame escort!"

I turned to him calmly; I had not spoken before. "George," I said, "if you say another word I shall go home alone, or burst into tears on the spot, and disgrace myself and you, one or the other. I cannot bear another word like this. I warn you, George Gaston!"

"Dear Miriam, forgive me; I am a fool I know," he said, as soon as he could recover himself. "Lend me your handkerchief, Laura, mine has mysteriously disappeared. There—Richard's himself again! (Sorra to him!) He ought to have a bullet through his head for his pains" (*sotto voce*).

This stroke of bathos brought about good-humor again, and soon our whole attention was absorbed in that magical music which to this hour electrifies me more than that of any other opera excepting "Norma." "Bad taste this," connoisseurs will say; but the perfection of human enjoyment is to pursue one's own tastes independently of Mrs. Grundy, whether musical, or literary, or artistic, according to my mode of thinking. In all the pauses of the opera, however, I saw that handsome and agitated face, that had last caught my eye at the box-door, rise before me like a spell; and anxiety for the safety of my strange champion—some curiosity too, mingled therewith, I do not deny, to know his name and lineage—beset me during the whole of a sleepless night and the dreaming day that succeeded it.

We were sitting around a cheerful spring fire in the front parlor, our ordinary sitting-room, opening as this did into the dining-room beyond on one hand, and the wide intersecting hall of entrance on the other, on the opposite side of which lay the long, double-chimneyed drawing-room, less cheerful than our smaller assembly-room by half, and therefore less often used (there, you have our whole first-floor arrangement now, my reader, I believe, and I must begin over again, to catch the clew of my long sentence). We were sitting, then, around the cheerful fire in the parlor in question, when Morton, my father's "own man," announced "Mr. Bainrothe and son," and a moment afterward the two gentlemen so heralded entered the room together. With one you are already somewhat familiar, reader mine, as a gentlemanly, handsome man, with deliberate movements and confident address. You have seen such men in cities frequently; but the word *distingué*, so often too hastily bestowed, was the chief characteristic of the appearance of his younger companion.

Tall, slender, graceful, strong—for strength alone bestows such easy perfection of movement, such equipoise of step as belonged to him—with a fine, clear-cut face and well-shaped head, nobly placed on his straight, square shoulders—wide for a man so slight—dark eyed, dark haired, with a mouth somewhat concealed by a long silken mustache, then an unusual coxcombry in our republic, yet revealing in glimpses superb teeth and the curve of accurately-cut lips, Claude Bainrothe stood before me, a young Apollo.

"I have brought my son here to-night, expressly to introduce him to you, Miriam, of whom he has heard so much."

He bowed low and silently, then tossed his curled head suddenly back again.

"We have met before, I believe, Mr. Bainrothe," I observed, when his eye rose to meet mine. "You were good enough to restore me my shawl and clasp last night at the opera, if I am not strangely mistaken."

"Ah! were you that lady?" he asked, with a slight yet somewhat embarrassed laugh. "Forgive me, if in the confusion of the moment I failed to remark your appearance. I only knew an outrage had been committed, and naturally sought to repair it."

"Now, that was really romantic," said Evelyn, who had caught the idea. "Miriam related her adventure, but was sorely puzzled to know to whom she was indebted for such chivalrous aid."

"I am glad to have been of service to Miss Monfort," he rejoined, deferentially, "but I merely obeyed an impulse strong with me. I should have been wanting to myself to have done otherwise than defend a helpless woman."

"There could not have been a more favorable opening to your acquaintance, certainly," observed Evelyn significantly; then, turning away and crossing the apartment, she applied herself to the entertainment of the elder Mr. Bainrothe, "Mr. Basil," as we called him after his son came, by way of distinction between the two, since the word "old" seemed invidious in his case, and we characterized them as we would have done two brothers.

Indeed, in manner, in bearing, in something of quiet repose entirely wanting in the father, and which usually seems the accompaniment of age or experience, the son seemed the elder man of the two. I had yet to learn that there is an experience so perfect and subtle that it assumes the air of ignorance, and triumphs in its simplicity over inferior craft itself.

When the mind has worked out the problems of life to its own satisfaction, like the school-boy who has proved his sums, it wipes the slate clean again and sets down the bare result—the laborious process it effaces. All is simplified.

"I was fearful that you had been hurt last night, Mr. Bainrothe," I hazarded, "from the expression of your face as I caught it at the box-door. I am glad to see you well this evening."

"I *was* hurt," he said, "to be frank with you. The scoundrel gave me a severe blow on the chest, which brought a little blood to my lips, and for the time I suffered. Had it not been for the faintness under which I was laboring I could not have failed to identify you. But you are generous enough to forgive this oversight I am convinced."

"Oh, surely! it was most natural under the circumstances. I have a habit of fixing faces at a glance that is rather uncommon, I believe. I never forget any one I have seen even for a moment, or where I have seen them, or even a name I have heard."

"A royal gift truly, one of the secrets of popularity, I believe. It is not so with me usually, though when my eye once drinks in a face" (and he looked steadily at mine while he spoke those words slowly, as if wrapped in contemplation), "it never departs again. 'A thing of beauty is a joy forever,' you know, Miss Monfort." He sighed slightly.

"Yes, that line has passed into an axiom, the only sensible one, I believe, by-the-by, that Keats ever wrote," I laughed.

"Oh, you do Keats injustice. Have you studied him, Miss Monfort?"

"Studied poetry? What an idea! No, but I have tried to read him, and failed. I think he had a very crude, chaotic mind indeed; I like more clearness."

"Clearness and shallowness most often go together," he observed. "When you see the pebbles at the bottom of a stream, most likely its waters are not deep."

"Yet, you can stir up mud with a long pole in the pool more readily than in the river. Keats wanted a current, it seems to me, to give him vitality and carry off his own mental impurities. His was a stagnant being."

"What a queer comparison," and he shook his head laughingly, "ingenious, but at fault; you are begging the question now. Well, what do you say to Shelley?"

"I have nothing to say to him; he has every thing to say to me. He is my master."

"An eccentric taste for so young a girl; and Byron? and Moore? and Mrs. Hemans? and Leigh Hunt? and Barry Cornwall?"

"Oh, every one likes *them*, but one gets tired of hearing lions roar, and harps play, and angels sing; and then one goes to Shelley for refreshment. He is never monotonous; he was a perennial fountain, singing at its source, and nearly all was fragmentary that he wrote, of course, wanting an outlet. The mind finishes out so much for itself, and the thought comes to one always, that he was completed in heaven. No other verse stirs me like his. You know he wrote it because he had to write or die. He was a poet, or nothing."

"You ought to write criticisms for *Blackwood*, really, Miss Monfort, and give a woman's reason for every opinion," with ill-concealed derision.

"You are laughing at me now, of course, but I don't regard good-natured raillery. I am sure I should not enjoy poetry as I do were I a better critic. I love flowers far more than many who understand botany as a science, and pull them to pieces scientifically and analytically."

"And paintings; do you love them?"

"Oh, passionately!"

"I confess I am *blasé* with art," he said, quietly; "I have seen so much of it, I like nature far better;" adding, after a pause, "now, that is your chief charm, Miss Monfort."

"What, being natural?"

"How well you divine my meaning!" with a little irony in the voice and eye. The tendency of his mind was evidently sarcastic.

"Ah! true. Papa thinks me *too* natural; he often checks my impulses. Your father, too, coincides with him, I believe, in this opinion; but don't talk about me. Tell me of your sojourn in Germany. How delightful it must have been to have lived in Heidelberg, and felt the very atmosphere you breathed filled with wisdom! Did you ever go to Frankfort? Did you see the statue of Goethe there? Can you read 'Faust' in the original? Oh, I should like to so much, but I know nothing of German. I never could learn the character, I am convinced.

French and Italian only. There was such a beautiful picture of 'Margaret' in the Academy of Fine Arts last year, I wanted papa to purchase it, but Evelyn and he did not fancy it as much as I did. They prefer copies from the old masters. I don't care a cent for Magdalenes and Madonnas and little fat cherubs. I prefer illustrations of poetry or fiction; don't you, Mr. Bainrothe?"

"Very frankly, Miss Monfort, I don't care for pictures at all, unless for good landscapes. I am cloyed with them. And as to German books, I never want to see another. The old 'Deer-Stealer' was worth all they have ever written put together, in my opinion. I love the vernacular."

"Oh, of course, Shakespeare and the Bible; there is nothing like them for truth and power. But to leave poetry for its sister art, you must have enjoyed the music in Germany. Do you love music, Mr. Bainrothe?"

"Not very much, except in opera; then the scenery and lights and people are half the charm. I don't care for science. Such an adventure as I had last night," he murmured low, "was worth a dozen operas to me;" and again I met his admiring, steady gaze, almost embarrassing, fixed upon me.

"What are you two talking about?" asked Evelyn, coming suddenly behind us. "Papa and Mr. Bainrothe are carrying on a little quiet flirtation, as usual, and have quite turned their backs on me, so I came hither, asking charity. I declare, Miriam's face is scarlet! What mischief are you two hatching?"

"I have been running on at a most unconscionable rate," I replied, "covering up my ignorance with many questions that have bored, rather than proved, Mr. Bainrothe, I fear. Take up the dialogue, dear Evelyn, for a few moments, while I go to superintend that elderly flirtation you speak of, and keep papa in order," and I left them abruptly.

"It will all be paid in before then," I heard Mr. Bainrothe say, as I approached them, "and you could not have a safer investment. It is as sound as the Federal Government itself. Indestructible as the solar system."

"I will bring the papers," papa said, rising. "Excuse me for ten minutes," and I dropped into his empty seat by Mr. Bainrothe.

"I hope I shall not interrupt your business meditations while papa is gone," I observed, breaking the silence first.

"Business is my pastime, and no food for meditation, my dear girl; for, like the Pontic monarch of old days, 'I live on poisons, and they have no power, but are a kind of nutriment.' Now, talking to a pretty young girl is far harder and more unusual work to me than transacting mercantile or financial affairs."

"Then I will not oppress you with my society," I said, with a feint to rise.

"Sit still, Miriam, and don't be foolish. You know what I mean, very well. Now, how do you like my son?"

"Oh, very much indeed; he is a little satirical, though, now and then; intolerant of youthful greenness, I perceive, and enthusiasm."

"All affectation, I assure you. He is as verdant himself as the Emerald Isle. Just from college, and very young; what can he know of life? As to enthusiasm, he is full of it."

"True, what *can* he know of life," I mused, and I glanced at him, as I questioned, sitting in front of Evelyn in a sort of humble, devoted way, very different from his easy, knightly air with me. She wore a cold, imperious expression of face not unbecoming to her haughty style of beauty, and fanned herself gently as she listened carelessly to his evidently earnest words, bowing superciliously in answer from time to time.

"The desire of the moth for the star," burst from my lips involuntarily.

"Nothing of the kind," said Mr. Bainrothe, quietly. "If Evelyn Erle were the last of her sex, *he* never could fancy *her*. She is much too old for my son, much too artificial; and, beautiful as she is, she wants some nameless charm, without which no woman ever secures the abiding love of man;" adding, abruptly, after a little pause, "*That charm is yours, Miriam.*"

"How strangely you talk, Mr. Bainrothe!" I replied, with evident embarrassment, which he pretended not to perceive.

"Had you remained one year longer at school, there would have been no grace, no perfection wanting. I am sorry to see you thrown so young, so unprotected, on the waves of society, as you must be soon."

"Oh, not necessarily. I rarely come into the parlor when Evelyn receives, rarely go to parties, and my studies are as dear to me as they ever were. Besides, Mabel absorbs much of my time, and I am quite infatuated with my new accomplishment."

"What is that, Miriam?"

"I am studying elocution, learning to read with Mr. Mortimer—you have heard of him—and he is pleased, so far, with my success. It is a very delightful resource."

"Yes, you have a good voice, an impassioned face and manner—all very suitable, no doubt; but what will it amount to, after all? You will never have to earn your bread in that way, and for a home circle you have always read well enough. It is time wasted, I imagine."

"But the reading is not *all*. I learn to know and comprehend so much that was sealed from me before; in this way, Shakespeare, Milton, Scott, all acquire new beauties. By-the-by, this is what your son meant by studying poetry, perhaps."

"The puppy! Has he been lecturing you, too? Really, there is no end to his presumption;" and he smiled, benignly, upon him.

"I must defend him from such a charge," I said, earnestly. "I find him very deferential—he has the courteous European manner, which, when high-bred, is so polite. Americans never learn to bow like foreign gentlemen. It is a great charm."

"Do you hear that, Claude? Miss Monfort approves of your bow. This is all I can extort from her; but she is very hard to please, very censorious by nature, so don't be entirely discouraged."

A bow of the approved sort, and wave of the hand across the room, in addition, were the only rejoinder elicited by this sally, and again the downcast head, the clasped hands, the low, entreating voice denoted the character of his conference with Evelyn. He was pleading a desperate cause, it seemed to me.

Mr. Bainrothe became unreasonably nervous, I thought. He fidgeted with his hat, and gloves, and cane, which he took from the table near him, dropping the last as he did so; he glanced impatiently at the door through which my father was to enter, and, when finally his friend came, after a brief conference in a corner with regard to the papers he had gone out to seek, probably, summoned his son abruptly and darted off in true Continental style, followed by his more stately junior.

"Mr. Bainrothe amuses me," observed Evelyn after we were alone again. He is so transparent, dear old butterfly! He need not be alarmed! I have put a quietus on all presumptuous hopes in that quarter forever, and now, Miriam, I hand him over to you signed and sealed 'Claude Bainrothe rejected and emancipated by Evelyn Erle, and ready for fresh servitude—apprenticed, in short.'"

"Thank you," I rejoined, dryly, speaking with a tightness at my throat.

"He thinks you quite good-looking, Miriam, I assure you; he was agreeably disappointed, even after what he had heard of your appearance—from the Stanburys, I suppose—and observed that there were fine elements in your character, too, if properly shaped and combined—a great deal of '*come out*.'"

"He is truly gracious and condescending," I replied. "I thank him humbly."

"It was very plain that you admired him, Miriam. Any one could see that. I noticed his internal amusement at your fluttered manner."

"Did he tell you what his thoughts were, Evelyn, or do you merely interpret them after your own fashion?" I asked, sternly.

"Oh, of course he said nothing of the kind; I would not have permitted it, had he wished to. Poor fellow! I hope you will be kinder to him than I have been," and she sighed heavily. "He is yours now to have and to hold, you know."

"You have not shown your usual good taste, Evelyn," I remarked, coolly, "in rejecting so handsome and fascinating a man, and making him over to another, unsolicited. Claude Bainrothe would suit you exactly, I think; and, as to money, he will have enough, no doubt, for both. If not"—I hesitated—colored—sighed.

"If not, what, Miriam?" she urged, stamping her little foot impatiently as my answer was delayed. "If not, what then, Miriam? Speak out!"

"If not, dear sister, *I* will try to make up the *deficiency*," I said, embracing her. "Now you understand my intentions."

I was learning to love my sister, and happy in the power to please her, unconscious that an invisible barrier was rising from that hour, never to be put aside.

## CHAPTER IV.

For a discarded lover heartlessly played with, as she herself confessed he had been, Claude Bainrothe bore himself very proudly and calmly in Evelyn Erle's presence, I thought. At first, there was a shade of coolness, of pique even in my own manner toward him as the memory of Evelyn's insinuations rose between us; but after the lapse of a few weeks all thought of this kind was put away, and he was received with a pleasure as undisguised, as it was innocent and undesigning on my part.

The repugnant idea of succeeding to Evelyn in his affections had stifled the very germs of coquetry, and my manner to him was unmistakable; nor was it without evident dissatisfaction that Mr. Basil Bainrothe surveyed the ruin of his hopes.

A sudden and painful change took place about midsummer in Claude's manner toward me (with Evelyn it was uniform). He became cold, restrained, embarrassed in his intercourse with me, hitherto so frank and brotherly. He made his visits shorter and at last at greater intervals; yet I knew, through others, that he remained strictly at home, eschewing all places of amusement, all society—"all occupation even," as Mr. Basil Bainrothe himself complained.

"I can't think what has got into Claude lately," he

said to my father one day at our dinner-table. "The boy mopes. He is in love, I believe, but with whom I can't conjecture," and he glanced askance at Evelyn and me.—"Can you assist me, ladies?"

"Not with me, I assure you," said Evelyn, proudly. "That measure has been trodden, and the dance is over."

"Nor with me," I faltered, for the careless words had struck to my heart. "That fancy dance has yet to be solicited. We both plead innocent, you see, Mr. Bainrothe," and I tried to laugh, but the glittering, kaleidoscopic eye was fixed upon me, and my face was crimson.

"Never *blush*, Miriam," whispered Evelyn, maliciously, "it makes you look the color of a new mahogany bedstead. You are best pale, child. Always remember that."

"It must be with Miss Stanbury, then," said Mr. Bainrothe, evasively. "She is a very pretty girl, and I don't wonder at Claude's infatuation. The old man is rich, too; it will answer very well, I think. What do you say, Mr. Monfort."

"Well, really, I think Claude could scarcely do better," rejoined my ever literal father. "She is an admirable young person, pious, and discreetly brought up—and —yes, quite pretty, certainly. Let us drink to his success in that quarter.—Ladies!—Mr. Bainrothe!—fill your glasses.—Franklin, the sherry.—Morton, the port. Which will you have, Bainrothe? or do you prefer Rhine wines?"

"A glass of Hockheimer, if you have it convenient, Franklin. Those heavy wines are too heating for our summers, I think, Mr. Monfort. You yourself would do well to follow my example."

"Thank you," said my father, loftily. "When you

feed lions on pound-cake you may expect to see Englishmen drink German acidulations instead of the generous juice of the grape—fostered on southern soil, above volcanoes even—to which they have been used since the time of the last Henrys. Beer were a better alternative. Give me claret or madeira."

Mr. Bainrothe had his limits, and usually took care not to exceed them. My father's easy good-nature was converted into frozen *hauteur* at any open effort to transcend the boundaries of his independence. He gloried in "*Magna Charta*," and never knowingly sacrificed his baronial privileges, yet he was wax in the hands of a skillful wheedler, and his "adamantine will" was readily fused in the fires of flattery.

We drank the proposed toast, much to Mr. Bainrothe's discomfiture. He had made the remark as a skillful feeler, and was mortified at my father's ready acquiescence in his plans. Of course, Evelyn and I both saw through the unskillful *ruse*, and pledged him with hearty malice; but he had yet another shot in reserve, which told with fatal effect.

"Mr. Biddle has offered me a cashiership for Claude," he remarked, carelessly, "in a thriving town in Georgia, and I shall accept for him forthwith. Then, if Miss Stanbury chooses to accompany him into exile, it will be all for the best; but, were he about to remain here, I would not suffer him to think of matrimony for years to come. 'A young man married is a young man marred,' as Shakespeare says somewhere, I believe; and I agree with him. A youth of twenty-one ought to be free for a season until he can shape his life."

I felt myself tremble from head to foot. I had never contemplated the possibility of his absence, and the conviction of my deep interest in him flashed across me for the first time with lightning force and vividness. Evelyn did not reproach me for blushing this time; I was pale enough to satisfy even her spleen. Indeed, some better feeling than she had before manifested seemed to inspire her now, for she filled another glass of wine and motioned me to drink it. I had merely sipped from mine when papa proposed his toast, and Franklin had borne it away with the others in making ready for the dessert.

"Don't let that man read you," she said, in a low, eager voice, not lost on me. I drank the wine, and met his glance steadily this time, and gave him look for look. My secret had nerved me well.

That evening Claude Bainrothe came.

"When do you enter the sacred bands of matrimony with Miss Stanbury, Mr. Bainrothe?" asked Evelyn, in her usual, cool, provoking way, sipping a glass of iced lemonade as she spoke, which Claude had brought her from the refreshment-slab and humbly offered.

"And when do you assume your office in Georgia?" I asked in the next breath, encouraged by her example, and perhaps, alas! eager to know the truth, scarcely lifting my eyes to his as I spoke.

He glanced from one to the other with a bewildered air, quite foreign from his usual self-possession.

"I protest, ladies, I do not understand your allusions," he replied at last, with such an air of truth that, taking pity on him, we explained the matter laughingly.

"My poor father is falling into that sear and yellow leaf, his dotage," he said, "that is evident; what could possess him to maunder so? I really believe he is in love with Miss Stanbury himself, and is wire-working merely to gain my consent. As to going to Georgia, I would as soon bury myself up to my neck in the sea-sand and bear the vertical sun for twenty sequent noons, as to dream of such a step. The old gentleman is a lunatic, and should be cared for without delay. I will get Dr. Parrish to see after him to-morrow."

"But I *did* hear you say you were going to Copenhagen with our minister," said George Gaston, who had swung himself softly up to our party on his crutches, unobserved by any one, while Claude was speaking, and now stood glaring upon him.

"Ah, that is a different matter. I *may* go there, George. I am told it is a very gay court; besides, I am curious about Denmark, naturally. Every one is who loves Shakespeare and the 'royal Dane,' you know."

Again that fatal pallor of mine swept from my heart to brow, and this time the large, dark-gray eye of the boy was fixed on me with agony unspeakable. He dropped it suddenly, wheeled on his supporting-sticks, and turned away, ghastly pale himself, to seek the shelter of the portico, where I joined him a few minutes later.

"Are you ill, George?" I asked. "I felt anxious about you when I saw you leave the parlor so suddenly. Have you had one of your spells?"

"A very severe spell, Miriam; but not of the usual kind." I understood him now. There was a dry anguish in the very tone of his voice that smote heavily on my ear, yet I felt impatient with him, provoked beyond endurance.

"George, you should be more of a man," I said, with asperity, "than to yield in this way to every impulse that besets you. Your whims are hard to bear with lately, and scarcely worth understanding, I am convinced."

"Would I were more or less of a man!" he answered, meekly. "I should suffer less, probably."

"Tell me what *does ail* you, George Gaston," I added, with a sudden revulsion of feeling, caused by his patient, deprecating manner. "You know you always have my warmest sympathy, and affection—sisterly interest."

"Ah, Miriam, it is that! You love that man; yes, you love him a thousand-fold more than you have ever loved me. I suspected it before—I know it now; and I would rather see you floating a corpse on the river, with your dead face turned up to heaven, than married to that man, I hate him so!"

The last words were ground between his set teeth, and he trembled with passion.

"George," I said, "you are still a child in years, in strength, in stature! I, but a few months older, am already a woman in age, experience, feeling, character. It is always thus with persons of our sexes who contract childish friendships—one outgrows the other. Then there are bitterness, reproach, suffering, resentment, on one part or the other. But is this just? Remember Byron and Miss Chaworth—how was it with them? He grasped too much, and lost every thing; he embittered his whole nature, his whole life, for the want of common-sense to guide him; but, with almost as much genius—more, in some things, than he possessed—you HAVE this governing principle. I know my dearest George will do me justice. I shall be an old, faded woman when you are of an age to marry—unlovely in your eyes, George,"—I hesitated. "I have always hoped you would be our Mabel's husband. You know you have promised me." I smiled tearfully this time.

He bounded off the bench, interrupting me with a low

cry. "Do not mock me, Miriam Monfort," he exclaimed, "if you can do no better. My God! a baby of five years old suggested as a wife by you, my idol! Oh, yes, wildly-beloved Miriam, the noblest, truest, as I have ever thought you—the most beautiful, too, surely, of all God's created beings!" and he caught my hand wildly.

"George, you are dreaming," I said; "your vivid fancy misleads you utterly. I am not beautiful—you cannot think so; no one has ever thought me so; you must not say such an absurd thing of me. It only humiliates me. But I do believe I still deserve your esteem. Let us separate now, and to-morrow come to me in a better mood."

"If I *must* give you up," he murmured, in a low, grieved voice, "let it be to a husband who loves and appreciates you—is worthy of you. I cannot tell you all I know—*have heard;* but of this I am certain: Claude Bainrothe loves you not! It is Evelyn he worships, and you are blind not to see it; Evelyn who has goaded him almost to madness already for her own purposes. I heard—but no, I cannot tell you this; I ought not—honor forbids;" and he laid his hand on his boyish breast, in a tragic, lofty manner, all his own, that almost made me smile.

"I know, I know all this, dear George," I said. "Claude Bainrothe addressed Evelyn before he knew me, and she refused him. Nor have I craved the honor, this is all that can be said as yet, of being her successor." I faltered here. "Let this satisfy you for the present. He has not spoken to me."

"But you love him—love him, Miriam!" he groaned. "Oh, I saw it plainly to-night, and, what is far more terrible and hard to bear, he saw it too! He was watching you from the corner of his furtive, downcast eye when he was speaking of going to Copenhagen, and a smile trembled around his mouth when you turned so pale—white as a poplar-leaf, Miriam, when the wind blows it over! If I were a woman I would cut out my heart rather than open it thus to the gaze of any man, far less one like that, shallow, selfish, superficial. O Miriam! not worthy of you at all—not fit to tie your shoe-latchet!"

"George, you overrate me, you always did, and—and—you undervalue Mr. Bainrothe, believe me; nay, I am sure you do. Let us part now, George. My father is calling me, you hear. Go home, my own dear boy, and rest and pray. Oh, be convinced that I love you better than all the world, except those I *ought* to love more.—Yes, yes, papa! I am coming.—Good-night, dear George."

And I kissed his clammy brow, hastening in the next moment to my father's side, who, missing me, could not rest in this new phase of his until I was forthcoming. Certainly, whatever tenderness I had missed in former years was amply lavished on me now. Evelyn, Mabel—all former idols sank out of sight in my presence, and the very touch of my hand, the sound of my voice, seemed to inspire him with happiness and a new sense of security. Sometime I flattered myself that I had earned this affection, since it had not seemed my birthright, nor come to me earlier; but no, it was the grace of God, I must believe, touching his heart at last, as the rod of Moses brought forth waters from the rock. Yet the simile is at fault here: my father's heart was never a stone, but tender and true and constant ever, even if locked away.

It may seem strange, but from the very evidences of his carelessness, as they seemed to others, I gathered, after a time, the blissful conviction that Claude Bainrothe was not indifferent to me. His reserve, his moroseness almost, the despairing way in which he spoke sometimes of his future life, his want of purpose, of interest in what was passing around him, his entire self-possession with Evelyn, so different from his embarrassment with me; his manner of pursuing me with his eyes, and holding me fast, and the long sidelong glances he often dropped at my feet like offerings, as I detected his vigilance—all persuaded me that what I most wished to believe was true, and that I had awakened interest if not passion in his heart, for—at last, I loved him!

The time came when his own lips confirmed my suspicions, my hopes—when faintly, and in broken accents, he related to me the story of his love; mine, as he declared, since the evening of our first meeting; and asked my troth in turn. I was so inexperienced in matters of this sort, I scarcely knew how to behave, I suppose; besides, I never thought of giving any other reply than the one he craved, for I too had inclined to him from the first. I recognized this now, and did not deny it when he urged me for the truth, holding my hands in his, and looking into my eyes in a deep and tender and devoted way peculiar to himself, that thrilled to my very life—an adoring expression that I have seen in no other gaze than his own, and which cast a glamour about him, I well believe, irresistible wherever it was exercised.

It was in September that we became engaged, with the joyful coincidence of Mr. Bainrothe, the somewhat reluctant consent of my father, the half-derisive approbation of Evelyn, the entire disapproval, expressed in eloquent silence, of the whole Stanbury family. For a time, this grave coldness on their part alienated me greatly from them all, George Gaston especially; and had it not been for Mabel, and the bond she proved between us, we might have been divided for life thereafter.

My father's declining health alone threw a bleakness over that rosy time of joy, and held in check the exuberance of my happy spirit, brimming like sparkling wine above the vase that contained it. Sometimes, when I met Evelyn's cold and gloomy eye, I felt myself rebuked for the indulgence of my perfect happiness. "She knows that my father is more ill than he seems!" I would conjecture—"Dr. Pemberton has told her what he conceals from me. I am making festal garlands in readiness for my father's grave, perhaps." Then with tears and entreaties I would question her: "I *cannot* be mistaken," I would say; "something is wrong with you. Is it about my father? If not of him, what is it, Evelyn, that makes your face like a stone mask of late—once all life and joy?" "Miriam, I am not quite well," she would reply evasively, or say, "I am meditating a step that will cost me dear. My uncle, the Earl of Pomfret, the head of our house since my grandfather's death, you know, writes me to visit him. It is this fatal necessity—for such for some reasons I feel it—that oppresses me so heavily."

"Why a necessity, dear Evelyn, why go at all? You certainly can never feel to any relative as you do to *my* father and *yours*."

"Your father does not find me as important to his happiness as he once did, Miriam. You have absorbed his whole affection of late; even Mabel, once his darling and plaything, is put aside."

"He surrendered her to me again, Evelyn, when I returned; this is all, believe me. He loves, he esteems you as much as ever; he consults you in all his arrangements. He has made you the mistress of his house; your judgment, your advice, are paramount with him as to all matters of outlay; and, Evelyn, suffer me to speak to you on one subject of great delicacy—sister! I must. Whenever you marry from this house, understand well that you shall not go empty-handed."

"Fortune is not *his* to bestow," she responded, "and large charities have absorbed, I know, much of his yearly income, princely as that is. Besides, he reinvests all that remains from that source for Mabel, as I know. I feel assured he will provide for me, but it must be in a very small way, and I must go to England and make my establishment there."

"Would you marry for money, Evelyn?" I asked gravely. "O sister, can you conceive of no higher happiness than this?"

"I can," she said with emotion, while her lips blanched to the hue of ashes. "I have dreamed such a dream in days past, but now the dark reality alone remains and sweeps all before it. I shall embrace my first eligible offer regardless of feeling, and I prefer to cast my destiny with my own people, however estranged they may be. Certainly, this letter is not very affectionate, nor even a courteous one from so near a relative," and she placed in my hand the cold and supercilious note of the Earl of Pomfret, containing a permission to visit his castle, rather than invitation.

"Yet you will go, Evelyn?"

"Miriam, I *must* go. I should go mad were I to stay here, or die in the struggle."

"Sister, what can this be? Evelyn, hear me: I swear to you, on the day of my majority, to endow you richly in your own right. It is independence you want—you shall have it. My father will consent to this I know, and consider it no more than your due."

"You are kind," she said; "generous, very. You are not like your mother's people in that respect, such as they are in these degenerate days, at least. She herself was unlike them, I have heard, for her hand was princely. But, Miriam, I could not receive such obligations from you—ought not. Besides—your husband!"

"Ah, Evelyn, there is nothing he would refuse me—nothing."

A gloomy mockery transfused itself into her eyes, her lips were fixed in a suppressed and sneering smile. Incredulity was written on her aspect. Her face at that moment was very repulsive to contemplate.

"You do not believe in men," I said, coldly. "I have always remarked it; yet there are *some* worthy of confidence, believe me."

"Very few, Miriam, and Claude Bainrothe is not unlike the majority of his fellows. Men count it no wrong to deceive women."

"O Evelyn, you are too severe, I think. Why seek to shake my confidence in the man I love? He did not happen to suit your fancy, and you rejected him. I took what you cast aside, humbly, thankfully, dear Evelyn. Why resent this, and scorn me for my humility? Let not your pride for me make you unjust toward him. You, of all women, can best afford to be generous to Claude Bainrothe."

But still the cold shadow veiled her face, and still she looked inauspiciously on our betrothal, which, owing to our youth, it was understood, should continue a year. In the interval I was to travel with my father to the different large cities of the Union which I had never seen, and abide awhile in Washington.

His health, Dr. Pemberton thought, required this change, but a darker one was in store for him.

On Christmas-day, of that year, he was smitten with paralysis, and his decline was sure and rapid from that hour. Let me pass over the agony of that period of six weeks, lengthened into years by the dread tension of anxiety, most relentless of the furies. But for the confidence I felt in Claude's affection, and the vista of hope it opened for me, I think I should have succumbed under the unequal struggle.

During this period, his attentions to me and to my helpless father were most kind and assiduous. Mr. Bainrothe and Evelyn, too, between whom some unexplained alienation had existed for some time, met in apparent harmony above his bed of death.

In addition to the services of our own dear and valued physician, we had others of eminence coming and going daily, with the knowledge in their own breasts that all was vain.

Still I never ceased entirely to hope until the very last. "He is not old, he is still vigorous," I would say to myself. "There may be—there *must* be—reaction. I have so often heard him boast of his English constitution, I cannot, oh, I cannot think that the end is yet!"

I wondered then at the inattention of the Stanburys, in whose disinterested friendship I had reposed so much confidence, even though a shadow of late had been thrown over our intercourse by my engagement with Claude Bainrothe, a shadow of which I thought I saw the substance in the bitter jealousy and rancorous, unreasonable love and hatred of the morbid George Gaston.

Later I found by the merest accident, through one note of his that had been left in a drawer of a desk long disused, that Mr. Gerald Stanbury and Evelyn had maintained a rather fierce correspondence on the subject of her refusal to accept his services at my father's pillow; founded, as she alleged, on the recent unexplained but deep-rooted aversion Mr. Monfort seemed to have imbibed for his neighbor and friend, and which his physicians said must be regarded.

Allusion was made, not unmixed with bitterness, in Mr. Stanbury's note, to this assertion of hers, which he pronounced, if true, to rest on the misrepresentations of villains who had interposed between the too confiding Mr. Monfort and himself for no good purpose. No names were given, but it was easy to see to whom his reference was made, and I had every reason to suppose that Evelyn had communicated these opinions to those most interested in knowing them long before this record accidentally fell into my hands.

On the day of the funeral, however, Mr. and Mrs. Stanbury were present, with Laura and George. All seemed deeply affected, and one by one came to me in my shadowed chamber with a few words of tender sympathy or kindly condolence, for I could not bear to go down into that crowded parlor and see *him* dead amid all that tide of life, who had so lately stood there powerful and beloved—Monfort the master!

It was a superb day, they told me, such as we often have at that season in our changeful clime, and the distant peal of military music, the chiming of bells, the firing of cannon, the roar of the awakened multitude, reached my ear even in that secluded street, that quiet room.

The people were celebrating an anniversary that in all times has brought joy and pride to millions of united hearts. It was the birthday of Washington.

Laura Stanbury remained with me while all the rest went to the stately funeral, Evelyn leading Mabel downstairs, they told me, attired in her little black dress, in sad contrast with her ivory skin, her yellow hair, her childish years, and her unconsciousness of the grave loss she had sustained; Mrs. Austin following these, her darlings, to go with them in the principal mourning-coach, in which Mr. Bainrothe also found himself ensconced, by some diplomacy of his own, no doubt, all clad in sables, and with his polished aspect fixed in woe!

After the funeral, Dr. Pemberton came up for a few minutes to my chamber. He found me reasonably calm and composed, and expressed his gratification at my condition.

"Now, do be very careful of yourself, my dear Miriam, or you may have one of your sleepy attacks, and they are exhausting to Nature, trying to both body and soul. We must guard against any thing of this sort at this time. You know how apt they are to supervene on excitement of any kind with you." He said this in his own kind, encouraging manner.

"Then they are strictly nervous?" I inquired.

"I don't know; can't say, indeed.—Here, Mrs. Austin, give Miriam one of these powders," and he drew them from his pocket-book, "every six hours until I come again, and keep her as quiet as possible. Some light nourishment she must take, but let there be no preaching and praying about her this evening, and advise Mr. Bainrothe to go quietly home for the present. She must not be excited, only soothed. Let Mabel come, of course."

He came again on the next day and the next, and so on until he was satisfied that all was going on very well, he said, but he would not suffer my father's will to be opened for a week, knowing that my presence would be necessary at the reading, and he permitted no disturbance of any kind to approach me during that interval of probation.

"Do you think you could get through with a few business details to-morrow?" he asked me on the last day of his visit. "They all seem very impatient, though I cannot see why."

"I think so, Dr. Pemberton."

"Well, then, notify Mr. Bainrothe to make ready for you in the library at any hour you may fix upon. He was your father's attorney, it seems, and had the will in his keeping. Of course it will be a very simple matter to carry out its provisions, since all was fixed before, as every one knows, but there may be some little agitation. Now, don't give way, I charge you."

"How can I help it, Dr. Pemberton?"

"Oh, with a will like yours, one can do a great deal. I had an obstinate patient once determined not to die, and she did not die, though death was due. Resistance is natural to some temperaments. Yours is one of them. Fight off those attacks, Miriam, in future."

"I will try," I said, half amused at his suggestion, "but, if all physicians gave such prescriptions, medicine would be at a discount."

"Not at all. Medicine is a great aid in any case—I have never thought it more. A doctor is only a pilot; he steers a ship sometimes past dangerous places on which it would founder otherwise, but he never pretends, unless he is a charlatan, to upheave shoals and rocks, or to control tempests. He can only mind his rudder and shift his sails; the rest is with Providence. Now, suppose the captain of this ship is calm and firm, and coincides with the pilot's efforts, instead of counteracting and embarrassing them. Don't you see the advantage to the ship?"

"Oh, certainly, and I admire the ingenuity of your allegory. You must have been studying Bunyan, lately.

"No, Miriam, I have little time for books, save those necessary to my profession. I study a mightier volume daily than scholar ever wrote—the wondrous mind and body of man, the one illustrated by the other, and both so mutually dependent that short-sighted people have occasionally confounded them, yet distinct after all as God and the universe."

"I am glad to hear you say this; doctors are so often accused of being materialists."

"No men living have less excuse for being so. The phenomenon of death alone ought to set that matter at rest in any reasoning mind. The impalpable is gone, and the material perishes. It is so plain that he that runs might read, one would think. That sudden change from volition to inertia is, in itself, conviction to every right-seeing mind."

"Yet I wish we knew more," I mused, aloud. "We ought to know more, it seems to me. God has not told us half enough for our satisfaction. It is so cruel to leave us in the dark, lit only by partial flashes of lightning. If we were certain of the future, we could bear separation better from those we love. It would not seem so hopeless."

"If we were certain of the future, we would not bear it all," he remarked, "but grow impatient and exacting like children who rise in the night to examine the Christmas stocking, rather than wait until morning. Most often we should join those we loved rather than bide our time if we were certain. Moreover, what merit would there be in faith or fortitude? No, Miriam, it is best as it is, believe me. Every thing is for the best that God has done; we must not dare to question the ways any more than the will of the Eternal."

"You ought to have been a preacher, Dr. Pemberton," I said, smiling sadly, "instead of a physician."

"No, my dear little girl, I ought to have been just what I am, since it was God's will. And now be calm and self-sustaining until I come again, which will be before long, I think."

I tried as far as in me lay to regard the instructions of my kind friend and physician (and happy are those who unite both in one person), but, prepare as we may to receive the waves of the sea when we bathe in its margin, and skillful as we may believe ourselves in buffeting or avoiding them, there comes one now and then with a strength and suddenness that sweeps us from our feet, overthrows us, and lays us prostrate at the sandy bottom of the ocean, to emerge therefrom half stifled with the bitter brine.

Such experience was destined to be mine before many hours.

## CHAPTER V.

Mr. Gerald Stanbury had been especially invited to attend the reading of my father's will, by a polite note from Mr. Bainrothe, in which the interest that both bore in this testament was plainly set forth. With the exception of our excellent old neighbor and the two Mr. Bainrothes, the circle assembled for the solemn occasion was composed entirely of Mr. Monfort's household and was truly a funereal one. I wore my deep-mourning dress for the first time that day, and Mabel, similarly attired, sat beside me. Claude Bainrothe was alone on a distant sofa.

Evelyn assumed my father's chair, and wore, with the weeds customary to widows, a demeanor of great dignity and reserve suitable to the head of the family. Mr. Gerald Stanbury had a seat near mine, on which he sat uneasily, and Mrs. Austin, Franklin, and Morton, were ranged together stiffly in chairs placed against the wall, likewise attired in deep mourning. Mr. Bainrothe was seated near the study-table, looking unusually pale and subdued, from one of the drawers of which he had drawn forth the will, unlocking and locking it again with a key suspended to his guard-chain.

"This key was placed in my hand," he said, "during my friend's last illness, and, although he could not speak to me at the time, his expressive eye indicated its importance and to what drawer it belonged. This was before he was removed from the study in which he was stricken, dear friends, as you may all remember, on Christmas-morning, and which he never again reëntered. From that day to this the key which I wear has not left my charge, nor been placed in the lock to which it belongs, and to the guardianship of which this will, as soon as made and legally attested, was probably committed. We will now, with your permission, break the seal that I see has been placed upon this document since I beheld it, the contents of which are already familiar to me." He then opened and read in a clear, monotonous voice my father's will and its provisions.

The property, as I knew already, was all mine by marriage contract, except such sums as my father had accumulated and set aside from his yearly income for his own purposes. With these he richly endowed Evelyn Erle, and comfortably the three servants or attendants, as he preferred to call them, who had followed him from England, and by their lives of fidelity and duty shown themselves worthy of his regard. Half of my estate was already in stocks of the United States Bank, and half loaned at interest on sound mortgages. This last was to be called in as speedily as possible and invested also in stocks of the above-mentioned bank, in that peculiar institution known as the Pennsylvania Bank, and still supposed to be under Mr. Biddle's superintendence. This was done, the testator said, to simplify his daughter's property, and render it more manageable to her hand, should she by her own will remain single, or by that of Providence be widowed, and he hoped in any case she would suffer it to remain in this shape as long as Mr. Biddle or Mr. Bainrothe lived.

All this I heard with satisfaction and even indifference, but the part that stung me almost to exasperation was reserved for the last. Mr. Bainrothe and Mr. Stanbury were named as executors conjointly with Evelyn Erle, in the last mentioned of whom all power over my actions was to vest until I should be of age, and in whose hands, as guardian, Mabel and her property were exclusively intrusted until that time should arrive; after that period her sisters were to act jointly, unless my marriage were made without consent of Evelyn, in which case Mabel was to be her charge alone.

No security was to be required of either executor, but, across Mr. Gerald Stanbury's name two lines in ink had been drawn with a wavering hand, as if for erasure.

I heard this last clause of the will with a beating, bounding, indignant heart. Evelyn, who so hated Claude Bainrothe, had us both completely in her power for the present, and might defer our marriage for years if it so pleased her. And Mabel, toward whom she did not disguise her indifference, was to be hers on this ground perhaps forever! Slavery for four of the best years of my life was entailed on me, and bondage forever on her, perhaps—my idol—my darling—mine—all mine by every right of man or God!

The injustice was too palpable. It was almost incomprehensible to me how he had been wrought upon to do these things—he, "a just man made perfect." All this flashed stunningly across my brain. Suddenly I threw my hand wildly to my head—the whirl of waters was in my ears; yet I struggled against the surging tide, and Claude Bainrothe's grasp upon my hand strengthened and revived me. I was roused from my apathy by hearing Mr. Gerald Stanbury's loud, sonorous voice speaking out clearly: "I decline to serve, Mr. Bainrothe, after that erasure. You understand that, of course. It was a farce to send for me to-day, under these circumstances."

"How could I know, my dear sir, that this erasure had been made?" was the soft and specious rejoinder. "It must have been done in the last few months. This will was drawn up in August last. I was ignorant of the whole subsequent proceeding, and at that time Mr. Monfort laid peculiar stress on your coincidence as executor. Has any thing occurred since that time to mar your good understanding?"

"Nothing of any consequence," said Mr. Stanbury, coldly—"nothing bearing on the esteem of man for man. Nevertheless, Mr. Monfort, as we all know, was a man easy to offend and difficult to appease, and I suppose" (he swallowed hard as he spoke) "he weighed old friendship and some good offices as nothing against his wounded self-love, and against the flatterers who beset him with their snares."

"Sir, you intend to be insulting, no doubt," Mr. Bainrothe observed, with a semblance of calm dignity; "but it is not on such an occasion as this, and in the disinterested discharge of my duty, that I will suffer myself to be ruffled by the bitter injustice of an irritable and disappointed old man."

"Be guarded, Mr. Bainrothe," Mr. Stanbury rejoined, "in your expressions to me, or I will look into that illegal erasure and still stand to my oar in this golden galley of yours, in which you expect to float with the stream, and so soon to have every thing your own way. I like plain sailing, sir; am a plain, straightforward man myself, to whom truth is second nature; and, were it not for the violence it might do the feelings of the person chiefly concerned in this testament, so soon to be allied to you and yours, if I understand things properly and report speaks truly, I would defy you, Mr. Basil Bainrothe, in the public courts, and claim my executorship under the wing of the law."

Mr. Bainrothe had turned ashy pale during the deliverance of this fiery rebuke. But he controlled himself admirably, merely contenting himself with saying, in a low voice: "No threats, if you please, Mr. Stanbury; act out your intentions when and where you choose, but have consideration just now for the feelings of others." And he waved his hand, trembling with rage, toward me, including in his gesture Evelyn, who by this time was beside me with her salts, chafing my hands. "I am sure we are all willing to yield our executorships if Miriam desires it," she said. "I, for one, should be glad to lift such a yoke from my shoulders, unaccustomed to such a burden. Mr. Stanbury, desirable as you seem to think it, this post of mine is no sinecure. But spare Miriam this scene, I beg of you; she is much overcome—much exhausted; excitement in her case is very injurious, Dr. Pemberton says. Let me beg you, my dear sir, to retire. All shall be done properly and in order. Her interest is our chief concern, of course."

"Evelyn Erle, I have nothing to say to you," I heard Mr. Stanbury exclaim, in a loud, excited tone. "It is not with women I wish to wage war, and so understand me! But there is One above to whom you will have to account rigidly some day for your stewardship and guardianship of these friendless girls, and be prepared, I counsel you, with your accounts, to meet Him when the day of reckoning comes! And it may come sooner than you suspect. I, for one, shall keep an unslumbering eye upon you and your devices while I live, even though at a distance.—Miriam, I am always ready to assist you, my dear, in any way possible to me—call on me freely. Remember, I am your friend." He came to me, he took me to his breast, he kissed my brow, his tears were on my cheek. I cast my arms about his dear, old, noble neck; I leaned my quivering face against his bosom. "I always loved you," I said. "I am so sorry, so sorry, Mr. Stanbury!" I knew no more—the words forsook my lips. Again that wild whirl of waters surged upon my ears; I seemed to be falling, falling down a black, steep, bottomless shaft, beneath which the sea was roaring—falling head-foremost—hurled as if with a strong impulse down the abyss to certain destruction.

Then all was still. The jaws of my dark malady had opened to receive me.

I woke as from a long, deep, and unrefreshing slumber. I was lying in my bed, with the curtains drawn closely around it—the heavy crimson curtains, with their white inside draperies and snowy tufted fringes. I had a vague consciousness that some hand had recently parted them, and the tassels on the valance were quivering still with the impulse they had thus received. Then I heard voices.

"How much longer will it endure, Evelyn?"

"Five or six hours, I suppose. What time is it now?" The clock in the hall struck ten before the question could be answered.

"Ten! It was about three when she was seized," rejoined the voice of Evelyn; "you can calculate for yourself—the turns are invariably twelve and twenty-four hours in duration; if one period is transcended the other is accomplished. Dr. Pemberton himself told me this."

"Might not the term in some way be shortened? I was very sure I heard her stirring just now, and my heart was in my mouth." After which a pause.

"I knew you were mistaken, but I examined to satisfy your mind. No, she still lies in a lethargy, and will lie in that comatose condition until after noon. Then Dr. Pemberton will be here, and she will revive."

"That seizure was very dreadful, but I saw no foam on her lips like most epileptics, and I watched narrowly."

"There are modifications of the disease, Claude; hers is of a passive kind, with very few or no convulsive struggles—more like syncope. Had you not better retire now?"

"Still, it *is* epilepsy? No, do not banish me yet."

"That is what the doctors call it, I believe, Claude. Dr. Pemberton is too guarded or politic, one or the other—all Quakers are, you know—to give it a name, however. Dr. Physick told papa what it was very plainly, years ago."

"Ah! he was good authority, certainly a great physician and a philosopher as well; but, Evelyn, it is very awful," with a groan, and perhaps a shudder. "Very hard to get over or to bear."

"Yes, and the worst of it is it will increase with age, and the end is so deplorable—idiocy or madness, you know, invariably. Early death is desirable for Miriam. Her best friends should not wish to see her life prolonged. It is an inheritance, probably. Her mother died of some inscrutable incurable disease, I suppose like this."

"O God! O God! it is almost more than I can stand."

I heard him pacing the room slowly up and down, and my impulse was to part the curtains, to call him to me and comfort him, but I could not; I was too weak even to speak as yet, and bound as with a spell, a nightmare.

A whirl of vivid joy passed through me like an electric flash, however, as I recognized in his disquietude the strength of his affection. Evelyn's malignant cruelty and falsehood were lost sight of in the bliss of this conviction; yet my triumph was but brief.

"Evelyn," he said, speaking low, and pausing in his slow, continued pace.—"Evelyn, just as she lies there sleeping, I would she could lie forever! Then happiness could dawn for us again."

"Never, Claude Bainrothe!"

"You are unforgiving, my Evelyn! you have no mercy on me nor my sufferings. You make no allowance for necessity, or the desperation of my condition. In debt myself, and so long a cause of expense and anxiety to my father, whose sacrifices for me have been manifold, and before whom ruin is grimly yawning even now, how could I act otherwise, consistently with the duty of a son? Nay, what manhood would there have been in consigning you to such a fate as awaited penniless wife of mine?

"I did not think of these things, did not know them even, when we first met, and when I told you of my sudden passion I was sincere, Evelyn, then, as I am now, for it is unchanged, and you know that it is so.

"When the dark necessity was laid bare to me, and I felt it my duty to cancel our engagement, you bore it bravely, you kept my counsel, you assisted me in my projects; you proved yourself all that was noble and magnanimous in woman. What marvel, then, that I more than ever loved you, and wished the obstacle removed that divides us, and yearn for my lost happiness now dearer to me than before, only to be renewed through you, Evelyn! that I still adore!—woman most beautiful, most beloved!"

"Claude, this is mockery; release my hand; arise, this position becomes you not, nor yet me. Go! I am lost to you forever! your own cowardice, your own weak worship of expediency, have been your real obstacles. For your sake I was willing to brave poverty, debt, expatriation. It was you who preferred the dross of gold, and the indulgence of your own luxury and that of the sybarite, your father, to the passionate affection I bore you. It is too late now for regret or recrimination. Go, I command you! accomplish your destiny; continue to beguile Miriam with the tale of your affection, and in return reap your harvest of deluded affection and golden store from her! and from me receive your guerdon of scorn. For I, Claude Bainrothe, know you as you are, and despise you utterly!" Her voice trembled with anger, I knew of old its violent ring of rage.

"No, Evelyn, you only know me as I *seem*"—he spoke mildly, humbly—"not as I *am*. I am not a very bad man, Evelyn, nor even a very weak one; in all respects, vile as I appear to you, only a very unhappy wretch, and as such entitled to your respectful compassion at least—all I dare ask for now. I will not receive your scorn as my fit guerdon. Is there no strength in overcoming inclination as I have done, in compelling words of affection to flow from loathing lips?—for those scars alone, Evelyn, in contrast to your speckless beauty, would of themselves be enough to shock a fastidious man like me, those hideous livid scars which I have yet to behold, and shudder over, marking one whole side as you assure me of neck, shoulder, and arm, things that in woman are of such inestimable value, of almost more importance than the divine face itself.'

"Yes, but the other side is statuesque enough to satisfy the requisitions of a sensuous sculptor," she rejoined, coldly; "you are wrong, Claude, let us be just! Miriam is very well formed, to say no more, and her skin is like a magnolia-leaf, where sun and wind have not touched or tanned it; then those scars will turn white after a while like the rest, and perhaps scarcely be visible."

"O Heavens! hideous white seams!" he exclaimed, passionately. "I have seen such, like small-pox marks, only ten times more frightful and indelible." In his impotent weakness he moaned aloud.

"Worse and worse! I will tell you frankly, had I known of *them*, the engagement never would have been contracted—no, not though the *inferno* had opened beneath me as my only alternative—but honor binds me now."

"You are fastidious truly, and your sense of honor supreme," she sneered.

"Beauty there was not," he continued, without regarding her rejoinder, "in any remarkable degree. I could have borne its absence with common patience, but absolute disfigurement, deformity, such as you assure me those burns have left behind them, is too dreadful! Had not Dr. Pemberton bared her arm in bleeding, as he did, I should never have known of it at all probably until too late. That one mark was suggestive."

"You attach too much consequence to mere externals, Claude," said Evelyn, coldly. "I trust such fastidious notions may be laid at rest before your marriage, or poor Miriam, with her warm, affectionate, and unsuspicious nature will be the sufferer. I pity her fate, sincerely."

"No, Evelyn, you wrong me there; I respect and esteem her far too much ever to wound her feelings. Against this I shall carefully guard. My bargain would be broken, otherwise. It is a clear case of barter and sale, you see. One's honor is concerned in keeping such an obligation. I shall never be ungrateful."

"You have European ideas, you tell me," she said, bitterly; "is this one of them?"

"It is, and the least among them, perhaps; yet it is, nevertheless, hard to overcome positive repulsion."

There was a pause now, during which I could count every throb of my heart, and throat, and temples—my whole frame was transfigured into an anvil, on which a thousand tiny hammers seemed to ring. Yet I could not move, nor speak, nor weep—no wretchedness was ever more supreme than this cataleptic seizure. Evelyn was the first to break the transient silence.

"Your path is a plain one, Claude Bainrothe; fulfill your contract, sealed with gold, and bear patiently your selected lot."

"Evelyn, one word—let it be sincere: do you hate and scorn me? Answer me as you would speak to your own soul."

"No, Claude, no, yet the blow was hard to bear—struck, too, as you must reflect, so suddenly! Only the day before abandonment, remember, you had made protestations of such undying constancy. Your conduct was surely inconstant, at least."

"I make them still, those professions you scorn so deeply."

"Away, false man, lest the sleeper awaken!"

"You say there is no danger of that, and that in their coffins the dead are not more insensible."

"To see you kneeling at my feet might bring the dead even to life," she laughed, contemptuously. "I am sick of this drama; be natural for once. We can both afford to be so now."

"Do not spurn me, Evelyn! Never was my love for you so wild as now." I heard him kissing her hands passionately, and his voice, as he spoke these words, was choked with grief.

"O Claude, let my hand go; at least consider appearances. Mrs. Austin will be here in a moment now; what will she think of you? What am I to think of such caprice?"

"One word, then, Evelyn—tell me that you forgive me—on such conditions I will release your hands."

"When I forgive you, Claude, I shall be wholly indifferent to you," she said, gently. "Do you still claim forgiveness? I am not angry, though, take that assurance for all comfort. Then, if you will have it" (and I heard a kiss exchanged), "this confirmation."

"Then you are not wholly indifferent to me, Evelyn?" he said, in eager tones, "you care for me still—a little?"

"A very little, Claude"—hesitatingly.

"Say that you love me, Evelyn, just once more—I can then die happy."

"Claude Bainrothe, arise—unhand me—this is child's play—let me breathe freely again. Well do you know I love you. O God! why do you return to a theme so bitter and profitless to both? Come, let us look together on Miriam sleeping, and gather strength and courage from such contemplation. Come, my friend!"

The curtains were lifted—still I lay rigidly and with closed eyelids before them—not from any notion of my own, but from the helplessness of my agony and the condition into which I was fast drifting. Once or twice during the progress of this conversation I had tried to lift my voice, my hand—both were alike powerless. I lay bound, for a while, in a cataleptic reverie, and then I passed away once more into darkness and syncope.

It was evening when I revived—Dr. Pemberton was sitting beside me, holding my pulse—Mrs. Austin and Mabel were at the bedside. This was, at last, the end I craved; of all, I hoped.

"The wine, Mrs. Austin," the doctor said, in low accents.

"Quick! one spoonful instantly. You know how it was before—you were too slow; she fell back before she could swallow it.—Now another, Miriam. Say, are you better?"

Most anxiously as my eyes opened and were fixed upon his face, were these words spoken:

"No, dying, I believe—at least, I hope so!"

The shrieks of the child aroused me to a sense of what I owed myself and her. "You shall not die, sister Miriam," she cried. "Papa does not want you—I want you—I will not stay with Evelyn and Claude—I will go down in the ground too, if you die. My sister, you shall not go to God! I will hold you tight, if He comes for you. He shall not have my Miriam—nor His angels either.

Her cries did for me what medicine had failed to do. They tried in vain to silence her. My pulse returned under the stimulus of emotion. I put out my hand blindly to Mabel.

"Hush, darling," I said, "I will live for you if I can—ask Dr. Pemberton to save me."

"You are better, already, Miriam," he whispered.—

"Mrs. Austin, take Mabel away until she can be quiet and behave like a lady; her sister is getting well—tell her I say so. Call Miss Evelyn here, instantly."

"No, no!" with an impatient movement of the hand. "Not Evelyn;" again my arm fell nervelessly.

"Well, then, don't call her, of course. I will stay a while myself; we don't want anybody at all, Miriam and I, only each other. Go you and make that panada ready, and sent it when I ring. Let Charity bring it, she will do. Keep every one else away."

His word was law in our household in times of illness, and Mabel's cries were hushed at once by his assurances, and she was led passively away. She was capable of great self-control on emergencies, like her own dear sainted mamma, who always thought *first* what was best for others, and *afterward* for herself, if there was room at all for such latter consideration.

"You must have revived hours ago," said Dr. Pemberton, after I had rallied sufficiently to prove to him that my crisis was over, and the usual symptoms of returning convalescence had been manifested. "I have marked your seizures narrowly, the periods are perfect—I have limited them to eighteen hours latterly—nay, sometimes to twelve; they used to be four-and-twenty. You were due back again in port, little craft, at nine or ten o'clock this morning."

"Back again from where, Dr. Pemberton?"

"How should I know, my dear? Some unknown shore—Hades, perhaps. Who knows what becomes of the soul when the body is wrapped in stupor or sleep, any more than when it is dead? You came partially to yourself at five this afternoon. I had just come in then, having been unavoidably detained. We administered, or tried to administer, wine—but too slowly; you fell back again into unconsciousness—drifted off to sea once more; but this last effort of Nature was successful. It is all very mysterious to me. Have you no memory of having revived before?"

"Yes, I was conscious for some time this morning—for nearly an hour, I think."

"At what hour? Who was with you?"

"At ten o'clock. I heard the hall clock strike that hour soon after I opened my eyes. I counted every stroke. There were persons in the room at the time, but no one knew of my recovery of consciousness. I lay as if spellbound. I heard conversation and understood it; I remember every word of it yet—I shall ever remember it. But, when they came to me, I was unable to speak or make a sign."

"Unable, or unwilling? I have said before, Miriam, the will has much to do with all this. It is a sort of magnetic seizure, I sometimes think."

"Both, perhaps, involuntary; but I certainly did not wish to grow unconscious again."

"Yet you wanted to die a while ago—child, child, there is something wrong here! What is it? Tell me frankly. I heard of the scene with Mr. Stanbury—the passionate old man was very unwise to excite you so; he meant well, though, no doubt—he always does. What more has occurred? Now, tell me candidly—much depends on the truth—has any one been unkind?"

"Whatever I say to you, Dr. Pemberton, must be under the pledge of confidence," I replied; "otherwise I shall keep my own counsel."

"Surely, Miriam."

"Well, then, I overheard some one saying, when I revived this morning, that I was epileptic, and it troubled me. Now, I call upon you solemnly to answer me truthfully on this point. Of what character is my disease?—speak earnestly."

"I do not know—not epilepsy, certainly; partially nervous, I think—one of Nature's strange safety-valves, I suppose."

"You would not deceive me?"

"Not under present circumstances, surely; not at any time after such an appeal as yours."

"Did Dr. Physick ever pronounce my disease epilepsy? You consulted together about it once, I believe. Do tell me the truth about this matter," laying my hand on his arm.

"Never, so help me God!" he said, earnestly.

"You have relieved me greatly," I said, pressing my lips on that dear and revered hand which had so often ministered to me and mine in sorest agony—a hand spotless as the heart within—yet, brown and withered as the leaves of autumn.

"Now you, in turn, must relieve me," he said, gravely. "Who was it that alleged these things? They were slanders, and deserve to be nailed to the wall, and shall be if power be mine to do so."

"I cannot tell you. Do not ask me. It was not asserted that you pronounced my disease epilepsy, but insinuated that you thought so. Dr. Physick's opinion was given to confirm this impression."

"Have you traitors in your own household, Miriam?" he asked, sternly.

I was silent—shedding quiet tears, however.

"I have thought so before," he said, low, between his set teeth. "But, thank God, you can put your foot on them all before very long!—This seems a nice young man you are going to marry, but I never liked his father. I say this frankly to you, child; but, in truth, I have had no sufficient reason for this distaste or prejudice—it is no more, I confess. You are very much in their hands for the present, I fear; but I hope they will do you justice."

"I shall not marry Claude Bainrothe," I rejoined at last, firmly. "Let this be perfectly understood between us two, Dr. Pemberton. That marriage will never take place!"

"Why, your own father told me you were engaged in October last!"

"I have changed my mind since then. Understand me, I admire Mr. Bainrothe for many qualities—I am attached to him even; and he is infinitely to be pitied for some reasons, certainly; but marry him I never will!"

"And this is your resolution?"

"It is. But, on second thoughts, I will ask you to keep your knowledge of it strictly to yourself. I cannot tell you my motives of action now, but they are good."

"Miriam, you must not ask me to be your confederate in any scheme of coquetry or caprice such as this concealment points to. You must deal with this young man openly—no double dealings, my child, or I shall come to the rescue."

"Have you ever known me to play fast and loose, Dr. Pemberton? Is that my characteristic? Ask Mr. Gerald Stanbury—ask all who know me—if I have ever been guilty of deceit, or time-serving, or caprice, or perfidy. No, Dr. Pemberton, it is on his own account solely that I wish to keep this matter quiet for the present. Should *he* wish to proclaim it, I surely shall not object. But I seek only to shield him from mortification, from reproach, in the line of conduct that I am adopting—best for both."

"And to give yourself margin for a change of mind again—little fox! Ah, Miriam, it is the old story—a lovers' quarrel! I understand it all perfectly now. Don't be too hard on the young fellow; he seemed very much in love. Relent in time; he will value your mercy more than your justice, perhaps."

"Have you ever seen us together, that you pronounce him very much in love?" I asked, in a hard, cold, subdued voice that startled my own ear, and made him serious at once.

"Never. But he wears the absent, dreamy air of a lover; even when alone it is noticeable, Miriam. I can always tell when a man is preoccupied in that way."

"If you could go a little further, and divine the object of such preoccupation, you would be better prepared to counsel me, dear friend. He is no lover of mine, I assure you!"

"Ah, the old story again, Miriam! Have patience, my dear child." And, strong in his belief that my change of resolution arose only from pique and jealousy, that would soon be over, the good doctor went his way, all the more ready to keep my secret for such conviction.

I passed a miserable night. The great bed seemed to inclose me like a sepulchre, which yet I was too feeble, too irresolute, to leave. The conversation I had heard seemed stereotyped on plates of brass, that rang like cymbals in my ears. Toward morning I slept. I dreamed that mamma came to me, and said, in tones so natural that they seemed to sound in my ears after I had awakened:

"Miriam, your mother and father have sent me to say

to you that they are united and happy. I, too, have found my mate at last. It was for this I was called. The sea has given up its dead, and I am blessed. Now, dearest, Mabel is all yours;" and then she kissed me.

I woke with that kiss upon my cheek.

The brief and distinct vision made a deep impression on me. I awoke refreshed and strengthened, as from a magnetic slumber.

At first, a sense of joy alone possessed me, but soon the great bitter burden came rolling back upon my soul, like the stone of Sisyphus, which my sleeping soul had heaved away.

It is a beautiful law of our being, that we rarely dream of that which occupies and troubles us most in the daytime. Compensation is carried out in this way, as in many others, insensibly, and the balance of thought kept equal. I have heard persons complain frequently that they could not dream of their dead, with whom their waking thoughts were ever filled. But madness must have been the consequence, had there been no repose for the mind from one engrossing image.

Relaxation comes to us in dreams at times when the brain needs it most, and to lose the consciousness of a sorrow is to cast off its burden for a time, and gain new strength to bear it.

I thought, when I first arose from my bed, that I would write to Claude Bainrothe, and thus save myself the trial of an interview. But the necessity of secrecy, in the commencement at least of the rupture, on his own account, presented itself too forcibly to my mind to permit me such self-indulgence. I felt assured in the first bitterness of feeling, that he would lay my letters before Evelyn, from whom I especially wished, for household peace, to preserve the knowledge of what had passed in my chamber between herself and him.

I had no wish either to mortify or wound the man I had loved so tenderly, but from whom I felt now wholly severed, as though the shadow of a grave had intervened between us.

Never again, never, could he be more to me than a memory, a regret.

Glaring faults, impulsive offenses, *crime* even it may be, I could have forgiven, so long as his allegiance had been mine, and his affection proof against change, but coldness, perfidy, loathing, such as he had avowed, these could never be redeemed in any way, nor considered other than they were, insuperable objections to our honorable union.

My heart recoiled from him so utterly, that I could conceive of no fate more bitter than to be compelled again to receive his profession of affection, his lover-like caresses; yet, in recoiling, it had been bruised against its prison-bars, bruised and crushed like a bird that seeks refuge in the farthest limits of its cage from an approaching foe, and suffers almost as severely as if given to its fangs.

I determined, after mature consideration, to see him once again, privately, and beyond the range of all foreign observation and hearing. In order to do this, I might have to wait, and in the mean time how should I deport myself, how conceal my change of feeling from his observant eyes?

I was relieved by an unlooked-for contingency. Evelyn announced her intention of going, as soon as I should be able to spare her, with a party of young friends, to hear a celebrated singer perform in an oratorio in the cathedral of an adjacent city, her specialty being vocal music, and her mourning permitting only sacred concerts. Her own highly-cultivated voice, it is true, had ill repaid the care that had been lavished on it, sharp and thin as it was by nature. I urged her to set forth at once, declaring myself convalescent, but I did not leave my room, nor see Claude Bainrothe, save for five minutes in her presence, until after she had gone. Then I was at liberty to work my will.

I wrote on the very evening of her departure, requesting him to defer his accustomed visit, until the next morning, when I hoped to have an hour's private conversation with him in the library, a room most dear to me, once as the chosen haunt of my father, but shunned of late as vault-like and melancholy, now that his ever-welcome and dear presence was removed from it forever.

Punctual as the hand to the hour or the dial to the sun, Claude Bainrothe came at the time I had appointed, and I was there to meet him, nerved and calm as a spirit of the past, in that great quiet sarcophagus of books—at least, I so deceived myself to believe. I had made up my mind, during the time I had been sitting alone in that sombre room, as to what I would say to him, and how clearly and concisely I would array my wrongs in words, and pronounce his sentence. But, when he came, all this was forgotten. A tumult of wild feeling surged through my brain. My very tongue grew icy, and trembled in my mouth. My eyes were dimmed, and my forehead was cold and rigid. I was silent from emotion. I felt like a dying wretch.

"You are very pale, Miriam," he said, as he advanced to me with outstretched hands, and wearing that beaming, candid, devoted look he knew so well how to assume;

"are you sure you are not going to be ill again, my love? You must be careful of yourself, my own darling; you must indeed, for my sake, if not your own."

I was strengthened now to speak, by the indignation that possessed me, at his perfidious words, his wholly artificial manner, which broke on me as suddenly and as glaringly on the eye as rouge will do on a woman's cheek in sunshine, which we have thought real bloom in shadow. I wondered then, how I ever could have been deceived. I wonder less now.

"Sit down, Mr. Bainrothe," I said, coldly, withdrawing my hands quietly from his grasp, and recovering with my composure my strength. "Do not concern yourself about my health, I beg. It is quite good just now, and will probably remain so for some time. My spells occur at distant intervals."

"I know how that is, or has been; but we must try to break them up altogether. We will go to Paris next year, and have the best advice; in the mean time Dr. Pemberton must try some new remedy for you, or call in counsel. On this point I am quite determined."

"I am satisfied that Dr. Pemberton, who understands my constitution thoroughly, is my best adviser. I shall decline all other medical aid," I replied. "Nature is on my side—I am young, vigorous, growing still, probably, in strength, and shall fling off my malady eventually, as a strong man casts a serpent from his thigh. I have little fear on that score. Nor do I think, with some others, that my disease is epilepsy; though, if it were, God knows I should have little need for shame."

"Miriam, what an idea! Epilepsy, indeed!" He was very nervous now, I saw. "Epilepsy, indeed!"—he faltered again.

"As to those scars, Claude," I said, fixing my eyes upon him, "they were honorably earned in my sister's service. Your father knows the details, which I spare your fastidious ear. I cannot wonder, however, that they shocked you, with your previous feelings to me. I do not like to look upon them myself, yet I have never felt them a humiliation until now." I knew that my forehead flushed hotly as I proceeded, and my lips trembled. The reaction was complete.

"Miriam, what does all this mean?" he asked, rising suddenly from his seat as pale as ashes, and clinging to the mantel-shelf for support as he did so.

"It means, Claude Bainrothe," I said, firmly, "it means simply this: that our engagement is at an end; that you are free from all claims of mine from this moment, and that henceforth we can only meet as friends or strangers—as the first, I trust!" I stretched forth my hand toward him kindly, irresistibly. He did not seem to notice it.

"Who has done this?" he asked, huskily. "Evelyn? This is her work, I feel; a piece of her bitter vengeance! Tell me the the truth, Miriam—who has done this devil's mischief?"

He suffered greatly, I saw—was terribly excited.

"So far from your surmise being just, Claude, I enjoin upon you, as a man of honor, never to let her know the subject of this conference, in which she has had no voluntary part. Placed as I am by my father's will, which I never will gainsay, however bitter it may be to me; bound hand and foot; indeed, in her power by its decisions for a term of years, her knowledge of the fact that I had overheard her conversation with you in my chamber when I lay stricken, helpless, if not unconscious (an unwilling listener, I assure you, Claude, to every word you uttered), would be a cause of endless misery to me and her. No, Evelyn has told me nothing, believe me."

He staggered back from the mantel to his chair, sat down again helplessly, and covered his face with his hands. The blush of shame mounted above his fingers and crimsoned the very roots of his silken hair. He trembled visibly.

O God! how I pitied him then! Self sank out of sight at that moment, and I thought only of his confusion. Had I obeyed my impulse, I would have cast my arms about his neck as about a brother's, and whispered, to that stormy nature, "Peace, be still!" But I refrained from a manifestation that might have deceived him utterly as to its source. I only said:

"I am very sorry, Claude, for all this; but bear it like a man. Believe me, no one shall ever know the occasion of this rupture—the management of which I leave entirely in your hands. Of what I overheard I shall never speak, I promise you, even though sorely pressed for my reasons for our separation. My own pride would prevent such a revelation, you know, putting principle aside." And again I extended my hand to him frankly, with the words, "Let us be friends."

He had glanced up a moment while I was speaking, evidently relieved by my voluntary promise. He took my hand humbly now, and reverently kissed it, bowing his head above it long and mutely.

"My poor, outraged, offended, noble Miriam!" I heard him murmur at last. The words affected me.

"I am all these, Claude," I said, withdrawing my hand gently but firmly, "but none the less your friend, if you will have it so. And now let us think what will be best for you to do. I wish to spare your feelings as much as possible, and I will say all I can with truth to exonerate you in your father's eyes. Go to Copenhagen, as you proposed at one time to do, and leave the rest to me. That will be best, I think."

"To Copenhagen!" he exclaimed. "You issue thus coldly your edict of banishment! Are you implacable then, Miriam?" and the cold dew stood in beads on his now pallid brow as he rose before me. He had not fully realized his situation until now.

"'Implacable' is scarcely the word for this occasion, Claude. It implies anger or hatred, it seems to me. Now, I feel neither of these—only the truest sympathy."

"Your anger, your hatred, were far more welcome, Miriam—more natural under the circumstances. This cool philosophy in one so young is monstrous! Mock me no longer with your calm compassion—it maddens me—it sinks me below contempt!"

He spoke gloomily, angrily, pushing away the clustering hair from his brow in the way peculiar to him when excited, as he proceeded, stamping slightly with his foot on the marble hearthstone in his impotent way. I could but smile!

"I will not offend you further, Claude," I said, mildly. "Receive your ring;" and I gave him back the diamond cross on a black enamel ground set on its circle of gold that he had placed upon my finger as a pledge of our betrothal; an ominous one, surely—for another cross was now to be borne.

"Understand me distinctly, Claude, all is finally at an end between us from this forever more! And now, farewell!"

"Go, Miriam, go!" he murmured. "Leave me to

my fate—I have deserved it all, and more. I have been weak and wicked—you shall not find me ungrateful. Go, queenly spirit! go, soul of tenderness, pity, and most unselfish faith, that ever folded its wings in human breast! go, and find a fitter mate! For me, the world is wide, I shall offend your gaze no more."

Without another word I left him. I could not trust myself to speak. Too much of the past returned to render any further intercourse between us wise, or other than torture at that season. Besides, my confidence in him was gone forever, and with it had vanished respect, esteem, affection!

## CHAPTER VI.

"WHAT is this Claude is talking of, Miriam?" asked Mr. Bainrothe a day or two after the interview I have described in my last pages. "Copenhagen again—and he seems quite dispirited. He says you have sent him into banishment for a year, Miriam—a long probation truly!"

"Our engagement was to have been for that length of time from the first," I said, evasively; "my father was not willing for me to marry before I had attained my seventeenth year, you remember, and it still wants some months of that period."

"Oh, yes! but all that is changed now by the force of circumstances. You are so well grown, so very womanly for your age, that I cannot see why it would not be just as well to shorten rather than lengthen the period of your engagement, especially as it seems Claude must go into exile until then, by some caprice of yours. You will be at the head of your own house too, after that ceremony takes place, which Claude is so impatient to have over. Evelyn would go to England for a time under such circumstances, for she will not oppose your views—your father's will was made before your betrothal to my son, or he would scarcely have made her your absolute guardian" (apologetically spoken). "For the matter of that," he pursued, "I cannot doubt that, were you settled in life, she would gladly transfer Mabel to your care. Indeed, I have heard her say as much."

"A great temptation, truly!" I said, grimly.

"Your manner is peculiar to-day, Miriam. I cannot understand it, I confess."

"For all explanation, Mr. Bainrothe, I refer you to your son. I prefer not to discuss the matter."

"Ah! it is just as I expected, from his behavior as well as your own. Some childish misunderstanding has taken place between you, which he was loath to acknowledge or explain, but which in your womanly candor you will reveal at once, and tell me all about it. I am the very best mediator you ever saw on such occasions," with a bland and confident air, taking my hand, smiling.

"Mr. Bainrothe, your mediation could effect nothing between me and Claude; we understand one another perfectly, I assure you."

He was very much excited now, evidently; he relinguished my unwilling hand coldly—on which he had, doubtless, missed the conspicuous ring, significant of my engagement. His chameleon eyes seemed to emit sparks of phosphorescent fire, as if every one of the dull-yellow sparks therein had become suddenly ignited. I saw then, for the first time, what his ire could be, and what reason I had to dread it.

"Have I been deceived in believing that you were attached to my son, Miriam Monfort, and that you meant to keep faith with him?" he asked, stiffly.

"You have not been deceived, Mr. Bainrothe, nor is it my wish to deceive you now. Again I beg to refer you to him for all explanation; whatever he alleges will be highly satisfactory to me."

"I will bet my life," he said, passionately, "that Evelyn Erle is at the root of all this! That girl," he soliloquized, "who knew so well, from the first, what our intentions were; to throw herself at his head in the shameless way she did! A woman, without a woman's modesty."

"Beware, Mr. Bainrothe," I interrupted; "it is of my sister you speak. I will not hear her slandered. Certainly, if propriety ever assumed female form, it is in that of Evelyn Erle. This was my father's opinion—it is mine."

"Propriety! The pale ghost of it rather," he sneered; "I thought you hated hypocrisy; you do not love that woman—have little right to; yet you praise and defend her. How is this! Are you sincere in such a course? Ask your own heart."

"Mr. Bainrothe, let us not discuss Evelyn, I beg, either now or hereafter; for some reason she is very sacred to me. I cannot say one word more on the subject of your son than I have said, without his own consent. As to our marriage, let me tell you frankly—" I hesitated—the stricture of my throat, for a moment, interrupted me, and I was ashamed of my weakness.

"That it is indefinitely postponed, I suppose you would like to say, Miriam," he added, ironically. "Well, I honor your emotion; don't be ashamed of it. Claude is to blame, no doubt; but the poor fellow suffers enough already, without prolonged punishment. Suppose I send him up to you; he will fall at your feet."

I shook my head silently.

"Now, don't be hard-hearted; I have never seen any

man more devoted than he is to you. A woman must forgive a few shortcomings, now and then, in one of our faulty sex. You lived so long with a man who was almost perfect, that you cannot make allowances for impulsive and indiscreet young manhood. What has poor Claude been guilty of?"

"I will tell you," I said, recovering myself by the time this speech was ended, by a mighty effort. "I will tell you: Guilty only of doing violence to his own inclinations, from a mistaken sense of duty to his father; that is all. I never felt more kindly—more affectionately to Claude Bainrothe than at this moment. If I can serve him in any way, but one, he may always command me. Let him go for the present to Copenhagen, I implore you; it will be best for him—for all of us. He will know his own mind better then, than he can now. When he returns, I would like to see him happy. I doubt if he will be so, if he remains here," I faltered; "I should dislike, very much, to see him make shipwreck of his happiness." I hesitated, choked again. "I acknowledge—"

"You have cut him off, Miriam, that is plain, for the present, at least," he interrupted. "Yet you speak in enigmas; but, if he be the man I think he is, he will make all clear to you at last, for I am sure he is incapable of any act radically wrong, and is the soul of chivalrous honor; always ready to repair a folly, and avoid it in future. The very best fellow living."

I had never seen Mr. Bainrothe so moved before as he now certainly was. The glitter of a tear was in his mottled eye, and it stirred me strangely. It was as if a snake should weep, and what in Nature could be more affecting than such a spectacle? Or, rather, what *out* of Nature?

There must have been, despite this tender showing, an

outbreak of some sort between father and son from the time of this call and the next visit of Mr. Bainrothe, which occurred some days later.

The expression of concentrated rage on his face was unmistakable on this occasion. Its usually placid, polished expression was laid aside, for one of unqualified displeasure. He was pale as marble too, which was a sign of excitement with him, with his complexion, usually clear and florid.

"Again I come to you, Miriam," he said, "and this time with his permission to mediate between you and my unhappy son. Believe me, you attach too much consequence to hasty and half-comprehended expressions, uttered, as he avers, to appease the offended vanity of an angry and implacable—ay, and dangerous woman. There are few things a man will not say for such a purpose. He went too far in his anxiety to conciliate malice, and allay an evil temper. This is all that can be imputed to him. Be reasonable, my dear girl! you are alone in the world; we are your truest friends. It shall be our study—mine, as well as his—to guard your life from every care, every anxiety even—precaution so necessary in your case, and with your peculiar constitution. You love my son, or have loved him—in this I could not be mistaken—and his affection for you is sincere and unaffected, despite the concessions a designing woman, who conceives herself slighted, has wrung from his unwary lips, on purpose to mar his prospects, and blight your happiness, I well believe."

"No, no, there was no design of this kind on her part, of that I am sure. She could not—did not know that I overheard them. You must do her justice there—I trust she may never know it. Claude promised me—"

"I know, I know—it was with this understanding," he interrupted, "that he confided to me the extent of his indiscretion, for which I have rated him soundly, I assure you. Evelyn is not to know that you overheard them. This is the compact—a very sensible and politic one on your part, under the circumstances, for Evelyn, we all know, is, excuse me my dear, the devil, when fairly aroused. Now, as to this overhearing of yours—might not your mind, laboring under recent coma, and a sort of mental mirage as it were, have had a tendency to magnify and only partially comprehend the conversation thus suddenly forced upon your attention? For I understand you were unable to make yourself heard at all, or even to give signs of life when the curtains of your bed were lifted by the interlocutors."

"This last is true—but that I could not have been mistaken, Claude's own admissions confirm. He denied nothing that I suggested—much was left by me unquestioned."

"Yes," catching wildly at this straw, "he finds himself quite in the dark still, I perceive—as to the accusations brought against him; suppose you make your charges one by one, as it were in the shape of specifications?"

"There are no charges, no accusations brought—nothing of that sort," I said, proudly; "and I must entreat that from this hour, Mr. Bainrothe, this subject be dropped between us utterly. It is wholly unprofitable, believe me."

"You are a person of extraordinary obduracy," he said, "for one of your years. I should like to know how much the Stanbury influence has had to do with strengthening your unwise, unamiable, and stiff-necked resolution! If I were Claude Bainrothe, I should lay heavy damages against you in the courts of law, for your unjustifiable evasion of a formal contract—one your father sanctioned, one of which all your friends are and were cognizant and proud, and which has subjected him, in its rupture, to so much distress and mortification; nay, even as I can prove, pecuniary loss."

"If *money* can repay your son Claude, for any wrong I have done him, he is welcome to a portion of mine," I said, deeply disgusted, "without intervention of law—a painful exposure of any kind. I cherish for him, however, even yet, too much regard and respect to believe him capable of such proceedings. The idea is worthy of the mind it springs from—worthy of the author of all this sorrow and confusion—worthy of Mr. Basil Bainrothe, the arch-conspirator himself."

He turned upon me with clinched hands and blazing eyes. "You shall answer for these words, girl! if not now, years hence," he said; "the seed of your insult has been thrown on fertile soil, I promise you!" and he laughed bitterly.

"I do not fear you," I replied; all disguise was thrown off—it was war to the knife between us now; "never have—never can, in spite of your unmanly threats. Evelyn must protect me henceforth from any further contact with you, however, until I am of age to take in hand my own affairs; Evelyn Erle, my guardian, and your fellow-executor, owes me this safeguard. I trust, Mr. Bainrothe, we shall meet no more."

I left the room—left him in possession of the library, in which he paced up and down for an hour or more, like a caged panther. There was a sealed note for me in his handwriting, under the massive paper-weight on the table, when I entered it again, which he had written and left there before his departure. It ran thus—for I read it derisively, and remember its contents still:

"We have both been wrong, dear Miriam. I, as the elder and more experienced offender—therefore, the more responsible one—claim it as my privilege to be the first to atone. I cannot think, from what I know of you, that you will be long in following my example. Let us forgive one another. Fate has thrown us together, and we must not afford a malicious world the spectacle of our inconsistency, or the satisfaction of seeing us quarrel, after so many years of harmony.

"As to Claude, you and he must settle your own matters. I wash my hands of the whole transaction from this hour, supposing that common-sense will triumph at last, and reconcile your differences.

"Yours as ever, truly and devotedly,

"BASIL BAINROTHE."

I did not answer this note—I could not discreetly, although I tried to do so several times. I could not conquer sufficiently my deep disgust of his insupportable behavior to respond kindly, at that time, to any overture of Mr. Bainrothe's, nor did I wish to write one rude word to him in connection with so delicate a subject as that of our late discussion.

He came no more until after Evelyn's return, and then only on necessary business; inquiring for her alone, and holding on such occasions secret conclaves with her invariably in the library. Whenever we met casually, however, whether in the street or my own house, he was polite and easy in his deportment, even gracious.

With Claude it was otherwise; he avoided me sedulously, and, although I have reason to think he met and joined Evelyn frequently, and even by appointment in her long walks, he never called to see her or paid her open attentions. Yet I found that he had followed my counsels.

A day or two before he sailed for Copenhagen to join the legation in Denmark, an exception to this rule of avoidance was made by both father and son, who came in as had been usual with them in other days, informally, in the evening.

This was Claude's farewell visit—a very unpleasant necessity evidently on his part. I was unconstrained in the cordiality with which I received both his father and himself—for it was heart-felt on this occasion. Old feelings came back to me so vividly that night, and my own dear father seemed so visibly recalled by the presence once more of our unbroken circle, that I lost sight, for a season, of my wrongs and sufferings in the memory of the past, and broke temporarily through the cloud that oppressed me and dimmed my existence.

I saw Mr. Bainrothe gazing at me several times, in the course of his visit, with an expression of interest and surprise.

He had expected very different manifestations, no doubt, and he told Evelyn afterward that "no woman of thirty could have carried off matters with a higher hand than did that chit of sixteen, Miriam Monfort."

"All that talk of yours, Miriam, about 'Hamlet,' 'Elsinore,' 'Wittenberg,' and the 'fiery Dane,' probably imposed on those two unsophisticated men; but I saw through the whole proceeding; you were afraid of yourself, my dear, that was evident, and ashamed, as you ought to have been, of your capricious conduct to poor Claude, who shows, however, as uncompromising a spirit as your own, I perceive. What *was* the matter, Miriam? I can get nothing out of him, and I have waited, until my patience is exhausted, for a voluntary communication from you."

"Why have you not asked me before, Evelyn?" I questioned, calmly, in reply. "You have shown more than your usual forbearance, on this occasion."

"My dear child, 'Least said is soonest mended,' is proverbial in quarrels of all kinds. I have no wish to pry or play mischief-maker, and, if Mr. Basil Bainrothe with his diplomatic talents could do nothing to mend the difficulty, I had no right to suppose that I could succeed better, with my very direct, straightforward disposition."

"You were right, Evelyn, certainly, in your conclusion, and, if you please, will never ask for any explanation of the breach between Claude and myself. It is irrevocable; but I am sorry to see him so resentful. He cannot conceal his displeasure against me, and yet I have never offended him willingly, I am sure."

"Caprice and coquetry are not so lightly estimated by every one, as you hold them, nor yet counted causes for gratitude by most men, let me assure you, Miriam."

"Who has accused me of these?" I questioned, with a flashing eye, a flushing cheek.

"Does your own heart acquit you?" she asked, evasively.

"It does," I answered, solemnly, "as does the God who reads all hearts, and to whom I am now alone answerable for any motives of mine."

"Since when have you grown so independent, Miriam?" she asked, ironically.

"Since the death of my father," I replied.

"Ah! you do not accredit delegated allegiance it seems," turning her face aside.

"Not as far as my own feelings and their sources are concerned. As to my acts, I hope never to commit one of which all just men might not approve."

"We shall see. However, a year more or less makes little difference. Claude Bainrothe, improved, will return within a year, probably, and all may still be well. Matters will then, I fancy, be in his own hands, pretty much.

"All *is* well, Evelyn, if you could only think so, and now, once for all, make up your mind, definitely, to let *well* alone, for I must not be approached again on this subject, I warn you!"

I spoke with a decision which, at times, had its effect even on the "indomitable Evelyn," as my father often had called her, playfully, and again the broken engagement was consigned to silence.

Yet on my mind, my feelings, the effect of this severe and sudden trial was far more bitter and profound than met the outward eye.

I had been sustained at first by a sense of pride, self-respect, and womanly indignation, that prevented me from feeling the whole extent of the wound I had received; but with reaction came that dull, dumb, aching of the heart, which all who have felt it may recognize as more wearing than keener pain, or more declared suffering.

I suppose the Spartan who felt the gnawing of the hidden fox was a mere type of this species of anguish, which reproduces itself wherever wounded pride underlies concealment, or wherever injustice and ingratitude render us uncomplaining through a sense of moral dignity.

The first six months succeeding my rupture with Claude Bainrothe went by like a leaden dream. My heart lay like a stone in my bosom, and the gloss had dropped from life, and the glory from the face of Nature for me, in that dreary interval, as though I had grown suddenly old.

In routine, in occupation alone, I found relief and companionship. I compelled myself to teach Mabel, and pursue my own studies, lest my mind should fall back on my body, and destroy both.

A nervous peculiarity manifested itself about this time, that was singularly distressing to me, and which I confided to no one, not even that excellent physician who kept a quiet and observant eye fixed upon me during all this period of my probation.

I became nervously but not mentally convinced of the want of substance in every thing around me, and have repeatedly risen and crossed the room, and touched an article on the opposite side, to compel my better judgment to the conviction that it was indeed tangible and substantial, and not the merest shadow of a shade.

I was sustained in my resolution to conquer this besetting weakness, from a vague horror and fear that, should I suffer it to gain further ascendency, I might fall back into habitual lethargies, and, remembering what Dr. Pemberton had said, I was determined, if possible, to throw off that incubus of my being, by the strength of my own will, aided by God's mercy.

There were no uttered prayers to this effect, that I remember, but an unceasing cry for strength, for light, went up from my heart, as continuously as the waters of a fountain, to the ear of my Creator. I have thought sometimes that, in this persistent wrestle of mind with matter, enduring so many weeks and months, so many weary, woful days and sleepless nights, the physical demon was exorcised at last, that had ruled my life so long, or was reduced to feeble efforts thereafter.

Once when Dr. Pemberton's attendance had been necessary to me, during a severe spell of pleurisy, he said when I was recovering: "There is some favorable change at work in your constitution, Miriam, it seems to me. We hear no more of the 'obliteration spells,'" for thus he called my seizures.

"Your drops have banished them, dear doctor, I suppose," I rejoined, with a faint smile.

"They may have aided to do so," he said, gravely, "but I think I have observed, Miriam, that you were doing good work lately for yourself. You have been struggling manfully, my little girl. Now, I am going for recreation to Niagara, and the Northern cities, for a few weeks, next month, and I want you to go with me, in aid of this effort of yours. Quite alone, with Charity as sole attendant. My niece will be with me—a good, quiet girl, you know, some years older than yourself, and also in feeble health; and I will see that you are both well taken care of, medically at least, while you are absent. How would you like this, Miriam," patting my shoulder, "just for a change?"

"Oh, very much!" I said, eagerly. "Yes, I will go gladly, in this quiet way, for I do not wish to visit gay places, or to make strange acquaintance, under the circumstances. My deep mourning must be respected, you know, and—" I hesitated; looked in his kind, sympathizing face; then hid mine on his shoulder—weeping. The first tears of relief I had shed for months.

He did not check me, for he knew full well the value

of this outlet of feeling, to one situated as I was, physically as well as mentally.

"I would offer to take Mabel," he added, after a time, "were I not solemnly convinced that it would be better for you both that she should stay here. Mrs. Austin seems necessary to her very existence; and that old woman is your vampire, I verily believe."

"No, no, she is very good, indeed. You are mistaken."

"No, I am not mistaken. There are persons who do suck away, unconsciously, the very life of others, from some peculiarity of organization in both. I have strong faith in this theory. I have been obliged sometimes to decree the separation of wife and husband for a time, to save the life of one or the other; of mother and child even. Every time you fall ill, I believe Mrs. Austin gains strength and energy at your expense. She absorbs your nervous fluid. It was from this conviction that I requested you two years ago to change your room, which, until then, she had shared on the pretence of your necessities, and to substitute a younger and less sponge-like attendant. You remember the stress I laid on this?"

"Yes, yes, one of your crotchets, dear doctor, nothing else. You are full of such vagaries—always were—but there is not another such dear old willful physician in Christendom for all that."

"Little flatterer! But here is a piece of cassava bread, I brought you, as you thought you would like to taste it. My old West Indian patient keeps me well supplied. I fancy to nibble it as I drive about in my cabriolet, or whatever they call this French affair of mine."

"For a wonder, you have the word right;" and I laughed in his honest face.

"I am going to France, next spring, when the Stanburys go over, just to see what strides medicine is making across the waters, and to rest myself a little, improve my Gallic pronunciation, and get the fashions, and I will take you as my interpreter, if you promise to be very good and obedient in the interval."

"Oh, thank you; I would like it of all things. But what takes the Stanburys abroad? I have heard nothing of this plan of theirs before."

"Pleasure and business combined, I believe. They will remain abroad some years, for the education of George Gaston. What an idol Mrs. Stanbury is making of that boy, to be sure, and Laura is just as foolish about him as her mother! By-the-by, she is to be married, they say, to that young Prussian nobleman, who was there so much last winter. I forget his unpronounceable name. They will reside in Berlin, I understand, should the marriage be '*un fait accompli*,' as the French have it. Is not that right, Miriam?"

"Oh, admirably pronounced! You are becoming quite a Gaul in your old age."

"I hope I shall never become gall and wormwood, in any event, like some old folks. Now, is not that being literal, Miriam?"

"And witty, as well! You must have been associating with Dr. C.....n, lately."

"So you can't give me credit for a little originality, because my facetious vein is new to you. Now, do your old friend justice, and believe even in his puns; if not pungent, he is self-sustaining and independent; but, remember, I count on you absolutely, next week. One trunk apiece and no bandboxes or baskets. A green-silk travelling-bonnet and pongee habit. This is my uniform, for my female guard. Carry Grey knows my whims, and will observe them. By-the-by, you will like my niece."

We made a delightful tour, which occupied the whole month of August, and I came back refreshed, soul and body; as for Carry Grey, she revived, like a plant that had been newly tended and watered after long neglect. For the poor girl had been making a slave of herself for two years in her widowed brother's household, consisting of many little children, and needed repose from her multifarious duties.

He was going to marry again soon, she told me, and then she hoped to feel at liberty to fulfill her own engagement of five years' standing. Carry Grey was quite this many years over twenty-one, and was going to emigrate with her husband to Missouri, and to settle in the thriving young town of St. Louis, fast growing up then into a city. He was to have a church there, and they might be so happy, she thought, if God only smiled upon them! But all depended upon that.

It was a wholesome lesson to my morbid discontent and pride to hear what trials she had surmounted already, and how many more she was ready to encounter.

She had once been engaged to a very brilliant young man, she told me, but he was dissipated and careless of her feelings, and she let him go; since that he had drifted fast to destruction, and sometimes she reproached herself for not having held to him through thick and thin. It was just possible she might have saved him, she thought, but her friends had persuaded her that he would only drag her down, and so she broke with him forever.

"Did he love you?" I asked, eagerly. "Were you sure that he was not perfidious?"

"Oh, I believe he was true to me—however false to himself."

"Then you were wrong," I said. "Wrong, believe me, Carry Grey! A woman should bear every thing but infidelity of heart for the man she loves—every thing!"

"I am sorry to hear you say so," she replied, somewhat coldly. "There is a great deal more than blind affection needful for a woman's happiness, Miss Monfort—so experience tells us. What I mean is, perhaps he *might* have reformed had I not broken with him; but it was the *merest* chance—one too feeble to depend on; and I did wisely to discard him, I am convinced."

"Forgive me! I did not mean to censure you," I said; "I was only speaking generally—too generally, perhaps, for individual courtesy. This is a theory of mine which as yet I have had no opportunity to put in practice, for I have never been attached to a dissipated man." I smiled. "I dare say I too should drop such a man like a pestilence."

"I hope so. But the best way is to avoid all intimacy with such men from the first. You are very young. Let me give you my advice on this subject before you form any attachment: keep your affections for a worthy object, if you keep them locked up forever. Better be alone than mismated."

"This is to shut the cage after the bird has flown," I thought, sadly; but I thanked her, and promised to profit by her good counsel.

We were fast friends ever after, and, when she went away to her distant Western home, Carry Ormsby bore some memorials of her summer friend away with her, in the shape of books, plate, and jewels, such as her simple means could have ill afforded. I felt that I could not have devised any means more sure to gratify her worthy uncle, to whom such gifts had been dross. He was a widower—the father of sons—indifferent to show, and, besides that, unwilling to incur obligations from any one, such as gifts entail on some minds.

There are persons made to give and others to receive, and neither can do the work of the other gracefully. He and I were both of the same order, so we accorded perfectly.

The autumn and winter passed very quietly. In Mrs. Stanbury and Laura I again found my chief consolation. George Gaston was in the South, for his health, on his own decayed plantation, with his uncle, who took charge of it. But, in the spring, as Dr. Pemberton had stated, they were all to go to Europe for some years. Laura would be married in Paris, if at all. Every thing depended on some investigations Mr. Gerald Stanbury was to make in person as to the character and position of her betrothed. "For a Prussian nobleman may be a Prussian boot-black for aught I know," he observed, "and without derogation to his dignity, no doubt, in that land of pipes and fiddlers. But an American sovereign requires something better than that when he gives away the hand of the princess, his relative, and endows her with a goodly dowry. Every man, we feel, is a king in America."

Our circle of society was much enlarged by Evelyn after our first year of mourning had expired. She insisted on taking me with her in turn to Washington, Boston, and Saratoga Springs, then at their acme of fashion. Mr. Bainrothe, who had by this time glided back into his old grooves of apparent sociability in our household, accompanied us, and did all in his power, it seemed, to promote our enjoyment and success.

Yet it was astonishing what an icy barrier still remained between us two, and how perfectly I managed, without a conscious effort, to set a limit to his approaches, even while treating him with apparent courtesy and confidence.

Something in his eye, his manner, had become extremely unpleasant to me since our social relations had been resumed. There was a controlled ardor in his expression of face and even in his demeanor that I could not reconcile with his position toward me nor understand, and yet which froze my blood in spite of my best endeavors to repel the thoughts suggested.

"I am very morbid and fanciful, certainly," I said to myself, "even to think such a thing possible. At his age, and knowing full well my opinion of him, my sentiments toward him—he surely would not dare—!" I could not even in my own heart finish out a conjecture that dyed my face and throat crimson, or mahogany-color, as Evelyn would have averred contemptuously could she have witnessed my solitary confusion.

"I have clung to him too much," I thought; "it is my own fault if he throws too much of the tone of tenderness in his manner, when, distasteful as he is to me, his arm, his protection, have seemed to me preferable to those of a stranger, and I have accepted them merely to avoid the advances of others.

"I am not in the mood to be sentimental, or susceptible either, after my bitter experience, and the idea he so carefully instills is ever present to me—strive as I will to repel it—the thought that I am sought alone for my fortune!

"Yet I am not wholly unattractive, probably, though less beautiful than Evelyn. But what, after all, is beauty?

Plainer women than I are loved and sought in marriage, who possess no gift of fortune or accomplishment.

"Why should I suffer him to fill my mind with suspicions that embitter it against all approaches? Why should I seal my soul away in endless gloom, because one man, out of all Adam's race, was faithless and false-hearted?"

Thus reasoning, I gained strength and self-reliance to receive other attentions and mingle with the multitude. Nor should I have known to what extent Mr. Bainrothe had carried his injustice and perfidy toward me, but for the loquacity of Lieutenant Raymond, a young adorer of mine, who revealed to me, the very evening before I left Saratoga, along with his passion—a hopeless one of course, which, but for this connection, would not be noted here—the strategic course of my guardian.

"I ought to have been warned, by what I saw and heard, that my suit was a hopeless one," he said; "I had been told of your engagement, but could not believe it possible, although confirmed by Mr. Bainrothe's manner. A rival of his age and experience, possessed too of such physical attractions, and such charm of manner, seldom fails to carry the day over a raw, impulsive youth—who can only adore—bow down and worship his idol, and who possesses no arts of conquest."

"Pause there, Lieutenant Raymond; of what are you speaking?" I asked, coldly; "you have probably confounded matters, names, and—"

"No, no, it is all too evident now to admit of a doubt! You are affianced to Mr. Bainrothe—your own timid and dependent manner might have enlightened me long ago, as well as his devoted one—but a man in love is blinder than the blindest bat even! He is the maddest fool certainly! Forgive me for my presumption, and forget it if you can;" and he turned away, smiting his brow impatiently.

I laid my hand on his arm—I drew it down from his face again, which he turned upon me with an expression of surprise. I felt that I was pale with rage and scorn as he looked at me. He misunderstood my feelings evidently, for he said, earnestly: "I am sorry to have caused you so much pain, Miss Monfort! I was premature, I have been indiscreet in my remarks. Your engagement is surely no concern of mine. I should have confined myself to my own disappointment exclusively, and respected your reserve;" adding, "I beg that you will pardon and look less angrily upon me, in this our parting."

"I am not offended with you, Mr. Raymond." (His boyish passion had, indeed, swept over me as lightly as the wing of a butterfly across a rose. I felt that it amounted to nothing but pastime on either hand—a careless throw of the dice on his part, that might, or might not, have resulted to his advantage. He probably staked but little feeling in the enterprise—I certainly none at all.) —"I am not angry with you, Lieutenant Raymond, nay, grateful rather for your impulsive homage, which I regret not to be able to reward as you deserve; but this you must tell me, as a true, as an honorable man, if you care one iota for my regard, or the cause of truth and justice: what has that man been saying about me?" And I laid my hand upon his arm and shook it slightly.

"What man, Miss Monfort? I—I, scarcely understand you! You surely do not mean Mr. Bainrothe—your—"

"Guardian, nothing more, scarcely that," I interrupted, almost fiercely; thus finishing out his sentence as he probably might not have done. "Answer me truthfully, honorably, as you are a gentleman, has he propagated this vile slander, for as such I feel it, and as such shall resent it?"

"I do, do—not know positively—but I have reason to think that, either directly or indirectly, the rumor comes from him. You know some men have a way of insinuating things. I—I—cannot recall any thing positive or definite. I cannot, indeed. He never spoke to me on the subject at all. There was only an expression at times, as he bore you off, that seemed to tell me that all my efforts to win you were vain. I can't see why you lay such stress on the matter at all, Miss Monfort."

He had evidently the gentleman's true reluctance to make mischief.

"Lieutenant Raymond, I simply dislike to be placed in a false position, or grossly misinterpreted or misrepresented. Do you see that unfortunate person there?" I asked suddenly, "with his head drawn completely to one side, and his arms and legs swathed in flannel bandages, hobbling feebly along, followed by a youth (a relation, probably, bearing a camp-stool) and a dingy little terrier-dog, on his way to the pool of Bethesda?" As if he knew that he was the object of our attention, the man alluded to stopped, and turned just then a face grotesquely hideous in our direction, and, seeing me, smiled, and nodded feebly—disclosing, as he did so, long, fang-like teeth, yellow, as if cut from lemon-rind, and fantastically irregular

"You have the oddest acquaintance, Miss Monfort, for a young lady of fashion, certainly! This old man keeps a little one-horse book-store somewhere, I am told, and makes it his constant theme of conversation."

"Yes, he has his hobby, like more distinguished men. I have known him from my childhood, however, and esteem him truly. He kept the choicest collection of children's books I ever saw in former days, and was a child at heart himself, and an especial crony of mine. But I have other reasons for asking you to remark him now. He is old, diseased, and poor; yet, just as good and honorable as he is, I would rather put my hand in his as betrothed or married a thousand-fold, than become the wife of Basil Bainrothe. Repeat this, if you please, whenever you hear this very unpleasant and absurd report and subject agitated. It will be a simple act of justice to me, and a tribute to truth, such as I am sure you will be pleased to render and illustrate."

"I will do so," he said, quietly; "but I confess you surprise me. I have always refused to give credit to the matter myself, blinded, I was assured, by my own impetuosity, but I acknowledge this engagement is very generally canvassed and believed at Saratoga; nor has Miss Erle in any instance refuted the impression. Of this I am quite certain, and deem it my duty now to tell you so."

"Is it possible," I thought, "that this can be one of Evelyn's subtle schemes, reacting on Mr. Bainrothe? The father for me, the son for herself! My God! the grave would be preferable to me, to marriage with either one or the other, the loathed or the loathing! O papa, papa! why was I ever placed in hands like these? It must be so sweet, so delightful, to trust and love one's associates, whether natural or accidental! I feel as if Fate had raised up for me this band of mocking fiends, to guard me from my kind, and mar my happiness. Day by day I hate and distrust them more and more—nay, learn to tremble through them at myself.

"You are silent, Miss Monfort," he said; "will you not bid me a kind, a pardoning farewell?"

"Oh, surely, Mr. Raymond; and let me beg that, when you are near me, you will come freely to my house. I shall be most happy to entertain you." And I gave him my hand, frankly.

"One word more, Miss Monfort. Are you engaged to any other and more fortunate man than Mr. Bainrothe and myself? Is it for another's sake you have felt so very indignant? Forgive a sailor's frankness, and a sailor's interest, even if bestowed in vain. I fear you will add to these, a sailor's undue curiosity."

"No, Mr. Raymond, neither engaged nor likely to be. But hinge no hope on this declaration of mine. I am probably destined to walk through life alone, and, like many better women, to live for the good of others, in self-defense, if for good at all. I shall never marry, Lieutenant Raymond."

The hand that held mine, trembled slightly, relaxed, relinquished its eager hold, and fell listlessly to his side. He believed me, evidently, as I believed myself.

"I have loved you," he said, hoarsely, "far more than you will ever understand. Do not forget me!"

"That is scarcely probable," I murmured; "but we shall meet again," and I spoke cheerfully and aloud, "and under happier auspices, I trust. The world is fair before you, Mr. Raymond; this much let me counsel, and the counsel is drawn from experience: do not surrender your freedom too lightly—it is a precious gift to man or woman, and those who drag broken fetters wear woful hearts. Farewell!"

We left Saratoga on the following day. It was autumn when we reached our home again—sad and strange September—my birth-month, and the grave of many hopes. Mabel was well, and finely grown for a child of her years; and the joy of seeing her, and holding her to my heart again, made me oblivious of all else for a season. After our brief separation even, her loveliness struck me afresh. How beautiful she was! not with the white radiance of Evelyn, but lovely as a young May rose, blushing among its leaves and peerless in grace, sweetness, and expression. She had her sainted mother's great blue, soulful eyes, with finer features and more brilliant coloring, and her father's gleaming teeth and clustering hair, "brown in the shadow, gold in the sun," falling, like his, over a brow of sculptured ivory. I was not alone in my appreciation of her loveliness. It was a theme of universal remark. Even Mr. Bainrothe, who could never forgive my father for having married his children's governess, confessed that she had the "air noble," which he valued far above beauty. "And where she got it from, Miriam, is sufficiently plain," he said, one day, glancing at me with undisguised admiration as he spoke. "Her mother was simple and unpretending enough, Heaven above knows, but you Monforts, and you, especially, Miriam, are truly *distingué*, which is a word that cannot often be justly applied in any land to man or woman either."

"By-the-by, Miriam," he continued, "you are growing into a very beautiful woman, after a somewhat unpromising childhood. You surpass Evelyn as rubies do garnets, or diamonds *aqua marine*, or sapphires the opaque turquoise. You do, indeed, my dear," and he attempted to take my hand in the old fashion. I murmured something indicative of my disapprobation.

"It is an exquisite hand!" he remarked, as I coldly

drew it away; "I have an artist's eye, and can admire beauty in the abstract, even though I am an old man, you know."

"Admire it also at a distance, I beg, hereafter," I said, bowing coldly, smiling very bitterly, I fear, with lips white with anger and disgust.

"Those scars, Miriam!" he went on, as if unobservant of my manner, yet with the old sarcastic gleam in his eyes, in the most audacious way, "have nearly disappeared, have they not? I think I understood so from Dr. Pemberton. Let me see that on your arm, my dear," and he extended his hand to grasp it.

"They are indelible, Mr. Bainrothe," I replied, folding my arms tightly above my heart, "as are some other impressions; never allude to them again, I request you. It offends me." And I left him, coldly and abruptly.

I give this little scene only as a specimen of his occasional behavior at this period, and of the humiliation to which his presence so often subjected me. But matters had not yet culminated.

## CHAPTER VII.

EVELYN's fortune and Mabel's were, like much of my own, invested in the Bank of Pennsylvania, and deemed secure in that gigantic bubble. At twenty-three Evelyn, of course, consulted no one as to the disposition of her income, which she spent freely and magnificently on herself alone. Her jewels, silks, laces, were of the finest quality and fabric; she drove a peerless little equipage, had her own ponies and tiger and maid; travelled frequently, entertained splendidly, though this last, it must be confessed, was not at her expense, if redounding to her credit.

To her my father had decreed the first position in his household until my marriage (with her sanction) or majority should occur, and she kept it bravely. She possessed a leading spirit, and loved to rule whether by right or sufferance. Lovers she had in plenty; suitors, such as they were, manifold; yet she preferred so far her single estate to aught that could be or had been offered. I began to think that her constancy deserved to be rewarded, and to withdraw on such score the objection I had felt so strong in the outset against her union with Claude Bainrothe.

He had been already more than a year in Copenhagen when I discovered how it was between them, or rather thought I had done so, from seeing one night when she came into my room in her night-dress, which was accidentally parted at the bosom, the betrothal-ring, so peculiar as not readily to be mistaken, which Claude Bainrothe had once given to me, suspended from the button of her chemisette by a small gold chain, so as to lie constantly against her heart. How her pride had ever stooped to receive and wear the pledge originally given to another it was difficult for me to conceive, and little less bitter, I confess, at first to know. I thought all care was over as to Claude Bainrothe and his affairs, but a qualm of anguish surged through my whole being, the dying throe, I well believe, of trust and affection, when I beheld this carefully-guarded token.

As Evelyn raised her hand to fasten her night-robe, through the accidental opening of which I had caught sight of my repudiated treasure, I noticed on one of her slender fingers, from which all other incumbrances in the way of rings had been removed for the night, a circlet of plain gold such as is generally used for the symbol of the marriage-rite, an engagement-ring, I then supposed it.

"Let me see your wedding-ring, Evelyn," I said, laughingly, to conceal my embarrassment. She colored slightly.

"What, that little affair of a philopœna?" she rejoined. "Oh, I promised not to take it off until certain things were accomplished, nor to tell the name of the giver either, so don't question about it, 'an you love me, Hal!'"

"Was it sent from beyond the seas?" I questioned, seriously, "I shall ask nothing more."

"What an idea! No, on my honor, it was not. There! I will not tell you another word about it, so don't bore me, Miriam. I thought you, yourself, despised a catechist, and undue curiosity. What I came here, to-night, for, was not to be catechised, or 'put to the question,' but to ask a favor which you must grant, dear prophetess, whether you will or no. Now, don't refuse your Eva," and she kissed me affectionately; "I am going to give a grand fancy ball, or rather, *we* are, the same thing of course, and I want you to lay off your deep mourning for a time" (hers had been already entirely put aside), "and appear as night. You can still wear black, you know; I shall be Morning, and Mabel, Hesper. Now, won't it be a lovely idea? Hesper, you know, is both morning and evening star, and can hover between us, bearing a torch, and dressed *à la Grecque.* Is not that appropriate—our little link of sisterhood? It cannot fail to make an impression. I consider it, myself, a capital idea. You can wear your mother's diamonds at last, which Mr. Bainrothe means to hand over to you to-morrow as your birthday gift—not that, exactly, either," seeing my rising scorn, "but as a token of respect suitable for the occasion. He might hold on to them two years longer you know, legally," she added, carelessly.

"He is very magnanimous," I remarked, coldly; "I shall be glad to have my diamonds though, in my own possession, I acknowledge, but why does he make any parade about it at all? They are mine all the same, whether in his hands or my own. Every thing that man does seems theatrical and affected to me!"

"I thought you were beginning to incline very favorably to Cagliostro! I am sure this was the opinion of all who saw you together at Saratoga, and I believe, between ourselves, it is his own."

"Evelyn Erle, you know better than this! People, of themselves, would never have dreamed of such a thing, and he, too, knows my sentiments thoroughly. He only feigns ignorance."

"My dear, dear girl! worse things than this have been said frequently, and stranger ones have come to pass. Mr. Bainrothe is certainly a splendid financier, that was your own father's opinion. You will never marry any man who will take better care of your money, and that is a consideration with you, or ought to be, Miriam. Your estate is your chief distinction, child, if you only knew it; besides, with a knowledge of your constitutional malady, you should be very careful what hands you fall into. No woman that I know of demands such peculiar care and tenderness from a husband, nor such choice in her surroundings. After all, Mr. Bainrothe is still a very handsome man, and admirably well preserved if not exactly young; he does not look forty, he has not a gray hair, a false tooth, nor a wrinkle."

"Have you done, Evelyn Erle?" I asked, almost ferociously. "Have you completed your catalogue of insult? Then listen, in turn, to my counsel. Marry him yourself by all means; he would suit you, body and soul, far better than me. Indeed, I have never seen any one else who seemed so thoroughly your counterpart, match and mate, as Cagliostro!"

"Thank you," she said, furiously; "if I thought you were in earnest"—here she hesitated, clinching her hand, and biting her white lips.

"I am in earnest," I rejoined, quietly; "what then?" and I looked coldly, resolutely in her face.

"Why I would perhaps marry the son, just to correct your fallacious idea about the father, that is all! This course is shut out from you, however, entirely, by your own folly, so *you* must take what you can get now, for

Claude Bainrothe, let me assure you, is lost to you forever." And she went out, smiling triumphantly.

I suspected from that hour what I knew later, and I had suffered the last pang to agonize my heart that my broken troth should ever cost me. The corpse of my dead love had bled at the touch of its murderer, in accordance with ancient superstition. Now, calm and quiet oblivion and the sepulchre should surround and enshroud it forever more.

I think I kept my determination bravely from that hour, but others must judge of this for me. We are not gods, to say to the tide of feeling, "Thus far, and no farther shalt thou come." We are only mortal Canutes at best, to lift back our chairs as the tide advances, and seat ourselves securely thereon beyond the surf. We all remember how it fared with the quaint old monarch and moralist when he tried the plan of the immortals, and commanded the sea to obey him—we perish if we arrogate too much when the surges sweep around us; but we can, we must avoid them if we hope to escape their force, and plant ourselves beyond them firmly on the shore.

Evelyn's fancy ball was a magnificent affair, and a complete success, as the word goes. She chose to call it my *début* party, but I never felt that it was so, or that I was more than any other guest. I would not have chosen a fancy dress for my first appearance, and she certainly was the queen of the occasion.

She was dressed as Aurora, in exquisite, fleecy gauze draperies of white, azure, and rose color, so artistically arranged as irresistibly to remind the observer of those delicate, transparent tints of morning that greet the rising sun. On her brow was a diadem of opals and diamonds arranged in a crescent form, from beneath which, her fleecy white veil flowed backward to the hem of her garments like a mist of the early day-spring; a rosy exhalation of the dawn enveloping but not obscuring the radiance of her raiment, over which dew-drops seemed to have been shed by the lavish hand of wakening Nature.

Her face, so fair as to gain from this marble-like radiance its chief characteristic, was delicately tinted to-night on either cheek so as to emulate the early blushes of Aurora. Her colorless hair, of a tint so neutral as to defy description, curling in light spiral ringlets so as to drop profusely on her bosom, had been richly powdered with gold-dust for this occasion, and glistened like the sunlight, or, to fall in my comparison, the tresses of Lucretia Borgia, as her historians portray them.

Nothing could be more refined, more refulgent, more ethereal, than her whole appearance, nor had I ever seen the light-blue eyes so clear and brilliant, the thin, writhing lips so scarlet and smiling, the pearly teeth so glistening by contrast with the first, as on this occasion.

Her arms and neck, which wanted contour, and yet were of snowy whiteness, were skillfully draped in her many-colored robe so as to cover all defects; and a chaplet of pearls, mingled with diamonds, concealed the slight prominence of the collar-bones, and descended low on the white and well-veiled bosom. Every eye was turned on her with admiration, and the low murmur that followed her through the halls she trod so proudly, proclaimed her triumph far more loudly than more open flattery could have done.

"You, too, look well to-night, in your black-velvet robe and diamonds, Miriam, better than I have ever seen you!" said a low voice in my ear, as I echoed the passing praises lavished on Evelyn's beauty by one of her admirers. "It is scarcely a fancy costume though, after all."

"Thank you, Mr. Baïnrothe," I replied coldly. "For reasons of my own, I have preferred to make my costume as subdued as possible."

"By Jove! I wish our young exile could see you this evening," he went on, disregardful of my brief explanation. "He would strew his hair with ashes, and wear sackcloth in penance for the past, I doubt not; for I tell you frankly, Miriam, you have improved wonderfully of late, and you bear inspection far better than Evelyn with all her beauty; your figure is absolutely faultless; your face the most attractive woman ever wore, if not the most absolutely regular. I tell you simple truths. I am a disinterested critic, you see, and stand apart gazing upon women simply as specimens. Your hands and feet are models, your smile enchanting, your voice musical, your manner witchery itself, when you choose to let out your nature; what more could heart desire?" and he gazed steadily in my face, insolently I felt it!

I had been listening indignantly to this cool summary of my attractions, and the arrogant idea manifestly uppermost, that Sultan Claude Bainrothe had only to appear on the scene, and throw his handkerchief, for me to succumb, and I had been so confounded by this tirade of compliment and commonplace that I scarcely knew how to stay its tide without absolute rudeness, such as no lady should ever be guilty of—when he coolly continued his remarks as if wholly unobservant of my displeasure.

"Evelyn, with all her arts, is a little faded already; don't you see it, Miriam? There is no corrosive poison equal to envy, and that, by-the-by, is her specialty. She is bitterly envious by nature. Most of those thin-lipped, sharp-elbowed, sharp-nosed women are, if you observe. Faded at twenty-three! Sad, but true of half our American morning-glory beauties. For my part, I love the statuesque in women, the enduring! those exquisitely-moulded proportions on which the gaze reposes with such delight, and that set a man to dreaming, whether he will, or not." And his eye dwelt on me from throat to waist in a manner that made my flesh crawl as if the worms that tortured Herod were passing over it. At this point I rebelled—I ground my teeth resolutely—my face flushed to the temples—I could willingly have stricken that audacious scrutinizer in the face with my clinched hand, and he knew it! How coarse coarseness makes us, even when most disinclined to it naturally! His sensuous brutality made me almost fiercely brutal in turn. As it was, I could only put him away with a gesture of contempt I sought not to command, and with which I swept past him into the thickest of the crowd, cursing at heart the bitter fate that had cast me bound and helpless, for a season, into such unscrupulous hands.

There was no one to turn to now. I knew Mr. Lodore thought Evelyn perfect, and me a sinner, because in the matter of church duties she was the more observant. Besides, my Jewish pedigree had always been a barrier between us. Dr. Pemberton, Mr. Stanbury, Laura, George Gaston, all that truly loved and believed in me, were gone for an indefinite time to Europe. I had not been suffered to accompany them, on many pleas and pretences, as I had wished to do, and this was the end of it all. Licentious persecution!

Evelyn, too! a blinded confederate in such schemes as should have nerved her woman's heart to indignation rather! Marry that man! I would have cut off my own right hand, or burnt it to a cinder like Scævola; sooner gone out to service—played chambermaid on the boards, or the tragedy-queen of the commonest melodrama, far rather! It was all insult, injury, degradation, in whatever light I could view it, and every feeling in my nature was stung to exasperation.

It was well understood that I was an heiress, and I did not want for adulation. I was surrounded by fashion and beauty, and wreathed with approbation from the noblest and most exalted, on that night of festal splendor; and again that beautiful face that had cast its spell above me in my inexperienced childhood, and that age never seemed to change nor chill, bent above me with its gracious and genial sweetness, and the princely banker on this occasion condescended to manifest his kindly and approving interest in the daughter of his dead friend. At any other time, such tribute would have been most grateful and acceptable to me, for this man was almost my *beau idéal* at this period, but now the bitterness with which my heart was filled, permeated my whole being, and dashed every draught of enjoyment untasted from my lips.

Yet the memory of that time—that face—returned to me later with emotions irresistible, when the being who was then the idol of society, became its ostracized outcast, and, among all who bowed before him in his pride of place and power, were found, before two years had elapsed from this period,

> "None so poor
> To do him reverence."

Already is the injustice of that decision forced on the convictions of his fellow-men. Our scales are not wisely balanced in this world—we cannot weigh motives against acts, thought against deeds, with atom-like precision, nor measure the tempted with the temptation grain by grain, hair by hair. Ambition was the fault of the seraphim in the commencement—be well assured that some of the old angelic leaven lingers still about all of its votaries and victims.

Ay—victims!—for he who was said to have made so many, was himself the victim of the society that spoiled and flattered him, and fostered his foibles, in the beginning, with its false and fawning breath, and, later, blew on him a blast of ice from its remorseless, pestilent jaws, that froze him out of his humanity.

He could not live—moulded, as he was, of all sweet elements—apart from social influences, from the regard, the affection, the approbation of his kind—and he died of heart-starvation; fortunate, indeed, in that he was mercifully permitted so to die, rather than have lived, as less fervent natures might have done, in cold and cheerless apathy.

I do not defend his errors; I only seek to extenuate them. Pity and justice are not the same; but one may still so temper the other that Mercy, the appointed angel of this earth, may be the result.

Let us, who are mortal and fallible, be wary how we condemn one whose head was rendered giddy by his very pinnacle of power! Peace be his!

I have diverged so widely from my subject—a most bitter and revolting one to me, eventually—that I will not return to it just now; nor, indeed, do I even in thought revert to it with any thing like patience or pardon. There are some things, paradoxical as this may seem, we must forget, in order to forgive.

I am lingering too long on this period of my story, uneventful as it is just yet, and circumscribed as I am in space; but, as the boldest rider draws rein with a beating heart beside the dark abyss over which he must fling his horse, or perish, so I pause here, on the threshold of despair, and take breath for a flying leap—for I shall clear it, reader, believe me!

It will be remembered that, at my father's death, half of my means were invested in the stocks of the Bank of Pennsylvania; and that his directions were that, as the different loans he had made became due, they should, one after the other, be drawn in and invested in like manner by Mr. Bainrothe.

No details of my business had ever been discussed before me, nor had I any insight into the periods at which these loans were due, or how the money was cared for when paid in by my father's executors, of whom, to my regret, Mr. Gerald Stanbury had refused to be one.

One thing alone I had heard them say, and it was said, I doubt not, expressly for my hearing. All debts should be paid in gold, as, according to law, this was the only legal tender. Paper, however excellent, should never be received in discharge of any liability of my estate, since it might render the executors responsible to me, to depart a hair's-breadth from the very letter of the law, which enjoined specie payment.

"But why not receive bank stocks instead?" I had ventured to suggest, a little indignantly, "seeing all moneys are to be immediately reinvested in that form. Pennsylvania Bank stocks, I mean."

"You know nothing about the matter, Miriam," Evelyn had remarked, with some asperity. "Had your father deemed you capable of conducting your own affairs, he would not have appointed *us* to manage and direct them during your minority. No sinecure, I assure you!"

But Mr. Bainrothe had only laughed, and turned away tapping his boot with his rattan cane, amused, it appeared to me, by my sister's assumption of importance, and, probably, as well by her entire ignorance of his true motive in exacting gold, of which secret spring of action she, knowing nothing, still tried to make so profound a mystery.

Yet he flattered Evelyn very much, I saw, on her business qualifications, and her insight into financial matters, of which abilities, indeed, she was more proud than of her accomplishments, or even beauty.

The last she took as a matter of course; but it was something new and unexpected to her to be considered sagacious and strong-minded, and very gratifying to her arrogant and exacting spirit—ever alive to the delight of controlling the affairs of others, as well as her own—to have the reins of government given apparently into her hands.

My father had placed an iron chest in a secure niche in the dining-room, behind the great central mirror, made for the purpose of concealing it, and to which he alone had access. Here he had kept a store of plate, money, jewels, and papers, so as to defy all burglarious interference or foreign scrutiny, and, in dying, had bequeathed the secret of the patent lock to Mr. Bainrothe alone. Old Morton even was ignorant of the contrivance.

I knew of the niche and the iron chest by the merest accident, and had been requested, nay, commanded, by my father, not to speak of either; so, in silence the mystery had almost died out of my recollection, when it was rather singularly revived again in this wise:

During one of the hottest nights early in September, after our return from Saratoga, I descended, parched with thirst, to the dining-room, about four o'clock in the morning, to seek a glass of iced-water, always to be found there, I knew, by night or day, on the sideboard, in a small silver cistern.

The dawn was dimly breaking through the great window in the hall as I passed down the broad stairway, still in my night-dress and unslippered feet; but, on approaching the dining-room, I was surprised to see the gleam of a candle falling athwart the mirror, which had been swung from its place (as I had seen it once before swung by my father), so as to screen my advancing form from the person evidently at work behind it. The massive shutters of the room were closed and securely barred, as was the habit of the house, and the room was, consequently, still in darkness, or deep shadow.

As I stood half hidden now, by the arch of the hall, behind which I shrank instinctively, and uncertain how to proceed, I saw Mr. Bainrothe suddenly emerge from behind the mirror, and take from the table near it a canvas bag, small but evidently weighty, from the manner in which he carried it to its place of concealment.

Then I heard the slow, heavy fall of a shower of gold coins, dropping on others, the same sound that had greeted my ear on the day when I first detected this treasure-cave of my father, and as different from the sound of falling silver as is the gurgling of rich old wine from the dash of crystal water.

"The wretch is faithful to his trust, after all. So this is where he keeps my gold," I thought; "but how did he find ingress into our castle, supposed at least to be inaccessible by night? Has he a false key I wonder, and are we above-stairs, with unlocked doors, subject to his visitations, should it occur to him to make them?"

I shuddered at the suggestions of my own fancy.

8

Women only, who have been similarly situated, can know how dark these may become, even in an innocent mind, from circumstances like those that surrounded me, and what a nameless horror there is about the insidious and licentious approaches of the man we would fain dash away from us, and trample under foot like a serpent, did we dare openly to do so.

Yet I lingered under the archway, determined to observe to the last Mr. Bainrothe's proceedings. When he had locked the chest and replaced the mirror, which swung out from its place, as I have said, like a door on invisible hinges and fastened with a spring, he passed hastily out of the dining-room into the pantry beyond, opening for convenience on a covered paved court, which divided the kitchen from the house and which led directly into the yard beyond. After that, all was silent.

Yet, the next day, Franklin assured me that he had carried the key of the pantry away with him, when he went home at night (he was a married man, and slept at his own house usually), and that he found it locked in the morning just as he had left it.

This was in answer to a question which I tried to make as careless as possible, with regard to some burglaries that had lately been committed in a neighboring street, adding, by way of caution: "Don't forget to lock us up carefully at night, Franklin; remember we are all women in the house, except Morton, and he is old and sleeps like a top, no doubt having a good conscience for his pillow."

"If you would have an *inside* bolt put upon the pantry-door, it would be best, Miss Miriam," he remarked; "that is, if your mind is really troubled about robbers. Then you could draw it yourself in my absence at night."

"And who would let you in, in the morning, Franklin, if I did this? Our household would sleep until noon, were it not for your early summons, I verily believe."

"I will throw a pebble at the cook's window, miss, if she is not on foot by that time. But she usually is; cooks has to stir earlier than the rest, you know, by reason of the light rolls and muffins."

"Oh, yes! true, I had forgotten this. Go at once, then, Franklin, for a smith, and let him put a massive bolt on the pantry-door, and I will be jailer of Monfort Hall in future, in your absence, for I am quite sure some one was trying that lock last night. I came to the dining-room for water just before daylight, and heard it distinctly."

"One of your lady-like notions," said Franklin, shaking his head, with an incredulous smile; "young ladies is always nervous like, and fearful about robbers, all but Miss Evelyn Erle—I never seen the like of her, for true grit! All was safe when I came, Miss Miriam, any way, and, if robbers had been about, it stands to reason the silver chest, setting out in the pantry, would have stood a poor chance."

Again he smiled provokingly. "There are all sorts of robbers in this world," I said, a little sternly; "some come for one purpose, some for another. Attend to the bolt, Franklin, at once; I am very sure of what I have said." And so the parley ended.

I am certain that Mr. Bainrothe came no more by night to his treasure-cave, but there was a mocking smile on his lip—when Evelyn told him, before me, some time later, that I had caused a bolt to be placed on the pantry-door, for fear of burglars—that was significant to my mind.

"What is the use of this mystery with me," I thought, "when I alone am concerned? Why not reveal to me at once the secret of the spring and the lock, as I only am to be the beneficiary of all this gold? The man's cunning is short-sighted. Suppose he were to die suddenly, how does he know that I would ever be the wiser or the better of these deposits? Years hence, when the house was crumbling to decay, some stranger might be enriched by this concealed gold, for aught he knows, which is legitimately mine. Evelyn, too, is in complete ignorance of this hidden chest, I am convinced, and, as far as I am concerned, will probably remain so. After all, does Bainrothe mistrust her honesty or mine? Good Heavens! what a mole the man is by nature, how darkly, deeply underhand, even in his responsibility! And there are two long years yet, nay more to wait, before I can openly defy him and put him away forever. Loathing him as I do, patience, patience! Rome was not built in a day. I shall still prevail."

Months after this occurrence, months that passed swiftly because monotonously to me, for by events alone we are told we measure time, I was roused one night from my early slumber by the sound of bitter weeping in Evelyn's chamber. I had left her engaged over accounts with Mr. Bainrothe, having withdrawn rather than spend a long, lonely evening in the parlor, somewhat indisposed as I felt.

I rose from my bed and went to her precipitately. I found her indulging in a passionate burst of grief, almost choking with sobs of hysterical indignation.

"All gone—all gone!" she exclaimed, wildly, as I entered the room. "Your estate—mine—Mabel's—all swept away with one fell swoop, Miriam! The Bank of

Pennsylvania has failed; it is discovered that Mr. Biddle has proved defaulter, and we are ruined!"

"I will never believe it, Evelyn!" I exclaimed, vehemently, "until he tells me so with his own lips. This is one of Mr. Bainrothe's fictions; he is trying to wake us up a little, that is all. Mr. Biddle is the Bayard of bankers—'*sans peur et sans reproche.*' As to that bank, did not my father believe it to be as indestructible as the United States, the government itself? Nay, did not Bainrothe himself do all he could to convince him of it, and induce him to invest in its stocks? The wily fox had his motive, no doubt, but it surely could not have been our ruin! Our own fortunes are too intimately involved in his prosperity for this. Besides, why have not the newspapers told us of this?"

All this time Evelyn was sobbing convulsively, and what I have told continuously here was said by me in a far more fragmentary way between her bursts of grief. She ceased now, and looked up, with some effort at calmness.

"The newspapers *have* been discussing it for months past, all but Mr. Biddle's organ, and that alone was permitted to enter our doors. Mr. Bainrothe acknowledges this now. Have you not noticed the irregularity of our Washington papers?"

"No; I so rarely read them, you know."

"Mr. Bainrothe, with mistaken charity," she resumed, "I fear, sought to shield us as long as possible from the blow, which was inevitable sooner or later; or perhaps he hoped still for an adjustment of affairs, that might have left us a competence at least. But he was deceived, Miriam; we are worth nothing—a round naught—" and she suited the action to the word by the union of the tips of her thumb and finger—" is the figure whereby to describe our fortunes now; and the heiress and her once dependent friend and sister are alike—beggars! All brought to one level at last—there is comfort in that thought, at least! Ha! ha! ha!" and she laughed wildly, horribly. I never before heard such laughter.

"Beggary is a word I repudiate, Evelyn, in any case," I said, firmly; "and we, it seems, if this frightful thing be true, are not alone in ruin. Be calm, dear Evelyn! Learn to bear with dignity our fate. We must sustain each other now—be all in all to one another, as we have never been before. Thank God! let us both thank God, Evelyn, from our inmost hearts, that we still have this shelter—and—yes—I have reason to believe, much more."

And, kneeling beside her bed, I told her impulsively of our concealed treasure behind the mirror (though I had once determined never to reveal this to her or any one)—treasure guarded so long by me with bolt by night and vigilance by day!

Oh, fatal error, never to be repaired or sufficiently repented of! Oh, utter misplacement of confidence, not warranted, surely, by any thing that had gone before, and the results of which I had subsequently such bitter cause to deplore!

She listened to me with an interest and zeal that were unmistakable. She sat up in her bed, with her large, blue, distended eyes fixed on mine, turning paler and paler, brighter and brighter, as she gazed, until their lustre seemed opaline rather than spiritual, and with her slender white hands wreathed together like the interlacing marble snakes in the grasp of the Laocoon, so long, and lithe, and sinuous, seemed the polished, flexile fingers. Her lips were livid, but on her cheek burned two flame-like spots, indicative ever with her of intense excitement. Surely the god Mammon has rarely possessed so sincere a worshiper! Let us do her this justice, at least. So far she was consistent; so far she was devout!'

"You are sure of the truth of what you utter, Miriam?" she questioned, eagerly.

"Sure as that I live," I replied.

"It is wonderful! Why did he not mention this to me? I cannot conjecture his motive. But perhaps he has already removed and invested this gold, Miriam, of which you say there was such a quantity as to have represented a large portion of your landed estate, I think!"

"No, no; that is simply impossible. By night he has never done this, I know. By day he could not effect this unseen or unsuspected. That dining-room is so public, you know, that Morton sees every thing; besides, I gave him directions which he blindly obeyed, I am certain (you know his almost canine obedience to me, Evelyn), to remain, when engaged with the plate, in the adjoining pantry, with the door ajar between, and to be always on guard. Papa always allowed him the privilege of that room, and I love to continue it, you know, since we never use it except for meals. You remember I said this when you objected to his sitting there, Evelyn, and remarked that he might as well sit with the other servants, to whom he is so superior. But of late, I confess, I have had a motive, and Morton knew this"—I hesitated—"must have known it."

"Do you mean to say you confided the secret of the mirror to Morton, and kept it from me? Thank you, Miriam!" loftily. "I might have expected this, however."

"Not wholly this," I replied, with embarrassment,

for I saw how the matter looked externally. "Morton simply knew that I wanted, for purposes of my own, to exclude every one except himself from solitary possession of the dining-room as much as possible, Mr. Bainrothe especially. Yes, I told him this, but I kept papa's secret. Believe me, Evelyn, I did this, and you know well enough what Morton's devotion is to me not to believe that he religiously fulfilled my request without asking for an explanation."

"Yes," she mused, "I saw him perched up there to-night, as usual, with his old English newspapers, and I have observed that he never leaves his post there, while Mr. Bainrothe remains. You could not have procured a better watchman, surely; but why have you watched at all?"

"Because," I said, "I felt sure that mystery lurked behind those nocturnal visits. You cannot doubt this yourself, Evelyn, and, with your opinion of Mr. Bainrothe, must see that I felt I had good reason for mistrust. I was determined to be present when that chest should next be opened by him."

A smile quivered across her face. "I had not suspected you of so much diplomacy," she observed, dryly; "but, after all, Miriam, how does this change the posture of affairs to me? I shall be all the same, poor and dependent."

"No, Evelyn, no indeed! I promise you faithfully.—But what is this?" I exclaimed, rising hastily from my knees, "I am faint—blind! Quick, the drops Dr. Pemberton left for me, Evelyn, or I am lost again."

I threw myself across the foot of her bed, sick and bewildered, yet feeling myself gradually—after a few moments of oppression—growing better, in spite of the dark effort of my evil genius to gain his fatal ascendency.

When she came with the drops, after some delay, I was, to her surprise, able to sit up and look around me. The spell was over.

"I believe I have troubled you uselessly," I said; "I will go to bed without medicine to-night, I think, and strive to be calm, as Dr. Pemberton enjoined me to do, and there was good sense in his advice, certainly. We have so much to do to-morrow, Evelyn—we two must remove these deposits ourselves. But not a word to Bainrothe!"

"Miriam," she said, eagerly, "can you doubt my discretion when you know, too, what your own promises have been now and long ago—to divide with me, ay, to the last cent, like a sister? Now, I insist on the drops! You are pale again, Miriam—collapsing visibly in my sight. Do take your remedy—so efficacious of late in warding off these distressing attacks. I have taken the trouble, too, to go after them. I was at some pains in hunting them up; they were not in the usual place. Come, now, as a punishment for your carelessness, I proclaim myself dictator, and command you to swallow them at once," and she poured the medicine into a spoon.

"No, Evelyn," I averred, putting the spoon aside, "I am better without the drops. I wish to see what my unaided *will* and constitution can do, this time."

"There is too much at stake to depend on these, Miriam. We must unearth this treasure-trove to-morrow at daylight, and defeat Bainrothe on his own grounds, or he may be beforehand with us. Take your drops, dear, and have a good night's rest, and be ready for the contest. There, now, that is a good sister," embracing me tenderly.

Persuasion and reason accomplished with me what *com-*

*mands* could not have done. I took the drops, went quietly to bed, and was soon lost to a sense of misfortunes, hopes, and the world itself.

I slept profoundly and long. When I awoke, the slant rays of the evening sun were pouring through the blinds of my window, in lines of moted light. Mrs. Austin was sitting close to the sash, with her invariable knitting-work, her aquiline profile and frilled cap strongly relieved against the jalousied shutters.

On the mantel-piece were the inevitable spirit-lamp and bowl of panada, recognized at once as part and parcel of my malady. In the chamber the usual smell of ether, the remedy so often ineffectually administered during the period of my lethargic attacks.

I understood everything now—I had experienced another seizure, and I had lost a day.

Whether it was this conviction that cleared my brain at once of those mephitic fogs that usually clung around it after a spell of lethargy, long after my consciousness returned, I never knew, but certain it is, I sat up in my bed like one refreshed by sleep, instead of feeling exhausted, and, greatly to her surprise, accosted Mrs. Austin in clear, strong accents.

"How long have I slept? And where is Evelyn?" I asked.

"You have not opened your eyes to-day, dear child, until just this moment; and Miss Evelyn has not been able to sit up in her bed since she went to it last night, that shock yesterday overcame her so completely." By this time she was standing by my pillow, after laying aside her knitting, in a leisurely manner peculiar to her at all seasons. "But Mabel is in the next room; let me call her to you."

"Let her stay there," I interrupted, in a manner so unusual with me, whose first inquiry on reviving from illness had always been for Mabel, instead of Evelyn, that Mrs. Austin looked surprised and startled.

"What ails you, Miss Miriam? I thought Mabel was always your first thought; the little angel! She has been hanging over you tearfully all day; never going near Miss Evelyn at all. It is so strange she shows such partiality!"

Strange that one being on earth, and that one my sister, should love me better than Evelyn, in the eyes of her partial affection; and yet Evelyn treated her with positive disrespect every day of her life, as I never did; and often with severity as well. It was incomprehensible!

"Give me the panada," I said, grimly; "I am half starved, and must grow strong again to do my work. I am not nearly so weak as I usually am, though, after one of my seizures."

"You see you are outgrowing them, as Dr. Pemberton predicted you would. I declare, you *are* hungry, poor child; you have not left a drop—pint-bowl too—with a gill of wine in it. Not going to get up, Miss Miriam? Oh, no; you must not venture to do that yet."

And she tried gently to restrain me.

"Yes, I must get about again; I have much to do, and Evelyn must aid me, if able. Is she ill or only nervous?"

"Very ill, I think; she wrote a note to Dr. Craig and sent it last night, after you went to sleep; but he did not come."

"Quite naturally, since he had been absent some weeks. I could have told her," I said, sententiously; "indeed, I thought she knew it. Who carried her note?"

"Morton."

"Poor old man! The idea of sending him on such a wild-goose chase, after night. Papa would turn in his grave could he know he had been forced out in the rain at such an hour, for a woman's whim. I would have suffered tortures till morning first. Where was Franklin?"

"Franklin had gone home earlier than usual, and did not return to-day. He is sick with a chill, we hear, and his wife is again ill."

"Who did the marketing?"

"Morton."

"Morton again! Why, the old man seems to be becoming a *factotum* in his declining years—he whose duties have always been so few, so simple! I am provoked, for some reasons, that he should have been sent away to-day. Fortunately, I bolted the pantry-door myself, before I came to bed last night," I murmured, "and the front door is self-fastening. The house was well secured, at least, by night."

"How long did Morton remain absent?" I asked, recommencing my system of cross-questions, very abruptly.

"About an hour, I believe; but what makes you so particular, all at once, Miss Miriam?"

"Some day you shall know, perhaps. In the mean while tell me, has Mr. Bainrothe been here to-day?"

"He called about one o'clock, but, as all were poorly, went away again without entering the house at all. I saw him go down-street, after dinner, in his phaeton, with another gentleman, and have not heard wheels since."

"You are sure he was not here, this morning—while —while Morton was absent?"

"Quite sure; he breakfasted later than usual, I think,

for I saw him throw open his side bedroom window at nine o'clock, and he was in his shirt-sleeves then. He sleeps in a large room in the ell, you know. I was standing at the pantry-door, and saw him distinctly, and he nodded to me, and called something, but I could not hear what it was at that distance."

"Where was Charity at that time, Mrs. Austin?"

"Cleaning the house, Miss Miriam—hard at work in the parlors, washing windows—this is her cleaning-day, you know."

"And cook, what was she about?"

"She got breakfast early, for us people, and went to mass, but was back by ten. Miss Evelyn had her breakfast after she returned, with Miss Mabel, and there was no one to eat dinner down-stairs so she thought—"

"Never mind what she thought," I interrupted, "or who went and came, so that all be well."

"You do ask such strange questions, this morning, Miss Miriam, and your eyes are so big! Do you feel light-headed at all after your turn—maybe you have fever?"

"Not at all—hard-headed, rather, Mrs. Austin—not even heavy-headed—though leaden-hearted enough, God knows! We are ruined, you know—or at least Evelyn tells me so. The rest I have still to learn—I must see Mr. Bainrothe this evening. There is a positive necessity for me to exert myself now, but first I have some examinations to make. Give me a shawl and wrapper, good nurse, and my slippers. Don't disturb Evelyn, or call Mabel till my return; and stay where you are until then, if you wish to serve me."

I sped rapidly down-stairs, and entered the dining-room so noiselessly that old Morton, who was a "little thick of hearing," did not hear my steps nor move from his position by the fire, where he sat apparently absorbed by his newspapers. "Morton," I said, and laid my quivering hand upon his arm, "the time has come to act. Come help me to secure my treasure." He rose silently to obey me.

I touched the spring of the mirror; it swung silently open, and revealed to the astonished old man a square niche built in the wall—unsuspected before by him—in which fitted an iron chest, the existence of which he had never dreamed of until now. But the contents were gone—gone since yesterday! The chest was empty, with its lid propped open. There was not even a paper within.

With a bitter groan I tottered back against the wall, while the cold dew stood on my brow, and my limbs trembled under me. This was indeed despair!

"What ails you, Miss Miriam?" he asked, with an expression of anguish upon his kind, old, quivering face. "Do you miss any thing—what have you lost, Miss Miriam?"

"You left your post, Morton," I said, at last, "and this is the consequence—I have lost every thing! Old man! old friend! did you think I charged you to watch every one who came, so earnestly, to stay here so constantly, without a good and sufficient reason? Some one has been here before us—my gold is gone! we are ruined, Morton!"

## CHAPTER VIII.

Whatever my flash of conviction might have been, all suspicions against Evelyn must have been allayed by the manner in which she received the information of the loss of the deposits behind the mirror.

Her shrieks filled the house; another physician was hastily summoned in Dr. Craig's absence, who gave her disease or seizure a Latin name—wrote a Greek or Hebrew prescription—or something equally unintelligible, and vanished ghost-like, in the manner most approved of by modern practitioners.

There was no hard epithet that Evelyn did not apply to Mr. Basil Bainrothe during her hysterical mania, and before the doctor's arrival; but, on her recovery, she begged me to repeat nothing of the sort, if she had been indiscreet enough to let out her true opinion of him and his measures, in a moment of irrepressible emotion. "For," she pursued, "it is expedient for us to keep on terms with the man, at least for the present, and in no way harass or exasperate him—we are completely in his hands now, Miriam—we must watch our opportunity—"

"I do not see that," I interrupted; "less now than ever, it seems to me. What more can he do for or against us now? Our property is all gone—except this house, plate, and furniture, and my mother's diamonds—all of which are tangible and visible, and in our own possession. We have no debts—you pay house-bills monthly, and I, fortunately, have just settled off every account I have in the world, and have five hundred Spanish dollars to start anew with—my savings during papa's lifetime. I hoarded it, fortunately, in this form for a missionary purpose you remember, Evelyn, but afterward changed my mind."

"Yes, I remember; merely because the person it was intended for prayed that the Jews might finally be exterminated."

"Was not that enough, Evelyn? The man who could utter such a prayer was no Christian, and unfit for religious teaching. Since then I have come to the conclusion that there is a great deal of undue and very impertinent meddling with the heathen; who are entitled to their own mode of worship as well as of government, and who I think are not yet ripe for Christianity."

"You have strange notions, Miriam; you talk like an old French philosopher."

"I never knew there was such a thing—a French sophist I am afraid you mean. No, I am not a sophist, Evelyn; any thing else than that! I wish sometimes I did not see so clearly. I love, I idolize the truth alone!"

She colored—sighed. God knows I was not thinking of her at that moment, or speaking with that reference, however I may have had reason to do so.

Is it not strange that our dreams often present to us, in our own despite, the vivid, photographic pictures struck by sleep from the dim, unconscious negative of our waking judgment, which we refuse to recognize as verities in the light of our open-eyed, daytime responsibility? I, who had declared myself no sophist, knew later that I had deceived my own heart, which spoke out so truthfully in dreams of sleep, and refused to be silenced in the dead hour of night, however I might stifle its suggestions by day.

In one of these suggestive, or rather reflected, visions, I saw Evelyn groping through darkness to the side-gate which gave into the grounds of Mr. Bainrothe from our own, made years before by my father's permission for the convenience of his friend; the night was a dark and stormy one, yet she went forth alone, or seemed to, in my vision, to seek a man she detested, and with him connive the destruction of the fortunes of the child of her benefactress, whose confidence she abused.

Then I saw them returning together, through that pantry-door which she had left unbolted, though locked when she went out by another egress, and which the man, who returned with her, readily unlocked with the duplicate key he carried, *not* by my father's permission. This last I knew.

Now the scene was changed to the dining-room. Again I saw the mirror swing back on its invisible and noiseless hinges, and now the glare of a shaded lamp fell in bands of light across its surface. But I was inside this time, by the glamour of my dream, and I saw them emptying the open chest painfully, laboriously, stealthily; stopping now and then to listen, to breathe, again working silently, industriously, at their vocation of theft and crime!

At last all seemed accomplished. A large, covered basket was partially loaded with the contents—heavy as lead—and, between them, they bore it out into the storm and darkness again, and I heard the sound of the spade and mattock at work on the graveled road.

Presently Evelyn came in again. Her air was wild and frightened; her trembling hands were stained with mud, seen by the light of the lantern she bore, and which she again hung in its accustomed place, stealing quietly away into the darkened hall, to grope her way up-stairs. All this while the farce of sending for Dr. Craig was being enacted, and Morton was out on his fruitless mission in the rain!

Again it was morning, and I saw them together in the library, while I still slept, consulting, planning, plotting, writing, erasing, whispering; soon to separate, however, this time. Their arrangements being completed without restraint, for again the old man was absent, doing the duties of another, who, knowing not the motive of such request or bribe, was content to work the will of a conspirator, and pass the day in idleness at home, for the sake of a purse of gold. Here ended my clairvoyance, if such it was.

All this may have been imaginary—part of it probably was—but the sense of the dream was no doubt what my untrammeled judgment would have suggested as truth, and what later—but let me not digress or anticipate here, in the thickest of my troubles, the jungle-pass of my story as it were, but strike on through a self-made path, it may be, to the light that shines beyond the forest, even if it lead into the desert!

Something in Evelyn's suggestion had struck me as the best to pursue under the circumstances, although at first I so boldly repudiated the idea of Mr. Bainrothe's power. Unless I could prove that he had removed the treasure for unworthy uses—why speak of it at all? I should only irritate and set him on his guard by such allusions; whereas, by a course of reticence, I still might learn, as she had suggested, the truth when he least suspected my purpose.

It would be so easy for him to deny all knowledge of the concealed chest—so easy to lay the robbery on Morton, even if the first were proved—or even on Evelyn!

I had sent impulsively for Mr. Bainrothe to come to me on the evening of my discovery, but his visit was delayed by a necessity that kept him from home all night, so that I had time to revolve and resolve on my course of action before I saw him, which was not until the following afternoon, and by this time my mind had undergone a change. He came, but not alone—his son accompanied him.

I have reason since then to think that Evelyn and Claude Bainrothe had met before their cold and measured interview in my presence. It was to me a painful and embarrassing one, and this time the graceful ease was all on the other side—I was preoccupied and agitated, Claude courteous and self-possessed, Evelyn lofty and confident, as though she had lived or trodden down her emotions, and, to my surprise, Mr. Basil Bainrothe wore his accustomed deliberate and self-poised demeanor, making no reference, not even by his expression of face or a glance of his kaleidoscopic eyes, to the sad catastrophe with which by this time I was but too well acquainted.

I had been reading newspapers eagerly all day, when he came, and, from a contradictory mass of evidence, had gleaned some grains of truth. One fact was beyond contradiction—a second Samson had drawn down the ruins of a temple, not on the heads of his foes alone, but his friends as well, blinded, as he of old, by the treachery of that basest of all Delilahs, a fawning public!

Yes, we were ruined; the only hope now was in the honesty of Mr. Basil Bainrothe. Should the gold I saw him hiding away not have been appropriated to the purchase of bank-stocks—should it have been saved for me—we might still rejoice in wealth beyond our deserts, and equal to our desires.

We still might keep the old, beloved roof above our heads, preserve one unbroken circle of family domestics—live without labor, or terror of the future. But would this be? I waited, as I still think I should have done, for Mr. Bainrothe to take the initiative in this proceeding.

Impatient and sick-hearted, I saw day after day glide past, without an effort on his part to explain or ameliorate my condition—one now of excessive and wearing anxiety.

At last he came. For the first time in his life when a matter of business was in question, he asked for me. I went to him alone at my own instance, and somewhat to Evelyn's chagrin, I thought.

I found him in the library, of late our sole receiving-room; the rest were closed and fireless. For, since the certainty of our misfortune, we had received no society, and would not long be obliged to *decline* it, Evelyn thought. Her opinion of the world little justified the pains she had taken to conciliate it.

I found Mr. Bainrothe buried in the deep reading-chair, always in his lifetime occupied by my father, his hand supporting his head, his hat and delicate ivory-headed cane thrown carelessly on the floor beside him—his whole attitude one of deep dejection.

He started a little when I addressed him by name, as if reviving from deep reverie—then arose and extended his hand to me, grasping mine firmly when I gave it to him, which I did unwillingly I confess.

"Miriam," he said, "this is all very dreadful!" subsiding into his seat again with a groan, and looking steadily and silently into the fire for some minutes afterward. "Very dreadful!" he repeated, shaking his head dismally; "wholly unforeseen!"

He glanced at me furtively once or twice to observe the effect of his words—his manner. Disappointed probably by my silence and coolness, he again affected to be absorbed in contemplation.

"Have we any thing left?" I asked quietly, at last—weary as I was of this histrionic performance of his, and anxious for the truth.

"Nothing," was the gloomy reply that fell on my ear—on my heart like molten lead; "nothing but what you know of. This house, this furniture, well preserved it is true, but old and out of style. Your carriage and horses—diamonds—in short, what you have in hand. That is all you have left of the great estate of your mother."

"It is enough to keep the wolf from the door, at all events," I remarked quietly, "and I am thankful for a bare competence; but why, under existing circumstances, were you in such haste to remove the contents of the iron chest behind the mirror, a portion of which you added to in September?"

He rose with dignity and advanced to the corner of the mantel-shelf, on which he leaned in a perfectly self-possessed position, one foot crossed lightly over the other, I remember, and one hand at his side—a favorite attitude of his. He interrupted my interrogatory with another, ever an effectual aid in browbeating.

"How did you become possessed of the knowledge that I kept gold there?" he asked, coolly; "I had meant to have preserved the secret of that spring until your majority, but you women penetrate every thing. No, my dear Miriam," he continued, without waiting for an answer, "unfortunately, the gold you refer to was exchanged for worthless bank-stocks in September last, according to the requisitions of your father's will; and, as that was the latest paid in of the loans he had made, and as all other means had been invested in like manner (and with a promptness characteristic of me, I believe I may say without vanity), as they fell into my hands. You will perceive, very clearly, that every thing, beyond the property I have here pointed out to you, is swept away."

I sat confounded by his consummate mendacity. His manner was entirely changed now—from one of gloomy depression, and absence of mind, to jaunty self-complacency, and even a degree of defiance was blended with his habitual coolness. It was only from his lurid and kaleidoscopic eyes, on which the light from an opposite window fell sharply, as he was speaking, that a glimpse of the inner man could be obtained. There was something confused and excited in their expression that did not escape me, but I kept my counsel, bewildered as I was.

"She has betrayed me!" was my involuntary reflection; "he was on his guard for my question or accusation; unconscious of my daily examination, he has borne away my gold, and it is lost to me forever!" And I clasped my hands more closely.

All that I have stated in the last two paragraphs, of my observation and reflections, passed through my mind like a flash—so that there seemed scarce a momentary interruption between his last remarks and those which followed—although so much had been recognized in the interval.

"It is unfortunate—" I said, merely eying him calmly.

For the first time during our interview, his eyes quivered—drooped—fell before mine; but, recovering instantly, he gave me a clear, cool stare in return for the quiet look of scorn he encountered. I saw at once the hopeless nature of the case.

"You will show me your accounts, Mr. Bainrothe," I observed, haughtily; "I require this at least!"

"When you have attained your majority, certainly, Miriam, not before. At present, I have only Evelyn Erle to satisfy on that score, and the law; I refer you to your guardian."

"Or whomsoever I choose to substitute as my guardian," I said; "I believe that privilege vests in me, being over eighteen."

"There are outside provisions in your father's will that debar you, unfortunately, from that usual privilege of minors of your age," he rejoined, quietly. "I regret this for many reasons: I should be glad to quiet any doubts you may entertain at once, but it is impossible that, compatibly with self-respect, I can do this, after what you have insinuated this morning; so you must wait, with what patience you can command, for the coming of your majority."

"Nearly two years to wait!" I cried; "I should die before then, if only of impatience. No, I will know at once. I will write to Mr. Gerald Stanbury—I will go to the president of the bank—nay, to Mr. Biddle himself. I will resolve this matter."

"You will do no such thing, my very dear young friend," said Mr. Bainrothe," advancing and laying his hand lightly on my arm—I shook it off, as if it had been a cold, crawling serpent. He retreated quietly but quickly. "You will do no such thing, Miriam," he repeated, resuming his post by the mantel-shelf, without evincing the least discomposure at my behavior to him; "your own good sense, your own good feeling will come to your assistance when you look this matter fully in the face, and dispassionately, which I must say you are not doing now. I have not earned at your hands mistrust and obloquy like this, Miriam; but, for the sake of the past, I shall strive and bear with the present. Who has inspired you with such opinions of me?"

Accomplished hypocrite! He tried to assume a much-injured air, to mingle forbearance with his reproachful words; but my heart was as hard toward him as a nether millstone, and his words made no impression on my flinty feelings, not even enough to strike fire therefrom, or sparks.

"No one," I replied, "no one; I judge for myself in all instances. Why did you secrete gold in the dead hour of the night, which, unless you bore it away in the same mysterious, or even more subtle manner, ought still to be in its hiding-place? Why did you preserve, even from Evelyn, your knowledge of that retreat, and the payment of the loan, which she asserts you have never communicated to her, from first to last? Why make mysteries of business transactions which, by the tenor of my father's will, she had a right to participate in, and be consulted about. Why?"

"I will tell you," he interrupted, gravely, and not without emotion. "Pause, and I will explain my reasons, painful as it is to me to do this, and greatly as I compromise myself by so doing, for, should you choose to be indiscreet, I shall have gained a dangerous enemy. I have no confidence in Evelyn Erle, in her truth, her sincerity, her honesty, even. I would not place temptation in her way. There, that is why I concealed the secrets of the spring-lock and recess in the wall from her, to secure them for you. As to the depositing of gold in that iron chest, I did it simply because I knew of no other place so safe and secret. In my own house none such exists, and, as I never kept gold for more than a few days after it was received, I thought it scarcely worth while to place it in the vaults of the bank. As I tell you, it was removed in September."

Surely no art was ever greater of its kind than that he manifested on this trying occasion, yet it fell to the earth, like the shedding scales of a serpent, before my simple discernment. Yet his words, his manner, did in some strange and unexplained way greatly exonerate Evelyn in my estimation, at least for a time, of complicity.

How could I consistently believe that two persons, entertaining of each other such similar and degrading opinions, could trust one another sufficiently to become confederates? Alas! I did not reflect that it is of such conflicting elements conspirators and conspiracies themselves are usually made, and that union of guilt creates eternal enmity.

I could not penetrate such depths of guile! I surrendered myself readily, I confess, to these fresh convictions. Evelyn was narrow, selfish, scheming, but, at all events, was not in league with this vampire. That was much. We might still make common cause against him—she with her injuries to avenge, I with mine—and preserve intact, and without his hated interference, that which was left to us at least.

There was comfort in the thought.

While these considerations were photographing themselves on my brain, with that indescribable rapidity of process whereby the action of the mind excels even that of light, Mr. Bainrothe was again settling himself down in my father's deep chair, and now once more addressed me in a sad and broken voice, perfectly well suited to the occasion.

"Miriam," he said, "I too have been an extensive loser through the failure of the Bank of Pennsylvania. Like yourself, with the exception of the house I now reside in, and some few small tenements I hold for rent, I find every thing swept away from me. Claude, it is true, is comfortable, and on his slender estate we must both now manage to support ourselves. You see marriage on his part is now simply out of the question. He has his father to take care of."

He said this last in so significant a tone, and apologetic a manner, that its intent was unmistakable, little dreaming how transparent my conviction of his crime had made his motives.

"As far as I am concerned, it was so eighteen months ago," I responded, and the blood rushed indignantly to my brow. "Yet I hope," I added, after a moment's hesitation, "that Claude may still marry and be happy."

"You are still vexed with that boy of mine, Miriam, I see that. Oh, you are wrong, there! It was not for him, unfledged and inexperienced, to weigh the precious diamond against the paste pretense! He could not see you with the eyes of riper judgment and deep feeling accorded to those who have studied life, and learned its loftiest lessons. Had he looked through my eyes, Miriam—" (he was standing before me now, his arms extended, his eyes blazing, his cheeks and lips strangely aglow), "he would have seen you as you are, the rose, the ruby of the world." He seized my hand impetuously, and pressed it to his lips, then rushed wildly away. A moment later, he returned, silently. I was standing before the silver cistern, I remember, washing away with my handkerchief an invisible stain from my hand, child-fashion, a loathsome impress, when I felt his audacious arms thrown suddenly around me, and his hot, polluting kisses on my face.

"I love—I love you!" he hissed in my ear, "and sooner or later I will possess you!"

Before I could strike him, spit upon him, strangle him with my hands—the thief, the midnight robber, the slave of lust—he was gone again. I heard my own wild shrieks resounding through the house, like those of some strange lunatic. I was for a time frantic with rage and shame. But no one came to my succor, except poor old Morton. He crept feebly from the pantry, and found me sobbing in my father's chair. As he stood meekly before me, leaning on his staff, and looking in my face, my only friend, so powerless to aid, the whole desolateness of my position burst upon me, like an overpowering avalanche. I bowed my head and wept.

"Bear up, bear up, my lamb," he said, in his weak, tremulous voice; "we have the promise of the Lord to rely on. Has he not said the seed of the just man should never know want or beg bread? We must believe in the Gospel, and be strengthened, Miss Miriam."

And he laid his quivering hand lightly on my head. I took it between both of my own, and kissed it fervently, bathing it with my tears. "Morton," I said, "dear old Morton, I have had such a terrible blow to bear—shame!" and again I was choked with sobs.

"Shame! Oh, no, my dear young mistress! my birdie child; ruin is not shame! This could never come near a Monfort, poor or rich! See! such as these old hands are, they shall work for you to the bone, and, if I understand matters aright, we still have the good roof left over our heads, and some little means for all immediate wants. God will put some good thought in your mind before long. Consult with Miss Evelyn ; she is wise. You are not the first high-born young ladies who have had to teach a school."

"Oh, bless you, bless you, Morton, for the thought!"

All idea of telling him (helpless, as he was, to avenge it) of the degrading treatment I had received was now laid at rest, and the practical good sense of a suggestion, that, if successfully carried out, would take us so completely out of the hands of Mr. Bainrothe, and insure such complete independence, was felt at once.

At a glance I saw the expediency as well as the feasibility of the scheme.

Our large and secluded establishment was well fitted for a boarding-school. Our father's spotless name, and our undeserved misfortunes, were calculated to enlist popular respect and sympathy.

Evelyn's decided manners and liberal accomplishments, my better principles and more solid attainments (I viewed things with the naked eye of truth that day, and thus the balance was struck in its rapid survey), might all be brought to bear on our new vocation.

"This is the very thing for us to do, Morton," I said, after a pause, wiping my eyes, and smiling up into his dear, old, withered face. "I will acquaint Evelyn with it before I sleep. Ay, and with other matters as well," I added, mentally. "God help me now!—upon her verdict every thing depends."

I met Mabel on the stairway as I ascended to my chamber. She hung about my neck, in a childish way she had, and kissed me fondly. Perhaps she had observed my agitated face, in which many emotions contended, probably (as in my heart), but I only said, "Let me pass now, darling!—One thing will," I thought, "be secure, under the contemplated circumstances—your welfare and education, whatever else betide—beautiful, and good as an angel, you shall be wise as well."

"Oh! I forgot to tell you, sister Miriam," she cried, running up-stairs, after we had parted, "Evelyn has gone out, and left this note for you;" and she placed one in my hand, adding:

"Mr. Claude Bainrothe was here, while you were in the library with his father, and they went away together."

"Where did she receive him, Mabel?—the parlors are closed, you know."

"Yes, but she was all ready when he came. It was an appointment, I think he said, to take a walk, and he stood at the front-door, until she went down, only five minutes, sister Miriam. He did not mind it at all. He sent her up the letter he had brought from the office, and she read it out loud to Mrs. Austin. I was there—it was very short."

"What letter, Mabel?"

"Oh, about her aunt! This note tells you, I suppose. Evelyn is rich now; but she had to go to New York to see the lawyer, so Mr. Claude Bainrothe said, before she could claim the fortune."

More and more bewildered, I made haste to tear open the sealed note which Mabel had given me. Its contents were scanty, and not fully satisfactory.

"My dear Miriam: The ways of Providence are truly strange and inscrutable, and its balance ever shifting. This morning I rose in despair, to-night I shall lie down rejoicing; for a way is again opened to us that will put it beyond *his* power to annoy or oppress us further. God knows we have both suffered enough, already, at his hands! My maiden aunt, Lady Frances Pomfret, is dead, and makes me her heir. I will show you the lawyer's letter when I return. The legacy is spoken of in the letter as small, because English people compute property so differently from ourselves. The attorney lives in New York, who is empowered by my aunt's English executor to transact this business, and it seems I must go to him, Mohammed-like, as this mountain cannot come to me.

"Claude Bainrothe is polite enough to offer to escort me to the boat, which I shall barely reach in time; so, farewell for the present, dear Miriam. I shall stay with Emma Gilroy, and return in a very few days. Write to me, however, if I should be detained, to her father's care, and keep a good heart, until the return of your fortunate

"EVELYN.

"P. S.—You know it is little matter, between sisters, which possesses the property, so all share it. E."

Claude Bainrothe called that afternoon, and placed in my hand the copy of the codicil that had been sent to Evelyn, together with the lawyer's letter to which she had alluded, and which, on consulting with him, she found it unnecessary to take with her to New York, her identity being already established, beyond a doubt, with that of the legatee, in the eyes of the American agent in possession of all the facts of the case from the London attorney. I examined the codicil closely, and could find no flaw! It purported to be the last will of the Lady Frances Pomfret, who revoked all other bequests, in order to bestow her whole property on her niece, Evelyn Erle.

I confess I had felt some doubts as to the existence at all of such a person, of whom I had never before heard mention made, until I read her last bequest, and saw with my own eyes the business-like letter, confirming the whole transaction of Mr. James Mainwaring, the London attorney, with its foreign post-mark, and huge office seal. This was accompanied by one from a legal gentleman of New York, whose name was familiar to me, as my father's agent, and which confirmed the truth of the matter in the most effectual way; for, in his letter, Evelyn was advised to come to New York and receive her legacy.

There was nothing more to be said, certainly; still I had strange misgivings even then, which I felt to be both unjust and ungenerous, yet could not wholly banish, and again I examined the codicil.

Claude Bainrothe smiled; it was the first time, let me state *en passant*, that we had found ourselves alone together since his return. "You scrutinize that will as if you were a legal flaw-finder, Miss Monfort, instead of a very confiding young lady of poetical proclivities."

"It is very short!" I said, sententiously, comparing at the same time the handwriting with that of Mr. Mainwaring, who had in his letter declared himself the copyist, the original codicil remaining in his hands, together with the will it had annulled, and finding them the same unmistakably.

"Short, but sweet," he remarked curtly, yet smiling again, and extending his hand for it. "I suppose one of Earl Pomfret's children had trodden on the tail of the old maid's poodle—she lived with him it seems—and offended her beyond repair, or something similar had occurred, to make her change her intentions, which were at first all in his favor, and revoke her first bequest."

"Mr. Mainwaring does not say so," I remarked, again glancing over his letter. "He merely observes that it is only important to send a copy of the codicil, since it revokes all previous bequests. How did you know her first intentions—have there been other letters?"

"I suppose so," he replied, coloring slightly, "but what a lawyer you are! I scarcely know how I got the idea, to be frank with you; it may be incorrect after all, but Evelyn will tell you every thing, of course, when she comes."

"Let me see the codicil again, Mr. Bainrothe," and I examined it once more closely, as if by some fascination I could not resist. I remarked only one peculiarity in the document. One word was written in a cramped manner, as though space had been wanting—yet much of the sheet of paper on which it appeared was unoccupied—this was the word "thirty," at the beginning of the enumeration of moneys, for thirty thousand pounds (repeated below in figures) was the sum set forth in the codicil as the bequest of the Lady Frances Pomfret to her niece Evelyn Erle! The five numerals that represented the same idea as the written words occupied half of the last portion of the last line, and seemed to my invidious eyes to make an ostentatious display of the power that may lie in a cipher, or an array thereof.

I gloated over the record, with something perhaps of that spirit which may have lurked in my blood, from the time of Jacob, and which, so far, had not evinced itself, except perhaps on that occasion when my ear thrilled to the music of falling gold.

As I gazed, I mused on the strange fate that took from one sister to enrich the other so providentially, as it might have seemed.

The paper had fallen from my nerveless hand before I knew it, and I was aroused from reverie by Claude's action in stooping for it, and his voice saying:

"I will fold up this record, Miriam; it seems to render you gloomy."

"Thoughtful, certainly," I said, recovering myself, with that impulse of self-command that belonged to me by nature; "no more—not envious, Claude, I assure you, however appearances may be against me."

"Of such a feeling no one could suspect Miriam Monfort," he said, gallantly; whispering low in the next moment, "one year has made strange improvement in your beauty, Miriam—you are hardly the same little dark, quick, yet quiet girl, I parted with when I went to Copenhagen. There is so much more pose and majesty —more sweetness about you now—and Evelyn too is changed—oh! sadly—sadly!"

"I have sometimes feared," I said, keeping down, as best I might, the emotions conflicting in my bosom— "feared that she might be delicate, and that her energies consumed her; you must control these, Claude!"

"I!—why, what on earth can I have to do with Miss Erle and her energies? you speak in enigmas, Miriam!"

He was evidently embarrassed by the cool, incredulous look I dropped upon him. "I had supposed every thing was settled some time ago," I observed, quietly; "however, I will not bore you with conjectures or questions, I shall hear every thing, of course, when the proper time comes; until then, I shall hope to act out Milton's noble line, and 'stand and wait.' And now, if you have a few minutes to spare, do give me the *résumé* of your experience at Copenhagen. What of the climate—what of the people—what of the court? Are the women pretty or plain, as a general thing—and had Hamlet light or dark hair, think you, from present indications in the royal family? Or is it the same blood? For you know that I have an enthusiasm about Denmark! It is such a little, valiant, fiery, dominant state, and their *sagas* of the sea-kings set my blood on flame. This always was a weakness of mine, you remember."

"Yes, I recollect perfectly how you used to run on about Elsinore. Well, I went there frequently, Miriam, and can tell you all about the dreary, decayed old town, to your utmost satisfaction. Even your romance would fail, could you behold it now."

And Claude evinced considerable power, as a word-painter, in the hour that followed, during the early part of which Mabel appeared at the door, was silently beckoned in by me, to remain a quiet and delighted listener, almost to the end of the interview, when Mrs. Austin suddenly summoned her away; and again Claude Bainrothe and I were left for a few minutes *tête-à-tête.* When my visitor departed, or rose to do so, we shook hands frankly; and I thought, on the whole, he seemed grateful for my mode of treatment, and the interest I had shown in his narrative—so entire a proof of the disinterested nature of my feelings, could he only have thought so! It had probably been his intention to test and probe them in the beginning, and he had succeeded.

He lingered a moment, however, on the threshold, gazing at me earnestly.

"Miriam," he said, reëntering and closing the door, "Miriam, I wish I could be certain of your friendship. I may put it to fiery proof before long. Can I rely on you to support me then?"

"Claude," I rejoined, gravely, "if I can assist you in any useful or honorable way, I shall be glad to do so, on general principles alone. You did not respond fairly to my friendly manifestations in times past, after—after a certain explanation, and the impulse has died away since then, I confess. Our future lives can have very little in common, I imagine."

"Would you not help me to break a loathed chain?" he asked, almost fiercely. "Bonds are often forced upon a man," he continued, "by the very reason of his superior strength. It is so hard to resist a pleading woman! O Miriam! more than any one living, I respect—revere—love—yes, love you. Pity me! You can assign no secondary reasons now to professions like these. You are no longer rich—no longer—"

"Miss Kilmansegg, with the golden leg," I interrupted, derisively. "Truly you surprise me."

"O Miriam! how can you treat me with such heartless levity?" and he wrung his hands bitterly. "I am pushed to desperation already. I never knew, until I lost you, what you were to me; how superior to all other women, how pure, how unworldly, how strong, how rich in all mental and womanly endowments! Hear me, Miriam," and he attempted to take my hand, an error of which he was soon made conscious.

"Claude Bainrothe," I said, sternly, "I can tolerate you on one condition alone—that you respect me. You cease to do this, you, the betrothed husband of another woman! the moment you sully my ear with your addresses, your effusions of sentiment. They are no more, I know; but even these I will not endure from you, nor yet from—" I hesitated; a hated name had risen to my lips, but I repressed it. He, the son, surely was not the father's keeper.

"You do me injustice; before Heaven, you do!" he exclaimed, flinging back his long curling locks impetuously, by a toss of his superb head, and bending his blazing eyes upon me. "Hear me, Miriam, I hold the clew to a secret by means of which I can compel wealth to flow back to your feet, in the old channels, if you will be mine. You would not have thought this condition hard a year ago. What has occurred to change you? You loved me then—by Heaven you love me still! Oh, say so, Miriam, and make me doubly blessed! Am I deceived in the expression of that beaming eye? You will pardon, bless me;" and he knelt humbly at my feet, and clasped my hand.

"Rise, Claude," I said, "and forgive me if a momentary feeling of triumph, that may have lit my eye, was mingled with the feeling of entire emancipation from all past weakness, which this hour so surely proves, and so satisfactorily, to my own spirit. You are to me like any other stranger."

He was standing sullenly before me now, his head dropping on his breast, his hands loosely clasped before him.

"You are deceived," I pursued, calmly, "if you imagine from any expression of mine that one ray of love survives the ruin of other days. I told you the truth when I said all was over between us forever. Did you suppose me a woman to sit down in the ashes because one man—one woman of all God's manifold creation—had proved false, or treacherous, or ungrateful? I should have wronged my youth, my soul, my descent, my God, had I so yielded. Go and fulfill your contract faithfully this time; a second rupture might not go so well with you as the first. There are persons who are singularly tenacious of their possessions, and who number their bondsmen as a principal portion of their property. Beware how you anger such! Your father too. He would be conciliated now, by what would once have incensed him. Evelyn Erle is rich, Miriam Monfort is poor; why need I add another word? The suggestion is perfect."

Coldly, silently, angrily, he left the room. I heard him stamp impatiently at the hall-door, at some delay apparently in undoing its fastenings—his childish habit when provoked—such was his haste to be gone.

Yet I could scarcely judge, from what had just occurred, taking this, too, in connection with what had passed long before, when I alone was the injured and forgiving one, that I had drawn down upon my head his eternal enmity.

But thus it proved.

## CHAPTER IX.

MONTHS passed away—months of dreary, monotonous despondency, through which ran a vein of anxiety that banished peace. During all this time matters went on pretty much as they had done before, with one exception, I held no further intercourse with Mr. Basil Bainrothe. Claude was absent most of this time on business, for a firm with which he had lately connected himself, and on the few occasions of his presence at Monfort Hall treated me with marked formality.

Evelyn had affected to make light of Mr. Bainrothe's outrage toward me, though far from defending him. "Men of his years do these things sometimes," she said, "under the mask of playfulness and fatherly feeling, and, however unpleasant it may be to bear them, one has to pass them over. You are right, of course, to be reserved with him henceforth, Miriam. By-the-by, dear child, your prudery is excessive, I fear, and it makes a young girl, especially if she is not beautiful, so ridiculous! But, of course, that even is far better than the opposite extreme. Now, I flatter myself, I know how to steer the *juste milieu*, always so desirable."

"But, Evelyn," I had rejoined, "his manner was atrocious! I could not—I would not if I could—give you any idea of its *animality;* yes, that is the very word! it makes my blood creep to think of it, even!"

And I hid my face in my hands, crimson as it was from the retrospection.

"Then don't think of it at all. That will be the best way, decidedly," she had said, tapping me playfully with her fan, then whispering: "This lover of yours may be useful to us, you know; let us not goad him to rebellion. You can be as cool as you please, Miriam, but be civil all the same."

I surveyed her with flashing eyes. "Such advice," I retorted, "falls but poorly from your lips, Evelyn Erle, whom my mistaken father dubbed 'propriety personified.' One woman should feel for another's wounded delicacy, even if a stranger; but, when it comes to sisters, O Evelyn!"

"And such insolence falls very absurdly from you, Miriam Monfort, under the circumstances. Sisters, indeed!" she sneered. "It was a claim you repudiated once!" and, with a sweeping bow, she left me, to repeat "sisters, indeed!" in my bitter solitude.

What were these circumstances to which she so haughtily referred? With my heavy head resting on my weary hands, I sat and contemplated them—ay, looked them fully in the face! Outwardly, matters stood just as they had ever done.

The same circle of servants—of acquaintances—revolved around us. The house was unchanged, the living identically the same, even to the one bottle of fine wine per day, carefully withdrawn from the cobwebbed cellar by Morton, and as carefully decanted for our table.

But this alone, of all the viands set before us, was furnished at my expense. My own small hoard of silver-pieces had, it is true, from the time of our ruin, more than sufficed for my absolute wants and Mabel's, confined, as they were, to mere externals of necessary dress; but all other outlay, even to the payment of Mabel's masters (I taught her chiefly myself, however), was met by Evelyn.

We, the children of a proud man, were dependent on strangers. Look upon it as I would, the revolting fact stared me out of countenance. Charity, the chambermaid, had more right to lift an opposing front to Evelyn than I had; for she earned the bread she ate, while I—there was no use concealing the mortifying truth any longer—served the apprenticeship of pauperdom!

True, the house was legally mine—the furniture I used, the plate I was served from, the carriage I occasionally drove out in, were all my own possessions—though, with a slow and moth-like process, I was gradually consuming these. For, at my majority, it was my determination to pay for my support in the intervening years, even if I sacrificed every thing in order to wipe out obligations. Ay, the very corn my horses were eating (what mockery to keep them at all!) was now furnished by another, and must eventually be paid for, with interest.

Then, how would it fare with me, beggared indeed? I would take time by the forelock; I would begin at once.

"Evelyn," I had said, not long after the conversation reverted to, "is there no way in which my property may be fixed, so as to leave the principal untouched, and still yield an income sufficient for my support, and that of Mabel? The bread of dependence is very bitter to me."

"I ate it long," she said, "and found it passing sweet. You are only receiving back the payment for an old debt, Miriam. Your father's lavish generosity can never be repaid, even to his children, by me, who was so long its happy recipient."

The words seemed unanswerable at the time, inconsistent as they were with her past reproaches. Again she said—when the same murmur left my lips upon a later occasion—looking at me sorrowfully as she spoke, and with something incomprehensible to me in her expression that affected me strangely: "Wait until you are of age, Miriam: all can be arranged definitely then; but now, the waves might as well chafe against the rocks that bind them in their bed, as you against your condition;" adding with a tragic look and tone, half playful, of course, "Votre sort, c'est moi. You remember what Louis XIV. said, 'L'État, c'est moi;' now be pacified, I implore you—all will still be well," and she patted my shoulder kindly, and kissed my forehead.

Her forbearance touched me; but the time came when all this was thrown aside. It was the old fable again of the bee and the bee-moth. Having failed in her first efforts, she was now very gradually gluing me against the hive.

Evelyn, as I have said, had always been at the head of my father's house and mine, and, by his will, was still to remain so until my marriage, or majority—one, usually, in the eyes of the law, in most respects. So it pained me infinitely less than it must have done had a different order of things ever existed, to see her supreme at Monfort Hall, and to feel that every thing emanated from her hand.

Of all the servants, old Morton alone seemed to feel the difference. Mrs. Austin had always openly preferred Evelyn to me, and Mabel to either—so that matters worked very well between those three. For, though I do not think Evelyn loved Mabel, nor Mabel Evelyn, yet, with this link between them of servile affection, they managed very well, without much feeling on either side.

Mrs. Austin certainly spoiled Mabel, yet she only rendered her self-indulged, not selfish—for this difference arises out of temperament and disposition—and no mother could have been more tender or vigilant of her comfort or welfare, than was this ancient and attached nurse and servitor. I mention this here, for it reconciled me later, somewhat, to an inevitable separation, that must have been else thrice bitter. But the culmination approaches!

I was lying, one evening, on a deep velvet couch in the library, now rarely used except for business purposes—for, again, fires and lights sparkled, in their respective seasons, in the several receiving-rooms of Monfort Hall, maintained by Evelyn's bounty—when, overpowered by the influence of the hour, and the weariness of my own unprofitable thoughts, and perhaps the dreary play of Racine's that I was reading, I dropped asleep.

The sofa was placed in a deep embrasure, surrounded with sweeping curtains, for the convenience of reading in a reclining posture, by the light of the window, and quite shut away, by such means, from the remainder of the room.

To-night, a chilly one in August, very unusual for that season, the window was down, and the drawn curtains kept off the light of the dim lamp that swung from the centre of the apartment immediately above the octagon centre-table.

I was roused to full consciousness by the sound of voices, which I had heard indistinctly mingling with my dreams for some time before.

Mr. Bainrothe and Evelyn were conversing or discussing some subject, somewhat angrily.

"You had the lion's share," I heard him say; "you have no reason to complain. The rest came in afterward, and was all merged in that sinking ship, and went down with it into the deep waters. It would not have been as much as you received, had it been saved, which it was not."

"That is not my concern," she rejoined, dryly; "but for my communication, Miriam would have secured all next morning. She was bent upon it. You ought never to forget this."

"Nor do I; but, after all, you are the chief beneficiary, Evelyn."

"And your son—do you count his welfare as nothing? Will he not share with me? Nay, was it not for his sake, chiefly, I warned you, knowing how implacable else you might be toward us both, and how 'gold would gild every thing' in your estimation."

"True, true; but still something is due to me. Undertake this office—succeed—and command me, eternally. I love that girl, as you know, as Claude could never love any one, and it will go hard with me if I do not still inspire her with somewhat of the same sentiment—that is, with your coincidence."

"Never, never!" she exclaimed with asperity; "her hatred is too implacable—the Judaic principle is too firmly grafted in her life. Truly, she is one of a stiff-necked generation. Her heart is especially hard toward you, Basil Bainrothe—and, I confess, you were precipitate."

"I know, I know—but that error can be repaired. I did not think of marriage *then*, I confess; after her bankruptcy and scorn to me, things had not gone so far; her own severity has made me consider the subject seriously. She is not one to be treated lightly, Evelyn!"

"Your son found that out to his cost!" was the bitter rejoinder, and I heard her draw in her breath hard between her closed teeth, with the hissing sound so familiar to me, and peculiar to her when she labored under excitement—a sound like that of a roused serpent.

"Yes, to his cost; but there is no question of that now. Though, I must say, I think he erred. He, like the base Judean, cast away a pearl richer than all his tribe!"

"Thank you!" was Evelyn's curt, ungracious reply.

I rose from the couch, my hand was on the curtain; painful as it was to me, I would go forth and confront them both with the acknowledgment of their conspiracy, their fraud. I would not again listen to bitter truths as I had done before, involuntarily, when bound hand and foot by the weakness of my condition. I was strong and courageous now. I had no excuse for hearing another syllable—I would defy them, utterly!

All this passed like a flash through my mind.

On what slight pivots our fate turns sometimes! How small are the guiding-points of destiny! A momentary entanglement of my bracelet, with one of the tassels of the curtain, delayed me an instant, inevitably, in my impulsive endeavor to extricate myself from its meshes, and what I then heard, determined me to remain where I was, at any cost to my own sense of pride and honor.

Fear, abject fear, obtained complete ascendency over every sense, and personal safety became my sole consideration. I, who had boasted so lately of my courage, felt the cold dew of cowardice bathe my brow, its tremor shake my frame.

They were plotting—deliberately plotting, as the price of secrecy on one part—to shut me up in a lunatic asylum until my consent could be obtained to that ill-starred marriage!

"Every thing is favorable to this undertaking," I heard

Mr. Bainrothe say; "her own moody and excitable condition of late—the absence of her physician (meddlesome people, those conscientious medical men sometimes prove, even when not asked for an opinion!)—Mrs. Austin's testimony as to those lethargies, which would be conclusive of itself—our own disinterestedness, so fully proved by our devotion to her and Mabel, under difficulties—her mother's mysterious malady—all these things will make it easy to carry out this plan in which your cheerful coincidence, and perhaps Claude's even, will be essential."

"I doubt whether you succeed in gaining him over," she remarked, coldly; "and, as to me, I shall act as you desire, perhaps, but any thing but 'cheerfully,' I assure you. I consider it a mighty price to pay for—" she hesitated.

"A fortune and a husband?" he queried. "Claude has his suspicions, I well know, but they rest on me alone so far. Could he be convinced of your part in distracting Miriam's gold from its legitimate channel, believe me, he would turn his back on you forever! I know the man."

"Yet he saw me—he must have seen me—alter that word in the codocil to my aunt's legacy—asking no explanation at the time, receiving none thereafter."

"That was different; he thought it a piece of vainglory on your part alone, amounting to nothing, if, indeed, he observed it at all. No, no, Evelyn Erle! if you expect to carry out your views, you must aid me in executing mine. I shall keep your secret from my son on no other conditions. We are confederates or nothing in this matter, you see."

"And suppose, in return, I publish yours to the world," she suggested, coolly; "brand you with baseness? What then, Basil Bainrothe—what then?"

"You dare not!" was the prompt reply. "I hold written propositions of yours on the subject—you have not a scratch of a pen of mine to show. I should declare simply that you were a frustrated rogue, that is all. Who could prove otherwise?" He laughed in his derisive way. There was a bitter pause.

"What is it you want me to do?" she asked, hoarsely, at its expiration. "State definitely what you exact from me in return for your forbearance—your *honorable* secrecy?" There was exquisite irony in her tone.

"Simply this," he said, calmly, taking no notice of her emphasis—"you are to accompany Miriam to the asylum and act as her nurse and guardian until my point is gained. You shall be present at every interview, and you shall both be made perfectly comfortable—treated like ladies; in short, every propriety shall be sacredly observed, and, on the day on which her marriage with me is solemnized, you may both return to Monfort Hall—you as its head, and Claude as its master; Miriam will go home with me, her husband, of course, and all will be settled. Now, I give you twenty-four hours wherein to consider this proposition. At the end of that time, if you still hesitate, Claude shall know every thing. You can then take your chances with him—he may be ready to take a felon for a wife, for aught I know, after all!"

"Come, then, to-morrow evening," she acceded, after a second pause, and in low, angry accents, "and I will acquaint you with my determination — my necessity rather." They parted thus and there.

## CHAPTER X.

NEARLY dead with terror and indignation, I crept stealthily to my own chamber, in which I locked myself up securely, resisting all friendly overtures of the enemy, except one cup of tea, received from the hand of a servant through the half-opened door (which was instantly relocked) of my citadel.

My resolution was formed that night. I would leave Monfort Hall, and even forsake Mabel, until I could return and legally claim both. At my majority, Mabel would be of age to select between her guardians, by that time, according to law, and—we should see! As for poor Morton, I would write to him and claim his prayers alone. Age like his is so irresponsible. I dared not trust him farther!

It was all very brief and bitter!

As yet I had digested no plan of action. I would go westward, I thought, but just as far away as my money would carry me from these fiends, trusting to God for the rest, just as a boat puts off from a blazing ship.

Of course, I must adopt another name—what should it be? I should need clothing; and *how* secure and convey away my trunk unseen by Evelyn? My diamonds must be secreted or disposed of—how should this be done? Could I trust Mrs. Austin—Mabel?

No, the suggestion was discarded at once as unworthy of consideration.

One was too old, too self-indulged, too selfish; and in age people usually worship expediency alone. The other far too young not to be necessarily indiscreet and impulsive. To have been otherwise at her tender age would have been simply monstrous!

No, I must forego even the sweet satisfaction of saying farewell to Mabel; we must part perhaps forever, as we might meet again within an hour, and all her distress and anxiety must pass unshared and unheeded.

There was no one else I cared very much about leaving, but the love of locality was a strong feature in my disposition, and every room in my father's house was dear to me, as was every book in his study, and every plant in our deep-green, shadowed garden.

The very streets were sacred in my sight, that I had trodden from childhood, but my liberty was more precious to my heart than scenes of old associations, and to gain one the other must be sacrificed. There was no hesitating now: I was on the tread-mill of fate, and must proceed, or fall and be crushed beneath.

And here again I repeat, what I have said so recently: "On what slight pivots our destiny often turns!—through what small channels Providence works its wondrous ways!"

A pair of shoes had been sent home for me that day, which still lay on the table, wrapped and corded. In truth, they came very opportunely; "I shall want these soon," I thought, as I examined the strong and elastic bootees, which had been made for me in view of my morning walks, a part of dear Dr. Pemberton's regimen, which I strenuously and advantageously carried out.

As I spoke, the paper in which they had been enveloped rustled down on the floor by my side. I stooped, languidly, to pick it up, merely from a sense of order, and my eye fell on a long column, headed "Wanted," and, almost for lack of resolution to withdraw it, wandered down its paragraphs, step by step.

It was a Democratic paper, such as was never patronized by Evelyn—herself a zealous conservative in politics, as our father had been before us—and, as I cared little for newspaper-reading, I had never suggested a subscription to any sheet that she did not fancy, although I inclined to democracy.

I was somewhat amused by the quaintness of some of the advertisements of this sheet for the people, that style of literature being new to me; and found myself smiling over the perfections set forth as necessary, by the paragons of the earth, in both wife and servant, when I came to a dead stand. Here was the very thing I should have selected, could I have chosen my own destination instead of depending on *chance* (as if, indeed, there were such a thing *possible* with God—the predestinator of the universe), or necessity (is the name a much better one as applied to the all-seeing Deity?), or fate (a more comprehensive but little less-abused term, perhaps), to do this for me!

The advertisement ran thus, and quite fascinated me with its eccentricity, as well as congeniality to my condition:

"A gentleman and lady, now sojourning for a short time at the Mansion House, wish to employ, immediately, for the benefit of their children, an instructress, who must be, *imprimis*, a lady—and young; secondly, soundly constituted and well educated; thirdly, a good reader, and able to teach elocution, and entertain a circle; fourthly, willing to reside with cheerfulness on a Southern plantation; fifthly, content with a moderate *modicum* as salary. None other need apply—no references given or asked. Inquire for "*Somnus.*"

I laid down the paper, and drew a long, free breath; then rang a peal of merriment, startling under the circumstances. It was the first hearty laugh that had left my lips for many days. "What an oddity, one or the other of these people must be!" I thought, "the man most probably—yes, I am sure it is he—no woman ever was so independent of references, or made youth a *sine qua non*, nor elocution either. But am I soundly constituted? ay, there's the rub! suppose my terrible foe sees fit to interfere, 'Epilepsy,' as Evelyn called it, and perhaps with reason—God alone knows!—what then? Well, I will hazard it—that is all—I will charge nothing for lost days, and try to be zealous in the interval; besides, it is a long time since one of these obliteration spells occurred; for I shall ever believe Evelyn dosed me for her own purposes on that last occasion! Fiend!—fiend!—and yet my little sister *must* remain in such hands for a season, protected by her guardian angel only.

I passed a feverish night, employing the first part of it in quilting my diamonds into a belt which I placed about my waist; and the remainder in putting together as many useful, as well as a few handsome clothes, as my travelling-trunk would contain; bonnets, evening-dresses, which require room to dispose of, and the like vanities, I abandoned to Evelyn's tender mercies. I rose early and, as usual whenever the weather permitted, sallied forth before breakfast, but this time unaccompanied by my usual attendant, Charity.

The "Mansion House" was at no great distance from our own residence. The beautiful home of the Bingham family, then converted into an hotel, destroyed by fire at a later period, like our own house, was situated in the ancient part of the city, from which fashion had gradually emerged, and shrank away to found new streets and dwellings.

I rang at the private door, and asked the porter for "*Somnus;*" at the same time sending up a card, on which was written:

"'Miriam Harz,' applicant for the post of teacher."

A few moments later a grave, copper-colored servant, respectably clad, and with an air of responsibility about him that was almost oppressive, invited me solemnly to follow him up the winding marble stair—so often trodden by the feet of Washington and his court, when a gracious assemblage filled the halls above—and ushered me into a small but lofty parlor at its head, in which a gentleman sat reading the morning journal.

Very wide awake, indeed, seemed he who affected the title of the god of sleep, as he arose courteously from his chair, still holding his paper in one hand, and waved me to a seat on the worn horse-hair sofa between the windows.

He was a tall, thin, sallow, hooked-nosed gentleman, of middle age, with a certain air of distinction about him in contrast with his singular homeliness.

"Miss Harz?" he said, interrogatively, glancing at the card over the mantel-shelf—near which he had been sitting—above an unseasonable, smouldering coal-fire.

I bowed affirmatively for all reply. "And I," he continued, "am Prosper La Vigne, of the '*Less durneer*' settlement" (for thus he pronounced this anglicized French name) "Maurice County, Georgia," with an air that seemed to say, "You have heard of me, of course!" and again I bowed, as my only alternative.

"Lay off your bonnet, if you please," he said, coolly; "I would like to see the shape of your head before proceeding further. Mine, you see, is an ill-balanced affair," smiling quizzically in his effort to be condescending, perhaps. "This is a mere business transaction, you know," seeing that I hesitated to comply, "and your phrenological developments must atone for my deficiencies, or all will go wrong at once—but do as you like. Now that you have thrown back your veil, I can see that the brow is a good one. That will suffice, I suppose. I will take the moral qualities on trial for the nonce. My wife is wholly occupied with her domestic and private affairs, you must understand, when we are at home, and much will devolve on you; that is, if we suit one another, which is dubious. That reminds me! I have not heard the sound of your voice yet; I am much governed by intonation in my estimates of people, and usually form a perfect opinion at first sight. Be good enough to read this item," and he handed me the morning paper, formally indicating it with his long, lithe forefinger. It was from one of Mr. Clay's speeches. I did as he requested, without hesitation.

"People trot out horses and negroes when they wish to purchase; why not governesses?" I questioned, dumbly. "He did well to ask no references; his examination is thorough, I perceive," and I laid the paper down, half amused, half provoked, when I had finished. He was gazing at me open-mouthed—no unusual thing with him, I found later—and was silent for a few moments.

"Splendid! admirable!" he exclaimed, suddenly;

"both voice and elocution perfect—you possess the greatest of all accomplishments, madam, next to conversational excellence," rising to his feet, and bowing low and seating himself again, in a formal way of his own. "Music is a mockery compared to such reading! as well set a jew's-harp against the winds of heaven! You understand my meaning, of course; it is not precisely that, however. Now let us converse a little."

"The advertisement did not refer to that, I believe, as a condition," I said, somewhat indignantly, and flushing hotly as I spoke. "I really cannot converse to order. I am a person of moods, and do not feel always like talking at all," and I rose and prepared to draw down my veil, take up my parasol, and depart.

"I like you none the worse for a proper exhibition of spirit," he said, nodding kindly, and settling himself once more to his paper composedly. "Sit still, miss, and compose yourself by the time Madame La Vigne comes in, or she *may* think you high-tempered, and I am sure you are nothing of the kind—only very properly proud. There, now, that is right! You seem to be a very sensible, well-conditioned young person indeed, and I think you will suit. You are the tenth since yesterday morning," smiling and bowing blandly, "and the only one that could read intelligibly. Elocution, you see, is my hobby. I forgot to say," looking up from his paper, after a pause, "the salary is six hundred dollars—not enough, perhaps, for a lady of your merit—but quite as much as we can afford to give. This I call a *modicum*."

"It is not very important," I remarked, "what I receive in the shape of money, so that I am at no expense beyond my clothing, and other personal matters, and that I find myself well situated. My engagement will, in no case, extend beyond a year. You have your peculiarities, I see, and I have mine. The question is, might they not jar occasionally?"

"Oh, never, never! '*noblesse oblige*,' you know," with a wave of the hand, soft and urbane. "I hope I shall know how to treat a lady and a teacher, both in one, and a member of my household. Besides that, I shall have very little to do with you, indeed. Just now it is different—we are coming to terms; we have not made them yet, however. I always save my wife this trouble, if possible.—Ah! there she comes, at last," as a mild, lady-like looking woman emerged from an adjoining chamber, somewhat elaborately dressed for that early hour, and followed by a stream of pale, pretty little girls. "Madame La Vigne," he said, rising ceremoniously, "permit me to introduce to you Miss Miriam Harz," reading the name slowly from the card again, which he took from the wall, "'a candidate for the position of instructress at Beauseincourt.'—Say, how do you like her looks?"

I had come to the conclusion by this time that Mr. La Vigne was decidedly as eccentric as his advertisement, and that his vagaries and personalities were not worth minding or estimating in the consideration in question.

So, when Madame La Vigne replied to his abrupt query, "Oh, very, *very* much, indeed!" and held out her kind hand to me, I took it without misgiving, and the first glance we interchanged contained freemasonry. From that time Colonel Prosper La Vigne fell gracefully back into his proper position, and I talked away fluently enough with his lady, as he pompously called his wife. In short, at the end of an hour it was settled that I was to join them the same evening, at their hotel, and proceed with them thence to New York, there to take the packet for Savannah (their first destination) on the same night. The plantation on which they lived, they informed me, was nearly a day's journey, by carriage-conveyance, beyond that city, but eligibly situated for health (though not for productiveness), among a low range of hills known as the "Les Dernier" Mountains, the name being anglicized into "Less derneer," with the accent on the last syllable, so as to metamorphose it completely to the ear, instead of translating it.

"It is a very lonely place though, Miss Harz, in the winter-time—mamma ought to tell you that," whispered Marion, the eldest daughter, as she nestled so closely to me, and looked so kindly in my face, that the intruding thought of her unwillingness for my society was instantly banished. "In the summer it is pleasant enough, so many people come to their cottages in the hills; but, during eight months of the year, we have but one near neighbor, and not a very social one either."

"From circumstances alone unsocial, Marion," said Madame La Vigne, flushing slightly (her usual complexion was of a fair sallowness, common to Southern ladies). "Cousin Celia is certainly devoted at heart to every one of us, but she cannot, you know, leave home often."

"Oh, I know, mamma! I only meant to keep Miss Harz from being disappointed."

"Miss Harz has internal resources, I have no doubt," rejoined Madame La Vigne; "and, even if she had not, I fear her duties would preclude much longing for excitement.—It is a very onerous task you are undertaking, my dear young lady, certainly," turning kindly to me. "Five ignorant little Southern girls, well disposed but imperfectly trained, will fill your hands to positive overflowing, I fear. You will find me exacting, too, sometimes. I am sure I shall enjoy your society whenever you choose to bestow it on me, and Colonel La Vigne as well."

To which declaration on the part of his wife, that gentleman responded by laying his hand on his breast, complacently, and bowing profoundly from his chair, ending the ceremony by a flourish of his delicate cambric handkerchief, and the exhibition at the same time of a slender, sickly, and peculiarly-shaped hand, decorated with an onyx seal-ring. He looked the gentleman, however, unmistakably plain and peculiar as his appearance was, and pompous and pretentious as was his manner.

If words could do the work of the photographer, I should like to show him to my readers, as he appeared to me on that first interview; though later his whole aspect underwent a change in my sight, reflected from the cavernous depths within, so that, what seemed somewhat ludicrous in the beginning, came to be solemnly serious and even sophistically tragical and awful on later acquaintance.

We have all more or less witnessed this phenomenon of transformation in some familiar aspect, either through love or hatred, respect or contempt, fear or admiration, until we find ourselves marveling at past impressions, received, in ignorance of the truth, in the commencement of our observations.

I remember that Mr. La Vigne struck me on that occasion as a superficial man in every way, but kindly, courteous, and vivacious, though certainly eccentric and somewhat absurd. One would have supposed him even a flippant, whimsical person, seen casually; but, on later examination, the droop of his eyelids and under lip, and the depressed corners of his mouth, gave to the close observer a surer indication of his character.

The shape of his narrow, conical, and somewhat elegantly-placed head, denoted an inclination to fanaticism, which had been skillfully combated by a perfectly skeptical education, so as to turn this stream of character into strange channels.

Hobbyism was his infirmity, perhaps, and he was essentially a man of one idea at a time. The word "odd" applied to him peculiarly, which is in itself a sort of social ostracism when attached to any one, and raises a barrier at once between a man and his fellow-bipeds that not even superiority could surmount.

He was emphatically a tawny man as to coloring—hair, skin, and eyes, being all pretty much of the same hue of "the ribbed sea-sands." Yet there were vestiges about him of an originally fair complexion. His wrists and temples were white as those of a woman. His face was long, lank, and cadaverous; his eyes shone with a clear, amber, and steady light, and had an abstracted expression usually, accompanied with a not unfrequent and most peculiar warp of the pupils.

His hair was singularly shaggy and picturesque in its tawny grayness, and wavy, wiry length. Above his eyes his heavy brows of the same texture and color seemed to make a pent-house, from which the high, pale brow receded gradually; his profile was aquiline to absolute grotesqueness. The idea of "Punchinello" presented itself irresistibly at the sight of his parrot-like nose and suddenly-upturned chin.

His gait was as peculiar as his countenance and manner; he glided, in walking, carrying himself erectly, with his arms closely pinioned to his sides. He was altogether so extraordinary looking that I felt myself staring almost rudely at him on our first interview; yet his dress was in no way remarkable except for an air of old-fashioned and speckless neatness.

Madame La Vigne was a pretty and well-preserved woman, of about thirty-five, a fair brunette, originally, to whom most of her daughters bore a close resemblance. One alone, the plainest of the band, presenting a resemblance, most unfortunately for her, of "Colonel La Vigne," as his wife called him, with scrupulous punctilio.

One son, the eldest of their family, they spoke of as the pride of their hearts even on that first interview. He was in the navy, and, consequently, much from home. They regretted this for many reasons, they said, and, among others, on my account. He was so genial, so companionable—their own dear Walter—"such a delightful fellow," as his sister Madge declared exultingly—the second of this band of sisters—and, as far as I could observe, on first acquaintance, the brightest. Marion, the elder, was extremely pretty and gentle; and Bertie, the third, taciturn and unprepossessing, yet evidently sensible. She it was who alone resembled her father.

Fortunately, for the uninterrupted success of my scheme, Evelyn had one of her sick turns that day, and remained closely shut up in her room. At one o'clock, I summoned Franklin to my chamber.

"There is a trunk," I said, "that I wish you would take to the Mansion House—to the care of a Mr. Somnus lodging there—here is the card attached, with his name; place it with his baggage. It is to go to New York, for a Miss Harz, a relation of mine—a teacher, I believe, who has applied to me for assistance; but he understands all that, so you need not be at any trouble to explain.

Be quiet, Franklin, in removing it, as Evelyn is very nervous to-day, and dislikes noise; and go with the drayman yourself to insure its safe delivery."

So passed my first lesson in deception, but I schooled lip and eye to obedience, so that Franklin suspected nothing, and, being a discreet servant, who never let his right hand know what his left was doing, especially when gold crossed the palm, I was sure of silence on the subject, at least until after my own departure.

Mabel and I dined *tête-à-tête* at two; I had caused dinner to be served earlier than usual for my own convenience, though indeed I found it a mere form—for how could I swallow a morsel, choked as I was with grief, while the fair child I worshipped, yet was forsaking, sat so calmly and unconsciously in my sight!

After dinner I sought Mrs. Austin, leading Mabel by the hand. I had been kissing her, almost wildly, every foot of the way up-stairs, and she gazed on me, I could not help perceiving, with a sort of fond surprise, for it was not my habit to lavish such passionate caresses, even on her, without occasion.

"I am obliged to go out now," I said, in a broken voice, which I vainly tried to command. "Take our darling, Mrs. Austin, and keep her very safely until I come again. Promise me this!" I added, eagerly seizing her hand.

"La! Miss Miriam, what's the use of promising for one afternoon, when I have taken the best of care of her all her life? You act so singularly to-day!" she added, pettishly, and she began to smooth Mabel's hair, grumblingly. I turned away without another word, murmuring blessings in my heart on that dear head.

There was no time to be lost now! The carriage was

already at the door of the Mansion House to convey us to the steamboat when I reached it, and Colonel La Vigne standing, rather anxiously, on the pavement, looking up and down.

"I was afraid you had rued your promise and were not coming," said Marion, springing forth from the door-way eagerly, to greet me.

"And we had forgotten to ask your address," added Madame La Vigne, "or we might have called for you, and saved you a long walk, perhaps."

"We should not have carried off your trunk, even had you not appeared, Miss Harz," said Colonel La Vigne, blandly. "There it is you see, distinctly labeled, on the baggage-wagon in front, directed to the care of 'Mr. Somnus!'—a good deal of waggery about you, I perceive, or had you forgotten my name?"

"No, no! I had reasons—but, you remember, no questions were to be asked; you must wait for voluntary communications."

"I am so glad—so glad you are going with us!" said little Louey La Vigne, pressing my hand, as she sat before me in the carriage by Aunt Felicité, her nurse—Colonel La Vigne and three of his daughters having been consigned to another hack—Louey and her sable attendant, stately with her large gold ear-hoops, and brilliant cotton handkerchief, being inseparable accompaniments of his wife.

"I have banished Mr. La Vigne, I fear," I said, in a broken voice; "it would have been best for me, perhaps, to have gone with the young ladies. Let me begin at once."

"No, it is much best as it is," she answered, affectionately; "think of yourself just now, and take no charge until we all get home. You are our guest until then, remember. I know it is a sad trial to go with strangers, but you will find us friends, I hope;" and she clasped my hand in hers, and so held it until we reached the wharf.

Tears rained down my face, beneath the friendly shelter of my veil, but Madame La Vigne, with the tact of good-breeding, affected not to remark them. Once little Louey, a child of eight years old, the youngest and prettiest of all, leaned forward, as if to soothe or question me, but she was plucked quickly back into her place by the decorous Aunt Felicité, who had not lived so long with quality without acquiring some delicacy of behavior, at least, even if it struck no deeper root.

I had commanded myself, before the carriage stopped beside the panting steamboat, and soon we were gliding along the placid river toward the point whence the railroad was to carry us on to our goal. At New York, we found ourselves hurried for time to reach the packet Magnolia, and went directly from the depot to the quay, for embarkation.

By the pilot, who left us at the Narrows, I sent back a few lines to Mabel, also enjoining him, with the gift of a piece of gold, to mail my letters on the following day, and receiving his promise to do so.

In this brief communication, I promised my dear child that we should meet at my majority, and enjoined her to patience. "You will hear from me again before long," I said, in conclusion; "and I will try and arrange some plan of correspondence. Bad people have obliged me to this step. Do not forget me, my darling, nor my lessons and counsel, and believe ever in the honor and devotion of your sister. *Pray for me, Mabel!* MIRIAM."

My letter to Evelyn Erle, without date, written on the ship, and sent back by the pilot to be mailed also at New York, revealed my acquaintance with a portion of her duplicity, and Mr. Bainrothe's dark design.

I promised her my forgiveness on two conditions alone: one was, that she should not seek to trace me, since all effort to regain me would be fruitless; another, that she would be kind to Mabel, and my father's ancient servants until my return, and, of these last, especially Morton.

I uttered no threats nor reproaches—asked no favors, beyond those which I had a right to demand at her hands as my father's ward—long supported by him, and even cherished with paternal tenderness—and the guardian of his child. I knew that the use of my house and furniture would amply compensate her for all Mabel's expenses, among the principal of which would be that liberal education which I demanded for her, as her right.

I was very nearly twenty, now; Mabel, ten. There was still time to redeem the past, and carry out all my frustrated intentions, after the expiration of one year of abeyance and exile. Yes! I would "stand and wait," trusting so "to serve."

*LIFE AT "LESDERNIER."*

"Break the dance and scatter the song,
Some depart, and some remain;
*These* beyond heaven are borne along,
Others the bonds of earth retain."

SHELLEY.

# PART II.

## *LIFE AT "LESDERNIER."*

---

### AN INTERLUDE.

I PURPOSE here to give only a brief sketch of my sojourn under the roof of the La Vignes. In another book, and at another time, when some that now live shall have passed away, or years shall have made dim the memory of results rather than events (for until *then* the last must continue, with their causes, to be *mysteries*), I may unfold the tissues of a dire tragedy enacted, by some strange providence, under my peculiar view alone, and thus inexplicable to others.

Of this no more, not even a hint, at present; lest, dropping the substance for the shadow, the reader should cease to find interest where I most wish to concentrate it for a season. The heroine so far of my own story, I cannot yet voluntarily relinquish the privilege of sympathy, so dear to the narrator of adventure, though I did, indeed, for a time forget my own identity in the dark shadow, the mysterious crimes, the unprecedented and speedy retributions that followed quickly on the heels of guilt at Beauseincourt.

The picturesque old place, with its quaint French

name and architecture and antique furniture, did truly at first enchant my fancy (which learned to shudder at its aspect later), as did, in the beginning, the contiguous estates of "Bellevue" with its exquisite grounds, fountains, and white-stuccoed mansion closely simulating the finest Italian marble. Later, in accordance with the law of associations, this, too, became as sorrowful in my sight as was the Hall of Vathek to those who mingled in its mournful yet magnificent pageantry.

The denizens of this lonely abode were a most interesting couple. Still young comparatively, virtually childless, and bearing the name (also a Huguenot appellation) of "*Favraud*," the husband was bright, intelligent, frivolous—the wife, an invalid of rare loveliness and sweetness of character, who seldom emerged from her solitude. Both were perfectly well bred.

These were relatives of Colonel La Vigne, whose son Walter was the residuary legatee of Bellevue, with but one imbecile life, after that of Madame Favraud, between him and enormous wealth. Great intimacy existed between the families, although from circumstances—nameless here—the ladies seldom met, and never at Bellevue.

Major Favraud was a constant visitor at Beauseincourt, when on his estates. He was, however, of a roving disposition, and, though tenderly attached to his wife, was often absent, negligent, and careless of her feelings. He was a renowned duelist, and deemed a challenge the essential element and result of every unsettled discussion. A typical Southerner of his day, I felt keen interest in the scrutiny of his character, until events developed those venomous tendencies which came very near destroying my peace of mind forever, with the life of the noble man whom, after a brief acquaintance, I had learned to love against my own desires.

The occasion of this belligerent demonstration was afforded at the Christmas festival, held yearly at Beauseincourt, by Colonel and Mrs. La Vigne—in the great, many-windowed drawing-room with its waxed parquet—its ebony-framed mirrors, its pier consoles, and faded damask furniture.

There were assembled around the bright pine-fire, on the occasion of this universal anniversary, neighbors, and guests from a distance, invited specially for a certain number of days, among whom the unexpected advent of a troop of engineers, of Northern extraction, made a desirable variety.

One of these gentlemen only, the chief-engineer, who came to make new roads for Lesdernier,[1] by order of government, had already been a visitor of some weeks, and a strong attachment, vital from the first, had sprung up between us; so far, unacknowledged by either.

During the dessert which succeeded the sumptuous Christmas-dinner, where old and young took part, and "all went merry as a marriage-bell," the health of John C. Calhoun, then heading the nullification party, was formally proposed by Colonel La Vigne, as "first of men, and greatest of statesmen."

This toast Captain Wentworth (the chief of the corps of engineers) tacitly refused to drink, and was seconded in this resolve by all of his party. There was, however, no active demonstration of unwillingness.

The representatives of government contented themselves with pressing their hands above their glasses, and so refusing to fill them with the wine that flowed freely

[1] Pronounced popularly "*Less der-neer.*"

to the welcome pledge, standing rigidly and silently while it was drunk with enthusiasm by the remaining guests—all Southern and sectional.

This defalcation to the common cause was apparently unnoticed at the time, but was made the subject of remark, and subsequently of a challenge by the Mars of the family, as Gregory denominated Major Favraud—a challenge which circumstances compelled Captain Wentworth reluctantly to accept.

No fire-eater, yet truly brave, he weighed the matter well, and decided on his course; the one most expedient, if not absolutely necessary for a stranger whose character for courage had still to be proved. In the interval of the pending duel, of which all the inmates of Beauseincourt were unconscious, save its master, who considered it as a mere matter of course, Gregory (to whom I have alluded, the evil genius of the house henceforth) arrived to reënforce the engineering corps.

Subtle, accomplished, versatile, graceful even in his singular homeliness, and peculiar insolent style of address, he yet made himself so acceptable to the family as to dare to seek the hand of the second daughter of Colonel La Vigne, and, though at first tolerated by her parents only, at last came to be well received.

At the very time that he was enlisting the innocent heart of Madge, he was making to me, the governess, whenever he could find the slightest opportunity, avowals of a desperate and audacious passion, which waxed the stronger for the absolute loathing vouchsafed in return. In this place it may be as well to reveal the end of this ill-fated and unsuitable courtship, which never had my sanction, nor even toleration. When the cloud gathered over Beauseincourt, so soon to burst in fury and destruction, when ruin was imminent, Gregory withdrew on frivolous pretexts, and turned his back on Lesdernier, and her who had so loved him, forever!

While pretending to be the devoted friend and even abject servant of Captain Wentworth, he was seeking, in every way, and on every hand, secretly to undermine him. This effort produced in my mind only mistrust and disdain; but with others it was, unfortunately, more successful.

Soon after my arrival at Lesdernier, I found, in one of the papers that I had ordered to be sent there from my native city to the address of "Miss Harz," an atrocious advertisement, describing me personally as an escaped lunatic, and offering a reward for my apprehension. Fortunately, these papers were not objects of interest to the family in which I found myself, where periodicals of all sorts were rife, as well as books, ancient and modern, and newspapers were thick as leaves in Vallambrosa.

In the silence of my chamber I read and destroyed, or concealed this evidence of enmity, malice, and all uncharitableness. I would trust no one with my identity—none save God—until the hour should come of my majority and emancipation; then, armed with Judaic vengeance, I would return to claim my sister, my fortune, and my rights.

Soon afterward I read in the same sheet, sent weekly to Lesdernier, the notice of the marriage of Claude Bainrothe and Evelyn Erle. This was the test of truth! I bore it bravely. Not a heart-beat gave tribute to the love of other days. The fire was dead, and ashes alone remained on the deserted hearth-stone. Lower down in the columns of the same paper, however, was something that smote my soul. The Parthian dart was there, and it quivered in its target! I saw that the wedding-party had sailed for Europe on the same day of the nuptials, to be absent a year, and had taken with them my dear one!

So far away! Seas rolling between us! Foreign lands, foreign laws intervening, which might, for all I knew, deprive me of her presence forever, who was my hope, my life!

"O little sister," I groaned, "was I right, after all, in forsaking you for a season? Should I not have dared every thing, rather than have so openly yielded my authority?"

. . . . . . .

In the mean while, the sanguinary preparations went silently on. In the gray of a foggy February morning the duel was fought, and Captain Wentworth fell, as it was at first thought, mortally wounded.

At the request of his excellent physician, Dr. Durand, when the watchers were exhausted, and vigilance was all-essential in his case, I accepted, rather than proposed to take, the post of watcher for one night, in company with his devoted friend and coadjutor Edward Vernon, and discovered, in my anguish, and in my power over his distracted senses, my so-far-hidden gift of magnetism.

Insomnolency was destroying him; opiates had been tried in vain to compose him, and now, under my waving fingers and strained will, he slept the sweet, refreshing magnetic slumber. He lived, some were pleased to say, and among others, his physician, through my agency—my admirable nursing—for none save Vernon ever knew the secret of my sway. We became engaged during his convalescence, simply, quietly, unostentatiously.

In due time we made our troth-plight known to the

household of Beauseincourt, all of whom, from its formal master to my best-beloved, brightest, and ever-tantalizing pupil, Bertie, accorded me their heart-felt congratulations. Gregory alone—the evil genius of the place—cast his poisonous sneers and doubts above our happiness — a structure too firmly based, too far removed from him, however, for his arrows to reach or destroy. Circumstances seemed later to favor his malicious designs, as shall be shown in the conclusion of this work; but, together, and in the full flush of our happiness, we were invincible.

A sudden summons from the seat of government compelled Captain Wentworth to leave Lesdernier a few hours after its reception — hours of which he passed, through the necessity of speedy preparation, but one with me. So far I had delayed the revelation of my true history and name, preferring to postpone this to my majority and our marriage-day; but, after his departure, I rued my resolution, and concluded to write to him a hasty summary of my life and motives of action. This letter was, as a matter of necessity, confided to the care of Luke Gregory (never a chosen depositary of mine in any way), who followed him to Savannah to receive some parting instructions for the conduct of their work, and who was to return to Lesdernier after the interval of a week.

In the ardor of my impulse, I could not slight an opportunity of so soon receiving a reply to my somewhat startling and, I felt now, too-long-delayed communication, and thus testing my lover's trust and confidence in me. When Gregory returned to Beauseincourt, he assured me he had delivered my letter punctually (I never doubted this, for he knew the man he had to deal with), adding, carelessly, that it was well Wentworth had said he would write soon, as he had been unfortunate enough to lose the hastily-pencilled reply, with his own pocket-book, at the Lenoir Landing, where both were food for fishes.

My disappointment was extreme, and many weeks of constrained silence passed before I received the promised letter from Captain Wentworth—so gloomy, so incomprehensible, so portentous, that it filled me with despair. In this letter he spoke of obstacles between us—in which blood bore part—of the wreck of all earthly happiness for him—perchance for me. Yet he conjured me to be calm and patient, as he could not be, and alluded to my silence as conclusive of his misery. He referred frequently to the letter he had intrusted to the care of Gregory as explanatory of all that might otherwise seem inexplicable—that letter at rest beneath the dark waters of the Bayou Noir—if—if, indeed! But no! not even of Gregory could I harbor on slight grounds such suspicions. "Let the devil himself have the full benefit of—doubt!" says Rabelais. I wrote to Wentworth that I would come and make all plain, as he desired, in June.

Suffering severely myself, I saw clouds gathering and rising around a happy household that for a time drew me from the depths of my own affliction in the vain effort to solace their woes.

Father and son and infant in one house, wife and imbecile daughter in another, at last fell at one dread swoop. To dishonor was added the crime of suicide, and poverty and breaking hearts were there, for the heritage of Beauseincourt was, by reason of debt and mismanagement, to pass, after the death of its master, into strange hands—the cruel hands of creditors!

Walter La Vigne was dead, and the succession of Bellevue passed over the daughters of the house, to vest in a distant kinsman. He came, toward the last of my stay, to take his own; and, unexpectedly, George Gaston, the playmate of my childhood, the lover of my first youth, stood before me in the residuary legatee of Armand La Vigne!

His advent was a revelation of my secret, through the necessity of surprise; and as, when the banquet is announced and the ball draws near its close, the maskers, so far unknown to each other, lay by their disguises, glad to be so relieved, draw breath and clasp hands once more in the freedom of social reality, so I, who had played too long a weary part, felt a new life infused into my veins when my mask was suddenly laid aside, and the necessity of disguise was over.

The time was so near at hand now, I felt, when I could claim my own from Bainrothe, and cast off all shackles of guardianship and minority, that I no longer feared the consequences of this revelation. In September we should meet on new ground. I, no more a minor, would be beyond the reach of his subtle mastery; and, until then—the time assigned for the expiration of his year of trust—he would remain in Europe, with the wide sea between us, and little probability of information through the medium of public rumor.

I would be secret, cautious, abide in the shadow, until the hour arrived to emerge therefrom, and, with the aid of God and Wardour Wentworth, defeat his schemes and vindicate the truth!

Alas for human foresight! Alas for Fate!

*SEA AND SHORE.*

"No fears hath she! Her giant form
Majestically calm would go
O'er wrathful surge, through blackening storm,
'Mid the deep darkness, white as snow!
So stately her bearing, so proud her array,
The main she will traverse forever and aye!
Many ports shall exult in the gleam of her mast—
Hush! hush! thou vain dreamer, this hour is her last!"

WILSON, "*Isle of Palms.*"

---

"Then hold her
Strictly confined in sombre banishment,
And doubt not but she will ere long, full gladly,
Her freedom purchase at the price you name."

---

"No, subtle snake!
It is the baseness of thy selfish mind,
Full of all guile, and cunning, and deceit,
That severs us so far, and shall do *ever.*"

---

"Despair shall give me strength—where is the door?
Mine eyes are dark! I cannot find it now.
O God! protect me in this awful pass!"

JOANNA BAILLIE, *Tragedy of* "*Orra.*"

## PART III.

### *SEA AND SHORE.*

---

### CHAPTER I.

It was a calm and hazy morning of Southern summer that on which I turned my face seaward from the "keep" of Beauseincourt, never, I knew, to see its time-stained walls again, save through the mirage of memory. There is an awe almost as solemn to me in a consciousness like this as that which attends the death-bed parting, and my straining eye takes in its last look of a familiar scene as it might do the ever-to-be-averted face of friendship.

The refrain of Poe's even then celebrated poem was ringing through my brain on that sultry August day, I remember, like a tolling bell, as I looked my last on the gloomy abode of the La Vignes; but I only said aloud, in answer to the sympathizing glances of one who sat before me—the gentle and quiet Marion—who had suddenly determined to accompany me to Savannah, nerved with unwonted impulse:

"Madame de Staël was right when she said that 'nevermore' was the saddest and most expressive word in the English tongue" (so harsh to her ears, usually). "I think she called it the sweetest, too, in sound; but to me it is simply the most sorrowful, a knell of doom, and it fills my soul to-day to overflowing, for 'never, never more' shall I look on Beauseincourt!"

"You cannot tell, Miss Harz, what *time* may do; you may still return to visit us in our retirement, you and Captain Wentworth," urged Marion, gently, leaning forward, as she spoke, to take my hand in hers.

"'Time the tomb-builder'" fell from my lips ere they were aware. "That is a grand thought—one that I saw lately in a Western poem, the New-Year's address of a young editor of Kentucky called Prentice. Is it not splendid, Marion?"

"Very awful, rather," she responded, with a faint shudder. "Time the 'comforter,' let us say, instead, Miss Miriam—Time the 'veil-spreader.'"

"Why, Marion, you are quite poetic to-day, quite Greek! That is a sweet and tender saying of yours, and I shall garner it. I stand reproved, my child. All honor to Time, the *merciful*, whether he builds palaces or tombs! but none the less do I reverence my young poet for that stupendous utterance of his soul. I shall watch the flight of that eaglet of the West with interest from this hour! May he aspire!"

"Not if he is a Jackson Democrat?" broke in the usually gentle Alice Durand, fired with a ready defiance of all heterodox policy, common, if not peculiar, to that region.

"Oh, but he is not; he is a good Whig instead—a Clay man, as we call such."

"Not a Calhoun man, though, I suppose, so I would not give a snap of my fingers for him or his poetry! It is very natural, for you, Miss Harz," in a somewhat deprecating tone, "to praise your partisans. I would not have you neutral if I could, it is so contemptible."

A little of the good doctor's spirit there, under all that exterior of meekness and modesty, I saw at a glance, and liked her none the less for it, if truth were told. And now we were nearing the gate, with its gray-stone pillars, on one of which, that from which the marble ball had rolled, to hide in the grass beneath, perchance, until the end of all, I had seen the joyous figure of Walter La Vigne so lightly poised on the occasion of my last exodus from Beauseincourt. A moment's pause, and the difficult, disused bolts that had once exasperated the patience of Colonel La Vigne were drawn asunder, and the clanking gates clashed behind us as we emerged from the shadowed domain into the glare and dust of the high-road.

Here Major Favraud, accompanied by Duganne, awaited us, seated in state in his lofty, stylish swung gig (with his tiny tiger behind), drawn tandem-wise by his high-stepping and peerless blooded bays, Castor and Pollux. Brothers, like the twins of Leda, they had been bred in the blue-grass region of Kentucky and the vicinity of Ashland, and were worthy of their ancient pedigree, their perfect training and classic names, the last bestowed when he first became their owner, by Major Favraud, who, with a touch of the whip or a turn of the hand, controlled them to subjection, fiery coursers although they were!

Dr. Durand, too, with his spacious and flame-lined gig, accompanied by his son, a lad of sixteen, awaited our arrival, and served to swell the cavalcade that wound slowly down the dusty road, with its sandy surface and red-clay substratum. A few young gentlemen on horseback completed our *cortége*.

Major Favraud sat holding his ribbons gracefully in

one gauntleted hand, while he uncovered his head with the other, bowing suavely in his knightly fashion, as he said:

"Come drive with me, Miss Harz, for a while, and let the young folks take it together."

"Oh, no, Major Favraud; you must excuse me, indeed! I feel a little languid this morning, and I should be poor company. Besides, I cannot surrender my position as one of the young folks yet."

"Nay, I have something to say to you—something very earnest. You shall be at no trouble to entertain me; but you must not refuse a poor, sad fellow a word of counsel and cheer. I shall think hard of you if you decline to let me drive you a little way. Besides, the freshness of the morning is all lost on you there. Now, set Marion a good example, and she will, in turn, enliven me later."

So adjured, I consented to drive to the Fifteen-mile House with Major Favraud, and Duganne glided into the coach in my stead, to take my place and play *vis-à-vis* to Sylphy, who, as usual, was selected as traveling-companion on this occasion, "to take kear of de young ladies."

"I am so glad I have you all to myself once more, Miss Harz! I feel now that we are fast friends again. And I wanted to tell you, while I could speak of her, how much my poor wife liked you. (The time will come when I must not, *dare* not, you know.) But for circumstances, she would have urged you to become our guest, or even in-dweller; but you know how it all was! I need not feign any longer, nor apologize either."

"It must have been that she saw how lovely and *spirituelle* I found *her*," I said, "and could not bear to be outdone in consideration, nor to owe a debt of social gratitude. She knew so little of me. But these affinities are electric sometimes, I must believe."

"Yes, there is more of that sort of thing on earth, perhaps, 'than is dreamed of in our philosophy'—antagonism and attraction are always going on among us unconsciously."

"I am inclined to believe so from my own experience," I replied, vaguely, thinking, Heaven knows, of any thing at the moment rather than of him who sat beside me.

"Your mind is on Wentworth, I perceive," he said, softly; after a short pause, "now give up your dream for a little while and listen to this sober reality—sober to-day, at least," he added, with a light laugh. "By-the-way, talking of magnetism, do you know, Miss Harz, I think you are the most universally magnetic woman I ever saw? All the men fall in love with you, and the women don't hate you for it, either."

"How perfectly the last assertion disproves the first!" I replied; "but I retract, I will not, even for the sake of a syllogism, abuse my own sex; women are never envious except when men make them so, by casting down among them the golden apple of admiration."

"I know one man, at least, who never foments discord in this way! Wentworth, from the beginning, had eyes and ears for no one but yourself, yet I never dreamed the drama would be enacted so speedily; I own I was as much in the dark as anybody."

I could not reply to this *badinage*, as in happier moments I might have done, but said, digressively:

"By-the-by, while I think of it, I must put down on my tablet the order of Mr. Vernon. He wants 'Longfellow's Poems,' if for sale in Savannah. He has been permeating his brain with the 'Psalms of Life,' that have come out singly in the *Knickerbocker Magazine*, until he craves every thing that pure and noble mind has thrown forth in the shape of a song."

And I scribbled in my memorandum-book, for a moment, while Major Favraud mused.

"Longfellow!" he said, at last, "Phœbus, what a name!" adding affectedly, "yet it seems to me, on reflection, I *have* heard it before. He is a Yankee, of course! Now, do you earnestly believe a native of New England, by descent a legitimate witch-burner, you know, *can* be any thing better than a poll-parrot in the poetical line?"

"Have we not proof to the contrary, Major Favraud?"

"What proof? Metre and rhyme, I grant you—long and short—but show me the afflatus! They make verse with a penknife, like their wooden nutmegs. They are perfect Chinese for ingenuity and imitation, and the resemblance to the real Simon-pure is very perfect—externally. But when it comes to grating the nut for negus, we miss the aroma!"

"Do you pretend that Bryant is not a poet in the grain, and that the wondrous boy, Willis, was not also 'to the manner born?' Read 'Thanatopsis,' or are you acquainted with it already? I hardly think you can be. Read those scriptural poems."

"A very smooth school-exercise the first, no more. There is not a heart-beat in the whole grind. As to Willis—he failed egregiously, when he attempted to 'gild refined gold and paint the lily,' as he did in his so-called 'Sacred Poems.' He can spin a yarn pretty well, and coin a new word for a make-shift, amusingly, but save me from the foil-glitter of his poetry."[1]

[1] It need not for one moment be supposed that the opinions of the author are represented through the extremist Favraud. To her Mr. Bryant stands forth as the high-priest of American poetry.

"This is surprising! You upset all precedent. I really wish you had not said these things. I now begin to see the truth of what my copy-book told me long ago, that 'evil association corrupts good manners,' or I will vary it and substitute 'opinions.' I must eschew your society, in a literary way, I must indeed, Major Favraud."

"Now comes along this strolling Longfellow minstrel," he continued, ignoring or not hearing my remark, "with *his* dreary hurdy-gurdy to cap the climax. Heavens! what a nasal twang the whole thing has to me. Not an original or cheerful note! 'Old Hundred' is joyful in comparison!"

"You shall not say that," I interrupted; "you shall not dare to say that in my presence. It is sheer slander, that you have caught up from some malignant British review, and, like all other serpents, you are venomous in proportion to your blindness! I am vexed with you, that you will not see with the clear, discerning eyes God gave you originally."

"But I do see with them, and very discerningly, notwithstanding your comparison. Now there is that 'Skeleton in Armor,' his last effusion, I believe, that you are all making such a work over—fine-sounding thing enough, I grant you, ingenious rhyme, and all that. But I know where the framework came from! Old Drayton furnished that in his 'Battle of Agincourt.'" Then in a clear, sonorous voice, he gave some specimens of each, so as to point the resemblance, real or imaginary.

"You are content with mere externs in finding your similitudes, Major Favraud! In power of thought, beauty of expression, what comparison is there? Drayton's verse is poor and vapid, even mean, beside Longfellow's."

"I grant you that. I have never for one moment disputed the ability of those Yankees. Their manufacturing talents are above all praise, but when it comes to the 'God-fire,' as an old German teacher of mine used to say, our simple Southern poets leave them all behind—'Beat them all hollow,' would be their own expression. You see, Miss Harz, that Cavalier blood of ours, that inspired the old English bards, *will* tell, in spite of circumstances."

"But genius is of no rank—no blood—no clime! What court poet of his day, Major Favraud, compared with Robert Burns for feeling, fire, and pathos? Who ever sung such siren strains as Moore, a simple Irishman of low degree? No Cavalier blood there, I fancy! What power, what beauty in the poems of Walter Scott! Byron was a poet in spite of his condition, not because of it. Hear Barry Cornwall—how he stirs the blood! What trumpet like to Campbell! What mortal voice like to Shelley's? the hybrid angel! What full orchestra surpassed Coleridge for harmony and brilliancy of effect? Who paints panoramas like Southey? Who charms like Wordsworth? Yet these were men of medium condition, all—I hate the conceits of Cowley, Waller, Sir John Suckling, Carew, and the like. All of your Cavalier type, I believe, a set of hollow pretenders mostly."

"All this is overwhelming, I grant," bowing deferentially. "But I return to my first idea, that Puritan blood was not exactly fit to engender genius; and that in the rich, careless Southern nature there lurks a vein of undeveloped song that shall yet exonerate America from the charge of poverty of genius, brought by the haughty Briton! Yes, we will sing yet a mightier strain than has ever been poured since the time of Shakespeare! and in that good time coming weave a grander heroic poem than any since the days of Homer! Then men's souls shall have been tried in the furnace of affliction, and Greek meets not Greek, but Yankee. For we Southerners *only bide our time!*"

And he cut his spirited lead-horse, until it leaped forward suddenly, as though to vent his excitement, and, setting his small white teeth sternly, with an eye like a burning coal, looked forward into space, his whole face contracting.

"The Southern lyre has been but lightly swept so far, Miss Harz," he continued, a moment later, "and only by the fingers of love; we need Bellona to give tone to our orchestra."

I could not forbear reciting somewhat derisively the old couplet—

"'Sound the trumpet, beat the drum,
Tremble France, we come, we come!'

"Is that the style Major Favraud?" I asked. "I remember the time when I thought these two lines the most soul-stirring in the language—they seem very bombastic now, in my maturity."

He smiled, and said: "The time is not come for our war-poem, and, as for love, let me give you one strain of Pinckney's to begin with;" and, without waiting for permission, he recited the beautiful "Pledge," with which all readers are now familiar, little known then, however, beyond the limits of the South, and entirely new to me, beginning with—

"I fill this cup to one made up
Of loveliness alone,
A woman of her gentle sex
The seeming paragon"—

continuing to the end with eloquence and spirit.

"Now, that is poetry, Miss Harz! the real afflatus is there; the bead on the wine; the dew on the rose; the bloom on the grape! Nothing wanting that constitutes the indefinable divine thing called genius! You understand my idea, of course; explanations are superfluous."

I assented mutely, scarce knowing why I did so.

"Now, hear another." And the woods rang with his clear, sonorous accents as he declaimed, a little too scanningly, perhaps—too much like an enthusiastic boy:

"Love lurks upon my lady's lip,
His bow is figured there;
Within her eyes his arrows sleep;
His fetters are—her hair!"

"I call that nothing but a bundle of conceits, Major Favraud, mostly of the days of Charles II., of Rochester himself—" interrupting him as I in turn was interrupted.

"But hear further," and he proceeded to the end of that marvelous ebullition of foam and fervor, such as celebrated the birth of Aphrodite herself perchance in the old Greek time; and which, despite my perverse intentions, stirred me as if I had quaffed a draught of pink champagne. Is it not, indeed, all *couleur de rose?* Hear this bit of melody, my reader, sitting in supreme judgment, and perhaps contempt, on your throne apart:

"'Upon her cheek the crimson ray
By changes comes and goes,
As rosy-hued Aurora's play
Along the polar snows;
Gay as the insect-bird that sips
From scented flowers the dew—
Pure as the snowy swan that dips
Its wings in waters blue;
Sweet thoughts are mirrored on her face,
Like clouds on the calm sea,
And every motion is a grace,
Each word a melody!'"

"Yes, that is true poetry, I acknowledge, Major Favraud," I exclaimed, not at all humbled by conviction, though a little annoyed at the pointed manner in which he gave (looking in my face as he did so) these concluding lines:

"Say from what fair and sunny shore,
Fair wanderer, dost thou rove,
Lest what I only should adore
I heedless think to love?"

"The character of Pinckney's genius," I rejoined, "is, I think, essentially like that of Praed, the last literary phase with me—for I am geological in my poetry, and take it in strata. But I am more generous to your Southern bard than you are to our glorious Longfellow! I don't call that imitation, but coincidence, the oneness of genius! I do not even insinuate plagiarism." My manner, cool and careless, steadied his own.

"You are right: our 'Shortfellow' *was* incapable of any thing of the sort. Peace be to his ashes! With all his nerve and *vim*, he died of melancholy, I believe. As good an end as any, however, and certainly highly respectable. But you know what Wordsworth says in his 'School-master'—

"'If there is one that may bemoan
His kindred laid in earth,
The household hearts that were his own,
It is the man of mirth.'"

He sighed as he concluded his quotation—sighed, and slackened the pace of his flying steeds. "But give me something of Praed's in return," he said, rallying suddenly; "is there not a pretty little thing called 'How shall I woo her?'" glancing archly and somewhat impertinently at me, I thought—or, perhaps, what would simply have amused me in another man and mood shocked me in him, the recent widower—widowed, too, under such peculiar and awful circumstances! I did not reflect sufficiently, perhaps, on his ignorance of many of these last.

How I deplored his levity, which nothing could overcome or restrain; and yet beneath which I even then believed lay depths of anguish! How I wished that influence of mine could prevail to induce him to divide his dual nature, "To throw away the worser part of it, and live the purer with the better half!" But I could only show disapprobation by the gravity of my silence.

"So you will not give me 'How shall I woo her?' Miss Harz?" a little embarrassed, I perceived, by my manner. "I have a fancy for the title, nevertheless, not having heard any more, and should be glad to hear the whole poem. But you are prudish to-day, I fancy."

"No, there is nothing in that poem, certainly, that angels might not hear approvingly; but it would sadden you, Major Favraud."

"I will take the chance of that," laughing. "Come, the poem, if you care to please your driver, and reward his care. See how skillfully I avoided that fallen branch—suppose I were to be spiteful, and upset you against this stump?"

Any thing was preferable to his levity; and, as I had warned him of the possible effect of the poem he solicited, I could not be accused of want of consideration in reciting it. Besides, he deserved the lesson, the stern lesson that it taught.

As this could in no way be understood by such of my readers as are unacquainted with this little gem, I venture to give it here—exquisite, passionate utterance that it is, though little known to fame, at least at this writing:

"'How shall I woo her? I will stand
Beside her when she sings,
And watch her fine and fairy hand
Flit o'er the quivering strings!
But shall I tell her I have heard,
Though sweet her song may be,
A voice where every whispered word
*Was more than song to me?*

"'How shall I woo her? I will gaze,
In sad and silent trance,
On those blue eyes whose liquid rays
Look love in every glance.
But shall I tell her eyes more bright,
Though bright her own may beam,
Will fling a deeper spell to-night
*Upon me in my dream?*'"

I hesitated. "Let me stop here, Major Favraud, I counsel you," I interpolated, earnestly; but he only rejoined:

"No, no! proceed, I entreat you! it is very beautiful—very touching, too!" Speaking calmly, and slacking rein, so that the grating of the wheels among the stems of the scarlet *lychnis*, that grew in immense patches on our road, might not disturb his sense of hearing, which, by-the-way, was exquisitely nice and fastidious.

"As you please, then;" and I continued the recitation.

"'How shall I woo her? I will try
The charms of olden time,
And swear by earth, and sea, and sky,
And rave in prose and rhyme—
And I will tell her, when I bent
My knee in other years,
I was not half so *eloquent;*
I could not speak—*for tears!*'"

I watched him narrowly; the spell was working now; the poet's hand was sweeping, with a gust of power, that harp of a thousand strings, the wondrous human heart! And I again pursued, in suppressed tones of heart-felt emotion, the pathetic strain that he had evoked with an idea of its frivolity alone:

"'How shall I woo her? I will bow
  Before the holy shrine,
And pray the prayer, and vow the vow,
  And press her lips to mine—
And I will tell her, when she starts
  From passion's thrilling kiss,
That *memory* to many hearts
  Is dearer far than bliss!'"

It was reserved for the concluding verse to unnerve him completely; a verse which I rendered with all the pathos of which I was capable, with a view to its final effect, I confess:

"'Away! away! the chords are mute,
  The bond is rent in twain;
You *cannot* wake the silent lute,
  Or clasp its links again.
Love's toil, I know, is little cost;
  Love's perjury is light sin;
But souls that lose what I have lost,
  What have they left to win?'"

"What, indeed?" he exclaimed, impetuously—tears now streaming over his olive cheeks. He flung the reins to me with a quick, convulsive motion, and covered his face with his hands. Groans burst from his murmuring lips, and the great deeps of sorrow gave up their secrets. I was sorry to have so stirred him to the depths by any act or words of mine, and yet I enjoyed the certainty of his anguish.

I checked the horses beneath a magnolia-tree, and sat quietly waiting for the flood of emotion to subside as for him to take the initiative. I had no word to say, no consolation to offer. Nay, after consideration, rather did I glory in his grief, which redeemed his nature in my estimation, though grieved in turn to have afflicted him. For, in spite of all his faults, and my earlier prejudices, I loved this impulsive Southron man, as Scott has it, "right brotherly."

At last, looking up grave, tearless, and pale, and resuming his reins without apology for having surrendered them, he said, abruptly:

"All is so vain! Such mockery now to me! She was the sole reality of this universe to my heart! I grapple with shadows unceasingly. There is not on the face of this globe a more desolate wretch. You understand this! You feel for me, you do not deride me! You know how perfect, how spiritual she was! You loved her well—I saw it in your eyes, your manner—and for that, if nothing else, you have my heart-felt gratitude. So few appreciated her unearthly purity. Yet, was it not strange she should have loved a man so gross, so steeped in sensuous, thoughtless enjoyment—so remote from God as I am—have ever been? But the song speaks for me"—waving his gauntleted hand—"better than I can speak:

> "'Away! away! the chords are mute,
> The bond is rent in twain.'"

"I shall never marry again—never! Miss Miriam, I know now, and shall know evermore, in all its fullness, and weariness, and bitterness, the meaning of that terrible word—alone! Eternal solitude. The Robinson Crusoe of society. A sort of social Daniel Boone. 'Thus you must ever consider me. And yet, just think of it, Miss Harz!"

"Oh, but you will not always feel so; there may come a time of reaction." I hesitated. It was not my purpose to encourage change.

"No, never! never!" he interrupted, passionately; "don't even suggest it—don't! and check me sternly if ever I forget my grief again in frivolity of any sort in your presence. You are a noble, sweet woman, with breadth enough of character to make allowances for the shortcomings of a poor, miserable man like me—trying to cheat himself back into gayety and the interests of life. I have sisters, but they are not like you. I wish to Heaven they were! There is not a woman in the world on whom I have any claims—on whose shoulder I can lean my head and take a hearty cry. And what are men at such a season? Mocking fiends, usually, the best of them! I shall go abroad, Miss Harz. I am no anchorite. You will hear of me as a gay man of the world, perhaps; but, as to being happy, that can never be again! The bubble of life has burst, and my existence falls flat to the earth. Victor Favraud, that airy nothing, is scarcely a 'local habitation and a name' now!"

"Let him make a name, then," I urged. "With military talents like yours, Major Favraud, the road to distinction will soon be open to you. Our approaching difficulties with France—"

"Oh, that will all be patched up, or has been, by this time. Van Buren is a crafty but peace-loving fox! Something of an epicurean, too, in his high estate. What grim old Jackson left half healed, he will complete the cure of. Ah, Miss Harz, I had hoped to flesh my sword in a nobler cause!"

I knew what he meant. That dream of nullification was still uppermost in his soul—dispersed, as it was, in the eyes of all reasonable men. I shook my head. "Thank God! all that is over," I said, gravely, fervently; "and my prayer to Him is that he may vouchsafe to preserve us for evermore an unbroken people!"

"May He help Israel when the time comes," he murmured low, "for come it will, Miss Harz, as surely as there is a sun in the heavens! 'and may I be there to see!' as John Gilpin said, or some one of him—which was it?"

And, whipping up his lagging steeds as we gained the open road, we emerged swiftly from the shadows of the forest—between nodding cornfields, already helmed and plumed for the harvest, and plantations green with thrifty cotton-plants, with their half-formed bolls, promising such bounteous yield, and meadows covered with the tufted Bermuda grass, with its golden-green verdure, we sped our way toward Lenoir's Landing.

This peninsula was formed by the junction of two rivers, between which intervened a narrow point of land, with a background of steep hills, covered with a growth of black-jack and yellow-pine to the summit. Here was a ferry with its Charon-like boat, of the primitive sort—a flat barge, poled over by negroes, and capable of containing at one time many bales of cotton, a stage-coach or wagon with four horses, besides passengers *ad libitum.*

This ferry constituted the chief source of revenue of Madame Grambeau, an old French lady, remarkable in many ways. She kept the stage-house hard by, with its neat picketed inclosure, its overhanging live-oak trees and small trim parterre, gay at this season with various annual flowers, scarce worth the cultivation, one would think, in that land of gorgeous perennial bloom. But Queen Margarets, ragged robins, variegated balsams, and tawny marigolds, have their associations, doubtless, to make them dear and valuable to the foreign heart, to which they seem essential, wherever a plot of ground be in possession.

Mignonette, I have observed, is a special passion with the French exile, recalling, doubtless, the narrow boxes, fitted to the stone window-sill of certain former lofty lodgings across the sea, perhaps, situated in the heart of some great city, and overlooking roofs and court-yards—the street being quite out of the question in such a view, distant, as it seems, from them, as the sky itself, though in an opposite direction.

I have used the word "exile" advisedly with regard to Madame Grambeau, and not figuratively at all. She was, I had been told, a *bourgeoise*, of good class, who had taken part in the early revolution, but who, when the *canaille* triumphed and drenched the land in blood, in the second phase of that fearful outburst of volcanic feeling, had fled before the whirlwind with her child and husband to embark for America. At the point of embarcation—like Evangeline—the husband and wife had been separated accidentally, and on her arrival in a strange land she found herself alone and penniless with her son, scarce six years old. Her husband had been carried to a Southern port, she learned by the merest chance, and, disguising herself in man's attire, and leading her little son by the hand, she set forth in quest of him, carrying with her a violin, which, together with the clothes she wore, had been found in the trunk of Monsieur Grambeau, brought on the vessel in which she came, but which depository she had been obliged to abandon, when setting forth on her pilgrimage.

She was no unskillful performer on this instrument, and solely by such aid she gained her food and lodging to the interior of Georgia. Reaching her destination after a long and painful journey and delays of many kinds, she found her husband living in a log-hut, on the border of Talupa River, a hut which he had built himself, and earning his bread by ferrying travellers across that stream.

Yet here, with the characteristic contentment of her people under all circumstances, she settled down quietly to aid him and make his home happy; bore him many children (most of whom were dead at the time I saw her, as those living were separated from her at that period), reared and educated them herself, toiled for and with them, late and early, strained every nerve in the arduous cause of duty, and found herself, in extreme old age, widowed and alone, having amassed but little of the world's lucre, yet cheerful and energetic even if dependent still on her own exertions.

All this and much more I had heard before I saw Madame Grambeau or her abode—a picturesque affair in itself, however humble—consisting originally of a log-house, to which more recently white frame wings had been attached, projecting a few feet in front of the primitive building, and connected thereto by a shed-roofed gallery, which embraced the whole front of the log-cottage, along which ran puncheon-steps the entire length of the grand original tree-trunk, as of the porch itself. It was a triumph of rural art.

Over this portico, so low in front as barely to admit the passage of a tall man beneath its eaves, without stooping, a wild multiflora rose, then in full flower, was artistically trained so as to present a series of arches to the eye as the wayfarer approached the dwelling; no tapestry was ever half so lovely.

The path which led from the little white gate, with its swinging chain and ball, was covered with river-pebbles and shells, and bordered by box, trimly clipped and kept low, and the two broad steps, that led to the porch, bore evidence of recent scouring, though rough and unpainted.

Framed in one of those pointed natural cathedral-windows of vivid green, gemmed with red roses, of which the division-posts of the porch formed the white outlines, stood the most remarkable-looking aged woman I have ever seen. At a first glance, indeed, the question of sex would have arisen, and been found difficult to decide. Her attire seemed that of a friar, even to the small scalloped cape that scantily covered her shoulders, and the coarse black serge, of which her strait gown was composed, leaving exposed her neatly though coarsely clad feet, with their snow-white home-knit stockings, and low-quartered, well-polished calf-skin shoes, confined with steel buckles, and elevated on heels, then worn by men alone.

She wore a white habit shirt, the collar, bosom, and wristbands of which were visible; but no cap covered her silver hair, which was cropped in the neck, and divided at one side in true manly fashion. It was brushed well back from her expansive, fair, and unwrinkled forehead, beneath which large blue eyes looked out with that strange solemnity we see alone in the orbs of young, thoughtful children, or the very old.

Scott's description of the "Monk of Melrose Abbey" occurred to me, as I gazed on this calm and striking figure:

"And strangely on the knight looked he,
And his blue eyes gleamed wild and wide."

She stood watching our approach, leaning with both hands on her ebony, silver-headed cane, above which she stooped slightly, her aged and somewhat severe, but serene face fully turned toward us, in the clear light of morning, with a grave majesty of aspect.

Above her head in its wicker cage swung the gray and crimson parrot, of which Sylphy had spoken, and to which, it may be remembered, she had so irreverently likened her master on one occasion; bursting forth, as it saw us coming, into a shrill, stereotyped phrase of welcome—"*Bien venu, compatriote*," that was irresistibly ludicrous and irrelevant.

"Tremble, France! we come—we come," said Major Favraud; "there's your quotation well applied this time, Miss Harz! It is impressive, after all."

"Hush! she will hear you," I remonstrated, quite awed in that still, majestic presence, for now we stood before our aged hostess, who, with a cold but stately politeness after Major Favraud's salutation and introduction, waved us in and across her threshold. As for Major Favraud, he had turned to leave us on the door-sill, to see to the comfort and safety of his horses; not liking, perhaps, the appearance of the superannuated ostler, who lounged near the stable of the inn, if such might be called this rustic retreat without sign, lodging, or bar-rooms.

"Are we in the mansion of a decayed queen, or the log-hut of a wayside innkeeper?" I questioned low of Marion.

"Both in one, it seems to me," was the reply. "But Madame Grambeau is no curiosity, no novelty to me, I have stopped here so frequently. I ought to have told you, before we came, not to be surprised."

Pausing at the door of a large, square room, from

which voices proceeded, she invited us with a singularly graceful though formal courtesy to enter, smiling and pointing forward silently as she did so, and then, like Major Favraud, she turned and abandoned us at the door-sill, on which we stood riveted for a moment by the sound of a vibrant and eager voice speaking some never-to-be-forgotten words.

"For the slave is the coral-insect of the South," said the voice within; "insignificant in himself, he rears a giant structure—which will yet cause the wreck of the ship of state, should its keel grate too closely on that adamantine wall. '*L'état c'est moi,*' said Louis XIV., and that 'slavery is the South' is as true an utterance. Our staple—our patriarchal institution—our prosperity—are one and indissoluble, and the sooner the issue comes the better for the nation!"

Standing with his hand on the back of a chair near the casement-window of the large, low apartment, in close conversation with two other gentlemen, was the speaker of these remarkable words, which embraced the whole genius and policy of the South as it then existed, and which were delivered in those clear and perfectly modulated tones that bespeak the practised orator and the man of dominant energies.

I felt instinctively that I stood in the presence of one of the anointed princes of the earth—felt it, and was thrilled.

"Do you know that gentleman, Marion?" I whispered, as we seated ourselves on the old-fashioned settle, or rather sofa, in one corner of the room, gazing admiringly, as I spoke, on the tall, slight figure, with its air of power and poise, that stood at some distance, with averted face.

"No, I have no idea who it is, or who are his companions either," she replied; "unless"—hesitating with scrutiny in her eyes—

"His companions, I do not care to question of them! —but that man himself—the speaker—has a sovereign presence! Can it be possible—"

The entrance of Major Favraud interrupted further conjecture, for at the sound of those emphatic boots the stranger turned, and for one moment the splendor of his large dark eyes, in their iron framing, met my own, then passed recognizingly on to rest on the face of Major Favraud, and advancing with extended hands, made more cordial by his voice and smile, he greeted him familiarly as "Victor."

Major Favraud stood for a moment spell-bound—then suddenly rushing forward, flung his hat to the floor, caught the hand of the stranger between his own and pressed it to his heart. (To his lips, I think, he would fain have lifted it, falling on one knee, perchance, at the same time in a knightly fashion of hero-worship that modern reticence forbids.) But he contented himself with exclaiming:

"Mr. Calhoun! best of friends, welcome back to Georgia!" And tears started to his eyes and choked his utterance. Thus was my conjecture confirmed. I never felt so thrilled, so elated, by any presence.

There was a momentary pause after this fervent greeting, emotional on one part only.

"But why did you not meet me at Milledgeville?" asked Mr. Calhoun. "Most of my friends in this vicinity sustained me there. I have been discussing the great question[1] again, Favraud, and I should have been glad of your countenance."

[1] The tariff.

"I have been detained at home of late by a cruel necessity," was the faltering reply, "or I should never have played recreant to my old master."

"Good fortune spoiled me a fine lawyer in your case, Victor! But introduce me to your wife. Remember, I have never had the pleasure of meeting Madame Favraud," advancing, as he spoke, toward me, with his hand on Major Favraud's shoulder (above whom he towered by a head), courteously and impulsively.

"Miss Harz, Miss La Vigne, Miss Durand—Mr. Calhoun," said Major Favraud, pale as death now, and trembling as he spoke. "These ladies are friends of mine—one, a distant relative"—he hesitated—"within the last six weeks I have had the misfortune to lose my wife, Mr. Calhoun. You understand matters better now."

All conversation was cut short by this sudden announcement. Deeply shocked, Mr. Calhoun led Major Favraud aside, with a brief apology to me for his misapprehension, and they stood together, talking low, at the extreme end of the apartment, affording me thus an admirable opportunity for observing the *personnel* of the great Southern leader, during the brief space of time accorded by the change of stage-horses. For, with his friends, he was then *en route* for another appointment. He was canvassing the State, with a view to a final rally of its resources, preparatory to his last great effort—to scotch the serpent of the North, which finally, however, wound its insidious folds around the heart of brotherly affection, stifling it, as the snakes of fable were sent to do the baby Hercules.

No picture of Mr. Calhoun has ever done him justice,

[1] Since writing the above, the admirable picture of Mr. Healey has filled this void; and those who have seen good copies of this work, executed for

although his was a physiognomy that an artist could scarcely fail to make an extern likeness of, from its remarkable characteristics. It was truly an iron-bound face, condensed, powerful in every nerve, muscle, and lineament, and fraught, beyond almost all others, with intellect and resolution. But the glory and power of that glance and smile no painter could convey—those attributes of man which more fully than aught else betray the immortal soul!

Just as I beheld him that day, bending above Major Favraud in his tender, half-paternal dignity and solicitude combined, soothing and condoling with him (I could not doubt, from the expression of his speaking countenance), I see him still in mental vision; nor can I wonder more at the depth and strength of enthusiasm he awakened in the hearts of his friends.

It belongs not to every great man to excite this devotion, yet, where it blends with greatness, it is irresistible. Mohammed, Cyrus, Alexander, Darius, Pericles, Napoleon, were thus magnetically gifted. I recall few instances of others so distinguished in station who possessed this power, which has its root, perhaps, after all, in the great master-passion of mortality, the yearning for exalted sympathy, so seldom accorded.

This observation of mine was but a glimpse at best, for the winding of the stage-horn was the signal for Mr. Calhoun's departure, and I never saw him more. But that glimpse alone opened to my eyes a mighty volume!

and by the order of Louis Philippe, may have a clear idea of that glorious countenance, the like of which we shall not see again.

Perhaps it was from this very personal magnetism of which I have spoken that Healey succeeded better with the portrait of Mr. Calhoun than any of the others he was sent to this country to paint.

A few days before I should have rejected as wearisome the details to which I listened with eagerness now, and which I even sought to elicit as to Mr. Calhoun—his mode of life, his mountain-home, and his passion for those heights he inhabited, and which, no doubt, contributed to train his character to energy and strengthen his *physique* to endure its brain-burden. I heard with pleasure the account of one who had passed much of his youth beneath his roof, and who, however enthusiastic, was, in the very framing of his nature, strictly truthful with regard to the mutual devotion of the master and slaves, the invariable courtesy and sweetness of his deportment to his own family, his justice and regard for the feelings of his lowest dependant, his simplicity, his cheerfulness.

"A grave and even gloomy man in public life, he is all life and interest in the social circle," said Major Favraud. "His range of thought is the grandest and most unlimited, his powers of conversation are the rarest I have ever met with. Yet he never refused, on any occasion, to answer with minuteness the inquiries of the smallest child or most insignificant dependant. 'Had he not been Alexander, he must have been Parmenio.' Had fortune not struck out for him the path of a statesman, he would have made the most impressive and perfect of teachers. As it was, without the slightest approach to pedagogism, he involuntarily instructed all who came near him, without effort or weariness on either side."

"Does he love music—poetry?" I asked.

"Oh, yes; Scottish songs and classic verse, especially, are his delights. He has no affectation. His tastes are all his own—his opinions all genuine. He is, indeed, a man of very varied attainment, as well as great grasp of intellect. Yet, as you see, he likes his opposites sometimes, Miss Harz," and he laid his hand proudly on his own manly breast.

Talking thus in that large, low, scantily-furnished parlor, with its split-bottomed chairs, in primitive frames (and in somewhat strange contrast to its well-polished mahogany tables, dark with time, and walls adorned with good engravings), with its floor freshly scoured and sanded, while a simple deal stand in the centre bore a vase filled with the rarest and most exquisite wild-flowers I had ever seen (from the gorgeous amaryllis and hibiscus of these regions, down to wax-like blossoms of fragile delicacy and beauty, whose very names I knew not), and its many small diamond-paned casement-windows, all neatly curtained with coarse white muslin bordered with blue, time passed unconsciously until the noonday meal was announced.

We followed the Mercury of the establishment, a grave-looking little yellow boy, who seemed to have grown prematurely old, from his constant companionship, probably, with his preceptor and mistress, into a long, low apartment in the rear of the dwelling, where a table was spread for our party, with a damask cloth and napkins, decorated china and cut-glass, that proved Madame Grambeau's personal superintendence; and which elicited from Major Favraud, as he entered, a long, low whistle of approval and surprise, and the exclamation "Heh! madame! you are overwhelming us to-day with your magnificence."

I was amused with the response. "Sit down, Victor Favraud, and eat your dinner Christian-like, without remarks! You have never got over the spoiling you received when you lay wounded under this roof. I shall indulge you no longer." Shaking her long forefinger at him. "Your familiarity needs to be checked." Her manner of grave and kindly irony removed all impression of rebuke from this speech, which Major Favraud received very coolly, spoiled child that he really was, rubbing his hands as he took the foot of the table. At the sight of the *bouilli* before him, from which a savory steam ascended to his epicurean nostrils, he said, notwithstanding: "Soup and *bouilli* too! Ah, madame, I see why you absented yourself so cruelly this morning. You have been engaged in good works!"

"Only the sauces, Favraud!—*seulement les sauces.*"

"The sauces—it's just that!—Ude is a mere charlatan in comparison," turning to me. "Miss Harz, you never tasted any thing before like madame's soup and sauces. I wish she would take me in partnership for a while, if only to teach me the recipes that will otherwise die with her. What a restaurant we two could keep together!"

"You are too unsteady, Favraud, for my *maître d'hôtel.* Your mind is too much engrossed by the bubbles of politics, you would spoil all my materials, and realize the old proverb that 'the devil sends cooks.' But go to work like a good fellow, and carve the dish before you; by that time the soup will be removed. I have a fine fish, however, in reserve (let me announce this at once), for my end of the table."

"Here are croquets too, as I live," said Duganne, lifting a cover before him and peeping in, then returning it quietly to its place. "Are you a fairy, madame?"

"Much more like a witch," she said, with gayety. "You young men, at least, think every old, toothless gray-haired crone like me ready for the stake, you know."

"Not when they make such steaks," said Dr. Durand, attacking the dish, with its savory surroundings, before him.

"Ah! you make calembourgs, my good doctor.—What do you call them, Favraud? It is one of the few English words I do not know—or forget. I believe, to make them, however, is a medical peculiarity."

"Puns, madame, puns, not pills. Don't forget it now. It is time you were beginning to master our language. You know you are almost grown up!" and Favraud looked at her saucily.

"A language which madame speaks more perfectly than any foreigner I have ever known," I remarked. She bowed in answer, well pleased.

In truth, the accent of Madame Grambeau was barely detectable, and her phraseology was that of a well-translated book—correct, but not idiomatic, and bearing about it the idiosyncrasy of the language from which it was derived. She was evidently a person of culture and native power of intellect combined, and her finely-moulded face, as well as every gesture and tone, indicated superiority and character.

In that lonely wild, and beneath that lowly roof, there abode a spirit able and worthy to lead the *coteries* of the great, and to preside over the councils of statesmen, and (to rise in climax) the drawing-room of the *grande monde.* But it was her whim rather than her necessity to tarry where she could alone be strictly independent, a *sine qua non* of her being.

The son she had led by the hand from New York to Georgia, and who, standing by her side, distinctly remembered to have seen the head of the Princess Lamballe borne on a pole through the streets of Paris, was now a prominent member of the Legislature, and, through his rich wife, the incumbent of a great plantation.

But the teachings of Jean-Jacques Rousseau, that philosophic sign-post, still influenced his mother, in her refusal to live under his splendid roof, and partake of his bounty, however liberally offered.

"I have a home of my own," she said, "a few faithful servants, brains, and energy still, besides a small account with General Curzon, in his bank at Savannah, wherewith to meet emergencies; while these things last, I will owe to no man or woman for bread or shelter. And, when these depart, may the grave cover my bones, and the good God receive my soul!"

Books alone she accepted as gifts from her son, and of these, in a little three-cornered library, she had a goodly store in the two languages which she read with equal facility, if not delight.

She showed us this nook before we left, and I saw, lying face downward, as she had recently left it, the volume she was then perusing at intervals—one of Madame Sand's novels, "Les Mauprats," I remember, a singular and powerful romance, then recently issued, whose root I have always thought might be found in Walter Scott's "Rob Roy," and more particularly in the Osbaldistone family commemorated in that work.

On suggesting this to Madame Grambeau, she too saw the resemblance I spoke of, and she agreed, with me, that the coincidence of genius furnished many such parallels, where no charge of plagiarism could be attached to either side.

A few bottles of "wild-berry wine," as Elizabeth Barrett called such fluids, were added to the dinner toward its close, and Marion begged permission to have her basket of cakes and fruits brought in for dessert, which else had been wanting to our repast; to which request Madame Grambeau graciously acceded.

"I make no confections," she said, "but I have lived on the juices of good meats, well prepared, with such vegetables as the Lord lets grow in this poor region, many years, and behold I am old and still able to do his service!"

"And a little good wine, too, occasionally—eh, madame?" added Major Favraud, impertinently.

"When attainable, Favraud. You drank good wine yourself, when you were here, and I partook with you moderately. But I buy none such. I drown not, Clarence-like, even in butts of malmsey, my hard-earned gold; and I own I am not fond of the juices of the muscadine of your hills;" and she tapped her snuffbox.

"You are going to hear her talk now," whispered Favraud; "that is a sign—equal to General Finistere's—the snuffbox tapping, I mean. The oracle is beginning to arouse! Come! let me stir her further!" and he inclined his head before her.

"I'll tell you what, madame, you must take a little cognac to keep off the chills of age. I have some of the best, and will send you down a demijohn, if you say the word; and in return you shall pray for me. I am a great sinner, Miss Harz thinks."

"Miss Harz is correct; and we will both promise you our prayers. She, too, is Catholic, I hope. No? I regret so, for her own sake; but your brandy I reject, Victor; remember that, and offend me not by sending it. You must not forget the fate of your malvoisie."

"Ah, madame, that was cruel! but I have forgiven you long since. I think, however, that the grape-vines bore better that year than ever before—thus watered, or wined, I mean.—Just think of it, Miss Harz! To pour good wine round the roots of a Fontainebleau grape, rather than replenish the springs of life with it! Was there ever waste like that since Cleopatra dissolved her pearl in vinegar?"

"Miss Harz will agree with me that a principle that could not resist the gift of a dozen bottles of choice wine was little worth. Of such stuff was made not the fathers of your Revolution. But stay, there is an explanation due to me, yet unrendered," she pursued. "I am a puzzled *bourgeoise*, I confess," she said, shaking her head. "Come, Favraud, explain. Who is this young lady?"

"A *bourgeoise* also," I replied for him, anxious to turn the tide of conversation into another channel for some reasons. "I had thought you an expatriated marquise, at least, madame!" I continued. "As for me, I am simply a governess."

"It is my glory, mademoiselle, to have been of that class to which belonged Madame Roland herself, and which represented that *juste milieu* which maintained the balance of society in France. When the dregs of the *bas peuple* rose to the surface of the revolution, commenced by the sound middle classes, we regarded the scum of aristocracy as the smaller of the two evils. As soon as the true element had ceased to assert itself in France, I fled forever from a land of bloodshed and misrule, and took shelter under the broad wing of your boasted American eagle."

"Which still continues to flap over you shelteringly, madame," I rejoined, somewhat flippantly, I fear, "and will to the end, no doubt; for, in its very organization, our country can never be subjected to the fluctuations of other lands—revolt and revolution."

"I am not so certain of this," she observed, shaking her white head slowly as she spoke, and, lifting a pinch of snuff from her tortoise-shell box (the companion of her whole married life, as she acquainted us), she inhaled it with an air of meditative self-complacency, then offered it quietly to the gentlemen, who were still sitting over their wine and peaches; passing by Marion, Alice Durand, and myself, completely, in this ovation.

"Good snuff is not to be sneezed at," said Major Favraud. "None offered to young ladies, it seems," taking a huge pinch, and thrusting it bravely up his nostrils, as one takes a spoonful of unpleasant medicine. Then contradicting his own assertion immediately afterward, he succeeded in expelling most of it in a series of violent sternutatory spasms, which left him breathless, red-faced, and watery-eyed, with a handkerchief much begrimed.

But Madame Grambeau seemed not to have noticed this ridiculous proceeding, which, of course, created momentary mirth at the expense of the penitent Favraud, to whom Dr. Durand repeated the tantalizing saying, that "it is a royal privilege to take snuff gracefully"—giving the example as he spoke, in a mock-heroic manner, quite as absurd and irrelevant as Favraud's own.

Lost in deep thought, and gently tapping her snuff-box as she mused—the tripod of her inspiration, as it seemed—Madame Grambeau sat silently, with what memories of the past and what insight into the future none can know save those like herself grown hoary with wisdom and experience.

At last she spoke, addressing her remarks to me, as though the careless words I had hazarded had just been spoken, and the attention of her hearers undiverted by divers absurdities—among others the affected gambols of Duganne—anxious to place himself in an agreeable aspect before both of his *inamoratas*, past and present.

"I do not agree with you, mademoiselle. I am one

of those who think that in the very framing of this Constitution of ours the dragon's teeth were sown, whose harvest is not yet produced. Mr. Calhoun, with his prophetic eye, foresees that this crop of armed men is inevitable from such germs, as does Mr. Clay, were he only frank, which he is not, because he deludes himself—the most incurable and inexcusable of all deceptions."

And she applied herself again assiduously to her snuffbox, tapping it peremptorily before opening it, and, with a gloomy eye fixed on space, she continued:

"In all lands, from the time of Cassandra and Jeremiah up, there have been prophets. Prophets for good and prophets for ill—of which some few have been God-appointed, and the sayings of such alone have been preserved. The rest vanish away into oblivion like chaff before the wind—never mind what their achievement, what their boast.

"In this nation we have only two true prophets, Calhoun and Clay—both men of equal might, and resolution, and intellect—gifted as beseems their vocation, masterful and heroic; and to these all other men are subordinate in the great designs of Providence."

"Where do you leave Mr. Webster, John Quincy Adams, General Jackson himself, in such a category, madame?" I asked, eagerly.

"They are doing, or have done, the work God has appointed for them to do, I suppose, mademoiselle; but they are accessories merely of the times, and will pass away with the necessities of the moment."

"'The earth has bubbles as the water hath, and these are of them,'" said Major Favraud aside, between his short, set teeth, nodding to me as he spoke, and lending the next moment implicit attention to what Madame

Grambeau was saying; for the brief pause she had made for another pinch of snuff was ended, and she continued impetuously, as if no interval had occurred:

"Clay is, unconsciously, I trust, for the honor of mankind, fulfilling his destiny—this great prophet who still refuses to prophesy. He is entering the wedge for what he declines to admit the possibility of—yet there must be moments when that eye of power pierces the clouds of prejudice and party, wherewith it seeks to blind its kingly vision, and descries the horrors beyond as the result of the acts he is now committing; and when such moments of clear conviction come to him, the ambitious tool of a party, I envy not his sensations," and she shook her head mournfully. "Not Napoleon at St. Helena, not Prometheus on his rock, were more to be pitied than he! the man whose ambition shall never know fruition, whose measures shall pass and leave no trace in less than fifty years after he has ceased to exist—the splendid failure of our century!"

She ceased for a moment, with her eye fixed on space, her hands clasped, her whole face and manner uplifted, as if, indeed, on her likewise the prophet's mantle had dropped from a chariot of fire.

"As to Calhoun—he is God-fearing," she continued, fervently. "In the solitudes of a spiritual Mount Sinai, he has received the tablets of the Lord, and bends every energy to their fulfillment. He, too, foresees—not with an eye like Clay's, clear only at intervals—and clouded by vanity, ambition, and sophistry, at other seasons—he, too, foresees the coming of our doom! His clear vision embraces anarchy, dissension, civil war, with all its attendant horrors, as the consequence of man's injustice; and, like Moses, he beholds the promised land into which he can never enter! Would that it were given to him to appoint his Joshua, or even to see him face to face, recognizingly! But this is not God's will. He lurks among the shadows yet—this Joshua of the South, but God shall yet search him out and bring him visibly before the people! Not while I live," she added, solemnly, "but within the natural lives of all others who sit this day around my table!"

"She is equal to Madame Le Normand!" said Major Favraud, aside, nodding approvingly at me.

"If one waits long enough, most prophecies may be fulfilled," I ventured; "but, madame, your words point to results too terrible—too unnatural, it seems to me, ever to be realized in these enlightened times or in this land of moderation."

"Child," she responded, "blood asserts itself to the end of races. There are two separate civilizations in this land, destined some day to come in fearful conflict; and the wars of Scylla, of the Jews themselves, shall be outdone in the horror and persistence of that strife of partners—I will not say brothers—for there is no brotherhood of blood between South and North, of which Clay and Calhoun stand forth to my mind as distinct types. No union of the red and white roses possible."

"But you forget, madame, that Mr. Clay is a Western man, a Virginian, a Kentuckian, and the representative of slave-holders," I remonstrated. "His interests are coincident with those of the South. His hope of the presidency itself vests in his constituents, and the wand would be broken in his hand were he to lend himself to partiality of any kind. Mr. Clay is a great patriot, I believe, Jacksonite though I am—he knows no South nor North, nor East nor West, but the Union alone, solid and undivided."

"All this is true," she answered, "in one sense. It is thus he speaks, and, like all partial parents, even thinks he feels toward his offspring; but observe his acts narrowly from first to last. He has a manufacturer's heart, with all his genius. He loves machinery—the sound of the mill, the anvil, the spinning-jenny, the sight of the ship upon the high-seas, or steamboat on the river, the roar of commerce, far more than the work of the husbandman. We are an agricultural people, we of the South and West—and especially we Southerners, with our poverty of invention, our one staple, our otherwise helpless habits, incident to the institution which, however it may be our curse, is still our wealth, and to which, for the present time, we are bound, Ixion-like, by every law of necessity. What does this tariff promise? Where will the profit rest? Where will the loss fall crushingly? The slow torture of which we read in histories of early times was like to this. Each day a weight was added to that already lying on the breast of a strong man, bound on his back by the cords of his oppressors, until relief and destruction came together, and the man was crushed; such was the *peine forte et dure*."

"Calhoun is patriarchal,[1] and is now placing all his individual strength to the task of heaving off this incubus from the breast of our body politic, but with small avail, for he has no lever to assist him—no fulcrum whereon to rest it; otherwise he might say with Archimedes, 'With these I could move a world.' He is unaided, this eagled-eyed prophet of ours, looking sorrowfully, sagaciously down into the ages! South Carolina is the Joseph, that his cruel brothers, the remaining South-

[1] It was about this time that Mr. Calhoun made his famous anti-tariff crusade throughout the land, it may be remembered by some of my readers.

ern States, have sold to the Egyptians, as a bond-slave. But they shall yet come to drink of his cup, and eat of his bread of opinion, in the famine of their Canaan. Nullification shall leave a fitting successor, as Philip of Macedon left Alexander to carry out his plans. The abolitionist and the slave-holder are as distinct as were Charles I. and Cromwell, or Catharine de Medicis and Henry of Navarre. The germ that Calhoun has planted shall lie long in the earth, perhaps, but when it breaks the surface, it shall grow in one night to maturity, like that in your so famous 'Mother Goose' story of 'Jack and his Bean-stalk,' forming a ladder wherewith to scale the abode of giants and slay them in their drunken sleep of security. But he who does this deed, this Joshua of the Lord's, this fierce successor of our gentle Moses, shall wade through his oceans of blood to gain the stone. God knoweth—He only—how all this shall end, whether in success or overthrow. It is so far wrapped in mystery."

As if she saw from some spiritual height the reign of terror she predicted, she dropped her head upon her hands and closed her eyes, and I felt my blood creep slowly through my veins as I followed her in thought across the waste of woe and desolation. For there was something in her manner, her voice (august and solemn with age and wisdom as these were), that impressed all who heard, with or in spite of their own consent, and for a time profound silence succeeded this harangue.

Dr. Durand was the first to recover himself. "I trust, my dear madame," he remarked, "that the substantial horrors realized in your youth still cast their dark shadows over the coming years, and so deceive you into prophecies that it is sad to hear from lips so reverent, and which, let us all pray, may never be realized. You yourself will say amen to that, I am convinced."

"Amen!" she murmured.

"Nonsense, Durand! don't play at hypocrite in your old age, after having been a true man all your life," broke in Major Favraud. "What is a conservative, after all, but a social parrot, who repeats 'wise saws and modern instances,' until he believes himself possessed of the wisdom of all the ages, and is incapable of conceiving of the existence even of an original idea?"

"By-the-by," digressed Duganne, weary of discussion, "hear that old fellow outside, how he is going on, Favraud, *à propos* of poll parrots, you know, as if all else, but the name of the bird, had been lost on his ear. Just listen!"

"Yes, hear him, and be edified," was the sarcastic response of Favraud to Duganne, who took no other notice, even if he understood the point, than to lead the way to the portico, where swung the cage of the jolly bird in question; and, headed by Madame Grambeau leaning on her cane, we followed simultaneously, with the exception of Major Favraud, who continued at the table with his cigar and cognac-flask, in sullen and solitary state.

"Nutmegs and nullification!" shrieked the parrot, as we stood before him. "Ha, ha, ha!"

"That is condensing the matter, certainly," I observed.

"*Bienvenu, compatriote!*" he repeated many times, laughing loudly, the next moment, as if in mockery.

"What a fiend it is!" said Marion, timidly; "only look at its black tongue, Miss Harz! Then what a laugh!"

"Danton! Danton! have you nothing to say to this strange lady?" said Madame Grambeau, addressing her bird by name; "you must not neglect my friends, Danton Pardi!"

"Bird of freedom, moulting—moulting!" was the whimsical rejoinder. "Jackson! give us your paw, Old Hick—Hick—Hickory!"

"This is the stuff Major Favraud taught him," she apologized, "when he used to lie on his porch day after day, after his hostile meeting with Juarez, which took place on that hill," signifying the site of the duel with her slender cane. "It was there they fought their duel, *à l'outrance*, and I knew it not until too late! His wife was too ill to come to him at that time, and the task of nursing him devolved on me, since when, on maternal principles, the lad has grown into my affections."

"The lad of forty-odd!" sneered Duganne, unnoticed, apparently, by the aged lady, however, at the moment, but not without amusing other hearers by this sally. Dr. Durand was especially delighted.

"For he is a boy at heart," she said later, "this same Victor Favraud of ours," gazing reprovingly around. "Indeed, he is the only American I have ever seen who possessed real *gaieté de cœur*, and for that, I imagine, he must thank his French extraction."

"Calhoun and cotton!" "Coal and codfish!" shouted the parrot at the top of his voice. "Catfish and coffee!"—"Rice cakes for breakfast"—"All in my eye, Betty Martin"—"Yarns and Yankees"—"Shad and shin-plasters"—"Yams and yaller boys," and so on, in a string of the most irrelevant alliteration and folly, that, like much other nonsense, evoked peals of laughter by its unexpected utterance, and which at last mollified and brought out Major Favraud himself, from his dignified retirement.

"You have ruined the morals of my bird," said Madame Grambeau, reproachfully. "Approach, Favraud, and justify yourself. In former times his discourse was discreet. He knew many wise proverbs and polite salutations in French and English both, most of which he has discarded in favor of your profane and foolish teachings. He is as bad as the 'Vert-vert' of Voltaire. I shall have to expel him soon, I fear."

"Danton, how can you so grieve your mistress?" remonstrated Major Favraud, lifting at the same time an admonitory finger, at which recognized signal, a part of past instructions probably, the parrot burst forth at once in a series of the most grotesque and *outré* oaths ear ever heard, ending (by the aid of some prompting from his teacher) by dismally croaking the fragment of a popular song thus travestied:

"My ole mistis dead and gone,
She lef to me her ole jawbone.
Says she, 'Charge up in dem yaller pines,
And slay dem Yankee Philistines!'"—

ending with the invariable "*Bon jour*," or "*Bienvenu, compatriote*," and demoniac "Ha! ha! ha!"

"The memory of the creature is perfectly wonderful," I said. "Many parrots have I seen, but never one like this before. It must have sprung out of the Arabian Nights."

"I can teach any thing to every thing," digressed Major Favraud, "and without severity; it is my specialty. I was meant for a trainer of beasts, probably. I will get up an entertainment, I believe, in opposition to the industrious fleas, called the 'Desperate Doves,' and teach pigeons to muster, drill, and go through all the military motions. I could do it easily, and so repair my broken fortunes. I have one already at home that feigns death at the word of command. I have amused myself for hours at a time with this bird.—Don't say a word, Miss Harz," speaking low, "I see what you think of it all, but I have had to cheat misery some way or other. It was a wretched device and waste of existence, though. And when I see that great, distinguished man, who had such hopes of me as a boy, I feel that I could creep into an auger-hole for sheer shame of my extinguished promise."

"Not extinguished!" I murmured, "only under a cloud, still destined to be fulfilled."

"Only in the grave," he said, sadly, "with the promise common to all mankind;" and thus by gloomy glimpses I caught the truth.

We staid that night at the house of an aunt of Madame La Vigne's, who received us cordially, entertained us sumptuously, and dismissed us graciously.

The next morning at sunrise we again set out for Savannah, into which city we entered before the noonday heat, finding cool shelter and warm welcome at once under the roof of General Curzon, the South's most polished gentleman and finished man of letters, of whom it may be truly said that, "Take him for all in all, we ne'er shall look upon his like again."

## CHAPTER II.

BEFORE leaving the hospitable roof of General Curzon —beneath which I tarried for several days—awaiting the tardy sailing of the packet-steamer Kosciusko, bound for New York, circumstances determined me to leave in the hands of my host a desk which I had intended to carry with me, and which contained most of my treasures. First among these, indisputably, in intrinsic value were my diamonds—"sole remnant of a past magnificence;" but the miniatures of my father and mother, and Mabel, in the cases of which locks of twisted hair—brown, and black, and golden, and gray—were contained and combined (dear, imperishable memorials of vitality in most instances when all the rest was dust and ashes), and the early letters of my parents, together with the carefully-kept diary I had written at Beauseincourt, ranked beyond these even in my estimation.

The cause of this deposit of valuables was simply owing to the unstable lock of my trunk, the condition of which was detected too late to have it repaired before sailing. Madame Curzon had suggested to me the unsafe nature of such custody for objects of price, if, indeed, I possessed such at all. I told her then of my diamonds, and it was agreed between us that these, at least, had better be deposited in the bank of her husband, who would bring them to me himself a few months later—and on reflection I concluded to add my desk, pictures, and papers, to my more substantial treasures. These, at least, I felt assured no accident should throw into the hands of Bainrothe.

On my way to the ship I left the carriage for a moment, in pursuance with this idea, and, followed by King, the bearer of my large and weighty desk, entered the banking-house of my host, and was shown at once, by attentive clerks, to his peculiar sanctum. I told him my errand in a few words.

"Keep it until called for, unless you hear from me in the interval," I had said in allusion to my deposit, for he acknowledged the chances were slight of his leaving home until the following year, notwithstanding Madame Curzon's convictions.

"Called for by whom?" he asked, calmly.

"By Miriam Monfort in person or her order," I replied, laughingly, "This is a mystery that, by-and-by, shall be explained to you."

"I understand something of that already," he rejoined. "Marion has been whispering to the reeds, you know, or Madame Curzon, the same thing nearly; but let us be earnest, as your time is short, and mine precious to-day. Life is uncertain, and, young and strong as you are, or seem to be, you cannot foresee one hour even of the future, or of your own existence. Suppose Miriam Monfort neither comes in person nor sends her order for its restoration—what, then, is to become of this treasure-chest of hers?"

"You shall keep it then," I replied, unhesitatingly, "until my little sister reaches her majority, and cause it to be placed in her own hands, none other—or, stay, let her have it on the day before her marriage, should this occur earlier than the time mentioned, or when she reaches her eighteenth year in any case; but, above all things, be careful."

"So many conflicting directions confuse and mystify me, I confess. Come, let me write down your wishes, and the matter can be arranged formally, which is always best in any case. There, I think I have the gist of your idea," he said a few moments later, as he pushed over to me a slip of paper to read and sign, which done, I shook hands with him cordially, preparing to go. "But your receipt—you have forgotten to take it up!"

"O General Curzon! the whole proceeding seems so ominous," I said, turning back at the door to receive the proffered scrap, which, in another moment, dropped from my nerveless fingers, while these, clasped over my streaming eyes, forgot their office.

"My dear young lady," he remonstrated, "I am shocked. What can have occurred to impress you thus? Not this mere routine of affairs, surely?—Duncan, a glass of water here for Miss Monfort."

"I do not know, I am sure, why I should be so weak for such a trifle," I said, after a few swallows of ice-water had somewhat restored my equilibrium; "but I do feel very dismally about this voyage—have done so ever since I left Beauseincourt. This is the last straw on the camel's back, believe me, General Curzon. You must not reproach yourself in the least—nor me; and now let me bid you farewell once more, perhaps eternally!"

These words of mine were remembered later in a very different spirit from that in which they were then received (one of incredulous compassion)—remembered as are ever the last utterances of the doomed, whether innocent or guilty, in solemn awe and reverential tenderness, not unmingled with a superstitious faith in presentiment.

"Why, you look bluer than your very obvious veil, bluer than your invisible school-marmish stockings, bluer than the skies, or a blue bag, or Madame de Staël's 'Corinne,' or Byron's 'dark-blue ocean,'" said Major Favraud, as he assisted me again into the carriage, where Dr. Durand and Marion awaited me, for, as I have said, we were now on our way to the vessel which was to bear me and my destinies forever from that lovely Southern land in which I had seen and suffered so much.

Dr. Durand looked serious at the sight of my woful aspect, and Marion mutely proffered her *vinaigrette*, gratefully accepted, as was the good doctor's compassionate silence; but, as usual, Favraud, after having once gotten fairly under weigh, ran on. "What is the use of bewailing the inevitable?" he pursued. "We have all seen your *penchant* for Curzon, and his for you, for three days past; but Octavia is as tough as *lignum-vitæ*, I regret to assure you, my dear Miss Harz, and your chance is *as blue* as your spirits, or the flames of snap-dragon, or Marion's eyes. You will have to just put up with the captain, I fear, for even the doctor there is in harness for life. Southern women, you know, proverbially survive their husbands; and, as the suttee is out of fashion, they sometimes have to marry Yankees as a *dernier ressort* of desperation! Of course, there are occasional sad exceptions"—looking grave for a moment, and glancing at the black hat-band on the Panama hat he was nursing on his knees, so as to let the breeze blow through his silky, silver-streaked black hair—"but—but—in short, why will you all look so doleful? Isn't it bad enough to feel so?"

"The loveliest fade earliest, we all know," and the tears

were in his honest, frivolous eyes, dashed away in the next moment as he exclaimed, eagerly, "Why, there goes the Lamarque equipage, as I live! I had forgotten all about it. The pleasantest woman in Savannah, young or old, is to be your *compagnon de voyage*, Miss Harz, and the most determined widower on record her escort; a perfect John Rogers of a man, with nine little motherless children, her brother Raguet ('Rag,' as we called him at school, on account of his prim stiffness, so that 'limber as a rag' seemed a most preposterous saying in his vicinity). He is handsome, however, and intelligent, a perfect gentleman, but on the mourners' bench just now, like some others you know of"—heaving a deep sigh. "His wife, poor thing, died last autumn—a pretty girl in her day was Cornelia Huger! I was a little weak in that direction once myself—before—that is, before—O doctor! what a trouble it is to remember!"

And again the small, fleet hand was dashed across the twinkling, tearful eyes of this April day of a middle-aged man of the world—this modern Mercutio—merry and mournful at once, as if there were two sides to his every mood, like the famous shield of story. When we reached the quay the Kosciusko was already getting up her steam, and, in less than an hour afterward, the friends I loved were gone like dreams, the bustle of departure was over, and, with lifted canvas and a puffing engine, we were grandly steaming past the noble forts (poor Bertie's broach and buckle, be it remembered) on our path of pride and power toward the broad Atlantic.

The weather was oppressively hot, and, for the first thirty-six hours, scarcely a breath of wind lifted us on our way, so that the engine, wholly incompetent to the work of both sails and machinery, bore us very slowly on our northward ocean-flight. Indeed, the failure of this engine to do its duty, at first, had sorely disheartened both captain and crew as we found later, for upon its execution and energies, in the beginning, had rested our entire dependence.

On the evening of the second day's voyage, a sudden and violent thunder-storm occurred, not unusual in those latitudes; during the raging of which our mainmast was struck by lightning, and wholly disabled.

The fire was extinguished in the only possible manner, by cutting it away from the decks, letting it gently down upon them, deluging it, so that our mast lay charred and blackened after its bath of sea-water, like a mighty serpent stretched along the ship, from stem to stern, and wrapped loosely in its shrouds. It did us good service later, though not by defying the winds of heaven, nor spreading forth its snowy sails to catch the tropic breezes.

Before many hours, it was destined to ride the waves in a shape that was certainly never intended by those who chose it among many others—taper and stately in its group of firs—to be the chief adornment of a gallant ship, and lift a pointing finger to the stars themselves, as an index of its might, and, with this exception, the hope of those it served—that of a charred and blackened life-raft.

The renewed freshness of the atmosphere, and the joyful upspringing of the breezes, alone remained, at midnight, to tell the story of the recent hurricane.

These tropic breezes came like benevolent fairies, to aid our groaning Titan in his labors.

I can never rid myself for one moment of the idea that an engine really works, with weary, reluctant strength like a genii slave, waiting vengefully for the time of retaliation, which sooner or later is sure to come; or of the visionary notion that a graceful, gliding ship, with all sails set, receives the same pleasure from its own motion and beauty that a snow-white swan must do "as down she bears before the gale," with her white plumage and stately crest.

I think, if ever I am called to give a toast, it shall be "Sail-ships; may their shadows never be less!" They are, indeed, a part of the romance of ocean.

The moon was full, in the balmy summer night that succeeded the tempest, and the ship's quarter-deck was crowded with the passengers of the Kosciusko, enjoying to the utmost, as it seemed, the delicious, newly-washed atmosphere, the moonlit heavens and sea, the exquisitely-caressing softness of the tardily-awakened breezes that filled the white sails of the vessel, and fluttered the silken scarf of the maiden, with the same wooing breath of persuasive, subtle strength.

Around Miss Lamarque, the lady of whom Major Favraud had spoken so admiringly, and to whose kindness he had committed me, a group had gathered, chiefly of the young, not to be surpassed in any land for manly bearing, graceful feminine beauty, gayety, wit, and refinement.

There was Helen Oscanyan, fair as a dream of Greece, in her serene, marble perfectness of form and feature; and the lovely Mollie Cairns, her cousin, small, dark, and sparkling—both under the care of that stately gentleman, their uncle, Julius Sevère, of Savannah; and there were the sisters Percy, twins in age and appearance, with voices like brook-ripples, and eyes like wood-violets, and feet of Chinese minuteness and French perfection—the darlings and only joys of a mother still beautiful, though sad in her widowhood, and gentle as the dove that mourns its mate.

There was the brilliant Ralph Maxwell, whose jests, stinging and slight, just glanced over the surface of society without inflicting a wound, even as the skater's heel glides over ice, leaving its mark as it goes, yet breaking no crust of frost; and there was the poetic dreamer Dartmore, with his large, dark eyes, and moonlight face, and manner of suffering serenity, on his way to put forth for fame, as he fondly believed, his manuscript epic on the "Sorrows of the South."

All these, and more, were there gathering about the leader of their home-society, on that alien deck, as securely as though they were sitting in her own drawing-room at "Berthold," on one of her brilliant reception-evenings.

How could they know—how could they dream the truth —or descry the hidden skeleton at the festival, wreathed in flowers and veiled with glittering, filmy draperies, which yet put forth its bony fingers to beckon on and clutch them?

I too was joyous and unconscious as the rest, and for the first time for many days felt the burden literally heaved rather than lifted away that had oppressed me.

Was I not on my way to him in whose presence alone I lived my true life? and what feeling of his morbid fancy was there that my hand could not smooth away, when once entwined in his? Beauseincourt, and all its shadows, had I not put behind me? The sunshine lay before, and in its light and warmth I should still rejoice, as it was my birthright to do.

I was "fey" that night, as the Scotch say, when an unaccountable lightness of mood precedes a heavy sorrow, which it so often does, as well as the more usual mood, the presage of gloom. I felt that I had the power to put aside all ills—to grapple with my fate, and compel back my lost happiness. Truly my bosom's lord sat lightly on her throne, as of late it had not been her wont to do.

Against my inclination had I been drawn into the current of that youthful gayety, and now my bark floated without an effort on the stream. I was in my own element again, and my powers were all responsive.

The small hours came—the happy group dispersed—not without many interchanges of social compliment, much *badinage*, and merry plans for the morrow. The monster Sea-sickness had been defied on the balmy voyage, save in the brief interval of tempest, and his victors mocked him, baffled as he was, with their purpose of amusement.

"We shall get up the band to-morrow evening," said Major Ravenel, "and have a dance; the gallop would go grandly here. See what reach of quarter-deck we have! There are Germans on board who play in concert violins and wind-instruments."

"Suppose we dress as sea-nymphs," said Honoria Pyne; "enact a masque for old Neptune's benefit? It would be so complimentary, you know; bring down the house, no doubt. I have a sea-green tarlatan lying so conveniently. Colonel Latrobe looks exactly like a Triton, with that wondrous beard. A little alum sprinkled over its red-gold ground would do wonders in the way of effect—would be gorgeous—wouldn't it, now, Miss Harz?"

"But all that could be done on shore as well, Miss Pyne," I replied, in the way of reminiscence. "It is a pity to waste our opportunities of observation now, in getting up costumes; and, for my part, I confess that I have a wholesome dread of these sea-deities, and fear to exasperate their finny feelings by reducing them to effigies. Thetis is very spiteful, sometimes; and jealous, too, you remember."

Miss Pyne did not remember, but did not mean to be baffled either, she would let Miss Harz know, even if that lady *did* know more about mythology than herself; and, if no one else would join her, meant to play her *rôle* of sea-nymph all alone, with Major Latrobe for her Triton in waiting, tooting upon a conch-shell, and looking lovely! At which compliment, open and above-board, poor Major Latrobe, who was over head and ears in love with her, and a very ugly man, only bowed and looked more silly than before, which seemed a work of supererogation.

After the rest were gone, Miss Lamarque and I concluded to promenade on the nearly-deserted deck, in the moonlight, and let the excitement of the evening die away through the medium of more serious conversation. She was a woman of forty-five, still graceful and fine-looking, but bearing few traces of earlier beauty, probably better to behold, in her overripe maturity, than in the unfolding of her less attractive time of bud and blossom. Self had been laid aside now (which it never can be until the effervescence of youth and hope are over). She had accepted her position of old maid and universal benefactress; and sustained it nobly, gracefully. She was thoroughly well-bred and agreeable, very vivacious, astute, and intelligent, rather than intellectual, yet she had the capacity (had her training been different) to have been both of these.

I remember how it chanced that, after a long promenade, during which we had discussed men, manners, books, customs, costumes, and politics, even (that once tabooed subject for women, now free to all), with infinite zest and responsiveness that charmed us mutually, so that we swore allegiance on the strength of this one day's rencontre, like two school-girls or knights of old—I remember how the dropping of her comb at his feet caused Miss Lamarque to pause, compelling me to follow her example, by reason of our intertwined arms, in front of the man at the wheel, as he stooped to raise it and hand it to her with a seaman's bow. His ready politeness, unusual for one in his station, determined us to cultivate his maritime acquaintance, and in a short time we had drawn forth the outlines of his story, simple and bare as this was of incident.

His picturesque appearance had impressed us equally during the day, but until now we had not met in concert about Christian Garth, for such we soon found was the name of our polite pilot.

He was a Jerseyman, he told us, of German descent, married to the girl of his heart, and living on the coast of that adventurous little State, famous alike for its peaches and wrecks.

"Sall had a stocking full of money," he informed us, silver, and copper, and gold, when he married her, for her mother had been a famous huckster—and never missed her post in the Philadelphia market for thirty years, and this was her child's inheritance, and with this money he had fixed up his old hut, till it looked 'e'en a'most inside like a ship-captain's cabin.'"

And now Sall wanted him to stay at home, he informed us, with her and the children, but somehow or other he could never tarry long at the hearth, for the sea pulled him like it was his mother, and the spell of the tides was on him, and he must foller even if he went to his own destruction, like them men that liquor lures to loss, or the love of mermaids.

"All land service is dead when likened to the sea," he said, shaking his great water-dog head, and looking out lovingly upon his idol. "But ships a'n't like they oncst was, ladies," he added, "before men put these here heavy iron ingines to work in 'em—it's like cropping a bird's wing to make a river-boat of a ship, and a dead, dead shame to shorten sails till it looks like a young gal dressed in breeches or any other onnatural thing—for a sailing-ship and a full-flowing petticoat always rise up in a true man's mind together—God bless them both, I say."

"To which we cordially say amen, of course," said Miss Lamarque, laughing. "We should have been at a loss, however, Mr. Garth, but for our engine during the dead calm preceding the storm, when our ship's sails flapped so lazily about her masts, and she rocked like a baby's cradle without making progress. It is well the engineer manœuvred so successfully while we lay fireless on the low rolling waves; but we are speeding along merrily enough now, to make up for it all—I take comfort in that—"

"But not exactly in the right direction, though, to suit my stripe," he said, turning his quid in his mouth as he looked out to leeward, revealing, as he did so, a fine yet rugged profile relieved against the silvery purple sheen of the moonlit sky.

"Do you see that dark object lying beyond" (our eyes mechanically followed his), "so still on the water?" and he indicated it with the pipe he held in one sinewy hand—for the native courtesy of the man had involuntarily proffered us the homage of removing it from his lips, when we addressed him.

"Yes—what is it? a wreck? a whale? a small volcanic island? Do explain, Mr. Garth," said Miss Lamarque.

"Nothing but an iceberg, and we are bearing down upon it rather too rapidly, it seems to me."

And so speaking, he turned his wheel in silence warily.

"But you have the command of the helm, and have nothing to do but—"

"Obey orders," he interrupted, grimly. "Ef the captain was to tell me to run the ship to purgatory, I'd have to do it, you know."

"But surely the captain would not jeopardize the lives of a ship's company, even if he likes warm latitudes, by ordering you to run foul of an iceberg; and, if he did, you certainly would not dare to obey him with the fear of God before your eyes?" remonstrated Miss Lamarque, indignantly. "For my part I shall go to him immediately and desire him to change his course—but after all I don't believe that dingy black thing is an iceberg at all—an old hencoop rather, thrown over from some merchant-ship, or a vast lump of charred wood. You are only trying to alarm us."

"Ef you was to see it close enough, you would find it to shine equal to the diamond on your hand; but I hope you never will, that's all—I hope you never will, lady! I sot on a peak of that sort oncst myself for three days in higher latitudes than this here—me and five others, all that was spared from the wreck of the schooner Delta, and we felt our convoy melting away beneath us, and courtesying e'en a'most even with the sea, before the merchant-ship Osprey took us off, half starved, and half frozen, and half roasted all at oncst! Them is onpleasant rickollections, ladies, and it makes my blood creep to this day to see an iceberg in konsikence; but a man must do his dooty, whatsomever do betide. It was in the dead of night, and Hans Schuyler had the wheel, I remember, when we went to pieces on that iceberg, all for disregarding the captain's orders; you see, he meant to graze it like!"

"Graze it!" almost shrieked Miss Lamarque. "Did he think he was driving a curricle? Graze it—Heaven, what rashness!"

"Don't—don't! Mr. Garth," I petitioned; "I shall never sleep a wink on this ship if you continue your narrative."

"Do—do! Mr. Garth," entreated Miss Lamarque, whose penetration showed her by this time that the pilot was only playing on our fears, for want of a better instrument for his skill. "I quite enjoy the idea that you have actually been astride a fragment of the arctic glacier, and that we may perhaps make the acquaintance of a white bear ourselves when we get near our iceberg, or a gentle seal. Wouldn't you like one for a pet, Miss Harz?"

"It is very cold," I said, digressively. "I feel the chill of that fragment of Greenland freeze my marrow. I must go fetch my shawl; but first reassure us, Mr. Garth, if possible."

He laughed. "I have paid you now for making fun of me to-day," he said, saucily. "I saw your drawing of me in your books, and heerd the ladies laughing. I peeped as I passed when Myers took the helm, and I wanted to see what all the fun was about; then I said to myself, 'I will give her a skeer for that if I have a chance'—but, all the same, the chill you feel is a real one, for as sure as death that lump of darkness is an iceberg. I have told you no yarn, as you will find out to-morrow when you ask the captain. I'll steer you clear of the iceberg though, ladies, never fear. Hans Schuyler has not got the wheel to-night—you see he was three sheets in the wind anyhow, and the captain says, 'Hans,' says he, 'don't tech another drop this night, or we'll never see another mornin' till we are resurrected,' and so he turned into his hammock and swung himself to sleep—a way he had, for he didn't keer for nothin' where his comfort was concerned, having been raised up in the Injies."

"Come, Miss Lamarque," I interrupted. "I must not hear another word. 'Macbeth doth murder sleep,' and I shall be nervous for a month after this. So, good-night, Mr. Garth, and be sure you merit your first name by taking good care of us while we imitate the example of your worthy captain and 'swing ourselves to sleep,' or rather let the waves perform that office for us. I shall make it my care to-morrow morning early, if you still hold the helm, to show you my sketch, and convince you that it was never made for fun at all, but that it is a real portrait of a very fine-looking seaman, a real viking in appearance, and somewhat better than one at heart, I trust. I shall hope to earn your good opinion instead of ill-will, when you have only seen my sketch."

"You have it already, you have it already, young gal—young miss, I mean," he said, with a wave of the hand, which meant to be courteous, no doubt, but seemed only defiant. "An' this much I kin say without injury to Sall—that I'd rather hear you talk and see you smile, as I has been watchin' of you constant do to-day, than go to the circus in New York, or even to a Spanish bull-fight, or hear a Fourth-of-July oration, or 'tend camp-meetin'—and that's saying no little—an' no iceberg shall come near you while Christian Garth lays a hand upon this helm. But don't be skeered, ladies; no harm will come to the good ship Kosciusko."

"I declare our pilot is quite chivalrous, as far as you are concerned, for I marked his glance, Miss Harz," said Miss Lamarque, archly, as we turned our faces cabin-ward, under the protection of our helmsman's promised vigilance. "See what it is to be young and pretty, and remark the truth of the old proverb, as exemplified in his case, that 'extremes meet.' Victoria herself is not more independent of me or my position—established facts as both are in the eyes of some—than is Christian Garth. To him, this outsider of the world of fashion, I am only a homely old woman; no prestige comes in to garnish the unvarnished fact—a plain old maid, my dear—with not even the remembrance of beauty as a consolation, nor its remnant as a sign of past triumphs, 'only this and nothing more,' as that wonderful man Poe makes his raven say. We never find our level until we go among people who know and care nothing about us, who have never 'heard of us'—that exordium of most greetings from folks of our own class. It is absolutely refreshing to be so unaffectedly despised and slighted—it does one a world of good, there is no doubt of that, especially when one's grandfather was a Revolutionary notability, and other antecedents of a piece—but men are all alike at heart, only the worldly ones wear flimsy masks, you know, and pretend to adore intellect and ugliness, when beauty is the only thing they care for—all a sham, my dear, in any case."

"Yes, all alike," I repeated, making, as I spoke, one mental entire reservation. "All *vain* alike, I mean;

flatter their vanity ever so little and they are at your very feet, asking 'for more,' like Oliver Twist; more bread for *amour propre*, the insatiable! It was that sketch of mine that wrought the spell, though unintentionally, of course, and the sly fellow knew very well that it was no caricature—that is, if he peeped, as he pretends—but a tolerably correct likeness that might have satisfied Sall herself. By-the-by, I have a great mind to bestow it upon him as a 'sop for Cerberus,' should her jealousy ever be aroused by your reports of his devotion to me, or admiration rather, most unequivocally avowed, it must be acknowledged. I really had no intention of injuring Sally, and, if you think it best, will make the *amende honorable* by being as cross as possible to him to-morrow."

"No, no, carry out your first intention and conciliate him; for, remember, he has us in the hollow of his hand. Bestow the picture, by all means, and just as many smiles and compliments as he can stand, or you can afford to squander; for you are worse than a mermaid, Miss Harz, for fascination, all the gentlemen say so; and, as to Captain Falconer—"

"They are malignants," I rejoined, ignoring purposely the last clause of the sentence which I had interrupted; "and you are perfidious to hear them slander me so. I hate fascinating people; they always make my flesh crawl like serpents. The few I have known have been so very base." "Good specimens of '*thorough* bass,'" she interpolated, laughing.—"I am sure I am glad I have no attributes of fascination, if a strange old work I met with at Beauseincourt may be considered responsible. Did you ever see it, Miss Lamarque, you who see every thing? Hieronymus Frascatorius tells of certain families in Crete who fascinated by praising, and to avert this evil influence some charm was used consisting of a magic word (I suppose this was typical of humility, though related as literal). This *naïveté* on the part of the old chronicler was simply *impayable*, as Major Favraud would say, with his characteristic shrug. One *Varius* related (you see my theme has full possession of me, and the book is a collation of facts on the subject of fascination of all kinds, even down to that of the serpent) that a friend of his saw a fascinator with a look break in two a precious gem in the hands of a lapidary—typical this, I suppose, of some fond, foolish, female heart. Fire, according to this author, represents the quality of fascination; and toads and moths are subject to its influence, as well as some higher animals—deer, for instance, who are hunted successfully with torches; and he relates, further, that in Abyssinia artificers of pottery and iron are thus fearfully endowed, and are consequently forbidden to join in the sacred rites of religion, as fire is their chief agent. Isn't this a strange, quaint volume, to set before a king? and how do you like my lecture delivered *extempore?*"

"Oh, vastly! but I did not know that was your style before. Don't cultivate it, dear, if you hope to win manly hearts. Men like to do all the lecturing themselves, and I find it diplomatic to feign profound ignorance on all subjects outside of a bandbox; it delights them so to enlighten us. No wonder they fancy us fools when we feign foolishness so admirably—lapwings that we are!"

"But I never do, in such society. My experience is different from yours. I always pretend to know twice as much as I do, when they are about; it bluffs them off, and they are credulous sometimes as well as ignorant, notwithstanding their boasted acumen."

"Your lamp of experience needs trimming, my pretty

Miriam," she said, shaking her head, "if you really believe this. They never forgive superiority, assumed or real; none but the noble ones, I mean; who, of course, are in the minority. Give a pair of tongs pantaloons, and it asserts itself. Trousers, my dear, are at the root of manly presumption. I discovered that long ago. A man in petticoats would be as humble as a woman. This is my theory, at least; take it for what it is worth. And now to sleep, with what heart we may, an iceberg being in our vicinity;" and, taking my face in her hand, she kissed me cordially. "It is very early in our acquaintance for such manifestations to be allowable," she said, kindly, "but I am a sort of spoiled child of society, and dare to be natural. I consider that the best privilege that attaches to my condition, that of the 'bell-wether' of Savannah *ton*—the universally-accepted bore! You know—Favraud has told you, of course; he always characterizes as he goes."

"He has called you the most agreeable woman in Savannah, I remember, young or old, and was truly glad, on my account, to know that you were on board. Of your brother he spoke very kindly also, even admiringly."

"Oh, yes, I know; but of Raguet there is little question now. His wife's death has crushed him. I never saw so changed a man; he is half idiotic, I believe; and I am with him now just to keep those children from completing the work of destruction. Six little motherless ones—only think—and as bad as they can possibly be; for poor Lucilla was no manager. Isn't it strange, the influence those little cottony women get over their husbands? You and I might try forever to establish such absolute despotism, all in vain. It is your whimpering sort that rule with the waving of a pocket-handkerchief;

but poor, dear little woman, she is powerless now ; and I suppose the next will be like unto her. Raguet would never look at any thing feminine that hadn't white eyes and pink hair (yellow, I mean, of course)—his style, you know, being dark and stern, he likes the downy, waxy kind. All this is shockingly egotistical; but the question is, who that has a spark of individuality is otherwise? Good-night, again, and may all sweet dreams attend you; for my part, I never dream, being past the dreaming age, and realities fortunately disappear with daylight; even cross children are wheedled into quietness, and servants forget to fidget and giggle; and, for mosquitoes, there are bars. Adieu."

And thus we parted, never to meet again in mutual mood like this!

Yet, had the free agency of which some men boast been ours, we had scarcely chosen to face the awful change—to look into each other's eyes through gathering death-doom!

## CHAPTER III.

Before my dreaming eyes was the terror of a hungry, crunching tooth, fixed in the vessel's side, that of the iceberg, lying black in the moonlight like a great coal crystal, grimly awaiting our approach, but the reality, as well as the figment, had disappeared when I emerged at sunrise from the suffocating cabin, to the atmosphere of the cool and quiet quarter-deck, which had just undergone its matutinal.

Armed with an orange and a biscuit for physical refreshment, I depended on sea and sky for my mental entertainment; and in my hand I bore a slender scroll, destined as a propitiatory offering to our offended helmsman.

I was glad to find again at the wheel our pilot of yesterday.

"Your iceberg has disappeared, Mr. Garth," I said, as I extended to him the sketch I had made of his noble *physique* the day before, "and here is a picture for your wife, which she will see was not drawn for fun. Women are sharper than men about such matters. There, I bestow it not without regret." He received my offering with a smile, and nod of his great curly head, opened it, gazed long and seriously upon it, and, with the single word "Good," rolled it up again, and consigned it to some bosom pocket in his flannel shirt, into which it seemed to glide as a telescope into its case, revealing, as he did so, glimpses of a hairy breast, and vigorous chest, more admirable for strength than beauty, certainly.

"I will keep it there," he said, "young miss," pressing it closely against his side with his colossal hand, "until I get safe home to the Jarseys, and to Sall, or go to Davy's locker, one or other, but which it will be, young gal—young miss, I should be saying—is not for me to know."

"Nor for any one," I rejoined, solemnly; "all rests with God."

"With God and our engineer," he resumed, tersely; "them sails is of little account, now the mainmast is struck away; them floppen petticoats, wat the wind loves to play in and out, layin' along like a lazy lubber that it is, and leaving its work for others to do. It was a noble mast, though, while it stood—and you could smell the turpentine blood in its heart to the very last. It was as limber as a sapling, and never growed brittle, like some wood, with age and dryness. No storm could splinter it, and it would fling itself over into the high waves sometimes, raytner than snap and lash them like a whip. But there it lies, burned with the fire of heaven's wrath, at last, and leaving its fires of hell behind, in the heart of the Kosciusko."

"You have changed your mind on the subject of engines, Mr. Garth, I am glad to see. Truly, ours seems to be doing giant's work; now we are flying, to be sure."

"Rushing, not flying, young lady—that's the word; our wings are little use to-day, you see, such as are left to us. Runnin' for dear life, we'd better say, for that's the truth of the matter, and may the merciful Lord speed us, and have in his care all helpless ones this day!"

The lifted hand, the bared head, the earnest accents, with which these words were spoken, gave to this simple utterance of good-will all the solemnity of a benediction or prayer.

I noticed that, after replacing his tarpaulin, the lips of Garth continued to move silently, then were compressed gravely for a time, while his eye, large, clear, and expressive, was fixed on space.

"Do you still see an iceberg, Mr. Garth? Do you really apprehend danger for us now?" I asked, after studying his countenance for a moment, "or, are you again desirous to try the nerves of your female passengers? I think I must apply to the captain this time for information."

"Yes, danger," he replied, in low, sad tones, ignoring my last remark, or perhaps not hearing it at all—"danger, compared with which an iceberg might be considered in the light of a heavenly marcy. There is a chance of grazing one of them snow-bowlders, or of its drifting away from a ship, when the ripples reach it, or, if the wust comes, a body can scramble overboard, and manage to live on the top of one of them peaks, or in one of their ice-caves, with a few blankets, and a little bread and junk and water, fur a space, so as to get a chance of meetin' a ship, or a schooner; but, when there is something wrong in a ship's heart, there a'n't much hope for rescue, onless it comes from above."

He hesitated, smiling grimly, rolled his quid, crammed his hat down over his eyes, and again addressed himself to his wheel, and, for a few moments, I stood beside him silently.

"The ship is leaking, I suppose," I said, at last, "so that you apprehend her loss, perhaps," and my heart sank coldly within me, as I spoke; "but, if this be true, why does not the captain apprise us? No, you are quizzing me again, and very cruelly this time, very unwarrantably."

Yet I did not think exactly as I spoke, strive as I might to believe the man in jest. Too much solemnity and sorrow both were discernible in his worn and rugged features, hewn grandly as if from granite, to admit of a hope like this. His words were earnest, and some great calamity was in store, I could not doubt, or at least he apprehended such. For some time he replied not, then, slowing pointing to the base of the stricken main-mast, which still showed an elevation of some inches above the deck, he revealed to me the truth without a word.

As my eyes followed his guiding finger, I saw, with terror unspeakable, a thin blue wavering smoke-wreath, float upward from the floor, and, after curling feebly about the truncated mast, disappear in the clear sunlit atmosphere, again to arise from the same point, that of the juncture of the mast and deck, creeping through some invisible crevice, as it seemed to form itself eternally in filmy folds, and successively elude the eye as soon as it shaped to sight. I understood him then. There was fire in the heart of the ship, and I knew the hold was filled with cotton; it was smouldering slowly, and our safety was a question of time alone!

Pale, transfixed, frozen, I lifted my eyes to the man, who seemed to represent my fate for the moment. "Was it the lightning?" I asked, after a pause, during which his pitying eye rested on me drearily. "Did the fire occur in that way?"

"Yes, the lightning it was; and God's hand, which sent the shaft direct, alone can deliver us."

I seemed to hear the voice of Bertie speak these words. Things grew confused; I wavered as I stood, lifted my hand to my head; the face of Christian Garth grew large and dim, then faded utterly. I knew no more until I found myself seated on a coil of rope, leaning against the bulwark, while a young girl stood beside me, fanning and bathing my face, and offering me a glass of water.

"You are better now," she said, kindly; "the man at the wheel called me as I was passing, and pointed out your condition, and I led you here, and ran for water. Being up so early is apt to disagree with some people."

"What are these people crawling about the deck for? Is all hope over, or was it only a dream?" I asked.

"Oh, you are quite wild yet from your swoon; it is only the calkers stopping up the seams, one of the captain's queer whims they say; but how they are to dance to-night, those *magnificos* I mean, without ruining their slippers with this pitch, I cannot see! Thank Goodness! I belong to a church, and am not of this party, and don't care on my own account, nor does the captain, I believe. I was placed under his care at Savannah, and I suppose it is only to stop the ball that—"

She was interrupted by the approach of the officer under discussion, but he passed us gloomily and went on to inspect the workmen so unseasonably employed, as it seemed, in a labor that, save in a case of long voyages, is always performed in port.

His melancholy air, and the preoccupation of his manner, confirmed my worst fears.

Again I sought the Ixion of the vessel, who calmly and stolidly performed his duty as if, indeed, Fate directed, without a change of feature now, or expression.

"Has the captain no hope of rescue, Mr. Garth?"

"Oh, yes; he thinks we shall meet a ship or two between now and noon—we 'most always do, you know" —rolling his quid slowly, and hesitating for a while; "keep heart, keep heart! I had thought from your face you were stronger; besides, the pumps are doing good work in the hold: who knows what may come of it, who knows?"

Alas! alas! I could not rise to the level of this dim hope. "Think of the burning crowd, the sheet of flame, the terrible destruction!" I murmured; "I must go now and apprise those poor wretches below that their time is short; they have a right to know."

His vice-like hand was on my arm. "You do not go a step on such an errand," he muttered. "It is the captain's business; he will 'tend to it when the time comes, for he is a true man, and the bravest sailor on the line. He means to do what's right, never fear. It is my dooty to hold you here until he comes, onless you promise me to be discreet."

"I shall be discreet, never fear—" and his grasp relaxed. I sped me back to the coil of rope on which I had left my young companion, intending to partake with her there my biscuit and orange, so needed now for strength.

I found in her stead (for she had departed in the interval) a delicate-looking young woman, plain and poor, a widow evidently from the style of her shabby mourning and sad expression of face, bearing in her arms a weird and sickly-looking child, evidently a sufferer from spinal disease—an infant as to size, but preternaturally old in countenance.

The steady gaze of its large and serious eyes affected me magnetically—eyes that seemed ever seeking something that still eluded them, and which now appeared to inquire into my very soul.

"Is your little boy ill, madam?" I asked at last; and at the sound of my voice a smile broke over his small, sallow features, lending them strange beauty, but dying away instantly again into an expression of startled suspicion.

"Yes, very ill," she answered, clasping him tenderly as he clung to her suddenly. "He has some settled trouble that no medicine reaches, and you see how small and light he is. Many a twelve months' babe is heavier than he, yet he is three years old come Monday next, and he is 'cute beyond his years, it seems to me."

"You seem very weak and weary," I rejoined. "I noticed you yesterday with interest, sitting all the time with your boy on your knee. You must need exercise and rest. Go and walk now a little, while you can;" and I stretched my arms for her baby.

To her surprise, evidently, he came to me willingly—attracted, no doubt, by the gleam of the watch-chain about my neck, and still further propitiated by a portion of my orange, which he greedily devoured.

In the mean time the poor, pale mother took a few turns on the quarter-deck, and, disappearing therefrom a moment, returned with a small supply of cakes and biscuits which she had sought in the steward's room.

An inspiration of Providence, no doubt, she thought this proceeding later, which at the moment was only intended to anticipate the delay attendant on all second-class meals.

These cakes, with a pains-taking diligence, if not forethought—peculiar to all feeble animals, squirrels, sick children, and the like—did he one by one cram and compel into my pocket, unconscious as I was at the moment of his miser-like proceeding (instinctive, probably), which later I detected, to his infinite rejoicing. In company with my slender purse, and bunch of useless keys, a pencil, and a small memorandum-book, they remained *perdu* until that moment of accidental discovery arrived which was to test their value and place it "far above that of rubies."

Light as a pithless nut seemed this little creature in my strong, energetic arms, and yet his mother staggered beneath his weight.

She insisted, however, after a time, on resuming her charge of him, as it was proper she should do, and then sat beside me, delivering herself of a long string of complaints and grievances, after the fashion of all second-rate, solitary people when secure of sympathy.

She overrated my benevolence on this occasion, however. I was lost in painful reverie, and scarcely understood a word of her communication, which I was obliged at last to cut short, for I had resolved, now that my strength was recruited, on the only visible course remaining to me—I would seek Miss Lamarque, confide to her the statement of Christian Garth, relate to her what my eyes had seen, and be guided by her determination and judgment, with those of her brother, a man of sense, I saw, and whose instincts, no doubt, would all be sharpened by the jeopardy of his children.

She was sitting up in her state-room when I knocked at the door, still in her berth, the lower one—from which the upper shelf had been lifted so as to afford her room and air—looking very Oriental and handsomer than I ever had seen her, in her bright Madras night-turban and fine white cambric wrapper richly trimmed.

Her face broke into smiles as soon as she beheld me; and she invited me, in a way not to be resisted, so resolute and yet so kindly was it, to partake with her of the hot coffee her maid was just handing her in bed, in a small gilded cup, a portion of the service on the stand beside her.

"It is our Southern custom, you know, Miss Harz—always our *café noir* before breakfast, as a safeguard against malaria. To be sure, there is nothing of that sort to be apprehended at sea, but still habits are inveterate; second nature, as the moralists and copy-books say, as if there ever could be more than one. What nonsense these wiseacres talk, to be sure! But there is cream, you see, for those who like it—boiled down and bottled for the use of the children before leaving home—one of Dominica's notions;" and here the smiling maid, with her little, respectful courtesy, tendered me a reviving cup of Miss Lamarque's morning beverage, Mocha, made to the last point of perfection, dripped and filtered over a spirit-lamp by Dominica, the skillful and neat-handed.

"But you are very pale to-day, my child—what on earth can be the matter?—There, Dominica, I thought I heard Florry cry! Go and help Caliste get the children ready for a trot upon deck before breakfast, and don't forget to give each one a gill of cream and a biscuit—or, stay, twice as much for the two elder before they go up. It may be some time before they get their regular morning meal.—They have to wait, you know, Miss Harz, which is such rank injustice where children are concerned. Patience never belongs to unreasoning creatures, unless an instinct, as with animals; men have to learn its lessons through the teachings of experience—that strictest of school-masters. Now, you see, I have my lecturing-cap on, and am almost equal to you or Dr. Lardner in my way. But it takes you to define fascination! I suppose Mrs. Heavyside, however, could help you there—for nothing short of witchcraft could account to me for her elopement with that dreary man! To leave her sweet children, too, as if all the men on earth could be worth to a true mother her teething baby's little toe or finger!"

"Would she never stop—never give one loop-hole for doubt to enter?" I thought.

"But what in the world ails you—has Dunmore, the disconsolate, been making love again? Has Captain Falconer declared himself too soon? and do you hesitate, on account of Miss Moore? Don't let that consideration influence you, I beg, for she is the greatest flirt in Savannah, the truest to the vocation, and I like her for that, anyhow. Whatever a man or woman has to do, let him or her do earnestly. That isn't exactly Scripture, but near enough, don't you think so?" and she laughed merrily.

"I have been on deck this morning," I commenced, "Miss Lamarque, and saw Christian Garth, and—"

"He has been terrifying and electrifying you again with his tale of horrors—there, it is all out. Why, he is as sensational as 'Jane Eyre,' this new English novel I am just reading," drawing it from under her pillow and holding it aloft as she spoke. "Currer Bell is not more mysteriously awful, but Garth is not artistic. I detected his intention by the inconsistency of his expression of face, which bore no part in his narrative, and at once exposed him, you must remember—"

"Oh, yes—but this time—"

"Nonsense, Miriam Harz! the iceberg is gone, I know. Why, what a nervous coward you are, to be sure, with all that assumed bravery! I am twice as courageous, I do believe, despite appearances; I really begin to be of opinion that it is safer to be at sea than on land—now what do you think of that for a heterodoxy?—A second cup? why, of course, and a third, if you want it; I am delighted you like it. These little Sèvres toys are but thimbles, but I always carry them about with me by sea and land, and have for years; I feel as if there were luck in them, not one of the original three has been broken—there—there!—just as I was boasting, too!—never mind, such accidents *will* occur; but your pretty pongee dress is sadly stained with the coffee; besides, as *you* dropped the cup, it is *your* luck, not mine; and I want an odd saucer, anyhow, to feed Desirée out of; she sleeps in that willow basket you see in the corner of the state-room, Miss Harz, and is lazy, like her mistress, of mornings.—Desirée! Desirée! peep out, can't you, now you have your long-desired Sèvres saucer to lap milk from?—She won't touch delft, Miss Harz. She is the most fastidious little creature!"

"Alas! alas!" and I groaned aloud.

"Not taking on about that silly cup, I hope—no; what can it be then, a megrim? No. Well, I can't imagine any thing worse, to save my life. Here, let me read you this, it is fine—it is where Jane Eyre feels herself deserted, and this comparison about 'the dried-up channel of a river' thrills one. Just hear it;" and she was about commencing—

"Not now—not now, Miss Lamarque; stern realities demand our attention. Lay your book aside, be calm, be firm, but listen to me seriously. Christian Garth informs me, nor he alone—my own eyes have done the rest—that the cotton in the hold has taken fire from the lightning yesterday; has been slowly smouldering ever since the mast was struck—and that the ship's hours are numbered!"

"O God! O God!" and she bowed her head upon her clasped and quivering hands. "But, Captain Ambrose—he did not tell you so?" looking up suddenly. "Christian Garth, indeed! his impudence is surprising—another hoax, I suppose," and she tried to smile; "such a coarse creature, too!"

"We shall see, but for the present say nothing; only get up and dress as quickly as you can, but it is important to be very quiet, for fear of causing confusion. I have promised discretion."

"Call Dominica, then, for me, Miss Harz," gasping and stretching forth her arms. "I can do nothing for myself—nothing—I am so weak, so helpless. Yet I must believe he is—you are mistaken!"

"I trust it may prove so. But let me assist you; Dominica is best employed making ready the little ones and giving them food—strengthening them for the struggle. She will be nerveless if she knows the truth, and you are not in a condition to conceal it."

"Just as you will, then. My trunk—will you be so kind as to unlock it and give me out the tray—that picture? After that I can get along alone."

I silently did as she desired, and saw her place a covered miniature about her neck before she arose. Very few minutes sufficed this morning for her toilet—usually a tedious and fastidious one—her dress, her bonnet, her shawl, were hastily thrown on, her watch secured with the few jewels lying upon the night-table; the rest of her valuables were with other boxes in the hold, the repository of all unneeded baggage, and these, of course, she could scarcely hope to save in case of fire, even if lives were rescued.

Then, together, we went out, just in time to join the little troop of young children and nurses on their way to the deck. Miss Lamarque did not reply to their tumultuous greeting, but, silently taking the baby Florry, her namesake, in her arms, kissed her many times. I had told her while, she was dressing, of the smoke-wreaths about the base of the broken mast, and she believed in the testimony my eyes had afforded me far more than in the reports of Christian Garth. We did not encounter Mr. Lamarque when we first went on deck; he had gone forward to smoke, some one said; but Captain Ambrose was standing alone, telescope in hand, and to him we addressed ourselves, quietly.

He seemed startled when I disclosed the result of my observation—for I did not choose to commit the pilot—but he did not attempt to deny the truth of the condition of things, and conjured us both to entire quiet and composure, and, if possible, to absolute silence. The safety of five hundred people, he said, depended on our discretion; the ship might not ignite for days, if at all, he thought, so carefully had the air been excluded from the cotton by the process of tight calking, so as to seal it almost hermetically; indeed, the fire might be wholly extinguished by the pumps, which were constantly at work, pouring streams of water around and through the hold; and a panic would be equal to a fire in any case. Such were his calmness and apparent faith in his own words, that they did much to allay Miss Lamarque's fears. My own were little soothed—I never doubted from the beginning what the end would be.

Mr. Lamarque approached us while the conference

with the captain was going on, and, under the seal of secrecy, the condition of affairs was communicated to that gentleman.

I never saw a man so crushed and calm at the same time. His handsome face seemed turned to stone—he scarcely spoke at all, and made no inquiries. I think his mind, like mine, was made up to the worst. Yet he commanded himself so far as to go to the breakfast-table and superintend the meal of his little children, about whom he hung, like a mother-bird who sees the shadow of a hawk above her brood, from that moment until the *dénoûment* of the drama separated us two forever.

Miss Lamarque and I sat down together on a bench, while the host of hungry passengers crowded down to the cabin at the welcome summons of the bell, and I was aware again of the pale widow and her patient child standing near me.

A sudden thought occurred to me. This woman, more than any one among us, needed the strengthening stimulus of good food, and this meal might be her last on shipboard—on earth, perhaps—for a dull, low, ominous sound began to make itself heard to my ear as soon as the murmur of the crowd subsided.

"Trust me with your child again while you go down and eat your breakfast in my place to-day. It is a whim of mine. I have had coffee with this lady in her state-room, and shall not appear at the table. You may bring me a slice of bread, if you choose, when you come back, and one for baby. Do not refuse me this favor."

Much pleased at my attention, as I could see, she went to the grand first table, with its high-heaped salvers of snowy rolls and biscuit, its delicate birds and fowls, its fragrant coffee and tea, so different from the dregs of the humble board at which her second-class ticket alone entitled her to appear; and, to save her from possible humiliation, I wrote a line to the steward; so she feasted, no doubt, in state.

Again I enacted the *rôle* of self-appointed nurse to a creature that looked more like a fairy changeling than a flesh-and-blood creation.

"You are a strange woman, Miriam Harz! At such an hour as this, what matters the quality of food?" said Miss Lamarque, sententiously. "After all, what can that invalid and her child be to you in any case? They are essentially common and mean. You never saw them before, and may never see them again."

"In view of such a catastrophe as that before us, all distinctions fade, Miss Lamarque. This is the last meal any one will take on the ship Kosciusko—she is doomed! The woman might as well get strength for the chance of saving herself and child. I doubt whether any second table will be spread to-day!" I spoke with anguish.

"You cannot believe this! Why, after what the captain said, days may go by before any real danger manifests itself! Ships must pass in the interval—many ships may pass to-day, within a few hours, ready for our relief, if needed; and see, the smoke has ceased to curl about your broken main-mast! That shows convincingly that the fire is being gotten under—extinguished, probably."

"Oh, no! no! no! not with that low, terrible roaring in the hold. The fire is gaining strength, and our agony will soon be over."

I sat with clasped hands and bowed head before her, insensible to her words. I suppose she strove to strengthen me. I think she tried to soothe. Failing in both, she rose and went away, and in her place came Christian

Garth, relieved from the helm, and stood a moment beside me.

"Don't be down-hearted, young gal, an' wait for me. Ef the Lord lets me, I will save you, and the old lady, too; that is, ef she is your aunt or mother or near of kin."

I shook my head drearily.

"You have no hope, then, Mr. Garth?"

"Hope? yes; the best of hope—the Christian's hope. God can do any thing He pleases, we all know, and He may stretch forth his hand when all seems dark; but Captain Ambrose is not one to run a risk of that sort, so he has sent me to work upon a raft—one of two he is making for the seamen if the wust comes to the wust. But you see, I have been on lost ships afore now, an' I know there is no larboard nor starboard rules when men are skeered. So I shall make my raft to hold the womenfolk, for the boats will be for the sailors—mark my word—and them that's wise will wait till the press is over and take the rafts."

"There are little children," I said; "six of them belonging to that lady and Mr. Lamarque. Don't forget them, Mr. Garth, and the poor little widow coming now to claim her baby; this miserable little creature I am holding until she breakfasts. Don't lose sight of these, either, in the crowd, if, indeed, we are obliged to have recourse to your raft."

"Pray rayther that it may float us all to safety," he said, sternly, "for your best chance of being saved will be on that raft, if matters go as I think they will. Trust me, for I will come;" and he passed away just before the little widow came to my side again.

"I came up as soon as I could, to relieve you. I know

how cross baby is when he gets restless, and I was afraid you might tire of him. See! I have brought his bread, and this waiter of tea and toast for you; now you must take a mouthful."

She knew nothing of our danger, it was plain. "Did you leave the other passengers at table?" I asked; "the captain, was he there?"

The question was never answered, for the attention of my interlocutor was riveted now, as was my own, on the companion-way, from which a wild and frightened-looking crowd was densely emerging, with a confused hum of voices that announced their recognition of their impending danger. The change of age, of pain, of woe, seemed sealed upon each aspect, as one by one, and phantom-like, in rapid succession, those who had so lately gone down to feast returned to the upper day, like grim ghosts coming from a church-yard carnival.

It was a sight to stir the stoutest spirit.

At the close of the repast, the captain had announced the truth to his passengers, and followed them now to enjoin them to firmness and efficiency, both so greatly needed at this crisis.

Mounted on the capstan, he addressed them briefly, and not without influence. Such was the power of his simple and manly bearing over these distracted souls, that even the wildest listened with decorum.

This was no immigrant-ship, loaded with stolid or desperate men, insensible of high teachings, and alone desirous of personal safety. Yet the universal instinct asserted itself, and for the time courtesies were set aside, and family affections were all that were regarded.

Miss Lamarque, pale, yet collected, now stood surrounded by the children of her brother, leaning upon his arm while the captain spoke. Husbands and wives were together, sisters and brothers, servants and their masters —each group revealed its several household affinities. We only were alone—the dreary little widow, whose name I never knew, and Miriam Monfort; and on natural principles we clung together.

It is true that Miss Lamarque, by many signs, implored me to come to her, but I would not. It was like intruding on a bed of death, I felt, to break through ties of blood at such a time, by thrusting a foreign presence amid devoted relatives; and I was too proud, or perhaps too selfish, to intrude where I must be secondary, unless I took away another's rights.

The captain had promised, in his brief address, to protect his passengers to the utmost of his power—leaving the result with God. He had entreated them to be calm, and to preserve order—so essential to safety; had mentioned his confidence that a ship must pass before the catastrophe could possibly occur; but added that, to prepare for the worst, he had ordered the construction of two rafts—one for the use of the seamen, the other for the reception of food and necessaries.

His plan was to attach these to the larger boats, and so provide against want; in the certainty, however, that on such a route relief must soon present itself, in the shape of ship or steamer.

He called on all able to abet his exertions to present themselves forthwith, so that universal safety might be insured; not only by making the rafts, but the securing of food upon them, and comforts for the women and children, who represented so large a portion of the passengers. He answered for the fidelity of his seamen with his life. There was not one among them, he knew, who would lift a finger to disobey him. He said these words in conclusion:

"And now, if there is any one present sufficiently imbued with the grace of God to fix the anxious minds of these voyagers in prayer, such at least of them as are powerless otherwise to aid our exertions, let him appear and minister to their tribulation. This task is not for me, although the holiest. My duties call me elsewhere."

So adjured, a man, whose wild, fanatical appearance had given rise to the rumor that the famous "Lorenzo Dow" was on board, sprang on a bulkhead, and commenced to exhort the crowd about him, from which a file of pale, determined-looking men was slowly emerging to join the seamen at the other end of the vessel in their efforts for the public weal. But many lingered, either overcome and paralyzed by the stringency of circumstances, or unequal to exertions from personal causes—aged men, women, and children, chiefly—and to these the frenzied speaker continued to address his words of exhortation and warning.

Such a tirade of terrible objurgation I felt was entirely out of place in a scene like this, and calculated to excite the worst passions of the human mind, instead of persuading it to serenity and submission, so essential now; for to me the captain's last words represented the final grace of the preacher, when, with closed eyes and outspread hands, he dismissed his flock from the temple at the close of the services. From that vessel and all that concerned it we were virtually enfranchised from that moment—dismissed to destruction, so to speak, by fire or flood, or rescue from beyond, as the case might be, to life or death, as God willed—for the ship's mission was accomplished.

I shrank as far as possible from the wild, waving arms, the frenzied eyes, the gaunt and wolfish aspect, the piercing, agonized voice of the fanatic, who had assumed to himself the solemn office of soul-comforter in a time of extremity. I saw from a distance his long, lank figure writhing like a sapling in a storm, as it overtopped the crowd; but his words were lost on my ear, and I sat leaning back against the bulwark with folded hands, absorbed in my own thoughts, when a young girl, bursting from the throng, came and threw herself down before me, and buried her face in my lap, convulsed with sobs. When she looked up, I recognized the young person who had bathed my face in the morning during my partial swoon—a fair and lovely-looking girl of about eighteen years, pallid and ill now with excitement.

"Oh, it is so terrible!" she cried; "I cannot—cannot bear it, and he says we are all hopelessly lost unless we have repented; that there is no death-bed salvation; and this is our death-bed, you know, for the Spanish ship passed us without stopping, and we scarcely hope to see another. O cruel, cruel fiends! to pretend they did not understand our signals, and leave us to destruction."

And she clasped her hands in mute and bitter despair—no actress was ever so impressive.

"We must make up our minds to the worst," I said, as calmly as I could. "Then, if God sees fit to deliver us, we shall be all the more thankful. You must not believe what this ignorant and panic-stricken man tells you. Think of the thief on the cross whom Christ pardoned in dying."

"Then you hope to be permitted to see God! You dare to hope this?" she asked, gazing into my very eyes, so closely did she come to me.

"Oh, surely in his own good time! I have done nothing so very wicked, I hope, as to exclude me from my Father's face forever—have you? Now, don't be frightened; speak calmly."

"I don't know—I don't know. I should be afraid not to call myself desperately wicked at such a time; he says we all are, you know. We are all miserable sinners."

"It is very abject to talk and feel thus, and I don't believe that God approves of it," I said, indignantly. "He gives us self-respect, and commands us to cherish it. Such abasement is unworthy of Christian souls. It is very bitter to die, as young as we are; but, if we have done our best to serve Him, we need—we ought not to be afraid to meet our God."

She clung to my outstretched hand. She strengthened my spirit by the fullness of her need. The feeble widow with her child, too, crept close to me, weeping and trembling.

"Do not leave me," she entreated; "let us stay together to the very last."

"Nay, that may be a long time," I answered, smiling feebly, and nerved for the first time to encouragement; "for the captain will do his best to save his passengers—the women especially, I cannot doubt; and see what bounteous provision he is making for their support!"

And I pointed to the piles of flour and sugar barrels, the boxes of crackers and of hams, of figs and raisins, the hampers of wine and ale, which were profusely piled on the quarter-deck ready for lowering to the rafts.

"He means to take care of us, you see, by the permission of Providence," I said, almost strengthened by this dependence, "and we will remain calmly together, and drink whatever cup God offers us—humbly, I hope." Yet, even as I spoke, my heart rebelled against the fiat of my fate, and the young life within me rose up in fierce conflict with its doom.

At this moment of bitter strife of heart, Mr. Dunmore, the youthful poet of whom I have already spoken, stood before me.

"I have found you at last," he said, "deputed as I am to do so by Miss Lamarque. It is a point of honor with her to care for you personally in this crisis. You know Major Favraud placed you under her care; besides that, her regard for you impels this request. She bids me say—"

I interrupted him hastily.

"This is no time for ceremonials, truly, Mr. Dunmore; yet, had family concurrence been perfect, it seems to me that her brother might have undertaken this mission. I have no wish to thrust myself undesired into any household circle at such a crisis."

"He is wholly absorbed with his children."

"As he ought to be, Mr. Dunmore, and, when the time of peril comes, it is of their needs alone that he will and must think. I am alone in this vessel, as I shall remain. I did not leave Savannah under Miss Lamarque's care. She is very generous, very considerate, but I will not embarrass her motions, nor yours, nor any one's. It is the duty of Captain Ambrose to see to the welfare of his female passengers. I shall not be forgotten among these—"

He stood before me with his knightly head uncovered, his handsome face as calm as though he were a guest at a festival instead of a patient and interested watcher at a funeral-pyre. His birth, his breeding, his genius even, asserted themselves in that mortal hour. He was calm, collected, serious, but not afraid.

"The peril will be great to all, of course," he said, quietly, "but no gentleman will prefer his own safety to that of the most humble and desolate woman on the ship. To you, Miss Harz, I devote my energies to-day, to you and these ladies of your party, whoever they may be—," bowing gently as he spoke. "I may fail in delivering you from danger, but it shall not be for want of effort on my part. Believe my words, I have less care for life than most people, and now let me offer you my escort through that maddened crowd (the rest may follow closely), to reach Miss Lamarque."

"No, Mr. Dunmore, I *must* remain just where I am, I have promised myself to do so; this is much; and these unhappy women—they, like myself, are alone, or seem to be. Should you see fit to do so, and be willing to be so encumbered, you can return after a lapse of time; but make no point of this, I entreat you. I think that Captain Ambrose will observe good order and save his helpless ones first. You know he promised this—"

There was a moment's pause, and movement of eye and hand, and then he spoke again, very softly:

"Yes, and much more that can never be fulfilled, for already the cabin is in flames, the companion-way is closed, and the fire in the hold is making fearful headway. I have heard the seamen have sworn to secure the boats; you are strong and resolute—be prepared for the very worst." Then, speaking in his usual tone, he added: "Since the banner of Spain passed near enough to show us the rampant lions and castles on its crimson shield, and yet made no sign, I have had little hope of rescue from a ship. It was ominous!"

"Not intended, then," I said, eagerly. "Oh, I am glad of this, at least, for the honor of human nature."

"A strange consideration at such a time! You are a study to me, Miss Harz; yours is not apathy, like mine, but true courage, even in this death-struggle, and I will save you if I can, for you have a noble soul!"

All further dialogue was cut short by the wild shout that rose from the crowd, the delusive cry of "A sail, a sail!" and Dunmore rushed with the rest to descry its myth-like form, if possible. It was some moments before hope again died down to a flat level of despair.

Too remote for signal or trumpet was that distant, white-winged vessel gliding securely on its path of peace, unconscious of the extremity of the mighty steamer it distinguished dimly, no doubt, by the aid of telescopes.

However this might have been, for the second time on that day of direst exigency, a ship went by, observed yet unobserving.

Fainter and fainter grew the accents of the fierce, fanatical preacher; his excitement forsook him as the danger became more and more imminent.

The crowd broke into groups. Pale, stern men, with rigid features, who had been employed aiding in the construction of the rafts, returned now to the sides of their wives and children.

Through a vista on the deck I discerned Miss Lamarque, sitting quietly with her youngest nursling in her arms, beside her brother. His children and slaves were gathered around her knees. Dunmore was giving her my message, I could not doubt, from the glances she cast in my direction, as he stood near by. I knew that he would soon turn to come again, but my resolution was fixed.

Captain Ambrose, with a face grown old in half a day,

gray, abstracted, wretched, passed and repassed me several times, telescope in hand.

Ralph Maxwell on the round-house kept constant watch, his attitude dauntless, his face uplifted and keen, field-glass in hand. His West-Point training stood him in good stead now. Captain Falconer, a naval officer, had returned to the side of Miss Oscanyan, the woman he had loved hopelessly for years, and, before the scene closed between us forever, I saw him clasp her to his bosom; so that trying hour had for some high spirits its crowning consolations, its solace and reward, and, whatever else was in store, the martyrdom of love was over.

An eager hand caught my shawl. "He is coming back, coming to persuade you to leave us," said the young girl; "but you have promised not to part from us, and I feel that God will remember us if we remain together firm and fast, we three."

Then the pale widow spoke in turn: "Let me stay beside you too," she entreated; "it makes me feel stronger, I am so desolate—" and she bowed her head and wept.

I would have said in the strange, calm bitterness that possessed my soul: "What value has life to you and your deformed one? Poor, widowed, sickly, and despised, why should you wish to live? Why encumber me?"

But thoughts like these were not for human utterance now, and we sat together, hand locked in hand for a time, waiting for the end, as men may wait in years to come, when the earth is gray with sin, for the coming of the fiery comet that they know is destined to consume them.

For was not this ship our world, penned in as we were on every side, and separated from all else by an ocean inexorable and illimitable as space, and were not we likewise looking forward to a fiery doom—our finite, perhaps final, day of judgment?

I could understand then, for the first time, how condemned criminals feel—well, strong, yet dying! I knew how Walter La Vigne, the self-doomed, had felt, and some passages of Madame Roland's appeal rose visibly before me, as if written on the air rather than in my memory. I had read the book at Beauseincourt, and it had powerfully impressed me; and this, I remember, was the passage that swept across my brain:

"And thou whom I dare not name, wouldst thou mourn to see me preceding thee to a place where we can love one another without wrong—where nothing will prevent our union—where all pernicious prejudices, all arbitrary exclusions, all hateful passions, and all tyranny, are silent? I shall wait for thee, then, and rest!"

So centred were my dying thoughts on Wentworth—so calmly did I await the great change that men call sudden death!

All this time—a time much briefer than that I have taken in recounting my sensations—the glorious summer's sun, the sun of morning, was bathing the sea; the ship, with beauty, and a soft, fresh breeze, was fanning every pallid brow with a caressing, silken wing, that seemed to mock its wretchedness.

I thought not once of Christian Garth. I had ceased to strain my eyes for a distant sail, to seek to compromise with my fate or make conditions with my Creator. Dunmore was forgotten. I was composed to die—not resigned. These things are different; a bitter patience possessed me that I felt would sustain me to the end, but I was not satisfied that my doom was just or opportune.

"Farewell, sweet, young, vigorous life!" I moaned

aloud. "Farewell, Miriam! It will not be thou, but a phantom, that shall arise from dead ashes! Farewell, dear hand, that hast served me long and well!" and I kissed my own right hand. I had not known until that moment how truly I loved myself. "Sister, lover, farewell! Mother, father, receive me! Gentle Constance, reach forth thy guiding hand and lead me to my parents! Wentworth, remember me! Saviour, my soul is thine!"

I bowed my head. I had no more to say. Unwilling I was to die—afraid I was not; for, as I sat there, my whole life swept before me, as it is said to do before the eyes of the drowning, and rapidly as one may sweep the gamut on a piano with one introverted finger, and I saw myself as though I had been another. I had done nothing to make me afraid to meet my God; so, with closed eyes, I lingered in the shadow, conscious of nothing save exceeding calm, when the grasp of my gentle friend of the moment aroused me to a sense of what was occurring, and I saw, with horror indescribable, the fierce flames leaping from the deck, heard the hoarse shouts, beheld the lurid surging of an agonized and despairing multitude! But above all rang the clear, trumpet-tones of Captain Ambrose, soon to sink in death:

"To the boats—to the boats! but save the women first—the children—as ye are Christian men! So help ye, mighty God!"

I heard later how signally this noble charge was disregarded; how utterly self triumphed over generosity and duty; and how, in enforcing the example all should have followed, Captain Ambrose lost his valiant, valuable life. But this was thought nothing of then, and I sat patiently down to perish!

## CHAPTER IV.

It was sunset when I first felt able to sit up beneath the awning of sails which provident hands had stretched above the central platform reserved for the occupancy of the women and children, spread thick with mattresses on the raft, and look about me understandingly.

We were riding smoothly over the long, low, level billows of that summer sea, sustained beyond their reach on what seemed a rude barn-floor, composed as this was of the masts, booms, and yards, roughly lashed together by tarred ropes, no longer needed on the destined ship, and which had been assigned by the captain for that purpose to Christian Garth.

A mast was erected in the front of this hastily-constructed raft, on three sides of which were breastworks, with strong, loose ropes attached, so that those who clung to this refuge might support themselves with comparative safety, or rather have a chance for life, when our "floating grave" should hang suspended perpendicularly on the steep side of a mountain-billow, or drift beneath it.

Just below, and surrounding the small, elevated platform on which I found myself when I revived, stretched on a slender mattress by the side of my feeble widow and her moaning child, were rows of barrels, firmly fastened by cleats, so as insure, to some degree, not only the preservation of our food and water, but to form a sort of bulwark of protection for those who occupied the central portion of the raft.

The young girl, of whom I have spoken as having attached herself to me during the last moments of my stay on shipboard, and an old negro woman, whose crooning hymns made a strange accompaniment to the dashing waters, and whose stolid tranquillity seemed to reproach my anguish, were our only companions on the sort of dais assigned to his female passengers by Christian Garth.

The man himself, to whom we owed our deliverance, stood near his primitive mast, trimming his sail carefully, and looking out with his far-reaching, sagacious ken over the waste of waters, into which the blood-red, full-orbed sun seemed dipping, suddenly, as for his night-bath.

A few of the common passengers of the Kosciusko, and a knot of the seamen, comprising not more than twenty souls, composed the groups, scattered about the roughly yet securely lashed raft, silent and observant all, as men who face their doom are apt to be.

I looked in vain for one familiar face, and for a moment regretted that I had been withheld, as by some spell, for whose weird influence I could never sufficiently account, from having cast my destiny with theirs, who were so much nearer to me in station and congeniality of spirit than those around me. With Miss Lamarque's hand locked in mine, I should have vied with her, I felt, in cheerful courage; and the knightly calmness of Dunmore might have sustained my drooping, fainting soul. These were my peers, and, *with* them, I should have been better content to be tried.

But the white squall, which had in no way affected us (so small and partial was the sphere of its influence), had sufficed to separate ours irretrievably from our companion-raft, and the squadron of boats that had promised not to forsake us. And now the eye of agony was strained in vain over the weltering waste, for a vestige of those refugees from the Kosciusko—buried, perhaps, a thousand fathoms deep, by their sudden visitors, beneath the waves of that deadly Atlantic sea.

Tears rained over my face as I thought of this probability, and, hopeless as I was of rescue, the almost certain fate of my companion-voyagers fell over me like a pall. "Better, perhaps—far better had it been"—I thought so then—"had we all perished together in that terrific sheet of flame that rose up like a dividing barrier between us at the last. Fit emblem of the final day of doom. Our trials were but begun. What more remained? God in heaven only knew!"

And rapidly, and in panoramic succession, all the fearful adventures of raft and boat that I had ever read of, or heard related, passed across my mind, ending with that latest, and perhaps the most fearful of all—the wreck of the Medusa!

The night came down serene and beautiful. As the sun disappeared in ocean, up rose the full-orbed moon—crimson and magnified by surrounding vapors—that to the practised eye portended future tempest, calm as the ocean and the heavens then seemed.

The constellations, singularly distinct and splendid, had the power to fix and fascinate my vision—never felt before—as they shone above me, clear and crystalline as enthroned in space—judges, and spectators, cold and pitiless as it seemed to me, in the strangeness and forlornness of my condition—Arcturus, and the Ursas, great and little, and Lyra, and the Corona Borealis, Berenice, and Hydra, and Cassiopea's chair; these and many more. I marked them all with a calm scrutiny that belongs to terror in some phases. The stars seemed mocking eyes that night—smiling and safe in heaven—the moon, a cold and cruel enemy with her vapory train, so grandly sailing across the cloudless heaven—so careless of our fate—the wreck of a ruined world as many deem her—veiling in light her inward desolation.

A faint and vapory comet lurked on the horizon—like a ghastly messenger—scarcely discernible to the human eyes, yet vaguely ominous and suggestive—a spirit-ship it might be—watching in silence to bear away the souls of those lost at sea!

There was deep stillness—unbroken, save by the lapping and plashing waters. Even the crooning hymns of the old negro woman had died away; and the moans of the suffering child, and the sobs of the weary mother, and the eager exclamations of Ada Greene (for such I learned was the name of my young companion), were, for a season, lost alike in sleep.

Food had been distributed—prayer had been offered—all seemed favorable so far to our preservation. We were on the track of voyage—the pathway of ships—and the sea was tranquil as a summer lake; up to this point, the arm of God had been extended over us almost visibly. Would He forsake us now? I questioned thus, and yet I could not, dare not, hope as others hoped!

The morning came; I woke, aroused by Salva's song, from troubled sleep; and, as I rose to a sitting posture, a troop of sea-birds that had been swooping overhead, fled with a fiend-like screaming.

The mother and child were already consuming their scant allowance of food. Ada Greene was standing self-poised, swaying like a slender reed with the motion of the raft, so as never to lose her balance, like a young acrobat, with her folded arms, her floating hair, and fair Aurora face, uplifted to the day.

Over the raft were scattered groups of men taking their morning meal; but, as before, the stalwart form of Christian Garth was at the helm, or rather, mast and rudder merged in one, which he controlled with calm, sagacious power.

"Is there a ship in the distance, that you gaze so earnestly?" I asked of the young girl as I put back my hair that had clustered thickly over my face in my uneasy slumber, and followed eagerly the direction of her eyes.

"Oh! no; only a school of dolphins; but it is so pretty! Some came quite near just now; the men were harpooning them; but if we had them we could not cook them, you know, on this miserable contrivance."

"One we should be very grateful for, Ada, since it is all that lies between us and destruction!" I answered, sorrowfully, for the levity of her spirit grieved and shocked me.

"I don't know about that; I think we might as well have gone down at once as stay here, and be roasted and starved. How hot it is to-day! What would I not give for a good glass of ice-water! Don't look so shocked; we shall be saved, of course. I am not the least afraid about that, for Mr. Garth says we *must* see a ship before evening. Don't you mark the flag flying at the mast-head? He brought it on board on purpose, so that they might not mistake our country (the packets, I mean), and give us the go-by as that Spanish vessel did! But they do say that was a pirate; and that, instead of sitting on a plank, we should have been walking a plank by this time, had they rescued us. I'm rather glad they didn't, though, after all—things couldn't be much worse than they are, could they, now?—There, I came very near falling, I declare!"

The moans of the sick woman at my side became almost constant toward noon; and she was obliged to surrender her infant wholly to my charge, for the hæmorrhage of the day before had returned, and she was fast drifting into unconsciousness. "Water, water!" was the only intelligible cry that left her lips, and that we had to give was warm and brackish, from the occasional lapping of the sea against the barrels, into which it oozed insensibly.

The sun shone down hot and brazen, from the lurid heavens, covered with filmy clouds, so equally overspreading it that a thin, gray veil seemed to interpose between us and its scorching rays, scarcely tempering them by its diaphanous medium.

Beneath it lay the sea, like a copper shield, smooth and glowing, seething like a boiling caldron, with its level foam, for the long, low-rolling billows lifted themselves but lazily from Ocean's breast, and assumed no distinctness of form or motion. Not the faintest breeze came to relieve the stifling closeness of the atmosphere, or lift the collapsed sail, or furled flag, that clung around our mast. The air shimmered visibly around us, as though undergoing some transformation from the heat, some culinary process, through which it was to be rendered unfit for human lips to breathe. Birds flew low and heavily around the raft, as though their wings met such resistance as fish find in water, alighting occasionally to pick up languidly morsels of rejected food.

Still the old negro's crooning hymns went on, recommenced with morning light. To my sad heart, the refrain bore a mournful significance:

> "In the land of the New Jerusalem
> There shall be no more sea."

She sat, a wrinkled hag, with a leering, repulsive face, with her feet planted firmly on her mattress, her knees elevated, her long, ape-like arms closely embracing these —her fingers, strung with brass and silver rings, intertwined with snake-like flexibility.

On her head was the inevitable bright-colored handkerchief, the badge of her race, or rather of her condition in those days, and she wore the decent, blue-cotton frock, which marked her for a plantation-negro. Large hoops were in her flat, enormous ears, that seemed to suspend her shoulders as they touched them, drawn up and narrowed as these were, even beyond their natural hideousness, by her attitude, one which she maintained as stolidly as a dervish.

"You must help us," I said, at last, when the crisis came, and affairs waxed desperate. "You must take the child, at least, and care for him. See, it requires two persons to sustain his dying mother—one to wet her lips, one—"

"'Deed, honey," she interrupted, coolly, "you must 'scuse me dis oncst; I has jus' as much to do as I kin posomply 'complish, in keepin' of myself dry, comfable, and singin' ob my hyme-toones. We has all to take our chances dis time, an' do for our own selves, black and white; an' I don't see none ob my own white folks on dis raf', wich I is mighty proud of. Dar, now! I does b'leve dat is a ship sail way off dar. Does you see it, honey?"

And she pointed to a large white gull, skimming the

main at some distance. Disgusted with her selfishness, I vouchsafed her no further notice at the time, and her crooning went on during the whole period of the bitter death-struggle of that poor sufferer, whose name I never knew, but whose little, deformed waif, the orphan of the raft, remained my heritage.

"You will take care of him," she had said to me, in her last conscious moments, "my baby-boy, my little—" the name died on her lips, and she never spoke again.

When she was dead, Christian Garth caused her to be wrapped in sail-cloth, weighted with chains, and, with a brief prayer, consigned to the deep. His superstitious sailor's fears rebelled against the idea of keeping a corpse on board one moment longer than necessary, so the rites of sepulture were speedily accomplished.

When I remonstrated, feebly enough it is true, for exhaustion was supervening on long-sustained effort, at his haste, which, even under the circumstances, seemed to me indecent, he coolly spoke of it as a measure essential to the good of all.

Talismanic as were these words on such occasion, mine were the lips that murmured the brief prayer, a portion of the solemn Episcopal grave-service that I chanced to remember, above the poor, pale corpse, even while my weary arms inclosed the struggling child, who, understanding nothing of the truth, would fain have plunged after his mother into depths unknown.

A low, long roll of thunder smote on the ear, like a message to the ocean, from the heavens above, as we saw the waters close greedily over the form of our dead passenger. The men who had launched the body from the raft looked up and listened fearfully, and Christian Garth hastened to trim his sail.

It was sunset now, and the clouds gathered so rapidly about the sun, that he sank empalled in purple to his watery bed, leaving no trace behind to mark his faded splendor.

A sudden breeze sprang up, infinitely refreshing at first to soul and sense, and again the thunder lumbered and crashed about us. The billows heaved and leaped like steeds just freed from harness, tossing their white manes; the raft shuddered and reeled with a deadly, sickly motion, like a creature in strong throes, plunging with frantic suddenness into the troughs of the waves at one moment, as if impelled by fear, then rallying to their summits, only to cast itself wildly down again.

All was confusion, dire and terrible. Then burst the storm upon us—rain, wind!

I was conscious of clutching, with one hand, a rope which strained and swayed desperately, while with the other I grasped the affrighted baby to my breast.

Ada Greene and the old negro woman clung together, hanging to the same cord of safety, flung to them, to all of us, by the hand of Christian Garth.

The barrels strained and groaned, and broke from their fastenings; the awning was wrenched from its mooring, and swept away; the bitter brine broke over us and choked our cries; the anguish of death was upon us without its submission. We struggled instinctively to breathe, to live; we grappled desperately with circumstances; we fought against our doom.

Suddenly the sea dropped to rest—the storm was spent; a low, sighing, soughing gale swept around our nucleus of despair, and the surging of the sea was like a bitter funeral-wail. The air grew cold and chill; one vast, pall-like cloud enveloped the whole face of the unpitying heavens, that seemed literally "to press down upon our very faces like a roof of black marble."

No moon, no stars, were visible; we had no light of any kind, nor could we ascertain the damage done until the cold, gray morning broke in gloom and rain upon us. Then it was made plain to us that our food had all been swept overboard—together with six seamen and five of the passengers. There remained on the raft only three shuddering women and a little child—and a handful of weary and discouraged men, sustained and led to a sense of duty by the dauntless master-spirit of one alone—the presence of Christian Garth, indomitable through all hardships. So it had fared with us for six-and-thirty hours of our experience on "our floating grave."

We had been washed from our little platform, which ordinarily lifted us above the lapping of the sea during the prevalence of the storm—and we regained it now, glad to repose even on the sea-soaked mattresses bereft of awning. By the mercy of God some glutinous sea-zoophytes had been tangled among them, and by the help of the brine-soaked biscuit in my pocket (crammed there, it may be remembered, as a precious hoard for a time of dire necessity, on the morning of the fire, by the small, cunning fingers of the sickly child), we breakfasted, or rather broke our fast—we four, the child, the negress, Ada Greene, and I—and life was aroused again in every breast by means of a briny morsel.

"A cup of coffee would not be amiss just now," said the girl, laughing, "but the Lord knows we can wait."

There was a strange, bright light in the eyes of the young girl as she spoke these words, and she was arraying her hair coquettishly with some bunches of sea-weed, which had been cast up by the storm, and from which the eager, famishing lips of the little boy had been permitted to suck the gluten before discarding the skeleton stems.

That hair was in itself a grace and glory—rippling from crown to waist in sheeny, golden splendor, fine as silk, and glossy as the yellow floss threads of pale, ripe Indian-corn—beautiful, even in its dishevelled and drenched condition, as an artist's dream. Devoid as it was of regular beauty, the face beneath, with its clear blue eyes, red lips, and pure complexion, the pink and white that reminds one of a sweet-pea or ocean-shell, had struck me as very lovely from the first; nothing to support this groundwork of excellence had I discovered, however, either in the form of the head, which was ignoble, or the expression of the face, which was both timid and defiant, or the tones of the voice, which were shrill and harsh by turns—yet, as my fellow-voyager and sufferer, I was interested in this young creature, not forgetting, either, her attention during my pending swoon, of which mention has been made.

"I am going to the party, whatever the preacher may say, and whether Captain Ambrose wills it or no. I am under his care and protection, you see, to go to New York to my aunt, Madame Du Vert, the famous milliner, and I am to learn her trade. Her name is Greene, so they call her Du Vert, to make out that she is French—*vert* is *green*, in French, you see; or so they tell me. Now, Captain Ambrose is a church-member, too, and he does not want dancing on his ship, and so he made the calkers pitch the deck—that was to break up the ball, you know; but don't tell any one this for the 'land's sake,'" drawing near to me and whispering strangely, with her forefinger raised—"or all those proud Southern people would pitch into me—pitch, you understand?" and she laughed merrily—"their white satin slippers and all!"

"You must not talk so, Ada;" and I took her hand, which was burning.

"Why not? Who are you, to prevent me? I am as good as you any day—or Miss Lamarque either, or any of those haughty ones—though my father was a negro-trader. Well, whose business was that but God's? If He don't care, who need care?—An't I right, old mammy?" appealing to the ancient negress, who had suspended her croon to listen.

"Yes, indeed—that you is, honey; right to upholden your own dad—nebber min' what he did to serbe the debble. But you looks mighty strange, chile, outen your eyes. Wat dat you sees ober dar—is it a ship, gal?—or must we—" and her voice sank to a mutter—"must we fall back on dis picaninny, to keep from starvation?—"

I understood her dreadful suggestion even before the words fully left her cannibal lips, exposing her yellow fangs; from the glance of her cruel eye in the direction of the child, and the working of her long, crooked talons, rather than fingers, writhed like knotted serpents; I understood them with an instinct that made me clutch him closely to my breast, and narrowly watch his enemy from that hour until the time when my brain failed and my eyes closed in unconsciousness, and with the determination to plunge with him into the sea rather than devote him to such a fate or yield to such an alternative as this wretch in human form had more than hinted—even should the animal instinct, underlying every nature, presume to dictate to reason at the last!

We could but die—that was the very worst that Fate had in store for us—*but* die in the body! How infinitely worse that the soul should perish through the selfish sensuousness of cannibalism, which would degrade life itself below dissolution, even if preserved by such means!

"I am ready now to go to Captain Ambrose for assistance," said Ada Greene, poising herself before me, and having surrendered or forgotten her first idea, evidently, in the new mania of the moment. "Of course, he does not intend to leave us here to perish, and he is in the next cabin—but a step; see how easily I can get to him, and I shall be back before you can say 'Presto!'"

As nimbly as a sea-gull runs upon the sand, the young creature flew across the now level raft toward the sea, but a strong hand clutched her as she was about to step overboard, and compelled her back to her place on the platform, where, bound with cords, she lay raving, until sleep or unconsciousness mercifully supervened to spare me the spectacle of her agony, which no human power could alleviate.

Hours passed before this "consummation devoutly to be wished" took effect, and, at the end of that time, my reeling brain, my fainting energies, warned me that I, too, was probably approaching some dreadful crisis. With a view to the refreshment its waters could possibly afford my head, I crept quietly from the platform on which the old negro woman held enforced guard over the insensible form of Ada Greene, and, still clasping the poor helpless one, so mysteriously thrust upon my tender mercies, to my bosom, I gained the edge of the raft, unnoticed by Christian Garth, who might otherwise have apprehended me in turn, and borne me back to my allotted precincts, and hung above the ocean, so as to suffer its cooling spray to fall unceasingly across my burning forehead.

From some instinctive prompting I had lashed the poor, frail baby to my girdle with the scarf of knotted silk I wore about my neck, and, wan and exhausted, he lay upon my shoulder tranquilly as any Indian papoose might do on its mother's breast. A branch of sea-weed floated past as I looked down—some gracious mermaid's gift, perhaps, extended by her invisible fingers to greet our famishing lips—and I caught it eagerly, dividing the welcome nutriment with the perishing child, now patient from weakness and instinctive consciousness, perhaps, of the entire uselessness of cries and tears.

Whether the weed was a sort of ocean-hasheesh, or wholesome aliment, I never knew, but certain it is that, from the moment its juices passed my lips, a strange and delightful quietude stole over my weary senses, fast lapsing, as these had seemed, into unconsciousness when I left my place to seek the ocean's brink.

The rays of the declining sun seemed for a moment centred on one spot, immediately before my impending face, supported as this was on one hand, and my sight followed their lance-like rays to the very floor of ocean!

As the waters of the Red Sea divided for the passage of Moses and the Israelites, so seemed these to part for my mental eyes, sundered as they were by a golden sword of infinite splendor.

That power which neither pain nor peril can subdue had possession of me now, and, above all, the bitter circumstances that surrounded me, and, in the face of danger and of death, imagination asserted her supremacy. My dream was not of passing ship or harbor gained, or rich repast, or festival, or clustered grapes and sparkling wines, like other sufferers from shipwreck, fevered with famine, frenzied with despair; but hasheesh or opium never bestowed so fair, so strange a vision as that which, in my extremity, was mercifully accorded to me.

My eyes pursued the sea-shaft to its base, as a telescope conducts the mortal gaze to revel in the stars. Merman and mermaid, nereid and triton, were there, rejoicing in the sunbeams thus poured upon them through this subtle conduit of ocean, as do the motes of summer in her rays; but soon these disappeared, a motley crowd, confused and joyous, leaving the vision free to pierce the depths, glowing with golden light, in search of still greater marvels.

Then I saw outspread before me the streets, the fanes, the towers, the dwellings, of a vast, deserted city, one of those, I could not doubt, that had existed before the flood, and which had lain submerged for thousands of centuries; the fretwork of the coral-insect was over all (that worker against time, so slow, so certain), in one monotonous web of solid snow.

Statues of colossal size, and arches of Titanic strength and power, adorned the portals, the pass-ways, the temples of this metropolis of ocean, guarded as were these last by the effigies of griffin and dragon, and winged elephant and lion, and stately mastodon and monstrous ichthyosaurus, all white as gleaming spar.

Gods and demi-gods of gigantic proportions and majestic aspect were carved on the external walls of the windowless abodes and fanes; and, from the yawning portal of one of these, a temple vast as Dendera's self, came forth, fold after fold, even as I seemed to gaze, the monstrous sea-serpent of which mariners dream, more huge, more loathly, than fancy or experience ever yet portrayed him. I still behold in memory the stately, fearful head, with its eyes of emerald fire and sweeping, sea-green mane, as it reared its neck for a moment as if to scale the ladder the sunbeams had thrown down when first emerging from its temple-cavern ; and, later, the mottled, monstrous body, as coil after coil was gradually unwound, until it seemed at last to lie in all its loathsome length for roods along the silent, shell-paved streets—the scaly monarch of that scene of human desolation !

I recall the feeling of security that upheld me to look and to observe every motion of the reptile of my dream.

" He cannot come to me here," I thought. " The ark is sacred, and God's hand is over it ; besides, I hear the singing of the priests, and the dove is about to be cast forth ! Will the raven never come back ? Oh, the sweet olive-branch ! It falls so lightly ! We are nearing the mountain now, and we shall soon cast anchor ! "

Then, among choral chants of joy and thanksgiving, I seemed to sleep. How long this slumber lasted, or whether it came at all, I never knew. It is a loving and tender thing in our Creator to decree to us this curtain of unconsciousness when nerve and strength would otherwise give way beneath the intensity of suffering—a holy and gentle thing for which we are not half thankful enough in our estimate of blessings.

My sleep, or swoon, shielded me from long hours of agony, mental and physical, that must have become unendurable ere the close. As it was, I knew no more after the sea-shaft closed with its wondrous and mysterious revelations (which I yet recall with marveling and admiration, as we are wont to do a pageant of the past), until aroused from lethargy by the hand and voice of Christian Garth.

It was night. I saw the glimmer of the moonlight on the seas, a tranquil, balmy night; but some dark object was interposed between me and the stars which, I knew, were shining above, and the raft lay motionless upon the waters. I was aware, when my senses returned temporarily, that the bow of a mighty vessel was projected above our frail place of refuge, and that we were saved. The dove had come at last!

When or how we were lifted to the deck of the ship I knew not, for, having partially revived, I soon drifted away again into profound lethargy and entire unconsciousness, which for a time seemed death.

## CHAPTER V.

A WOMAN sat sewing near my berth in the state-room in which I found myself; a fan, lying on a small table at her side, betokened in what manner she had divided her attentions—between her needle and her helpless charge. I thought, indeed, that I had felt its soft plumes glide gently across my face in the very moment of my awakening, in the first amazement of which I but dimly comprehended the circumstances that surrounded me.

"What brought this stranger to my pillow? Who and what was she? Where was I?" These were my mental queries at the first. Then, as the truth gradually dawned over my sluggish and bewildered brain, I lay quietly revolving matters, and noticed my self-constituted nurse, and my surroundings, with the close yet careless observation of a child.

The woman, on whom my gaze was earliest fixed (while her own seemed riveted on the work upon her knee), was of middle age or beyond it, of medium size, of square and sturdy make, and homely to the very verge of ugliness. She was dressed plainly, if not commonly, in black, but there was a general air of decency about her that seemed to place her beyond the sphere of servitude. She wore spectacles set in tortoise-shell frames, and she wore her iron-gray hair straight back behind small, funnel-shaped ears, and gathered into the tightest knot behind. Her head was flat and narrow at the summit, though broad at and above the base of the brain. Her forehead, wide yet low, was ignoble in expression. The mouth, shaped like a horseshoe, was curved down at the corners, and was full of sullen resolution. The nose, pinched, yet not pointed, showed scarcely any nostril, and might as well have been made of wood, for any meaning it betrayed. Her eyebrows were short, wide, rugged, and irregular, though very black; the cast-down eyes, of course, so far inscrutable.

She was shaping a flimsy, black-silk dress, and doing it deftly, though it was a marvel to me how hands so stiff and cramped as hers appeared to be could handle a needle at all.

On one of these gnarled and unlovely fingers she wore a ring which, in the idleness of the mood that possessed me, I examined listlessly. It was an old-fashioned and slender circle of gold, so pale that it looked silvery, such as in times long past had commonly been used either for troth-plight or marriage-vows, surmounted by two small united hearts of the same dull metal by way of ornament. Mrs. Austin, I remembered, possessed one, the aversion of my childhood, that seemed its counterpart.

My weary eyes wandered from her at last, to take in the accessories of my chamber, tiny as this was, and I saw that against the wall were hanging a gentleman's great-coat and hand-satchel. Cigars and books were piled on the same table which held the spool and scissors of my companion, and a pair of cloth slippers, embroidered with colored chenilles and quilted lining, of masculine size and shape, reposed upon the floor. A cane and umbrella were secured neatly in a small corner rack. There were no traces, I saw, of feminine occupancy beyond the transient implements of industry alluded to.

Suddenly, in their languid, listless roving, my eyes encountered those of my attendant fixed full upon me, while a smile distorted the homely, sallow face, disclosing a set of yellow teeth, sound, short, and strong, like regular grains of corn.

In those eyes, in that mouth and saffron teeth, lay the whole power and character of this repulsive and disagreeable physiognomy.

Those feline orbs of mingled gray and green, with their small, pointed pupils, were keen, vigilant, and observing beyond all eyes it had ever before or since been my lot to encounter. After meeting their penetrating glance I was not surprised to hear their possessor accost me in clear, metallic tones, that seemed only the result of her gift of insight, and consistent with it.

"You are awake and yourself again, young lady, I am glad to see! You have slept very quietly for the last few hours, and your fever is wellnigh broken. Will you have some food now? You need it; you must be weak."

"Yes, very weak; but not hungry at all. I do not want to eat. Just let me lie quietly awhile. It is such enjoyment."

She complied silently and judiciously with my request.

After a satisfactory pause, during which I had gradually collected my ideas, I inquired, suddenly:

"How long is it since we were lifted from the raft, and where are the other survivors?"

"All safe, I believe, and on board, well cared for, like yourself. It has been nearly two days since your raft was overhauled. This was what the captain called it," and she smiled.

"The baby—where is he? I hope he lived."

"Yes, he is at last out of danger, and we have obtained a nurse for him. He would only trouble you now; but it is very natural you should be anxious about him."

"Yes, he was my principal care on the raft, and I do not wish to lose sight of him. When I am better, you must let him share my room until we reach our friends."

"Oh, certainly!" and again she smiled her evil smile. "No one, so far as I know of, has any right or wish to separate you; but, for the present, you are better alone."

"Yes, I am strangely weak—confused, even," and I passed my hand over my blistered face and dishevelled hair with something of the feeling of the little woman in the story who doubted her own identity. Alas! there was not even a familar dog to bark and determine the vexed question, "Is this I?"

Helpless as an infant, flaccid as the sea-weed when taken from its native element, feeble in mind from recent suffering, broken in body, I was cast on the mercies of strangers, ignorant, until they saw me, of my existence, yet not indifferent to it, as their care testified.

"You will take some food now," said the woman, kindly. "Your weakness is not unfavorable, since it proves the fierce fever broken; but you must hasten to gather strength for what lies before you. We shall be in port to-morrow."

I put away the spoon with an impatient gesture. "I cannot; it nauseates me but to see it, to think of it. Strength will come of itself."

"Oh, no; that is impossible. Besides, the doctor has ordered panada, and I am responsible to him for your safety. Come, now, be reasonable. This is very nice, seasoned with madeira and nutmeg."

Making a strong effort to overcome my repugnance, I received one spoonful of the proffered aliment, then sank back on my pillow, soothed and comforted, not more by the unexpectedly good effects of the compound, than the associations it conjured up, of my sick childhood, of Mrs. Austin, and of Dr. Pemberton.

"Ah! you smile; that is a good sign," said the woman; "favorable every way. We shall have no more delirium now, I hope; no more 'bears and serpents' about the berth; no more calls for 'Bertie' and 'Captain Wentworth,' and you will soon be able to tell us all about yourself and your people—all we want to know."

I must have lapsed again into reverie rather than slumber, from which I was partly aroused by whispering voices at the door, one of which seemed familiar to me. Yet this fact or fancy made little impression on me at the moment, feeble and wretched as was my will, undiscriminating as were my faculties.

And when the door opened, and a lady entered, I did not seek to inquire about her interlocutor. Respectfully rising from her seat beside me, my companion left it vacant for her, to whom she introduced me as her mistress, and stood, work in hand, sewing beneath the skylight, while the new-comer remained in the state-room.

A handsome woman, tall and fashionably attired, apparently between thirty and forty years of age, square face, dark-eyed, rosy-cheeked, and with curling hair, approached me with uplifted hands and eyebrows as I lay gazing calmly upon her; for my food and slumber together had strengthened and revived me wonderfully in the last few hours, and my senses were again collected.

"Awake, and herself again, as I live, even if we cannot say yet truthfully 'clothed and in her right mind.'—

Eh, Clayton?" with a sneering simper; "and what eyes, what teeth, to be sure! Then the dreadful redness is going away, though the skin will scale, of course; but no matter for that; all the fairer in the end. And what a special mercy that her hair is saved!—You have to thank *me* for that, young lady. I would not let the ship's doctor touch a strand of it—not a strand. 'One does not grow a yard and a half of hair in a month, or a year, doctor,' I observed, 'and a woman might as well be dead at once, or mad, or a man, as have cropped hair during all the days of her youth.' I had a fellow-feeling, you see! I have magnificent hair myself, child, as Clayton well knows, for it is her chief trouble on earth, and I would almost as lief die as lose it."

"Yes, indeed, Lady Anastasia's hair is one of her chief attractions," observed the sympathizing Clayton, behind her chair.

"So Sir Harry Raymond thought, my dear"—addressing me—"when I married him, ten years ago; and so somebody else thinks just now, for I am tired of my widowhood, and intend taking on the conjugal yoke again as soon as I reach—"

"New York," interpolated Mrs. Clayton, hastily and emphatically; clearing her throat slightly, by way of apology, perhaps, for her officiousness.

"And you shall stand bridesmaid, my dear. Yes, I am determined on it; so never make great eyes at me. There is a little bit of romance about me that will strike out in spite of all my worldliness; and it will be so pretty to have an 'ocean-waif' for an attendant—it will read so well in the papers! I suppose, when you reach your friends, there will be no difficulty about a dress, and all that sort of thing, meet for the occasion—a very splendid one, I assure you—conducted without regard to expense; for my *fiancé* is very rich, I hear, and my own jointure was a liberal one."

"You do me a great honor," I murmured, conventionally rebelling inwardly at the suggestion.

"Oh, not at all!" was the gracious rejoinder. "I see at a glance, in spite of your misfortunes, that you are one of us, which is not what I say to everybody. True blood will show under all circumstances, though there is such an improvement. Did any one ever see the like before? Why, my dear, you were blistered and black when we picked you up, and afterward sienna-colored; now you are almost a beauty!"

"I am better—much better, and have a great deal to be thankful for, I feel," I contented myself with murmuring.

"Of course you have. It was just a chance with you between our ship and death, you know. By-the-by, what name shall we give our 'treasure-trove?'"

"Miriam for the present, if you please. This is no time nor place for ceremony."

"Well, Miriam it shall be," she repeated with laughing eyes (hers were of that sort which close and grow Chinese under the pressure of merriment and high cheekbones combined). "Miriam, I like the name—there is something grand about it."

"But how shall we know where to find your friends when we get to port?" asked my first attendant. "We *must* know more than your Christian name for such a purpose. You must place confidence in us, you must indeed!"

"Be patient with me," I entreated. "I am much too feeble yet to give you the details that may be necessary.

When we reach New York, you shall know every thing: or is it, indeed, to that place this ship is bound?"

"I thought you knew all about your destination by this time," replied Lady Anastasia Raymond. "Yes, yes, New York of course!" and again she laughed. "Didn't you hear Clayton say so?"

Just then a sharp tap at the door was answered by Lady Anastasia, who went quickly from beneath the curtain hung across it (in consideration, no doubt, of the privacy my illness enjoined), but not before I had caught once, and this time clearly, the tones of a voice that thrilled to my life, the same that had haunted my delirious fancy, I now remembered, through the last four-and-twenty hours.

I rose to my elbow impulsively, only to fall back again utterly exhausted.

"Who was that speaking?" I asked, feebly; "can it be possible—" and I wrung my hands.

"It was the ship's doctor," interrupted the woman I had heard called Clayton by her mistress. "He had not time to do more than inquire about you, I suppose, there are so many ill in the steerage; but he has been very kind and will probably return."

"I hope so," I rejoined; "I should like to realize that voice as *his*. It has haunted me very disagreeably in my dreams, and the tones are those of an old, old acquaintance, one I should be sorry to see here."

"I do not believe you have an acquaintance on the ship," she said, simply. "Under the circumstances any such person would certainly have discovered himself; your situation would have moved a heart of stone."

"But it is sometimes wise for the wicked to lie *perdu*," I murmured, and conjecture was busy in my brain.

"I should be glad, too, to see the captain of this vessel at his earliest convenience," I added, after a pause. "Will you be so good as to apprise him in person of my earnest wish? It would be a real charity."

"Oh, certainly; but I am afraid he cannot come to-night. It is nearly evening now, and he never leaves the deck at this hour, nor until very late."

"To-morrow, then, I must insist on this interview, since I reflect about it, for several reasons."

"To-morrow he shall come," she said, sententiously; "and now try and sleep again. It is very necessary you should gather strength, for we shall be in port shortly, when all will be confusion."

I went to sleep, I remember, murmuring to myself: "The hands were the hands of Jacob, but the voice was the voice of Esau;" and my bewildered faculties found rest until the morning's dawn.

After a hasty toilet made by the careful hands of Mrs. Clayton, a matutinal visit made by Mrs. or Lady Raymond, who always rose early as she informed me, and a cup of tea, very soothing to my prostrated nerves, the potentate of the Latona was duly announced.

Our ship's master was a tall, gaunt, sandy-haired man, with steady gray eyes, hard features, and enormous hands and feet, the first freckled and awkward, the last so long as very nearly to span the space between his seat (a small Spanish-leather trunk) and the berth I reposed in. He entered without his hat; and the swoop of the head he made to avoid the entanglement of the curtain was supposed to do double duty, and serve as a bow to the inmate of his state-room as well, for his I supposed it to be at the time, and he did not contradict me.

"I hope you find yourself comfortable, marm, on board of my ship."

"And in your state-room, captain?" I interrupted promptly.

"Wall, you see it all belongs to me, kinder," he said, after seating himself, as he rubbed his huge, projecting knees, plainly indicated through his nankeen trousers, with his capacious, horny hands. "I'm not very particular, though, where I sleep on shipboard, but at home there's few more so."

"I thought a captain was more at home on shipboard than anywhere else," I pursued mechanically; "such is the theory at least."

"Oh, not at all, not at all; when he has a snug nest on land, with a wife and children waiting to receive him. You might as well talk of a man in the new settlements bein' more at home in his wagon than in his neat, hewn-log cabin."

"A very good simile, captain, and one that kills the ancient theory outright. Let me thank you, however, before we proceed further, for all the kindness and attention I have received in this floating castle of yours, both from you and others. I hope and believe that my companions in misfortune have fared as well."

"Wall, they have not wanted for nothing as far as I knew—the poor baby in particular;" and, as he spoke, he roughed his hair with one hand and smiled into my face a huge, honest, gummy smile, inexpressibly reassuring.

"The man is hideous and repulsive," I thought; "but infinitely preferable, somehow, to the specimen of English aristocracy and her maid who have constituted themselves so far my guardian angels"—a twinge of ingratitude here, which I resented instantly by settling my patriotic prejudices to be at the root of the thing, and rebuking my mistrust sternly though silently. "Yet that voice—how could I be mistaken?" and again I addressed myself to the task before me, having gotten through all preliminaries.

While I sat hesitating as to what I should say, so as to both guard against and conceal my suspicions from the captain's scrutiny, if, indeed, he might be supposed to possess such a quality, I observed that he drew from his pocket a long slip of newspaper, in which he appeared to bury himself for a time, when not glancing furtively at me, as if waiting impatiently for the coming revelation.

"I have sent for you, Captain Van Dorne," I said, at last, in very low and even tones, not calculated to reach outside ears, however vigilant, and yet not suppressed by any means to whispers—"I have sent for you," and my heart beat quickly as I spoke, "not merely to thank you for your hospitable kindness, but because I wish, for reasons that I cannot now explain, to place myself under your especial care until I reach my friends."

"Certainly, certainly; but you *air* among your friends already if you could only think so," he answered, evasively, still caressing his potato knees with large and outspread hands.

"Do not for one moment deem me unmindful of much kindness, or ungrateful to those who have bestowed it," I hastened to explain. "Yet I cannot deny that a fear possesses me that among your passengers may be found one whom I esteem, not without sufficient cause, my greatest enemy."

"Poor thing! poor thing! what put such a strange fancy into your head? An enemy in my ship! Why, there is not a man on board who would not cut off his right hand rather than harm one hair of your poor, witless, defenseless head! There was not a dry eye on the deck when you and the rest wuz lifted from the raft!"

"I understand this prevalence of sympathy for misfortune perfectly, and honor it; yet I have heard a voice since my immurement in this cabin which must belong"—and I whispered the dreaded name—"to Mr. Basil Bainrothe!"

As I spoke I eyed him steadily, and I fancied that his cheek flushed and his eye wavered—that clear and honest eye which had given him a high place in my consideration from the moment I met its gaze.

"You must have been delirious-like when you conceited you heerd that strange voice," he said, presently. "I'll send you my passenger-list if you choose, and you can read it over keerfully. I don't think you'll find *that* name, though, in its kolyums," shaking his head sagaciously.

"Captain Van Dorne, do you mean to say there is no such passenger in your ship's list as Basil Bainrothe?" I asked, desperately.

"That's what I mean to say."

"Give me your honor on this point. It is a vital one to me. Your honor!"

He hesitated and looked around. Just at this moment of apparent uncertainty, a slight tap was heard on the ground-glass eye above us that threw a sullen and unwilling light upon the scene of our interview. It seemed to nerve him strangely.

"On my word of honor, as an American seaman, I assure you that the name of Basil Bainrothe is not on the ship's list at this present speaking;" and, as he spoke, he held up his right hand, adding, as he dropped it, doggedly, "Ef the man's on board I don't know it!"

"It is enough—I believe you, Captain Van Dorne.

And now I want to ask you, as a parting grace, to convey me yourself to the Astor House, and place my watch" (detaching it from my neck as I spoke) "in the hands of the proprietors as a proof of my honest intentions. For yourself, I shall seek another opportunity."

"Not at all—not at all!" he interrupted. "Keep your watch, young lady. No such pledge will be required by them proprietors; and, as to myself, if it had not been for this paper," drawing from his pocket, and flattening on his knees as he spoke, the slip I had before observed, then glancing at me sharply, "I could never have believed that such a pretty-spoken, pretty-behaved young creetur could have been *non com.* But pshaw! what am I talking about? This paper is as old as last year's krout! You don't keer nothing about seeing of it, do you, now?" and he crumpled it in his hand.

"Not unless it concerns me in some way, Captain Van Dorne," I said, coldly. His manner had suddenly become offensive to me, and I longed to see him depart, having transacted my affairs, as far, at least, as I deemed it prudent to insist on such transaction.

"It may be," I added, "that, on reaching the port of New York, a friend or friends who expected me on the Kosciusko may be in waiting to receive me; that is, if the fate of that vessel be not already known. In that case, I shall not be obliged to avail myself of your services, and will acquaint you; but, otherwise, promise that you will conduct me from the ship yourself, either to the hotel or to your wife, as you prefer."

"Wall, I promise you," he said, doggedly, as he prepared literally to undouble his long frame before executing another dive beneath my door-guarding drapery, and with this brief assurance I was fain to rest content.

At all events, I was reassured on one subject—those honest eyes, that frank if ugly mouth had no acquaintance with lies, or the father of them, I saw at once; and the voice of the ship's doctor had for the nonce deceived my practised ear, overstrung by suspicion—enfeebled by suffering.

So I rested calmly until the afternoon, with Mrs. Clayton sewing silently by my side, when with a little tap Lady Anastasia (or Mrs. Raymond, as she declared she preferred to be called by "Americans") entered, bearing a basket in her hand, and wearing on her head a Dunstable bonnet simply trimmed, which she came, she said, to place, along with other articles of dress, at my disposal.

It had not occurred to me before that, in order to go on shore respectably clad, some attire very different from a bed-gown would be essential, and I could but feel grateful for such proofs of unselfish consideration on the part of strangers, pitying both my indigence and imbecility, and so expressed myself.

In accordance with their generous intentions, I submitted myself to be arrayed by Mrs. Clayton and her mistress: first, in the flimsy black-silk gown now completed, on which I had seen my attendant working when I first unclosed my eyes after long unconsciousness, and the measure which she had taken, while I lay in this condition, as coolly in all probability as an undertaker measures a corpse for its shroud; secondly, in a cardinal of the same material, a wrapping cut in the shape in vogue at that period; thirdly, in certain loosely-fitting boots and gloves with which I was fain to cover up my naked feet and blistered hands *in forma pauperis;* and, lastly, in the collarette and cuffs provided by the economic and considerate Lady Anastasia, composed of cotton lace!

The Dunstable bonnet was hung upon a peg in readiness, and I was kindly counseled to lie still, "accoutred as I was," and exhausted by means of such accoutrement as I felt, until evening should find us riding in our harbor.

Then there was a little, low consulting at the door with the renowned "ship's doctor," who positively refused to approach me because he had just come from a case of ship-fever in the steerage, which he feared to communicate to one in my precarious state, but who sent in his imperative orders that I should have soup and sherry-cobbler forthwith, and try and build up my strength for the time of debarkation—speaking in a low, growling voice divested of its former clearness, but still strangely resembling that of Basil Bainrothe!

"The poor man is so fagged out," said Mrs. Clayton, as she brought in my broth and wine, "that his very voice is changed. He is a good soul, and has shown you great interest. Some day you must send him a present, that is, if you are able; but just now all you have to think of is getting safe ashore. Lady Anastasia will go to her friends, probably, or to those of the gentleman she is engaged to; but I do not mean to forsake you until I see you better, and in good hands."

I know not how it was that my heart sank so strangely at this announcement. The woman was kind—tender, even—and had probably saved my life, and yet her presence to me was a punishment worse than pain, a positive evil greater than any other.

"I shall go to the Astor House," I faltered. "The captain has promised me his escort thither."

"Yes, yes, I know, he has told me all about it; but your friends may not be in waiting, and it is simply our duty to see you in their hands. And now drink your sangaree. See, I have broken a biscuit in the glass, and it is well seasoned with lemon and nutmeg. There, now, that is right; a few spoonfuls of soup, and you will feel strengthened for your undertaking. I will sit quietly in the corner until you have your rest."

"No, I prefer to see Christian Garth before I try to sleep—the man who steered our raft—and the young girl he saved, and the baby—let them all come to me, and we will go on shore together."

I spoke these words with a sort of desperation, as though they contained my last hope of justice or protection from a fate which, however obscurely, seemed to threaten me, as we feel the thunder-storm brooding in the tranquil atmosphere of summer.

"Christian Garth!" she repeated, looking at me over her tortoise-shell spectacles, and, quietly drawing out a snuffbox of the same material, she proceeded to fill her narrow nostrils therewith. "Why, that shaggy-looking old sailor, and the girl, and the old negro woman and child, went on shore at daylight this morning. He hailed a Jersey craft, and they all left together. It is perfectly understood, though, that the child is to be returned to you if you desire its company, but, if I were situated as you are, and sure of its safety, I would never want to see it again. It would be better off dead than living anyhow, under the circumstances, poor, deformed creaturé—better for both of you."

The words came to me distinctly, yet as if from an immense distance, and I seemed to see the small chamber lengthening as if it had been a telescope unfolding, and the sallow woman with her hateful smile and tightly-knotted, brindled hair seated in diminished size and distinctness at its farthest extremity.

So had I felt on that fearful night when Evelyn had made her revelation and received mine, and I did not doubt, even in my sinking state, that I was under the influence of a powerful anodyne.

"Call the ship's doctor—I am dying!" were the last words I remember to have articulated; then all was dark, and hours went by, of deep, unconscious sleep.

It was night when I felt myself drawn to my feet, and roused to life by the repeated applications of cold water to my face. "The anodyne was over-powerful," I heard Mrs. Raymond say. "It is a shame to tamper with such strong medicines."

"Oh, she has strength for any thing!" was Clayton's rejoinder. "I never saw such a constitution—and he knew what he was doing."

"No doubt of that.—But, dear Miss Miriam, do speak to me. I am so frightened at your lethargic condition.—I declare I am sorry I ever consented to have any thing to do with this matter! See how she stands. I cannot think it was right, Clayton, I cannot, indeed; I dislike the whole drama."

"Do be quiet! She is coming to herself fast, and what will she think of such expressions? You never had any self-control in your life, and you are playing for great stakes now." These last words in a hoarse whisper.

"Nonsense! mother."

"Again! How often must I warn you?"

"Well, Clayton, then, now and forever."

"Here! rouse up, little one! We are fast anchored in port, and the captain is waiting for us, for we go part of the way together, and our escorts have all failed us—yours and mine. Nice fellows, are they not?"

I sat up and looked about me bewildered; yet I had

heard distinctly every word spoken in the last few minutes, and remembered them for future observance, without having had the power to move or articulate a remonstrance.

"Now, drink this strong coffee, and all will be well again," said Clayton, putting a cup of the smoking beverage to my lips, which I swallowed eagerly, instinctively. The effect was instantaneous, and I was able to speak and stand, as well as hear and comprehend, while my bonnet was being tied on, and my throat muffled in a veil, by the dexterous fingers of Lady Anastasia.

When this process was completed, she stooped down and kissed me, and I felt a hot tear fall upon my cheek as she rose again. In the next moment I was clinging to the captain's arm, with a spasmodic feeling of relief for which I could ill account. We passed across the plank which connected the ship with the shore in utter darkness, guided by a twinkling light far ahead, borne by a seaman, reached the dusky quay, with its few flaring lamps, made dim by drizzling rain and summer mist, and before many minutes we paused before one of a long line of coaches.

The captain handed me in, then, standing before the open door, seemed to await the coming of some other person before taking his own place—the dreaded Clayton, I knew; but I could not remonstrate against what seemed an ordinary courtesy, and perhaps a step suggested by his innate notions of propriety.

At any other time I might have agreed with him; but, feeble as I was, and still bewildered, my whole object seemed to be to escape from the sphere and power of those women, who had been most kind to me, yet whom I instinctively dreaded and abhorred.

They came together, the mother and daughter, in their travesty of mistress and maid—enough of itself to excite suspicion of foul play—and climbed up the rickety steps of the hackney-coach, rejoicing over their victim. It mattered not; the captain would make the fourth passenger, and in his shadow I felt there were strength and security.

"What are you waiting for, Captain Van Dorne?" I had just feebly asked, as the door snapped-to, and the driver mounted his box. A hand was thrust through the window for all reply, and a card dropped upon my lap, which I hastened to secure in the depths of my pocket. By the merest chance, I found it there on the morrow, and later I comprehended its import, so mysterious to me at the moment of perusal.

"My poor young lady, you must forgive me for disappointing you, and hidin' the truth, for your own sake. May God bless and restore you, and bring you to a proper sense of his mercies, is the prayer of your servant to command, JOSEPH VAN DORNE."

My frame of mind was a very different one when I read this scrawl, from that which bewildered and oppressed me on that never-to-be-forgotten night of suffering and distress, both mental and physical. Formed of those elements which readily react, courage and calmness had returned to me before I read the oracle of our worthy shipmaster; for, in spite of his disastrous dealing with me on that occasion, misguided as he was by others, I have reason to so consider him.

But now the influence of the drug that had been given me so recently, doubtless through want of judgment, by the ship's doctor, was felt in every nerve; and, as the carriage rolled up the stony quay, I clung convulsively to Mrs. Raymond, and buried my face and aching forehead in her shoulder, with a strange revulsion of feeling.

"You dread the darkness," she said, kindly, putting her arm around me as she spoke; "but it is only for a time; we shall soon come out into the open lamplight of—"

"Broadway, New York," interrupted Clayton, sententiously; "a very poor sight to see, to one who has lived abroad. Have you ever crossed the waters, Miss Miriam? But I see you are quite faint and overcome. Here, smell this ether, that the ship's doctor put up expressly for your use, and recommended highly as a new restorative much in fashion in Paris."

Had the ship's doctor no name, then, that they never mentioned it, and that he spoke in a demon's voice? His doses I had proved, and was resolved to take no more of them, and I pushed away the phial, whose cold glass nose was thrust obtrusively against my own—pushed it away with all my strength, fast ebbing away as this was, even as I made the effort.

The cruel potion had possession of me, and entered into every fibre of my brain through the avenues prepared for it by the treacherous anodyne; so that, enervated and intoxicated, I yielded passively, after a brief struggle, to the power of the then newly-invented sedative, called chloroform.

When the carriage stopped, or whither it transported me, or who lifted my insensible form to the chamber prepared for me, I know not—never knew. There was a faint reviving, I remember; a process of disrobing gone through by the aid of foreign assistance (whose, I recognized not), then I slumbered profoundly and securely through the entire night, to recover no clearness of perception until a late hour on the following morning.

## CHAPTER VI.

I AWOKE, as I had done of old, after one of my lethargic seizures, from a deep, unrefreshing slumber, with a lingering sense about me of drowsiness and even fatigue.

I found myself lying on a broad, canopied bedstead, the massive posts of which were of wrought rosewood, bare of draperies, as became the season, save at the head-board, behind which a heavy curtain was dropped of rose-colored damask satin.

Of the same rich material were composed the tester and the lightly-quilted coverlet, thrown across the foot of the bed, over a fine white Marseilles counterpane.

The chimney immediately opposite to me, as I lay, was of black marble, and, instead of graceful Greek *caryatides*, bandaged mummies, or Egyptian figures, supported the heavy shelf that surmounted the polished grate. In the centre of this massive mantel-slab was placed a huge bronze clock, and candelabra of the same material graced its corners.

In either recess of this chimney rosewood doors were situated, one of which stood invitingly ajar, disclosing the bath-room, into which it opened, with its accessories of white marble.

The other, firmly closed, seemed to be the outlet of the chamber—its only one—with the exception of the four large Venetian windows, two on either side of me as I lay, the sashes of which, warm as the season was, were drawn closely down.

The furniture of this spacious chamber to which, as if by the touch of a magician's wand, I found myself transported, was throughout solid and of elegant forms, consisting as it did of *armoire*, toilet-table, book-case, *étagère*, writing and flower stands, tables and chairs, of the richest rosewood.

At the foot of my bed was placed a console, supporting a huge Bible and Prayer-book, bound alike in purple velvet, emblazoned with central suns of gold—an arch-hypocrisy that was not lost on its object. Freshly-gathered flowers were heaped in the vases of the floral stands, filling the close, cool room with an overpowering fragrance. The carpet of crimson and white seemed to the eye what it afterward proved to the foot—thick, soft, and elastic; and harmonized well with the rich, antique, and consistent furniture.

The sort of microscopic scrutiny that children manifest seemed mine—in my unreasoning, half-convalescent state; and for a time I observed all that I have described with a listless pleasure, difficult to analyze, a sort of dreamy acceptance of my condition, the very memory of which exasperated me, later, almost to self-contempt.

A crimson cord hung at one side of my bed, continued from a bell-wire at some distance, the tassel of which I touched lightly, and, at the very first signal, Mrs. Clayton appeared through the hitherto only unopened door, to know and do my bidding.

The clock on the mantel-shelf struck nine as she stood beside me, and made respectful inquiries concerning my wants and condition; understanding which, she disappeared, to return a few minutes later, followed by an ancient negress, bearing a silver waiter.

I recognized in this sable assistant (or thought I recognized at a glance) my companion in shipwreck; but, upon making known my convictions, was met with a prompt denial by the sable dame herself, who, shaking her head, gave me to understand, in a few broken words, that she "no understood English—only Spanish tongue!"

Her dress—handsome and Frenchified—her creole coiffure, and the long gray locks that escaped from her crimson kerchief bound over her ears, as well as her more refined deportment, did indeed seem to discredit my first idea, which came at last (notwithstanding these discrepancies) to be fixed, and proved one link in the long chain of duplicity I untangled later.

At the time, however, I gave it little thought, but partook with what appetite I might of the choice and delicate repast provided for me, in this truly princely hotel, whose fame I discovered had not been over-trumpeted. On my previous visits to New York, the Astor House had been unfinished, and had made in its completion a new era certainly in the "tavern-life" of that inhospitable city of publicans. When the delicious coffee and snowy bread, the eggs of milky freshness, the golden butter, the savory rice-birds, the appetizing fish, had each and all been merely tasted and dismissed, and the exquisite China, in which the breakfast was served, duly marveled at as an unprecedented extravagance on the part even of John Jacob Astor, Mrs. Clayton came to me with kindly offers of assistance in the performance of my toilet, still a matter of difficulty in my feeble hands.

My long hair, yet tangled and clogged with sea-water,

was to be at last unbound and thoroughly combed, cleansed, and oiled, so that the black and glossy braids, that had been my chief personal pride, might again be wound about my head in the old classic fashion.

Then came the bath, with its reviving, rehabilitating process, and lastly I assumed with the docility of a baby or a pauper the clean and fragrant linen and simple wrapper that had been mysteriously provided for me by the Lady Anastasia again, I could not doubt.

"All this must end to-day," I said, "when really clothed and in my right mind." I requested writing-materials and more light to work by, and composed myself to write to Dr. Pemberton (once again, I knew, in Philadelphia), and request his assistance and protection in getting home safely, and, if need be, in tracing Captain Wentworth.

"I suppose Captain Van Dorne has been too busy to call," I observed, carelessly, as I prepared to commence my letter, "and Mrs. Raymond too happy, probably, in getting safe to shore and her lover, to think of me."

"They have both inquired for you," said Mrs. Clayton, as she arranged pen, ink, and paper, before me, with her usual precision, while a grim, sardonic smile lingered about her features; "several have called, but none have been admitted."

"Who have called, Mrs. Clayton? Give me the cards immediately. I must, must know," I rejoined, eagerly, pausing with extended hand to receive them.

"Oh, there were no cards, and such as want to see you can come again. There, now! write away, and never trouble your mind about strange people. Have you sufficient light?"

And, as she spoke, she touched a cord which set at

right angles with the lower one the upper inside shutter of another window as she had adjusted the first.

I wrote two hasty notes, one on further consideration to Captain Wentworth himself, who might, after all, be at that very time in that same hotel—"*Quien sabe?*" as Favraud used to say with his significant shrug, which no Frenchman ever excelled or Spaniard equalled (albeit they shrug severally).

My spirits rose with every word I wrote, and, when I got up from my chair after sealing and directing my letters, a new and subtle energy seemed to have infused itself through my frame. "There, I have finished, Mrs. Clayton," I said, putting aside the implements I had been using. "Now go, if you please, and bring to me the proprietor of this hotel. I will give him my letters myself, since I have other business to transact with him," and I laid my watch and chain on the table before me, ready for his hand, not having lost sight of my early resolution. "But, stay—before you go, be good enough to open the lower shutters and throw up the windows. Cool as the weather is in this climate, I stifle for air, and this close atmosphere, laden with fragrance, grows oppressive. Who sent these flowers, by-the-by, Mrs. Clayton? or do they belong to the magnificence of this idealized hotel?" She made no reply to any thing I had been saying.

By this time, however, she had lowered the upper sashes of the windows about a foot, and the fresh air of morning was pouring in, curling the paper on the centre table and dispersing the noisome fragrance of the flowers, in which I detected the morbid supremacy of the tuberose and jasmine.

"I want to see the streets, the people," I said, approaching one of the windows; "this artistic light is not at all the thing I need. I have no picture to paint, not even my own face;" and, finding her unmoved, I undertook to do the requisite work myself.

The sashes were shut away below by inside shutters, which resisted all my efforts to stir them. After a moment's inspection, I perceived that they were secured by iron screws of great strength and size; not, in short, meant to be moved or opened at all. Again I essayed to shake them convulsively one after the other—as you may sometimes see a tiger, made desperate by confinement, grapple with the inexorable bars of his cage, though certain of failure and defeat.

Overpowered by a sudden dismay that took entire possession of me, I sank into one of the deep *fauteuils* that extended its arms very opportunely to receive me, and sat mutely for a moment, while anguish unutterable, and conjecture too wild to be hazarded in speech, were surging through my brain.

"I am too weak, I suppose, to open these shutters," I said at last, feebly. "Be good enough to do it for me, Mrs. Clayton, or cause it to be done immediately."

Was it not strange that up to this very moment no suspicion had clouded my horizon since I woke in that sumptuous room?

"I cannot transcend my orders by doing any thing of the kind," she said quietly, yet resolutely, as she pursued her avocation, that of dusting with a bunch of colored plumes the delicate ornaments of the *étagère* carefully one by one.

"Your authority! Who has dared to delegate to you what has no existence as far as I am concerned?" I asked indignantly. "I will go instantly."

"You cannot leave this chamber until you receive

outside permission," she interrupted, firmly planting herself at once between me and the door through which I had seen her enter. "You must not think to pass through my chamber, Miss Miriam. It is locked without, and there is no other outlet."

"Woman!" I said, grasping her feebly yet fiercely, by the arm. "Look at me! Raise those feline eyes to mine, if you dare, and answer me truthfully: What means this mockery? Why have you been forced on me at all? Where is Captain Van Dorne? What becomes of his promises? What house is this in which I find myself a prisoner? Speak!"

"You can do nothing to make me angry," she rejoined, calmly. "I know your condition, and pity and respect it, but I shall certainly fulfill my part of this undertaking. Captain Van Dorne recognized you as Miss Monfort by the description in the newspaper, as did my mistress, and for your own welfare we determined to secure you and keep you safe until the return of Mr. Bainrothe and your sisters from Europe. They will be here shortly, and all you have to do is to be patient and behave as well as you can until the time comes for your trial;" and she cast on me a menacing look from her green and quivering pupils, indescribably feline.

My trial! Great Heaven! did they mean to turn the tables, then, and destroy me by anticipating my evidence? I staggered to a chair and again sat down silent confounded. "Where am I, then?" I feebly asked at length.

"In the establishment of Dr. Englehart," she made answer, "a private madhouse."

"God of heaven! has it come to this?" I covered my eyes with my hands and sobbed aloud, while tears of pride and passion rained hotly over my cheeks. This outburst was of short duration. "I will give them no advantage," I considered. "My violence might be perverted. There are creatures too cold and crafty to conceive of such a thing as natural emotion, and passion with them means insanity. Thank God, the very power to feel bears with it the power of self-government, and is proof of reason. I will be calm, and if my life endures put them thus to shame."—"You say that I am in the asylum of Dr. Englehart?" I asked after a pause, during which she had not ceased to dust the furniture and arrange the bed in its pristine order, speckless, with lace-trimmings, pillow-cases smooth as glass, and sheets of lawn, and counterpane of snow. "If so, call my physician hither; I, his patient, have surely a right to his prompt services."—"It is just possible," I thought, "that interest or compassion may, one or both, still enlist him in my cause—I can but try."

A slight embarrassment was evidenced in her countenance as I made this request. It vanished speedily.

"He is absent just at this time," she answered, quickly. "When he returns I will make known your wish to him, if, indeed, he does not call of his own accord."

"Be done with this shallow farce," I exclaimed, harshly. "It shames humanity. Acknowledge yourself at once the faithful agent of a tyrant and felon, or a pair of them, and I shall respect you more. Confess that it was the voice of Basil Bainrothe I heard at my cabin-door, and that Captain Van Dorne was imposed upon by that specious scoundrel, even to the point of being conscientiously compelled to falsehood.

"I deny nothing—I acknowledge nothing," she said, deliberately. "You and your friends can settle this between yourselves when they arrive. Until then, you need not seek to tamper with me—it will be useless; and I hope you are too much of a lady to be insulting to a person who has no choice but to do her duty."

She could not more effectually have silenced me, nor more utterly have crushed my hopes. Yet again I approached her with entreaties.

"I hope you will not refuse to mail my notes, even under these trying circumstances," I said, extending them to her.

"You can ask Dr. Englehart to do so when he comes," she answered, gently; "for myself, I am utterly powerless to serve you beyond the walls of this chamber."

"And how long is this close immurement to continue?" I asked again, after another dreary pause. "Am I not permitted to breathe the external air—to exercise? Is my health to be unconsidered?"

"I know nothing more than I have told you," she replied. "I am directed to furnish you with every means of comfort—with books, flowers, clothing, musical instrument, even, if you desire it; but, for the present, you will not leave these walls, and you will see no society. The doctor has decided that this is best."

"And whence did he derive his authority?"

"Oh, it was all arranged between him and Mr. Bainrothe, your guardeen" (for thus she pronounced this word, ever hateful to me), "long ago; before he went to France, I suppose. Captain Van Dorne had nothing to do but hand you over."

"Captain Van Dorne! To think those honest eyes could so deceive me!" and I shook my head wofully.

When I looked up again from reverie, Mrs. Clayton had settled herself to work with a basket of stockings on her knees, which she appeared to be assorting assiduously.

There she sat, spectacles on nose, thimble on twisted

finger, ivory-egg in hand, in active preparation for that work, woman's *par excellence*, that alone rivals Penelope's. Surely that assortment of yellow, ill-mated, half-worn, and holey hose, was a treasure to her, that no gold could have replaced, in our dreary solitude (none the less dreary for being so luxurious). I envied her almost the power she seemed to have to merge her mind in things like these; and saw, for the first time in my life, what advantages might lie in being commonplace.

It was now nearly the end of July. My birthday occurred in the middle of September. I thought I knew that, as soon as possible after my majority, Mr. Bainrothe's conditions would be laid before me.

I could not, dared not, believe that my captivity would be lengthened beyond that time. I resolved that I would condone the past, and go forth penniless, if this were exacted in exchange for liberty at the end of a month and a half from this time.

Six weeks to wait! Were they not, in the fullness of their power, to crush and baffle me? Six weary years! For, during all this time, I felt that the unexplained mystery that weighed upon my life would gather in force and inflexibility. Death would have seemed to have set its seal upon it, in the estimation of Captain Wentworth, as of all others. He would never know that the sea, which swallowed up the Kosciusko, had spared the woman he loved, nor receive the explanation that she alone could give him, of the mystery he deplored.

Before I emerged from my prison, he might be gone to the antipodes, for aught I knew, and a barrier of eternal silence and absence be interposed between us. So worked my fate! These reflections continued to haunt and oppress me, by night and day, and life itself seemed a bitter burden in that interval of rebellious agony, and in that terrible seclusion, where luxury itself became an additional engine of torture.

Days passed, alternately of leaden apathy and bitter gloom, varied by irrepressible paroxysms of despair. Whenever I found myself alone, even for a few moments, I paced my room and wept aloud, or prayed passionately. There were times when I felt that my Creator heard and pitied me; others when I persuaded myself his ear was closed inexorably against me.

I suffered fearfully—this could not last. The accusation brought against me by my enemies seemed almost ready to be realized, when my body magnanimously assumed the penalty the soul was perhaps about to pay, and drifted off to fever.

Then, for the first time, came the man I had until then believed a myth, and sat beside me in the shadow, and administered to me small, mystic pellets, that he assured me, in low, husky whispers, and foreign accent, would infallibly cure my malady—my physical one, at least; as for the mind, its forces, he regretted to add, were beyond such influence!

For a moment, the wild suspicion intruded on my fevered brain that this leech was no other than Basil Bainrothe himself, disguised for his own dark purposes; but the tall, square, high-shouldered form that rose before me to depart (taller, by half a head, than the man I suspected of this fresh deception), and the angular movements and large extremities of Dr. Englehart, dispelled this delusion forever. After all, might he not be honest, even if a tool of Bainrothe's?

I took the sugared minature pills—the novel medicine he had left for me—faithfully, through ministry of Mrs.

Clayton's, and was benefited by them; and, when he came again, as before, in the twilight, I was able to be installed in the great cushioned chair he had sent up for me, and to bear the light of a shaded lamp in one corner of the large apartment.

Dr. Englehart approached me deferentially, and, without divesting himself of the light-kid gloves which fitted his large hands so closely, he clasped my wrist with his finger and thumb, and seemed to count my pulses.

"Ver much bettair," was his first remark, made in that disagreeable, harsh, and husky voice of his, while he bent so near me that the aroma of the tobacco he had been smoking caused me to cough and turn aside.

Still, I could not see his face, for the immense bushy whiskers he wore, nor his eyes, for the glasses that covered them, nor his teeth, even, for the long, fierce mustache that swept his lips; and when, after a brief visit, he rose and was gone again, there remained only in my mind the image of a huge and hairy horror—a sort of bear of the Blue Mountains, from the return of which or whom I fervently hoped to be delivered.

"Send him word I am better, Mrs. Clayton," I entreated; "I cannot see him again, he is so repulsive; and, if you have a woman's heart in your breast, never leave me alone with him, or with Mr. Bainrothe, when he calls, for one moment—they inspire me equally with terror indescribable," and I covered my face to hide its burning blushes.

"Look up, Miss Monfort, and listen to me," said Mrs. Clayton, at last, regarding me keenly, with her warped forefinger uplifted in her usual admonitory fashion, but with an expression on her face of interest and sympathy such as I had never witnessed there before.

"A new light has broken just now upon my understanding; I can't tell how or whence it came, but here it is," pressing her hand to her brow; "I believe you have been misrepresented to me—but that is neither here nor there. I shall watch you closely and faithfully until we part—all the more that I do not believe you any more crazy than I am; I half suspected this before, but I know it now." She paused, then continued: "I should have to tell you my life's secret if I were to explain to you why Mr. Bainrothe's interests are so dear to me, so vital even, and I will not conceal from you that I knew your guardeen's good name depends on your confinement here until you come of age. After that it will only be necessary for you to sign a few papers, and all will be straight again—no harm or insult is designed. To these I would never have lent myself in any way—ill as you think of me. And as long as we continue together I will guard your good name as I would do that of my own dear daughter—that is, if I had one. You shall receive no visitor alone."

She spoke with a feeling and dignity of which I had scarcely believed her capable, shrewd and sensible as I knew her to be, and far above the woman she called her mistress, in a certain *retenu* of manner and delicacy of deportment, usually inseparable from good-breeding.

I could not then guess how acceptable, to her and the person she was chiefly interested in, were these signs of my aversion for Basil Bainrothe, and what sure means they were of access to the only tender spot in the obdurate heart of Rachel Clayton.

Certain it is that, from these expressions, I derived the first consolation that had come to me in my immurement, and from that hour the solemn farce of keeper and lunatic ceased to be played between us two.

From such freedom of communication on my jailer's part, I began to hope for additional information, which never came. It was in vain that I conjured her to tell me where my prison was situated, whether at the edge of the city, or far away in the country, or to suffer me to have a glimpse from a window of my vicinity. To all such entreaties she was pitiless, and I was left to that vague and vain conjecture which so wears the intellect.

In the absence of all possibility of escape, it became a morbid and haunting wish with me to know my exact locality. That it could be no great distance from the city of New York, if not within its limits, I felt assured, from the expedition with which my transit from the ship had been effected.

During the first three weeks of my confinement the deep silence that prevailed about me had led me to adopt the opinion that I was the occupant of a *maison de santé*. I had once driven past one on Staten Island, where a friend of my father's—about whose condition he came to inquire personally—had been immured for years. I did not alight with him when he left the carriage to make these inquiries, but I perfectly remembered the old gray stone building, with its ancient elms, and the impression of gloom and awe it had left on my mind. But this idea was presently dispelled.

I was awakened one morning, in the fourth week of my sojourn in captivity, by the sound of chimes long familiar to my ear, the duplicate of which I had not supposed to be in existence. At first I feared it was some mirage of the ear, so to speak, instead of eye, that reflected back that fairy melody, which had rung its accompaniment to my whole childhood and youth; but, when, after the lapse of seven days, it was repeated, I became convinced that its reality was unquestionable, and that neither impatience nor indignation had so impaired my senses as to reproduce those sounds through the medium of a fevered imagination.

Were these delicious bells, a recent addition to the cupola of our grim asylum, bestowed by some benevolent hand that sought to mark and lend enchantment to the holy Sabbath-day—even for the sake of the irresponsible ones within its walls—or was I indeed—? But of this there could be no question—I dared not hazard such conjecture lest it drive me mad in reality—I must not!

I groped in thick darkness, and time itself was only measured now by those sweet chimes, so like our own, and yet so far away. My very clock one morning was found to have stopped, and was not again repaired or set in motion. Papers I never saw, had never seen since I came to dwell in shadow, save that single one so ostentatiously spread before me, announcing the loss of the Kosciusko and her passengers—a refinement of cruelty, on the part of those who sent it, worthy of a Japanese.

Rafts had been launched and lost, the survivors stated (the men who had seized the long-boat, to the exclusion of the women and children); the sea had swallowed all the remainder. A later statement might refute the first, but even then none could know the truth with regard to my identity, for would not Basil Bainrothe control the publication as he pleased, and make me dead if he listed—dead even after the rescue?

Yet Hope would sometimes whisper in her daring moods: "All this shall pass away, and be as it had not been. Be of good heart, Miriam, and do not let them kill you; live for Mabel—live for Wentworth!"

Then, with bowed head, and silent, streaming tears, my soul would climb in prayer to the footstool of the Most High, and the grace, which had never come to me before, fell over me like a mantle in this sad extremity.

## CHAPTER VI.

Unfaltering in her respectful demeanor toward me was Mrs. Clayton from the time of the little scene I have recently described. What new and sudden light had broken in upon her I never knew, but I supposed at the time that the flash of conviction had gone home to her mind with regard to the baseness of Bainrothe and the iniquity of his proceedings, founded on the fear I had expressed of his solitary presence, and the insight she had gained into my character.

Watching none the less strictly, she gradually relaxed that personal surveillance that is ever so intolerable to the proud and delicate-minded, and those suggestions that, however well intended, had been so irritating to me from such a source. She no longer urged me to read, or sew, or eat, or take exercise; but, retiring into her own work (whence she could observe me at her pleasure, for her door was always set wide open, and her face turned in my direction), she employed or feigned to employ herself in her inexhaustible stocking-basket or scollop-work, either one the last resource of idiocy, as it seemed to me.

Left thus to myself in some degree, I unclosed the leaves of the bookcase, and surveyed its grim array of "classics"—all new and unmarked by any name, or sign of having been read—and from them I selected a few worthies, through whose pages I delved drearily and industriously, and most unprofitably it must be confessed. The only living sensations I received from the contents of that bookcase were, I am ashamed to acknowledge, from a few odd volumes of memoirs, and collections of travels that I had happened to find stowed away behind the others. The rest seemed sermons from the stars.

Captain Cook's voyages and Le Vaillant's descriptions did stir me very slightly with their strong reality, and make me for a few hours forget myself and my captivity; but all the rest prated at me like parrots, from stately, pragmatical Johnson down to sentimental, maudlin Sterne.

I found them intolerable in the mood in which I was, nothing so exhausting as the abstract! and closed the book desperately to resume my diary, neglected since the awful events of Beauseincourt, but always to me a resource in time of trouble and of solitude. Of pens, ink, paper, there was no lack, and I wrote one day, Penelope-wise, what I destroyed the next. Yet this very "jotting down" impressed upon my brain the few incidents of my prison-house recorded here, that might otherwise have faded from my memory in the twilight of monotony.

I had no need to sew. Fair linen and a sufficiency of other plain wearing-apparel, including summer gowns, I found laid carefully in my drawers, and the creole negress brought in my clothes well ironed and carefully mended, to be laid away by the orderly hands of Mrs. Clayton.

Once, during the temporary illness of this dragon (whose bed or lair was placed absolutely across the door of egress from her closet, so as to block the way or make it difficult of access), the creole, in an unavoidable contingency like this, came with a pile of clothing in her arms to lay the pieces herself in the bureau, by direction of my jailer, and thus revealed herself.

By the merest accident I had found in the lining of my purse two pieces of gold (the rest of my money had been spirited away with the belt that contained it, or the leather had been destroyed by the action of the salt-water), and one of these I hastened to bestow on the attendant, signifying silence by a gesture as I did so.

I knew this wretch to be wholly selfish and mercenary, from my experience of her on the raft—for that she was the same negress I had long ceased to doubt—and I determined, while I had an opportunity of doing so, to enter a wedge of confidence between us in the only possible way.

"Sabra," I whispered, "what became of the young girl, Ada Lee, and the deformed child? It surely can do no harm to tell me this, and I know you understand me perfectly."

"No, honey, sartinly not; 'sides, I is tired out of speakin' Spanish," in low, mumbling accents. "Well, den, dat young gal gone to 'tend on Mrs. Raymond, and, as fur de chile, dey pays me to take kear of dat in dis very house ware you is disposed of. Dat boy gits me a heap of trouble and onrest of nights, dough, I tells you, honey; but I is well paid, and dey all has der reasons for letting him stay here, I spec' "—shaking her head sagaciously—"dough dey may be disappinted yit, when de time comes to testify and swar! De biggest price will carry de day den, chile; I tells you all," eying the gold held closely in her palm."

I caught eagerly at the idea of the child's presence, though the rest was Greek to my comprehension until long afterward, when, in untangling a chain of iniquity difficult to match, it formed one important but additional link.

"Poor little Ernie! I would give so much to see

him," I said. "Ask Dr. Englehart to let him come to see me, Sabra, and some day I will reward you"—all this in the faintest whisper. "But Mrs. Raymond—where is she? Does she never come here? I desire earnestly to speak with her. Can't you let her know this? Try, Sabra, for humanity's sake."

At this juncture the head of Mrs. Clayton was thrust forth from its shell, turtle-wise, and appeared peering at the door-cheek.

"You have been there long enough to make these clothes instead of putting them away, old woman," was the sharp rebuke that startled the pretended Dinah to a condition of bustling agitation, and induced her to shut up one of her own shrivelled hands in closing the drawer, with a force that made her cry aloud, and, when released, wring it with agony, that drew some words in the vernacular. "What makes you suppose Miss Monfort wants to hear your chattering, old magpie that you are?" continued Mrs. Clayton, throwing off her mask. "Now walk very straight, or the police shall have you next time you steal from a companion. Remember who rescued you on the Latona, and on what conditions, and take care how you conduct yourself in the future. Do you understand me?"

After this tirade, which sorely exhausted her, Mrs. Clayton relapsed into silence; and now it was my time to speak and even scold. I said:

"Now that the Spanish farce is thrown aside, it is hard indeed that I cannot even be allowed to exchange a few words with a laundress in my solitary condition—hard that I should be pressed to the wall in this fiendish fashion. This woman was telling me of the presence of a little child in the house, and I have desired permission to see it by way of diversion and occupation. I have asked her to apply to Dr. Englehart."

"The child shall come to you, Miss Monfort, whenever you wish," said Mrs. Clayton, with ill-disguised eagerness. "This woman is not the proper person to apply to, however, and it is natural you should feel concerned about it, now that you are able to think and feel again. You know, of course, it is the boy of the wreck."

"Yes, very natural. Its mother died in my arms, if I am not mistaken in the identity of the child; and fortunately—" I paused here, arrested by some strange instinct of prudence, and decided not to show further interest in his fate.

He might be inquired for, and traced even, I reflected, and thus my own existence be brought to light. Selfishly, as well as charitably, would I cherish him. Little children had ever been a passion with me, but this poor, repulsive thing was the "*dernier ressort* of desolation."

That very evening I heard the husky and guttural voice of Dr. Englehart in the adjoining chamber, or rather in the closet of Mrs. Clayton, a mere anteroom originally, as it seemed, to the large apartment I occupied.

It was very natural that in her ill condition my dragon should seek medical aid, and I paid no further attention to the propinquity of this unpleasant visitor than I could help—sitting quietly by my shaded lamp, absorbed in the Psalter, in which I found nightly refuge.

He came in at last, after tapping very lightly on the door-panel, unsolicited and unexpected, to my presence—the same inscrutable, hirsute horror I had seen before, with his trudging, scraping walk, his square and stalwart frame, his gloved extremities, his light, blue-glasses, hat and cane in hand, a being as I felt to chill one's very marrow.

"Is it true vat I hear," he asked, pausing at some distance, "dat you vant to have dat leetle hompback chilt for a companion, Miss Monfort?"

"It is true, Dr. Englehart."

"And vat can your motif be? Heh? I must study dat for a leetle before I can decide de question, or even trost him as a human being in your hands."

"Lunatics are rarely governed by motives at all," I replied, "only impulses. I want human companionship, however, that is all. I sicken in this solitude—I am dying of mental inanition."

"It is true, you look delicate indeed, I am pained to see." The accent was forgotten here for a moment, and an expression of real sympathy was perceivable in his low, husky voice. "Command me in any way dat accords wid my duty," he continued, "yes! de boy shall come! To interest, to amuse you, is perhaps—to cure!"

"Thank you; I shall await his advent anxiously; be careful not to disappoint me."

"Oh, not for vorlds!"

"You are very kind; I believe, though, that is all we have to say to one another, Dr. Englehart."

"You are bettair, then?" he said, advancing steadily toward me in spite of this dismissal. "You need no more leetle pill? Are you quite sure of dat?"

"Not now, at least, Dr. Englehart."

"Permit me, then, to feel your pulse vonce more. I shall determine den more perfectly dis vexing subject of your sanity."

"Thank you; I decline your opinion on a matter so

little open to difference. Be good enough to retire, Dr. Englehart. Let me at least breathe freely in the solitude to which I am consigned."

"I mean no offence, yonge lady," he said, meekly, falling back to the centre-table on which was burning my shaded astral lamp—for I had left it as he approached, instinctively to seek the protection of an interposing chair, on the back of which I stood leaning as I spoke.

He, too, remained standing, with one hand pressed firmly backward on the top of the table, in front of which he poised himself, gesticulating earnestly yet respectfully.

His position was an error of mistaken confidence in his own make-up, such as we see occur every day among those even long habituated to disguise.

As he stood I distinctly saw a line of light traced between his cheek and one of his bushy side-whiskers.

That line of light let in a flood of evidence. The man was an impostor, a tool, as criminal as his employer—not the footprint on the sand was more suggestive to Robinson Crusoe than that luminous streak to me, nor the cause of wilder conjecture.

Yet I betrayed nothing of my amazement I am convinced, for, after standing silently for a time and almost in a suppliant attitude before me, Dr. Englehart departed, and for many days I saw him not again.

An object that looked not unlike a small, solemn owl, stood in the middle of the floor, regarding me silently when I awoke very early on the following morning.

At a glance I recognized poor little Ernie, and singularly enough, he knew and remembered me at once.

"Ernie good boy now," he said as he came toward me with his tiny claw extended. "Lady got cake in pocket, give Ernie some?" Not only did he recall me, it was plain, but the incident that saved his life, and the rebukes he had received on the raft for his refusal to partake of briny biscuit, which no persuasion, it may be remembered, had availed to make him taste—even when devoured by the pangs of hunger. I tried in vain, however, to recall him to some remembrance of his poor mother. On that point he was invulnerable; the abstract had no charm for him or meaning. He dealt only in realities and presences.

A new element was infused into my solitude from this time. In this child I lived, breathed, and had my being, until later events startled my individuality once more into its old currents of existence. Not that I merged myself entirely in Ernie, sickly, wayward, fitful, ugly little mite that he was undeniably. Nay, rather did I draw him forcibly into my own sphere of being and find nutrition in this novel element.

So grudgingly had Nature fulfilled her obligations in the case of this poor stunted infant, that, at two and a half years of age, he had not the usual complement of teeth due a child of eighteen months, and was suffering sorely from the pointing up of tardy stomach-teeth through ulcerated gums.

To attend to and heal his bodily ailments occupied me entirely at first, and finally, finding him ill cared for, I made him a little pallet on my sofa and kept him with me by night and day. Surely such devotion as he manifested in return for my scant kindness to him few mothers have received from their offspring. To sit silently at my feet while I talked to him, or do my bidding, seemed his chief pleasures, as they might not, could not have been, had he been strong, and active, and more soundly constituted. As it was, no more loyal creature existed, nor did the Creator ever enshrine deeper affections or quicker perceptions in any childish frame. Weird, and wise, and witty as Æsop was this child, like him deformed; and to draw out his quaint remarks, read him fresh from his Maker's hand—this warped, and tiny, imperfect volume of humanity—was to me an ever-new puzzle and delight. Severity he had been used to of late, I saw plainly. He shrank with winking eyes from an uplifted hand, even if the gesture were one of mere amazement, or affection, and sat patiently, like a little well-trained dog, when he saw food placed before me, until invited to partake thereof. His manner was wistful and deprecating even to pathos, and I longed for one burst of passion, one evidence of self-will, to prove to myself that I, like others he had been recently thrown with, was not the meanest of all created creatures—a baby's despot!

Oh, better than this the cap and bells, and infant tyranny forever, and the wildest freaks of baby folly. He suffered silently, as I have seen no other child do, uncomplainingly even, and at such times would sink into moods of the blackest gloom, like those of an old, gouty subject. Hypochondria, baby as he was, seemed already to have fixed his fangs upon him. He had days of profound melancholy, when nothing provoked a smile, and others of bitter, silent fretting, inconceivably distressing; again there were periods of the wildest joy, only restrained by that reticence which had become habitual, from positive boisterousness.

All this I could have compelled into subservience, of course, by substituting fear for affection. It is not a difficult matter for the strong and cunning to cow and crush the spirit of a little child; no great achievement, after all, nor proof of power, though many boast of it as such.

Strength and hardness of heart are all one requires for this external victory; but human souls are not to be so governed (God be praised for this!), and love and respect are not to be compelled.

It is the error of all errors to suppose that, because a child has a sickly frame or imperfect animal organization, it is just or profitable to give it over to its own devices, and consign it to indolence and ignorance. Alas! the vacancy that begets fretfulness, and crude, capricious desires, the confusion of images that arises from partial understanding, are far more wearing to the nerves of an intelligent infant than the small labor the brain undertakes, if any, indeed, be needed, in mastering ideas properly presented, and suitable to the condition of the sufferer. One might as well forbid the hand to grasp, the eye to see, nay, more, it will not do to confound the child of genius with the fool, or to suppose that the one needs not a mental aliment of which the other is incapable. Feed well the hungry mind, lest it perish of inanition. It is a sponge in infancy that imbibes ideas without an effort; it is a safety-valve through which fancy and poetry conduct away foul vapors; it is an alembic, retaining only the pure and valuable of all that is poured into it, to be stored for future use. It is a lightning-rod that conducts away from the body all superfluous electricity. It does not harm a sensible child to put it to study early, but it destroys a dull one. Let your poor soil lie fallow, but harvest your rich mould, and you shall be repaid, without harm to its fertility.

Ideas were balm to Ernie, even as regarded his physical suffering. His enthusiasm rose above it and carried him to other spheres.

Some illustrated volumes of "Wilson's Ornithology,"

which I found in the bookcase, proved to be oil on troubled waters in Ernie's case; and before long he knew, without an effort, the name of every bird in the two folios of prints, and would come of his own accord to repeat and point them out to me.

I found, to my amazement, that, when a cage of canaries was brought in and hung in the bath-room at my request for his amusement, he discriminated and gravely averred that no birds like those were to be found in his big book, though yellow hammers and orioles were there in their native colors, that might have deceived a less observant eye into a delusion as to their identity with our pretty importation.

Verses, remarkable for rhyme and rhythm both, when repeated to him a few times with scanning emphasis, took root in that fertile brain which piled his compact forehead so powerfully above his piercing, deep-set eyes, and fell from his infant lips in silvery melody as effortless and spontaneous as the trickling of water or the singing of birds in the trees.

Day by day I saw the little, wistful face relaxing from the hard-knot expression, so to speak, of sour and serious suffering, and assuming something akin to baby joyousness, and the small, warped figure, so low that it walked under my dropped and level hand, acquiring security of step and erectness of bearing. I knew little of the treatment required for spinal disease, but common-sense taught me that, in order to effect a cure, the vertebral column must be relieved as much as possible from pressure, and allowed to rest. So I persuaded him to lie down a great part of the time, and contrived for him a little sustaining brace to relieve him when he walked.

I fed him carefully; I bathed him tenderly, and

rubbed his weary, aching limbs to rest, so that before many weeks the change was surprising, and the success of my treatment evident to all who saw him—the comprehensive " all " being myself and two attendants.

Dr. Englehart had been suggested in the beginning by Mrs. Clayton, as his medical attendant, but rejected by me with a shudder, that seemed conclusive; yet one evening, unsummoned by me, and as far as I knew by any other, he walked calmly into my apartment, ostensibly to see the little invalid—his charge as well as mine.

For a moment the extravagant idea possessed me that, in spite of appearances, I had done this man injustice, and that he came in reality for humane purposes alone; wore his disguise for these.

This delusion was soon dissipated, as with audacity (no doubt characteristic, though not before evidenced to me), he seated himself complacently and uninvited, and, disposing of his hat and stick, settled himself down for a *tête-à-tête*, an affair which, if medical, usually partakes of the confidential.

"Your little *protégé*, Miss Monfort," he said, huskily, "seems to be a serious sufferer," and for a moment dropping his accent while he rubbed his gloved hands together as with an ill-repressed self-gratification; "come, tell me now what you are doing for his benefit," again artistically assuming a foreign accentuation.

In a few words I described my course of treatment and its success.

"All very well," he responded, hoarsely, "as far as it goes; but I am convinced that much severer treatment will be necessaire—"

"I think not," I replied, curtly; "and certainly nothing of the kind will be permitted by me while I have charge of this poor infant."

"A few leetle pills, then, for both mother and child;" he suggested, humbly.

"You are mistaken if you imagine any relationship to exist between Ernie and myself," I answered, calmly, never dreaming at the moment of covert or intended insult. "I might as well inform you at once, that I am Miss, not Mrs. Monfort; you should be guarded how you make mistakes of that nature."

And my eye flashed fire, I felt, for I now heard him chuckling low in the shadow, in which he so carefully concealed himself.

"I shall remembair vat you say," he observed, "and try to do bettair next visit; but all dis time I delay in de execution of my mission here. See, I have brought you von lettair; now vat will you do to reward me?"

Holding it high above my head, in a manner meant, no doubt, to be playful, and to suggest a game of snatch, perhaps, such as his peers might have afforded him, he displayed his treasure to my longing eyes, but I sat with folded arms.

"If the letter brings me good news, I shall thank you warmly, Dr. Englehart; if not, I shall try to believe you unconscious of its contents."

"Tanks from your lips would, indeed, seem priceless," he remarked, courteously, as with many bows and shrugs he laid it on the table before me, bringing his shaggy head by such means much closer to my hand than I cared to know it should be, under any circumstances.

With a gesture of inexpressible disgust, regretted the next moment, as I reflected that, to bring me this letter, he might be overstepping common rules, I raised the envelope to the light and recognized, to my intense disappointment, the well-known characters of Bainrothe's—small, rigid, neat, constrained.

My heart, which a moment before had beat audibly to my own ear, sank like a stone in my breast, and I sat for a time holding the letter mutely, uncertain how to proceed. Should I return it unread, and thus hurl the gauntlet in the traitor's face, or be governed by expedience (word ever so despised by me of old), and trace the venom of the viper, by his trail, back to his native den?

After a brief conflict of feeling, I determined on the wiser course—that of self-humiliation as a measure of profound policy.

I broke the seal, the well-known "dove-and-vulture" effigy which he called in heraldry "The quarry" and claimed as his rightful crest. Very significantly, indeed, did it strike me now, though I had jested on the subject so merrily of old with Evelyn and George Gaston.

The letter was of very recent date, and ran as follows—I have the original still, and this is an exact copy:

"On September 1st, or as soon thereafter as feasible, I shall call to see you, Miriam, in your retirement, which I am glad to hear has so far been beneficial. Should I find you in a condition to *make* conditions, I shall lay before you a very advantageous offer of marriage I had received for you before your shipwreck. Should you accept this offer, and attach your signature to a few papers that I shall bring with me (papers important to the respectability of your whole family as well as my own), I shall at once resign to you your father's house and the guardianship of Mabel. The chimera that alarmed you to frenzy can have no further existence, either in fact or fancy. I am about to contract an advantageous marriage with a foreign lady of rank, wealth, and beauty, to whom I hope soon to introduce you. I need not mention her name, if you are wise. Be patient and cheerful; cultivate your talents, and take care of your good looks—no woman can afford to dispense with these, however gifted; and you will soon find yourself as free as that 'chartered libertine' the air, for which last two words I am afraid you will be malicious enough to substitute the name you will not find appended, of your true friend and guardian, B. B."

Had Wentworth spoken, then? Did he know of my immurement? Was it his beloved presence, his dear hand, that were to be made the prize of my silence and submission? Was the bitter pill of humiliation I was now swallowing to be gilded thus? No, no—a thousand times, no! He was not the man with whom to make such conditions—the man I loved—nay worshiped almost. He was of the old heroic mould, that would have preferred any certainty to suspense, and death itself to an instant's degradation.

He deemed me dead, and the obstacle that had risen between us needed no explanation now. The waves had swallowed all necessities like this. But, had he known me the inmate of a mad-house, no bolts or bars would have withheld him from my presence. His own eyes could alone have convinced him of such ruin as was alleged against me by these friends.

From this survey of my utter helplessness I turned suddenly to confront the deep, dark, salient eyes of the disciple of Hahnemann, real or pretended, fixed upon me with a glance that even his blue spectacles could not deprive of its subtle intensity.

Where had I seen before orbs of the same snake-like peculiarity of expression, or caught the outline of the profile which suddenly riveted my gaze as the light partially revealed it, then subsided into shadow again? I pondered this question for a moment while Dr. Englehart, silent, expectant perhaps, stood with his hand tightly grasping the back of a chair, on the seat of which he reposed one knee, in a position such as defiant school-boys often assume before a pedagogue.

As I have said, his head and body were again in shadow, as was, indeed, most of the chamber, for the rays which struggled through the thick ground glass of my astral lamp were as mild as moonbeams, and as unsatisfactory. But the light fell strong and red beneath the shade, and the full glare of the astral lamp seemed centred on that pudgy hand, in its inevitable glove, that had fixed so firm a gripe on the back of the mahogany chair as to strain open one of the fingers of the tight, tawny kid-glove worn by Dr. Englehart. This had parted slightly just above the knuckle of the front-finger, and revealed the cotton stuffing within. Nay, more, the ruby ring with its peculiar device was thus exposed, which graced the slender finger of the charlatan! I do not apply this term as concerned the profession he affected at all, but merely (as shall be seen later) as one appropriate to himself individually.

There must be beings of all kinds to constitute a world, philosophers tell us, and he, no doubt, so long in ignorance of it, had stumbled suddenly on his proper vocation at last. The *rôle* he was playing (so far successfully) had doubtless been the occasion of an exquisite delight to him, unknown to simpler mortals, who masquerade not without dread misgivings of detection. I for one, when affecting any costume not essentially belonging to me, or covering my face even with a paper-mask for holiday diversion, have had a feeling of unusual transparency and obviousness, so to speak, which precluded on my part every thing like a successful maintenance of the part I was attempting to play. It was as if some mocking voice was saying: "This is Miriam Monfort, the true Miriam; the person you have known before as such was only making believe—but the Simon-pure is before you, a volume of folly that all who run may read! Behold her—she was never half so evident before!"

But to digress thus in the very moment of detection, of recognition, seems irrelevant. The flash of conviction was as instantaneous in its action in my mind as that of the lightning when it strikes its object. I stood confounded, yet enlightened, all ablaze!—but the subject of this discovery did not seem in the least to apprehend it, or to believe it possible, in his mad, mole-like effrontery of self-sufficiency, that by his own track he could be betrayed.

"Vat ansair shall I bear to Mr. Bainrothe from his vard?" asked the Mercury of my Jove, clasping his costumed hands together, then dropping them meekly before him. "I vait de reply of Miss Monfort vid patience. Dere is pen, and ink, and papair, I perceive, on dat table. Be good enough to write at once your reply to de vise conditions of your excellent guardian."

"You know them, then?" I said, quickly, glancing at him with a derisive scorn that did not escape his observation.

"I have dat honnair," was the hypocritical reply, accompanied by a profound bow.

"Disgrace, rather," I substituted. "But you have your own stand-point of view, of course. The shield that to you is white, to me is black as Erebus. You remember the knights of fable?"

"Always the same—always indomitable!" I heard him murmur, so low that it was marvelous how the words reached my ear, tense as was every sense with disdainful excitement. Yet he simply said aloud, after his impulsive stage-whisper: "Excuse me! I understand not your allusions. I pretend not to de classics; my leetle pills—" and he hesitated, or affected to do so.

"Enough—I waive all apologies; they only prolong an interview singularly distasteful to me for many reasons. You are behind the curtain, I cannot doubt, and understand not only the contents of that absurd letter, but its unprincipled references. To Basil Bainrothe I will never address one line; but you may say to him that I scorn him and his conditions. Yet, helpless as I am, and in his hands, tell him to bring his emancipation papers, and I will sign them, though they cost me all I possess of property. My sister I will not surrender any longer to his care, nor my right in her, which, with or without his consent, is perfect when I reach my majority. As to the suitor to whom he alluded, he had better be allowed to speak for himself when this transaction is over. I shall then decide very calmly on his merits, tarnished, as these might seem, from such recommendation."

"He is one who has loved you long, lady," said the man, sadly, speaking ever in that made and husky voice (wonderful actor that he was by nature!), which he sustained so well that, had I not unmistakably identified him, it might have imposed on my ear as real. "Hear what has been written on this subject: When others have forsaken you and left you to your fate, he has continued faithful to your memory. The revelation of your immurement was made simultaneously to two men who called themselves your lovers, and its sad necessity explained by your ever-watchful guardian. One of these lovers repudiated your claims upon him, and turned coldly from the idea of uniting his fate to that of one who had even for an hour been a suspected lunatic; the other declared himself willing to take her as she was to his arms, even though her own were loaded with the chains of a mad-house! Penniless and abandoned by all the world, and with a clouded name, he woos her as his wife—the woman he adores!"

And, as he read, or seemed to read, these words, with scarce an accent to mar their impetuous flow, Dr. Englehart drew in his breath with the hissing sound of passion, and folded his arms tightly across his padded breast, as if they enfolded the bride he was suing for in another's name.

"And who, let me ask, is this Paladin of chivalry?" I inquired, derisively. "Give me his name, that I may consider the subject well and thoroughly before we meet at last."

"Excuse me if I refuse to give the name of eider of dese gentlemen at dis onhappy season," he rejoined. "Wen de brain is all right again"—tapping his own forehead — "your guardian will conduct the faithful knight to kneel at de feet of her he loves so well."

"And the other—where is he?" fell involuntarily from my lips—my heaving heart—an inquiry that I regretted as soon as it was uttered; for, affecting sorrowful mystery, the man inclined himself toward me and whispered in my ear confidentially:

"Plighted to another, and gone where no eyes of yours shall rest on him again."

"Pander—liar—spy!" burst from my passionate lips as in all the fury of desperation I turned from the creature who had so wantonly wounded my self-respect, and waved to him to begone. Another name quivered on my lips, but I checked it on their threshold after that first burst of indignation instantly subdued.

I was not brave enough nor strong enough to hazard a shaft like that which might have been returned to me so deathfully. I would let the barrier stand which he had erected between us, and which to demolish would be to lay myself open, perhaps, to insult of the darkest description.

Let the ostrich with his head in the sand still imagine himself unseen; the masquerader still conceive himself secure beneath his paper travesty; the serpent still coil apparently unrecognized beside the bare, gray stone that reveals him to the eye—I was too cowardly, too feeble, to cope with strategy and double-dyed duplicity like this!

So the man went his way with his silly secret undiscovered, as he deemed, and that it might remain so to the end, as far as he could know, I devoutly prayed. For I knew of old the unscrupulous lengths to which, when nerved by hate or disappointment or passions of any kind, he could go, without a particle of mercy for his victims or remorse for his ill-doing.

When Dr. Englehart was gone—for so I still choose to call him for some reasons, although I give my reader credit for still more astuteness than I possessed myself, and believe that he has long ago recognized, through this cloud of mystery and travesty thrown about him, an old acquaintance—the child Ernie rose from the bed on which he had lain tremulous and observant, with his small hands clinched, his eyes on fire. "Ernie kill bad man!" he exclaimed, ferociously, "for trouble missy. Give Ernie letter—he carry it away and hide it; bad letter—make poor Mirry cry."

"No, Ernie, I will keep it," I said, as I laid it carefully aside. "It shall stand as a sign and testimony of treachery to the end. Go to sleep, little child; but first say your prayers, so that the good angels may sit by you all night. Don't you hear Mrs. Clayton groaning? Poor Clayton! I must go and comfort her and soothe her pains, as Dinah cannot do. And, now that the bad doctor is gone home, and we are all locked up again securely, we shall rest peacefully, I trust; and so, good-night!"

## CHAPTER VII.

From being the most silent of children, a perfect creep-mouse in every way, Ernie had become fearfully loquacious under my care, and was now as talkative as he had ever been observant.

The action that most children develop through exercise of limb had been reserved for his untiring tongue. He had literally learned to talk from hearing me read aloud, which I did daily, much to Mrs. Clayton's delight and edification, for the benefit of my own lungs, which suffered from such confirmed silence, as I had at first indulged in. His exquisite ear—his prodigious memory—aided him in the acquirement of words, and even long and difficult sentences, of which he delivered himself oracularly when engaged with his blocks and dominoes.

He told himself wonderful stories in which the "buful faiwry" and "hollible" giant of the story-books figured largely. I am almost ashamed to acknowledge that I would hold my breath and strain my ear at times to listen to these murmured stories, self-addressed, as I have never done to receive the finest ebullitions of eloquence or the veriest marvels of the *raconteur*. There was something so sweet, so wondrous to me in this little, ever-babbling baby-brain fountain, content with its own music, having no thought of auditors or effect, no care for appreciation, totally self-addressed and self-absorbed, that I was never weary of giving it my ear and interest. Had the child known of or perceived this, the effect would have been destroyed, and a fatal self-consciousness have been instituted instead of this lotus-eating infantile *abandon*—the very existence of which mood indicated genius. What poor Ernie's father might have been I could only surmise from his own qualities, which, after all, may have flowed from a far-off source; but that his mother had been gentle, simple, and inefficient, I knew full well, from my slight acquaintance with her, and observation of her non-resisting organization. Ernie, on the contrary, grappled with obstacles uncomplainingly, and was only outspoken in his moments of gratification. His was the temperament that is the noblest and the most magnanimous in its very moulding. Whining children are selfish, as a rule, and petty-minded, and most often incapable of enjoyment—which last is a gift of itself that goes not always with possession.

Among other accomplishments self-acquired, Ernie had the power of mimicry to a singular degree. Mrs. Clayton had a slight hitch in her gait of late from rheumatic suffering, which he simulated solemnly, notwithstanding every effort on my part to restrain him.

Without a smile or any effort of mirth, he would limp behind as she walked across the floor, unconscious of his close attendance, and when she would turn suddenly and detect him, and shake her clinched fist at him, half in jest, he would retaliate by a similar gesture, and scowl, and stamp of the foot, that so nearly resembled her own proceedings as to cause me much internal merriment. But of course for his own advantage, as well as from regard for her feelings, it was necessary for me on such occasions to assume a gravity of deportment bordering on displeasure.

It may be supposed, then, that when, on the morning after Dr. Englehart's visit, before my chamber had been swept and garnished, and while Mrs. Clayton was busy in her own, Ernie brought me a letter and laid it on the table before me, as Dr. Englehart had done the night before in his presence, I was infinitely amused.

What, then, was my surprise in stooping over it to find this letter addressed to myself in the unfamiliar yet never-to-be-forgotten character of Wardour Wentworth!

After the first moment of bewilderment I opened the already-fastened letter—closed, as was the fashion of the day, without envelope, and sealed originally with wax, of which a few fragments still remained alone.

The date, the subject, the earnest contents, convinced me that I now held the clew of that mystery which had baffled me so long, and that the missing letter said to have been lost at Le Noir's Landing was at last in my possession. It needed not this additional proof of treachery to convince me that my suspicions had been correct, and that, next to the arch-fiend Bainrothe, I owed the greatest misery of my life to him who, in his ill-adjusted disguise, had dropped this letter from his pocket on the preceding evening—my evil genius, Dr. Englehart—*alias* Luke Gregory.

It was a gracious thing in God to permit me to owe the great happiness of this discovery to the little crippled child he had cast upon my care so mysteriously, and I failed not to render to him with other grateful acknowledgments "most humble and hearty thanks" for this crowning grace. Henceforth Hope should lend her torch to light my dearth—her wings to bear me up—her anchor wherewith to moor my bark of life wherever cast, and to the poor waif I cherished I owed this immeasurable good. Had Mrs. Clayton anticipated him with her infallible besom—that housewifely detective, that drags more secrets to light than ever did paid policeman—I should never have grasped this talisman of love and hope, never have waked up as I did wake up from that hour to the endurance which immortalizes endeavor, and renders patience almost pleasurable.

On the back of this well-worn letter was a pencil-scrawl, which, although I read it last, I present first to my reader, that he may trace link by link the chain of villainy that bound together my two oppressors.

It was in the small, clear calligraphy of Basil Bainrothe, before described; characterized, I believe, as a back-hand—and thus it ran:

"You are right—it was a master-stroke! Keep them in ignorance of each other, and all will yet go well. I sail to-morrow, and have only time to inclose this with a pencilled line. Try and head them at New York. My first idea was the best—my reason I will explain later.

"Yours truly, B. B.

"N. B.—The man could not have played into our hands better than by taking up such an impression. There is no one there to undeceive him."

THE LETTER.

"My Miriam: Your note, through the hands of Mr. Gregory, has been received—read, noted, pondered over with pain and amazement. The avowal of your name so uselessly withheld from me, lets in a whole flood of light, blinding and dazzling, too, on a subject that fills me with infinite solicitude.

"There have been strange reserves between us that never ought to have existed, on my part as well as yours. I should have told you that I once had a half-sister, called Constance Glen—older than myself by many years—who married during my long absence from our native land a gentleman much older than herself, an Englishman by the name of Monfort, and, after giving birth to a daughter, died suddenly. These particulars I gathered from strangers, but there were many wanting which you can best supply. I know that this gentleman had a daughter, or daughters, by an earlier marriage—and I can find no clew to the date of my sister's marriage—which might in itself determine the possible age of her own daughter. That this child survived I have painful cause to remember. I had sustained shipwreck, and was in abeyance for clothes and money both, when it occurred to me to call on my brother-in-law, present to him my credentials, and remain a few days at his house as his guest, in the enjoyment of my sister's society, until my needs could be supplied from certain resources at a distance. The reception I met with from his elder daughter, and the information she haughtily gave me, determined my course. I sought no more the inhospitable roof of Mr. Monfort, to find shelter beneath which I had forfeited all claim by the death of my sister, then first suddenly revealed to me. Her child, I was told, had been recently injured by burning and could not be seen, even by so near a relative, and the manner of the young lady, whom I now identify as Evelyn Monfort, was such as to lead me at the time to believe this a mere excuse or evasion, which I did not seek to oppose.

"It is just possible that there may be a third sister, yet I think I have heard you say you had but one, and this reminiscence is anguish to my mind. Even more, the careless and unwarrantable allusions of Mr. Gregory to certain scars, evidently from burns that he had the insolence to observe on your neck and arms, and remark upon as mere foils to their beauty, in my first acquaintance with you and before I had a right to silence him, recurred to me as a partial confirmation of my fears. Without explaining to him my motives, I questioned him on this subject again soon after he handed me your note, a proceeding that I should have shrunk from as gross and unworthy of a gentleman under any other circumstances. I did not stop to think what impression my inquiries would leave upon his mind, ever prone to levity and suspicion; but he must have seen that I was deeply moved, and that no impertinent curiosity could sway me to such a course with regard to the woman I loved and had openly declared my plighted wife. You will understand all this and make allowance for me. Write to me immediately, and relieve, if possible, my intense solicitude. At all events, let me know the truth, and look it in the face as soon as may be. Any reality is better than suspense. Yet I must 'hope against hope,' or surrender wholly. I have not time to write another line. My business is imperative, or I should certainly retrace my steps.

"Yours eternally, WENTWORTH."

The man who wrote this letter was capable of condensing in a few calm words a world of passion, whether he spoke or wrote them; but he had governed his pen carefully in his agonizing uncertainty. It was yet to be determined when he penned these lines whether he should be considered a lover addressing his mistress, or an uncle writing to his niece, and in this bitter perplexity he commanded his inclinations to the side of principle.

I wept with tears of joy and thankfulness above this constrained epistle—I pressed it to my heart, my lips, a thousand times, in the quiet hours of night, in the moments of retirement my jailer granted me. The child Ernie alone saw and wondered at these manifestations of which I first saw the extravagance through his solemn imitations thereof, which yet made me catch him rapturously in my arms and kiss him a thousand times, until he put me aside, at last, with decorous dignity, as one transcending privilege.

By some vicarious process, best understood by lovers, I lavished on little Ernie a thousand terms of endearment, meant only for another, and by the light of my own happiness he seemed transfigured. He was identified with the lifting away of a burden more bitter than captivity itself. They could but kill my body now—my soul was filled with a new life that nothing could extinguish; and believing in Wentworth, I felt that I could die happy, let death come when and how it would. I knew now that in the course of time, whether I lived or died, Wentworth would know that I was not his niece, and claim Mabel as his own, remembering my estimate of those who held her in charge. Then would the tide of love and passion, so long repressed, roll back in its old channel, and he would leave no stone unturned, no path unexplored, whereby to trace my fate.

To this, as yet, he held no clew. The sea had seemed to swallow Miriam Harz, by which name I had been registered in the ship's books and known to the passengers; nor could it be surmised that the young "mad girl," since spoken of, as I had been told, in the papers, as having been restored to her friends by the accident of meeting the Latona, and Miriam Monfort, were one and the same person. But if the time should come when all should be explained, either by my own lips or the revelations of others, good cause might Basil Bainrothe and his confederate have to tremble!

Like all cold, patient, deeply-feeling men, there were untold reserves of power and passion in the nature of Wardour Wentworth which might, for aught I knew to the contrary, tend naturally to and culminate in revenge. The wish to retaliate was, I knew, a fundamental fault in my own character, one I had often occasion to struggle with even in childhood, when Evelyn, my despot, was also my dependant, and generosity had been called to the aid of forbearance. Vengeance was a fierce thirst in my Judaic heart which only Christian streams could ever allay or quench, and I judged the man I loved by self—not always a fitting standard of comparison.

And Gregory! I could imagine well the fiendish delight with which he had seen me day by day writhing uncomplainingly beneath the unexplained and as I had deemed unsuspected alienation of Wentworth, the cause of which his act had wrapped in mystery! Afraid to tamper with the note I gave him for the cool, discerning eye of Wentworth, curiosity had at first led him to break the seal of that intrusted to his care in return, and dark malevolence to retain it rather than destroy, for the eye of his confederate. That he had dispatched it at once for Paris was very evident from the pencilling on the back of the letter; and that the snare was set for me already, in which the accident of the encountered raft proved an assistant, I could not doubt.

I fell into the hands of Bainrothe on shipboard instead of into those of Gregory in New York; this was the only difference, for subterfuge could have done its work as well, if not as daringly, on land as on sea; and the league of iniquity was made before I sailed from Savannah.

How perfectly I could comprehend, for the first time since this revelation, what Wentworth must have suffered beneath his burden of unrelieved doubt and conjecture! I could see how, day by day, as no answer came to change the current of his thoughts, conviction slowly settled down like a cloud upon his heart, his reason; and what stern confirmation of all he dreaded most, my silence must have seemed to him!

All this I saw in my mental survey with pity, with concern, with wild desire to fly to him, and whisper truth and consolation in his arms; for I loved this man as it is given to passionate, earnest natures to love but once, be it early or late; loved him as Eve loved Adam, when the whole inhabited earth was given to those two alone.

"You seem in very good spirits to-day, Miss Monfort," said Mrs. Clayton, with unusual asperity on one occasion, when, holding Ernie in my arms, I lavished endearments upon him; "your king, indeed! your angel! I really believe you admire as well as love that hideous little elf."

"Of course I do," Mrs. Clayton; "all things I love are beautiful to me;" and I remembered how Bertie's plain face had grown into touching loveliness in my sight from the affection I bore her.

"And do you really love this child?"

"Most certainly, and very tenderly too; is he not my sweetest consolation in this dreary life?"

"What if they remove him?"

"Ah! what, indeed!" and, relaxing my grasp, I clasped my hands together patiently; that thought had occurred to me before.

"It is a very strong affection to have sprung up from a short acquaintance on a raft," she remarked, sententiously.

"I saved his infant life, you know; and the benefactor always loves the thing he benefits. It is on this principle alone God loves his erring creatures, Mrs. Clayton, rest assured."

"If you had loved the child with true friendship, you would have pushed him into the sea, rather than have held him in your arms above it."

"Do you suppose he is less near to God than you or I—to Christ the all-merciful?" I questioned, sternly. "Much rather would I have that infant's yet unconscious hope of heaven than either yours or mine, Mrs. Clayton!"

"But his earthly hope—it was that I alluded to; what chance for him? Poor, weakly, deformed; he had better be at rest than knocked from pillar to post, as he must be in this hard, cold world of chance and change."

"And that shall never be while I live, Ernie," I said, taking him again in my lap, at his silent solicitation. "Why, Mrs. Clayton, with such a noble soul, such intelligence as this child possesses, he may fill a pulpit, and save erring souls, or write such beautiful poems and romances as shall thrill the heart, or draw from an instrument sounds as divine as De Beriot's, or paint a picture, and immortalize his name; there is nothing too good, too great for Ernie to do, should God grant him life to achieve; and, as surely as I am spared to be enfranchised, shall I make this gifted child my charge."

"You are perfectly infatuated, Miss Monfort; I declare, I shall begin to believe—"

"No, you shall not begin to believe any such thing," I interrupted her, smiling; "you are surely too sensible and just a woman to begin to believe fallacies thus late in the day."

"Have it your own way," she said, sharply; "you always get the better of me at last."

"Not always," I pursued, "or I should not be here, you know. It rests with you to keep or let me go—"

"To ruin my child's husband! There, now! you have my life-secret," she said, with a desperate gesture; "use it as you will."

I understood more than ever the hopelessness of my case from the moment of that impulsive revelation, to which I made no answer.

"What is more," she said, huskily, "I, too, am watched; I never knew this until two days ago: a negro man, an attendant of the house, an old servant of your guardian's, I believe, guards the doors below, and refuses to let me pass to and fro. Dinah, even, is employed to dog my steps. This is not exactly what I bargained for; yet, in spite of all, on her account I shall be faithful to the end." And for a time she busied herself in that careful dusting of the ornaments of the chamber, which seemed mechanical, so habitual was it to her sense of order and tidiness.

Her hand was on the gold-emblazoned Bible, I remember, and her party-colored bunch of plumes lifted above it, as if for immediate action, when her arm fell heavily to her side, and she heaved a bitter sigh, so deep, it sounded like a long-suppressed sob, rather, to my ear.

"If I could only think you did not hate me, Miss

Miriam," she said, "I believe I could be better satisfied to lead the life I do."

"Hate you! Why should I hate you, Mrs. Clayton? You are only a tool in the hands of my persecutor, I know, from your own confession, and I understand your motive better in the last few moments than I did before (inadequate as it seems to my sense of justice), for aiding this oppressor. You have been very kind to me in some respects; an inferior person could have tortured in a thousand ways, where you have shown yourself considerate, delicate even, and for all this I thank you more than I can express. I should be very ungrateful, indeed, were I to hate you. The word is strong."

"Yet you prefer even that hump-backed child to me or my society," she said, peevishly.

"The comparison cannot be instituted with any propriety," I responded, gravely, turning away and dismissing the boy to his blocks and books, as I did so, which made for him, I knew, a fairy kingdom of delight, through the aid of his splendid imagination.

A commonplace infant will tire of the choicest toys; they are to such minds but effigies and delusion, which last, the delight of imaginative infancy, to the cut and dried, dull, childish understanding is impossible.

I once overheard one little girl at a theatre—a splendid spectacle, calculated to dazzle and delight imaginative childhood—say to another: "It is nothing but make-believe! That house and garden are only painted. See how they shake! And the women are dressed in paste jewelry, like that our cook-maid wears to parties, and no jeweler would give a cent for them; and the fairies are poor girls, dressed up for the occasion; and the whole play is made up as they go. You see, I know all about it, father says."

I heard no more, but had a glimpse of a little, eager face suddenly dashed in its expression, and of small fingers pressed to unwilling ears to shut out unwelcome truths.

The discriminating child seemed a little monster in my eyes, who ought to have been sent out of the way at once of all companions capable of *abandon* and enjoyment; and, as to the "father" she quoted from, I could imagine him as the embodiment of asinine wisdom, so to speak—the quintessence of the practical, which so often, I observe, inclines its devotees to idiocy!

I knew very well that Wattie was not of the stamp to doubt the truth and splendor of "Aladdin and the Wonderful Lamp," or "Cinderella," as surveyed from the stage-box, in his confiding infancy, any more than to believing in baubles when the time came to justly discriminate. Woe for the incredulous child, too matter-of-fact to be enlisted in the creations of fancy, and who tastes in infancy the chief bitterness of age—the incapability of surrendering life to the ideal!

How fresh imagination keeps the heart—how young! What a glorious gift it is when rightly used and governed! Hear Charlotte Bronté's testimony, as recorded by her biographer: "They are all gone," she says, "the sisters I so loved, and I have only my imagination left to comfort me. But for this solace I should despair or perish." The words are not exact—the book is not beside me, but such is their substance. He who lists can seek them for himself in the pages of that wondrous spell woven by Mrs. Gaskell—that tragic and strange biography which once in a season of deep despondency did more to reconcile me to my own condition, through my pity and admiration for another, than all the condolences that came so freely from lip and pen. Every fabric that love had erected crumbled about her or turned to Dead-Sea ashes on her lip. See what a world of passion those French letters and themes of hers betray!

The brand of suffering and suffocating sorrow is on every one of them, plain to the eye of the initiated alone, they who have gazed on the wonders of the inner temple —the holy of holies—and gone forth reverently to dream of the revelation evermore in silence.

But, above every ruin of hope, or pride, or affection, like an imperial banner flung from "the outer wall," her imagination waved and triumphed. "The clouds of glory" she trailed after her were dyed in spheres unapproachable by death, or shame, or disappointment, and the gift described in the Arabian story as conferred by the genii's salve when he touched therewith the eyes of the traveler and caused him to see all the wonders of the earth, its gems, its gold, its gleaming chrysolites, its inward fires, unobscured by the interposition of dust and clay, which veiled them from all the rest of humanity, may stand as a type of her ideality.

## CHAPTER VIII.

THE six weeks which had been allotted to me as the term of my captivity were accomplished, and still Mr. Basil Bainrothe came not—wrote not. I had seen the month of August glide away, its progress marked only by the changing fruits and flowers of the season, and the more fervent light that pierced through the Venetian blinds when turned heavenward, for it was through these alone that the light of day was permitted to visit my chamber.

Where, then, was the place of my captivity situated? In the environs of a great city, possibly, for the wind often blew, laden with fragrance as from choice rather than extensive gardens, through my casement, and the shadow of a tall tree impending over the skylight of the bath-room was, when windy, cast so distinctly on its panes as to convince me of the neighborhood of an English elm, the foliage of which tree I knew like an alphabet.

And then, those fairy, Sabbath chimes! Were such musical bells duplicated in adjacent cities? or was I, indeed, near our old, beloved church, in which memory so distinctly revealed our ancient, velvet-lined pew, my father's bowed head, and the venerable pastor rising white-robed and saintly in his pulpit to bid all the earth keep silent before the Lord! Conjecture was rife! Thus August passed away.

My birthday had gone by, and the equinox was upon us, with its rapid changes of sun and storm, when one of these tempests, accompanied by hail of unusual size, shattered to fragments the skylight of the bath-room. This hail-storm was succeeded by a deluge of rain, which flooded not only the adjacent closet, but the chamber I occupied, among other evils completely submerging the superb Wilton carpet, concerning the safety of which Mrs. Clayton felt immense responsibility.

A glazier came as soon as the weather permitted, who was carefully escorted through my chamber by Mrs. Clayton to ascertain the repairs to be made—a fresh-looking, white-aproned Irish lad, I remember (for a human being was a novelty to me then), who found it necessary, in order to repaint the wood-work, to bear the sash away with him, leaving behind his tray of chisels and putty, and the light step-ladder he had brought with him on his shoulder, and on whose return I vainly waited as a chance for communication with the outer world.

While Dinah was busy with mops and brooms drying the carpet, and Mrs. Clayton thoroughly occupied with her active superintendence of the needful operations, little mischievous, meddlesome Ernie had made his way, contrary to all rules, beneath and behind my bed, and torn off a goodly portion of the gray and gilded paper which had so far effectually aided to conceal a closed door situated behind the bed-head, from which the frame had been removed. Then, for the first time since our acquaintance, did I slap sharply those little, busy fingers which I could have kissed for thankfulness, and, watching my opportunity, I replaced the paper, unseen by Mrs. Clayton, with the remains of a gum-arabic draught which had been prescribed for his cough. I knew that, after experiencing such condign punishment, he would return no more to the scene of his destruction, and that he might forget both injury and discovery, I devoted myself to his amusement during that active, long, rainy day with unhoped-for success.

The glazier had announced to Mrs. Clayton that his return might be deferred for four-and-twenty hours, and, as the succeeding day was clear and warm, I proceeded, in spite of broken sashes, to take my daily bath as usual at twelve o'clock.

Mrs. Clayton, with her prison-key in her pocket, and her snuffbox at hand, yielded herself to the delight of ginger-nuts and her stocking-basket, and rested calmly after her fatigues of the preceding day; and Ernie, attracted by the crunching noise—the sound of dropping nuts, perhaps, which betrayed the presence of his favorite article of food—hastened to keep her company—a thing he never did disinterestedly, it must be confessed.

An opportunity now presented itself for observation which I knew might not again occur during my whole captivity; and surely no sailor ever ascended to the masthead of the Pinta with a heart more heaved with emotion than was mine, as I placed my foot on the last rung of the ladder, and towered from my waist upward above the skylight. I had drawn the bolt within, as I invariably did while bathing, and with a feeling of proud security I stood and surveyed the scene beneath and around me. The angle of vision did not, it is true, embrace objects immediately below me, owing to the projecting cornices of the flat roof (a mere excrescence from the original structure, as this was), but beyond this the eye swept for some distance uninterruptedly.

Bathed in the golden light of that autumn noonday

sun, I saw and recognized a long-familiar scene, and for a moment I reeled on the slender step as I did so, and all grew dark around me. But, with one of those energetic impulses that come to us all in time of emergency, I recovered my balance in time to save myself from falling; and eagerly and wistfully, as looks the dying wretch on the dear faces he is soon to see no more, I gazed upon the paradise from which fiends had driven me.

There, indeed, just as I had left it, lay the deep-green grassy lawn, with its richly-burdened flower-pots, its laburnums, and white and purple lilacs, and drooping guelder-rose bushes, and its great English walnut-tree towering, like a Titan, in the centre. There was the hawthorn-hedge my father's hand had planted, and the fountain-like weeping-willow my mother had set, in memory of her dead, whose graves were far away; and there towered the lofty elm-trees, with their long, low, sweeping branches, meeting in friendly greeting, to two of which a swing had once been attached as a bond of union—a swing in which it had once been my childish pleasure to sway and read, while Mabel sat beside me with her head upon my shoulder, held securely in her place by my strong, loving, encircling arm.

Nor were these all to assure me that, after a year of melancholy and eventful absence, I looked again upon the precincts of home. A little farther on rose the gray wall and tower of the library and belfry, half concealed by its heavy coating of ivy, glossy and dark, and shutting away all other view of the mansion. Beyond these last was the pavilion my father had built for the play-house of his children, through the open lattice-door of which I saw a girl seated at her work, with graceful, bending neck, and half-averted face. A moment later,

Claude Bainrothe lounged across the sward, cigar in hand. At his approach, the face within was turned, and I recognized, at a glance, that of my young aurora-like companion of the raft, Ada Greene. Then gazing cautiously around, as if to elude observation (never dreaming of the eye dropped like a bird's upon him), he lifted the rosy face in his hand and kissed it thrice right loverly!

I saw no more—I would not witness more—for had I not learned already all that I asked or ought to know? Well might the dear old chimes ring out their Sabbath welcome to one who had obeyed their summons from her childhood up to womanhood! Well might the summer air bear on its wings greeting of familiar odors, lost and found!

This was no idle dream, no mirage of a vagrant brain like that sea-picture, or that wild vision at Beauseincourt, but sober, and sad, and strange reality. I understood my position from that moment, geographically as well as physically. I was a prisoner in the house of Basil Bainrothe (while he, perchance, reigned lordly in my own); that house whose hidden arcana I had never explored, and which, beyond its parlor and exterior, was to me as the dwelling of a stranger.

Derisively deferential, he had resigned to me this secluded chamber in the ell—his own particular sanctum, I remember to have heard—and betaken himself, in all probability, to the more spacious mansion of his former neighbor.

Far wiser, even if sadder, than I went up its rounds, did I descend that ladder!

Half an hour after I had entered it, and with new hope, I emerged from the bath-room as fresh as a naiad, having first abstracted from the tool-box of the glazier two tiny chisels of different sizes, and a small lump of putty, which I secreted, on my first opportunity, in my favorite hiding-place—a hollow in the post of my bedstead—an accidental discovery of mine, made during Mrs. Clayton's first illness, since which I had always insisted on making up my own bed, much to her relief.

My conscience so disturbed me on the score of this theft, that I hastened to secrete my only remaining piece of gold in the glazier's box; ill-judged, as this appeared to me on reflection. The boy was an apprentice, evidently, and might else, I thought, at the time, have been the loser. I feared to add a line, and dared not seek a passing word with him, so carefully was I watched.

I next examined, with the eye of scientific scrutiny, two massive rulers that lay on my table, one made of maple-wood, and the other of ebony, and, having selected the first as most available for my purpose, prepared to commence the most arduous undertaking of my life—the careful shaping of a wooden key!

I had read somewhere that, during the French Revolution, a young peasant-girl, by means of such an instrument, had set at large her lover, or her brother, in *La Vendée;* having taken with soft wax the outline of the wards of the lock, in a moment of opportunity.

That day my work began—three times a failure, but at last successful. With the aid of putty, gradually allowed to harden, I obtained the mould I desired, in the dead of night, and afterward, whenever privacy, even for a few minutes, was mine, I drew from my bosom my sacred piece of sculpture, and worked upon it with knife and chisel alternately, as devotee never worked on sculptured crucifix. Never shall I forget the rapture, the ecstasy of that moment, in which, ensconced between my bed-head and the wall, I slowly turned the key, first thoroughly soaked in oil, in the morticed wards, and knew, by the slight giving of the door, that it was unlocked.

Not Ali Baba, when he entered the robbers' cave, and saw the heaps of gold—all his by the force of one magic word; not Aladdin, when the genius of the lamp rose to his bidding, bearing salvers of jewels, which were to purchase for him the hand of the sultan's daughter; not Sindbad, when he saw the light which led him to the aperture of egress from the sepulchre in which he had been pent up with his wife's body to die—knew keener or more triumphant sensations than filled my bosom as I laid that completed key next my heart, after turning it cautiously backward and forward in my prison-lock!

I dared not, at that time, draw back the bolt above, that confined it loosely yet securely, or turn the silver knob sufficiently to set it even ever so little ajar; but I did both later, when oil had time to do its subtle work, and I could effect my experiment in silence. Yet I hazarded nothing of the sort when the quick ear of Mrs. Clayton held watch in the adjoining room. I was obliged to take advantage of those moments of rare absence, when, double-locking the doors of her chamber, both inner and outer, she would descend, for a few minutes, to the realms below, returning so suddenly and silently as almost to surprise me, on one or two occasions, at my work.

About the time of the completion of my experiment, I became aware of sounds in the room beneath my chamber, and sometimes on the great stairway (of which I now knew the largest platform was situated very near the head of my bed), that gave token of occupancy.

The rattling of china and silver might be discerned in

the ancient dining-room, at morn and night. The occupant probably dined elsewhere, but the regularity of these meals was unmistakable.

I recognized, faintly, the step of Bainrothe on the stairway, distinguishing it readily from any other, as it passed and repassed my hidden door.

October had now set in, with a chilliness unusual to that bland season, and I asked for and obtained permission to have a fire kindled in the wide and gloomy grate of my chamber, hitherto unused by me.

About this household flame, Ernie, Mrs. Clayton, and I gathered harmoniously; she with her unfailing work-basket, I with book or pencil, the baby with his blocks and dominoes and painted pictures—the only happy and truly industrious spirit of the group. My true work was done—else might it never have been completed.

The presence of fire was indispensable to Mrs. Clayton, and, from the time of its first lighting, she left me but seldom alone. Her rheumatic limbs needed the solace that I had no heart to grudge her, distasteful as she was to me, and becoming more so day by day—false as I now knew her to be—false at heart.

How hatred grows, when we once admit the germ—not, like love, parasitically—but strong, stanch, stern, alone throwing down fresh roots, even hour by hour, like the banyan, monarch of the Eastern forest. I am afraid I have a turn for this passion naturally, but for love as well, ten times more intense—so that one pretty well counterbalances the other.

To carry out the vine-simile, I might as well add at once that, in the end, the parasitical plant has triumphed, and stifled the sterner growth. In other words, Christianity has conquered Judaism.

"I suppose I may soon expect a visit from Mr. Bainrothe," I said one day to Mrs. Clayton. "I think my birthday approaches; can you tell me the day of the month? I know that of the week from remembering the Sabbath chimes."

I thought she started slightly at this announcement, but she replied, unflinchingly:

"The 5th, yes, I am quite sure it is the 5th of the month."

"Do you never see a newspaper, Mrs. Clayton, and, if so, can you not indulge me with a glimpse of one? I think it would do me good—remind me that I was alive. I have seen none since the account of Miss Lamarque's safety, for which God be praised."[1]

"No, Miss Monfort, it is simply impossible. I should be transgressing the rules of the establishment."

"Dr. Englehart's, I suppose, as if indeed there were such a person," I said, impetuously—unguardedly.

"Do you pretend to doubt it?" she asked, slowly, setting her greedy eyes upon my face, and dropping her darning-work and shell upon her knee. Why, what possesses you to-day, Miss Miriam?"

"I shall answer no questions, Mrs. Clayton—this right, at least, I reserve—but, the fact is, I doubt every thing

[1] The raft on which Miss Lamarque and her family had found refuge had been swept by the tempest of nearly every soul that clung to it, after a terrible night of storm and rain, during which that courageous lady—that Sybarite of society—sustained the fainting souls of her companions by singing the grand anthems of her Church, in a voice loud, clear, and sweet as that of a dying swan. One child was saved of the nine little ones, and the brother and sister remained almost alone on the raft. Let it be here mentioned that, at no period of her subsequent life, a long and apparently prosperous one, could Miss Lamarque bear to hear the circumstances of the wreck alluded to. Mr. Dunmore and his companions found a watery grave.

lately, except this child and God. I do not believe my Creator will forsake me utterly—I shall not, till the end." And tears rolled down my face, the first I had shed for days. I had been petrified, of late, by the resolution I was making, and the effort of mind it had cost me. I had felt, until now, that I was hardening into stone.

"You desire to see Mr. Bainrothe, I suppose," she remarked, after a long silence, during which she had again betaken herself to her occupation, without lifting her eyes as she asked the question.

"I desire to look my fate in the face at once, and understand his conditions," I replied, sullenly.

"But what if he is not here—what if Dr. Englehart—" lifting her eyes to mine.

"I cannot be mistaken," I interrupted, with impetuosity. "I have heard his step; he eats in the room below; I am convinced, for I know of old that bronchial cough of his—the effect of gormandism—"

Then suddenly, Ernie, looking up, made a revelation, irrelevant, yet to my ear terrible and astounding, but fortunately incomprehensible to my companion. What did that little vigilant creature ever fail to remark?

"Mirry make tea," he said, or seemed to say, and my face paled and flushed alternately, until my brain swam.

"Make tea?" said the voice of Mrs. Clayton, apparently at a great distance. "No, I will make the tea, Ernie, as long as we stay together. Mirry does not know how to draw tea like an Englishwoman."

Oh, fortunate misunderstanding! how great was the reaction it occasioned! From an almost fainting condition I rallied to vivacity, and, for long, weary hours, sat pointing out pictures to the boy, to win him to oblivion, and persuade him to silence. Singularly enough, but not unusual with him, he never resumed the topic. I had taken pains to hide my work from his observing eyes; and how he knew it, unless he lay silently and watched me from his little bed, when I worked at early dawn in mine, I never could conjecture. A few days later Mrs. Clayton announced to me that Mr. Bainrothe would call very shortly.

It was early morning, I remember, when she laid before me the card of "Basil Bainrothe," with its elaborate German characters, on which was written, in pencil, the addendum, "Will call at ten o'clock;" and, punctual as the hand to the hour, he knocked at the dressing-room door at the appointed time, and was admitted.

He entered with that light, jaunty step peculiar to him, and which I have consequently ever associated in others with impudence and guile. Hat and cane in the left hand, he entered; two fingers of the right raised to his lips, by way of salutation (he clinched his glove in the remainder), to be offered to me later, and ignored completely, then waved carelessly, as if condoning the offense.

He was quite a picture as he came in—a fashion-plate, and as such I coolly regarded him—fresh, fair, and smiling, looking younger, if possible, than when we parted a year before, and handsome, as that much-abused word goes, in his debonair, off-hand style of appearance.

He was dressed with even more than his usual care and trimness (wore patent-leather boots, my aversion from that hour, for these were the first I had ever seen), and lavender-colored pantaloons, very tightly strapped down over them; a glossy black coat and vest, and linen of unimpeachable quality and whiteness; while a chain of fine

Venetian gold held his watch, or eye-glass, or both, in suspension from his neck. Yet no beggar in rags ever appeared to me half so loathly as did this speckless dandy!

"You have come," I said, grimly, as he settled his shirt-collar to speak to me, after formally depositing his hat and cane, and a roll of paper he drew from his pocket, on the centre-table, and wiping his face carefully with his cambric, musk-scented handkerchief, unspeakably odious and unclean to my olfactories—"you have come at last; yet the greatest wonder to me is, how you dare appear at all before me," and I looked upon him right lionly, I believe.

"You were always inclined to assume the offensive with me, Miriam. Yet I confess you have a little shadow of reason this time, or seem to have, and I am here to-day for purposes of explanation or compromise" (bowing gracefully), and he rubbed his palms together very gently and complacently, looking around as he did so for a chair, which perceiving, and drawing to the table so as to face me where I sat on the sofa, he deposited himself upon, assuming at once his usual graceful pose.

It was a *fauteuil*, and he threw one arm over that of the chair, suffering his well-preserved white hand—always suggestive of poultices to me—with its signet ring, to droop in front of it—a hand which he moved up and down habitually, as he conversed, in a singularly soothing and mechanical fashion—his "pendulum" we used to call it in old times, Evelyn and I, when it was one of our chief resources for amusement to laugh at "Cagliostro," our *sobriquet* for this *ci-devant jeune homme*, it may be remembered.

"Let me premise, Miriam," he began, "by congratulating you on your improved appearance"—another benign bow. "You were so burned and blackened by exposure, and so—in short, so very wild-looking when I last saw you, that I began to fear for the result; but perfect rest and retirement, and good nursing, have effected wonders. I have never seen you so fair, so refined-looking, and yet so calm, as you are now (calmness, my child, is aristocratic—cultivate it!); even if a little thin and delicate from confinement, yet perfectly healthy, I cannot doubt, from what I see. Do assure me of your health, my dear girl. You are as dumb to-day as Grey's celebrated prophetess."

"All personal remarks as coming from you are offensive to me, Mr. Bainrothe," I rejoined; "proceed to your business at once, whatever that may be—a truce to preamble and compliments."

"You shall be obeyed," he remarked, bowing low and derisively. "Yet, believe me, nothing but my care for your fair fame and my own have led me to confine you in such narrow limits for a season which, I trust, is almost over. As to my persecutions, which, I am told, you allege as a reason for leaving your house and friends so precipitately, these are out of the question henceforth forever, I assure you"—with a wave of the velvet hand—"since I am privately married to a lady of rank and fortune, who will soon be openly proclaimed 'my wife,' and who will be found, on close acquaintance, worthy of your friendship."

While giving utterance to this tirade, Mr. Bainrothe was slowly unwinding a string from around the roll of papers he had laid on the table, and which he now proceeded to spread somewhat ostentatiously before me, still mute and impassive to all his advances as I continued to be.

"There are several," he said. "Your signature to each will be required, which, now that you are in your right mind again, and of age, will be binding, as you know. My witnesses shall be called in when the time comes. Dr. Englehart and Mrs. Clayton will suffice as proofs of these solemnities—these and others likely to occur."

"Solemnities! Levities, mockeries rather!" I could not help rejoining.

He felt the sarcasm. His florid cheek paled with anger, his yellow-speckled eyes glowed with lurid fire, he compressed his lips bitterly as he said:

"Marriage is usually considered a solemnity, Miss Monfort; and, let me assure you, it is only as a married woman I can conscientiously release you from confinement. You have shown yourself too erratic to be intrusted in future with your own liberties."

"Possibly," I rejoined. "Yet I mean to have the selection, let me assure you, in return, of the controller of my liberties—nay, have already selected him, for aught you know!"

My cool audacity seemed for a moment to paralyze even his own. He paused and surveyed me, as if in doubt of his own senses.

"*Impayable!*" I heard him murmur, softly, and, turning to the book-shelves, he left me for a time to master the contents of the three documents over which I was bending.

I read them in order as they were numbered, and became more and more indignant as their meaning opened upon my brain, and culminated at last in a sharp, sudden exclamation of utter disdain.

I started from my chair and approached him, paper in

hand. I think for a few moments the idea of personal danger possessed him, and the vision of a concealed dirk or pistol swam before his eyes, which he shielded with his hand, while he placed a chair between us; and, truth to say, there was murder in my heart, and in my eyes as well, I suppose, even if the mistrust went no further.

I could have obliterated him from the face of the earth at that moment as remorselessly as if he had been a viper in my path striking to sting me. Yet I advanced toward him with no demonstration or intentions of this kind, having the habits of lady-like breeding and usual innocence of weapons, and ignorance of the use thereof as well, to restrain me.

I forget. Close to my heart lay one of the sharp, shining chisels I had taken from the glazier in the bath-room.

"What is it you object to, Miriam?" he asked, in faltering tones, as his hand fell and his glimmering eyes encountered mine.

From that day I have believed the legend which tells that, when the Roman, helpless in his dungeon, thundered forth, "Slave! darest thou kill Caius Marius?" the armed minion of murder turned and fled, dropping the knife he held, in his panic, at the feet of the man he came to slay. Almost such effect was for a time observable in Basil Bainrothe.

It made me smile bitterly. "All, every thing," I answered. "The whole requisition, from first to last, is base, dastardly—crime-confessing, too—if seen with discriminating eyes. Why, if innocent of fraud toward me and mine, should you ask a formal acknowledgment on my part as to your just administration of my affairs, and a recantation of all I have said to the contrary, both with regard to yourself and Evelyn Erle? Such are the contents of this first paper, the only one that I could, under any possible circumstances, be induced to sign as a compromise with your villainy; for, not to gain my own life or liberty, will I ever put hand to the others, infamous as they are on the very surface."

"Miriam, this violence surprises me, is wholly unlooked for, and unnecessary," he remarked, mildly. "From what Mrs. Clayton has told me, I had supposed that my disinterested care and assiduity with regard to your condition were about to meet their reward in your rational submission to the necessities of your case and mine. Resume your seat, I entreat you, and let us calmly discuss a matter that seems to agitate you so unduly. Perhaps I may be able to place it before you in a better light ere we have concluded our interview. You will sit down again, Miriam, will you not?"

"Oh, surely, if you are alarmed; but, really, I should suppose, with Mrs. Clayton and Dr. Englehart no doubt in call, you need not be so tremulous. There, you are quite safe, I assure you, in your old place, with the table between us;" and I pointed derisively to the *fauteuil* he had occupied so gracefully a few moments before, and into which he now slowly subsided.

"Contemptuous girl," he broke forth at last, "you may yet live to regret this behavior; so far, nothing has been denied you; no expense has been spared for your comfort; in a tribunal of justice you could say this, no more: 'My guardian, thinking me mad from his experiences of my conduct and health, and regaining accidental possession of me at a time when, under a feigned name, I was thought to be drowned, deemed it best, before revealing my existence to the world, to try and restore me to sanity by private measures, rather than bring upon my malady the eyes of a mocking world. In doing this, he used all delicacy, all devotion, surrounding me with comforts, and many luxuries, and even humoring my insane whim to have the companionship of a year-old child found with me on the raft under circumstances suspicious —if no more—' "

"Wretch!" I gasped, "dare only asperse me in thought, and"—the menace hung suspended on my tongue. What power had I to execute it, even if uttered?

"As to my name, I feigned none. It was my mother's, is my own, and from her I inherited, or, from the race of which she sprang, the power to remember and avenge my wrongs; to hate, and curse—and blast, perhaps, as well—such as you and yours, granted to his chosen children through the power of Almighty God!" And again I rose and confronted him; then fiercely pointed down upon his ignoble head, now bowed involuntarily, either from policy or nervous terror, I never knew, a finger quivering and keen with scorn and rage, an index of the mind that directed it.

"I wonder you are not afraid to behave to me in this manner," he said, at length, lifting his head with a spasmodic jerk, and raising to mine his mottled, angry eyes, now cold and hard as pebbles, "seeing that you are, so to speak, in the hollow of my hand;" and, suiting the action to the word, he extended his long, spongy, right hand, and closed it crushingly, as though it contained a worm, while he smiled and sneered—oh, such a sneer! it seemed to fill the room.

"True, true—I am very helpless," I said, sitting down with a sudden revulsion of feeling, and, clasping my hands above my eyes, I wept aloud, adding, a moment later, as I indignantly wiped my tears: "Yes, if the worst betide, there will only be one more martyr; and, what is martyrdom, that any need shrink from it? The world is full of it!"

"Nothing, if you are used to it," he said, carelessly, "as the old woman remarked of the eels she was skinning alive; I suppose you know all about it by this time. But come, you are rational again, now, and I don't wish to be hard on you, Miriam; I don't, upon my soul!"

"Your soul!" I murmured—"your soul!" I reiterated louder; and I smiled at the idea that suggested itself—"have reptiles souls?"

"The memory of your father alone, my old, confiding friend, one of the most perfect of men, as I always thought him, would incline me kindly to his daughter, even if no other tie existed between us," he said calmly, unmindful of my sarcasm. "But other ties do exist, mistaken girl! The world looks upon us as one family—since the marriage of Claude and Evelyn, that uncongenial union which, but for your caprice, would never have taken place, and which is at the root of all our misfortunes, all our fatal necessities."

"Necessities!" I muttered, between my clinched teeth, drumming with my fingers impatiently on the table before me, and smiling scornfully a moment later.

"You seem in a mood for iteration, to-day, Miss Monfort."

"I make my running commentaries in that way, Mr. Bainrothe. But a truce to recrimination and reminiscence both. Let us adhere strictly to the letter and verse of our affairs. These papers form the subject of your visit, I believe. Know, at once, that the first I will sign, on certain conditions, bitter and humiliating as I feel it to be obliged to do this; but, that I will ever consent to yield the guardianship of my sister wholly to Evelyn Erle and her husband, or divest myself of my house and furniture, or my wild lands in Georgia, to you, here first named to me, in consideration of expenses already incurred and to be incurred for Mabel's education, and my own safe-keeping, during a long attack of lunacy; or that I will, to crown the whole iniquitous requisition, consent to give my hand in marriage to that scoundrel—Luke Gregory!—are visions as vain as those of the child who tried to grasp a comet or the moon—or, to descend in comparison, to catch a bird by putting salt on its tail! There, you have my ultimatum; now go and make the best of it!"

"I am prepared for your objections—prepared, too, to overcome them," he said, coolly. "Take time to consider all this. I do not expect an answer to-day, did not when I came, nor will I accept one signature without the whole. There is no compromise possible. As to your marriage—it must be accomplished before you leave this room. I, as a magistrate, can tie the knot—fast enough to bind all the other agreements to certain fulfillments, for Gregory is a friend of mine, and a man of honor, and will see them carried out to the letter. He loves you, too, and proves it, for he takes you penniless. Afterward a priest may complete the ceremony if you have any scruples. Then, of course, it rests between you and Gregory, whether you remain together or separate as wide as the poles—I shall wash my hands of the whole affair thereafter, having secured my good name and yours."

I stood with bowed head and moving lips before him—mutely, indignantly.

"I shall, however, make all this," he continued, "appear as well as possible to your friends and mine, especially, believe me, Miriam! I shall state, for your sake, that, after being rescued from the raft, you were partially insane, but still sufficiently mistress of yourself to coincide with me and your sisters in the wish to let your death as Miss Harz pass current with the world, until you should redeem your errors" (what errors?), "and be restored to health and perfect reason. You will see that your acknowledgment of the last paper includes these extenuating facts, when you have leisure to re-read it (for I saw how hastily you glanced over that one in particular); you must do me the favor to peruse it much more carefully," drawing on his gloves coolly, "before you make your final decision. You are very comfortable here, my dear girl," glancing around benignly, "but you have no conception of the frame of mind, bare walls, utter solitude, a fireless hearth and a frugal table, would bring about in a very few days or weeks, or even in one as resolute and defiant as yourself. I should be loath to try such an experiment *or deprive you of your child*—but *necessitas non habet legem*, the school-book says. I think you, too, studied a little Latin, Miriam?"

"Monster!"

"Not a very relevant or polite remark, I must confess. By-the-by, Miriam, as you stand before me with your well-poised figure—your blazing eyes—your quivering nostrils—your curling, compressed lip—your heaving chest (always a splendid feature in your *physique*), your folded arms, and the color coming and going in your pale-olive cheek, in the old flame-like way I used to admire so much in your girlhood—you are a splendid creature, by Jove! I could find it in my heart to love you still—there, it is out at last—if it were not for Mrs. Raymond—" glancing, as he spoke, in the direction of Mrs. Clayton, with a knowing smile. "It was your magnificent disdain that kindled the torch before. Beware how you revive that fanaticism of mine!"

I turned for one moment with an involuntary feeling of appeal to Mrs. Clayton, but her cold, green eyes were quivering in accordance with the smile that stretched her thin lips to a line of mocking mirth. One glimpse of sympathy would have carried me to her arms for refuge —distasteful as she was to me in every way save one. She, like myself, was a woman. But such perversion of all natural feeling estranged me from her irreconcilably and forever.

I was alone; shame, humiliation, despair, possessed me; indignation, for the insult I was forced to bear in her presence, filled my soul—I stood with my head cast down, tears raining on my bosom, my arms dropped nervelessly beside me, my hands clinched, my whole frame trembling with excitement.

Slowly and one by one came those convulsive sobs—that rend and wrench the physical frame as earthquakes do the earth. Then rose the sudden resolve—born of volcanic impulse, irresistible to mind as is the lava-flood to matter, sweeping before it all obstructions of reason, habit, expediency.

If it cost me my life I would avenge myself on this tiger, thirsting for my blood; I would anticipate him in his work of destruction, and the strength of Samson seemed to permeate my frame.

It was strange that at that moment of cold, impetuous energy I forgot the steel I carried in my bosom, and thought only of the power I bore in my own hands. I determined to strangle him with my strong, elastic fingers, of which I knew full well the powerful grasp.

The consequences were as cobwebs in my estimate—compared to the ecstasy of such revenge—for all this flashed through my brain with the swift vividness of lightning, and in less than thirty seconds after his last remark this matter was matured. The woman prevailed over the lady.

I raised my eyes slowly and dashed away my tears, preparatory to the onset. He was looking at me wonder-struck, and, perhaps, with something like compunction in his face as I met his gaze. He must have read an expression that appalled him in those dilated eyes of mine that confronted his, for, as I sprang toward him, he bounded backward and escaped through the door of Mrs. Clayton's chamber, which he shut after him with undignified alertness. I stood smiling, and strangely cold, leaning against the mantel-shelf, while my heart beat as though it would have leaped from my throat, and I could feel the pallor of my face as chill as marble.

Mrs. Clayton approached me, but I put her away with waving hands. "Go, wretch!" I said, "woman no more, you have unsexed yourself. Leave me in peace—your touch is poisonous."

She shrank away silently, and I stood for a while like one frozen; then cast myself down on a chair and gave way to bitter weeping. The flood-gates were open, and the "waters" had indeed "come in over my soul." I had restrained my passionate inclinations until now, not only from a sense of personal dignity, but from a determination not to play into the hands of my enemies and captors, and all the more from such long self-control was the revulsion potent and overwhelming.

The consciousness that Ernie was at my knee at last

aroused me from the indulgence of my grief, and I looked down to meet his compassionate and inquiring eyes fixed upon me with a masterful expression I have never seen in any other childish face. It thrilled me to the heart.

"What Mirry cry for—is God mad with Mirry?" he asked at length.

"It seems so, Ernie—yet oh, no, no! I cannot, will not believe in such injustice on the part of the Most High!" I pursued in sad soliloquy, with folded hands, and shaking head, and musing eyes fixed on the fire before me: "My God will not forsake me!"

"Did the bad man hurt Mirry?" he asked, leaning with both arms on my lap and putting up his hand to touch my face.

"Yes, very cruelly, Ernie."

"Big giant will come and kill him, and fayways put him in the river, and the old wolf wat eat Red Riding Hood eat him, and then the devil will roast him for his dinner."

I could but smile, albeit through my tears, at the climax of these threats which seemed to delight and stir the inmost soul of Ernie. His eyes flashed, his cheek crimsoned, his wide red mouth curled with disdainful ire, disclosing the small, pointed pearls within; he seemed transfigured.

"And Ernie! what will Ernie do for Mirry?" I asked, as I watched the workings of his expressive face. "Will Ernie let the wicked man kill Mirry?"

He looked at his small hands and arms, then extended them wistfully.

"Ernie will tell good Jesus," he said, "and he will make Ernie grow big—ever so big—to tie the man and put him in a bag like Clayton's cat."

The burlesque was irresistible, and none the less so that the child was so direfully in earnest. To his infant imagination no worse disaster than had befallen Clayton's cat could be devised. This animal, adored by him, had been bagged and exiled, perhaps drowned for aught I know, for stealing cheese from the cupboard sacred to Clayton, by that vengeful potentate, to the despair of Ernie. The idolized kittens, too, which had followed her, had disappeared with their mother, and days of infant melancholy ensued, during which the canaries before referred to were brought as substitutes. The faithful heart still clung to its feline passion, it was evident, though for weeks the memory of that hapless cat had been ignored and its name unmentioned.

I believe, after my momentary wrath was over, I should have been content with the punishment suggested by the child, as sufficient even for Basil Bainrothe.

## CHAPTER IX.

A NERVOUS headache, that confined me to my bed for several days, succeeded the degrading and exciting scene through which I had passed, and, as Mrs. Clayton had at the same time one of her prostrating neuralgic attacks, the services of Dinah were in active requisition. During my own peculiar phase of suffering, the small racket of Ernie, unnoticed in hours of health, grated painfully on my ear, and I caught eagerly at the proposition of the negress to take him down-stairs for a walk and hours of play in the sunshine, privileges he did not very often obtain in these latter days.

I was much the better for having lain silently for a time, when he returned with his hands filled with flowers, his lips smelling of peppermint-drops, and his eyes, always his finest feature, dancing with delight.

He had seen Ady, he told me, with eagerness, and she had kissed him, and tied a string of beads about his neck—red ones—which he displayed; and "Ady had a comb in her head, and her toof was broke"—touching one of his own front teeth lightly, so that I knew he was not pointing out any deficiency in the afore-mentioned comb. From this description, vague as it was, I identified Ada Greene as the person intended to be described; for I too had observed the imperfection he made a point of—a broken tooth, impairing the beauty of otherwise faultless ones.

"And who gave you the flowers, Ernie?" I asked, receiving them from his generous hands as I spoke, and raising the white roses to my nostrils to inhale their delicate breath. "Did Ady give you these?"

"No—Angy!" he answered, solemnly.

"Tell me about Angy, Ernie—had she wings?"

"No wings! Poor Angy could not fly. She was walking in the garden with Adam and Eve, with their clothes on," he said, earnestly.

"Mr. and Mrs. Claude Bainrothe, no doubt," I thought, smiling at the strange mixture of the real and the ideal—the plates of the old Bible evidently supplied the latter, from which many of his impressions were derived—and the practical pair in question the former, quietly perambulating together.

But "Angy!" Could I doubt for one moment to whom he applied that celestial title? The face of one of the angels in the transfiguration did, indeed, resemble Mabel's. I had often remarked and pondered over it.

"Tell me about Angy, Ernie," I entreated. "O Heaven! to think her hands have touched these flowers—her sweet face bent above him! Darling, darling! to be divided and yet so near! It breaks my heart!" and tears flowed freely while he tried to describe the vision that had so impressed him, in his earnest way.

"Poor Angy got no wings," he began again; "bu hair, and bu eyes, and bu dress"—every thing he admired was blue—"and she kissed Ernie and gave him peppermint-drops. Then Adam and Eve laughed just so"—grinning wonderfully—"and said, 'Go home, bad, ugly child, with a back on!' Then Angy pulled flowers and gave Ernie!"

"It is only the little gal next door—I means de young

lady ob de 'stablishment, wat de poor, foolish, humped-shouldered baby talking about," Dinah explained. "He calls her 'Angy,' I s'pose, 'cause she's so purty like; and you tells him 'bout dem hebbenly kine of people, so de say, mos' ebbery night. Does you think dar is such tings, sure enough, Mirry?"

"Certainly, Dinah—the Bible tells us so; but what is the name of the pretty little girl of whom you speak? Tell me, if you know"—and I laid my hand upon her arm and whispered this inquiry, waiting impatiently for a confirmation of my almost certainty. For, that my darling *was* Ernie's Angy, I could not doubt, and the thought moved me to tremulous emotion.

"Dar, now! you is going to hab one ob dem bad turns agin—I sees it in your eyes. You see," dropping her voice for a moment, "I darsn't dar to speak out plain and 'bove-board heah, as if I was at home in Georgy! Ebbery ting is wat dey calls a 'mist'ry' hereabouts; an' I has bin notified not to tell ob no secret doins ob deirn to any airthly creeter, onless I wants to be smacked into jail an' guv up to my wrong owners. My own folks went down on de 'Scewsko;' an' I means to wait till I see how dat 'state's gwine to be settled up afore I pursents myself as 'mong de live ones. We is all published as dead, you sees, honey, an' it would be no lie to preach our funeral, or eben put up our foot-board. He—he—he! I wonder wat my ole man 'll say ef he ebber sees me comin' back agin wid a bag full ob money? I guess it 'll skeer de ole creeter out ob a year's growfe; but dis is de trufe! Ef Miss Polly Allen gits de 'state (she was my mistis's born full-sister, an' a mity fine ole maid, I tells you, chile!), wy, den Sabra 'll be found to be no ghose; fur it's easier to lib wid good wite folks Souf dan Norf. We hab our own housen dar, an' pigs, an' poultry, an' taturs, an' a heap besides, an' time to come an' go, an' doctors wen we's sick, an' our own preachin', an' de banjo an' bones to dance by, an' de best ob funeral 'casions an' weddin's bofe, an' no cole wedder, an' nuffin to do but set by de light wood-fiah an' smoke a pipe wen we gits past work; an' we chooses our own time to lay by—some sooner, some later, 'cordin' as de jints holes out. But here it is work—work—work—all de time; good pay, but no holiday, no yams, no possum-meat, an' mity mean colored siety!"

"But what has all this to do with the name of the little girl next door? Whisper that, and tell me the rest afterward."

"But, if Master Jack Dillard gits de 'state," she proceeded, as though she had not heard my eager question, "wy, den Sabra Smif am as dead as a door-nail from dis time to de day ob judgment, an' de ole man 'll have to git anoder 'fectionate companion. I'se mity sorry for de poor ole soul, but I a'n't gwine to put myself in Jack Dillard's claws, not ef I knows myself. He's one ob dem young wite sort wat lubs de card-table, an' don't 'scriminate atween ole an' young folks. You see, he's my masta's nevy—for de ole folks had no chillun but Miss May Jane, an' she's bin dead dis fifteen yeer, and bofe her chilluns dun follered her to de grabe, so dere is only Miss Polly Ann lef, and—"

Here Mrs. Clayton groaned audibly, and, calling Dinah to her aid, broke up the *tête-à-tête*, if such might justly have been called our interview. It was not very long, however, before Dinah returned to my bedside, by Mrs. Clayton's directions, to offer to comb out my hair, which was tangled beyond my skill to thread in my prostrate condition. Yet, to make an effort so far as to rise and have this done, I knew would be of benefit to me.

We were sitting by the toilet, while the process of untangling my massive length of locks was going on, and the upper drawer thereof was half open, thus affording me a glimpse of its contents. Among these was my silent watch with its chain of gold, its pencil and seal attached. I wore it usually (though useless now in its silent condition—the mainspring was broken) from habit and for safe keeping, but had laid it there when I staggered to my bed, ill and weak after my terrible interview with Mr. Bainrothe.

It caught the eye of Dinah and stirred her master-passion, avarice, and she began to question me, I soon saw, with a view of getting it in her own possession. The selfishness of the old negress had struck me on the raft as something rare even in one of her shallow race, and my conviction of her cowardice and coldness prevented me from taking advantage of her cupidity, as I might have done otherwise.

She was fully capable, I felt convinced, of accepting my watch as a bribe, and failing afterward to come up to her bargain. Yet, dear as it was to me from association of ideas, I should not have weighed it an instant against the merest probability of escape. I knew if I could gain an hour upon my pursuers, I should be safe in the house of Dr. Pemberton, or even in that of Dr. Craig, another friend of my father's. I was comparatively at home anywhere in the city of my nativity, acquainted as I was with its streets and people, and I fully determined, when I found Sabra's avarice excited, to offer her as a reward this golden treasure, should she first place me in circumstances to gain my freedom.

"Dey calls you pore, honey," she said softly, "but wen I sees dat bright gole watch and chain I knows better. Now I reckon dey would bring enough bright silver dollars at a juglar's shop to buy my ole man twice over agin! He is but porely, and our chilluns is all dead and gone, anyway, all but one, way down in New Orleans, an' ef I could git his free papers he might come here and jine his wife in freedom, even if Massa Jack Dillard did heir masta's estate. How much would dat watch and chain be worth, honey?"

"Two or three hundred dollars, I suppose, I don't know exactly; but certainly enough to buy your old man at Southerners' value set upon aged negroes; but whether it be or not—"

An apparition, of which I fortunately caught the reflection in the glass before me, cut short the promise that hovered on my lips. It was that of Mrs. Clayton, in her bed-gown and swathed in flannel, peering, peeping, listening at the door of her chamber, as unlovely a vision, certainly, as ever broke up an *entretien* or dissolved a delusion.

I maintained my self-possession, though my agitation was extreme (the crisis had seemed so favorable!), while she limped forward and accosted me civilly, with a demand as peremptory as a highwayman's for my watch and chain, of which I took no notice.

"I should be doing you great injustice in your condition," she added, coolly, "to let you sell your watch, even to benefit Dinah and her old man, benevolent as is your motive; so I must take possession of it, or send for Dr. Englehart to do so, whichever you prefer."

"The watch is there," I said, rising haughtily, with my still unadjusted hair falling about me. "It was my father's and is precious to me far beyond its intrinsic value; and I shall hold you accountable for it some day. Take it at once, though, rather than recall the person before me with whose presence you menace me. Keep it yourself, however; I would rather deal with you than the others, false as you have shown yourself to every promise."

"I wish you would be reasonable," she said, "and do what your friends ask of you. This confinement is wearing us both out; it will be the death of me, and you will be to blame."

"The sooner the better," I rejoined, heartlessly.

"Ah, Miss Monfort, you have no better friend than I am, perhaps, but you are ungrateful."

"I hope not; but some things of late have shaken, I confess, what little faith I had in you; this confiscation of my property is one of them."

"You know why this is done; I need not explain, but I shall trust you fearlessly in Dinah's society in future. I believe you have no other treasure to bribe her with," and, smiling in her sardonic way, she turned and limped to her bedroom, which it had cost her so great an effort to leave. Her groans and moans during the remainder of the evening were piteous, and Dinah could do nothing to comfort her. A sudden determination possessed me. My own system recuperated rapidly, and after a nervous headache I was always conscious of renewed vital power and of keener sensations. I would try the experiment once more —hazarded under circumstances so different that it made me tremulous but to think of the vast abyss between my *now* and then—and essay to magnetize Mrs. Clayton.

She could not sleep naturally, and she feared evidently to avail herself of opiates, lest in her heavy slumber, perhaps, I should escape. In her normal condition this seemed impossible, for she slept habitually as lightly as a cat, or bird upon its perch, yet lying, and with her key beneath her head (never dreaming of other outlet) she felt at ease. I had already learned that since her illness there were additional precautions taken to insure my safety, and, as she had alleged, her own fidelity.

The Dragon was watched in turn by a Cerberus—no other than the long-trusted colored coachman of Basil Bainrothe, of whom mention has been made far back in these pages.

Thus secure and secured, Mrs. Clayton might have surrendered herself to slumber with all serenity, one would suppose, had it not absolutely refused to visit her eyelids, and the suggestion of an opiate, on my part, was received for some reason in dumb derision.

I went to her at last, and said: "Mrs. Clayton, I hear you groaning grievously, and I fancy I could relieve you. The laying on of hands is a sort of gift of mine; let me try by such means to ease your pain."

"Thank you, Miss Monfort," very dryly, "you are very kind, indeed, but I don't think you can relieve me. I have excruciating neuralgia in my eyebones and temples, and my hands are cramped again. Dinah has been rubbing, without bettering them, for the last half hour."

"Let me try," and, without farther parley, I sat down to my self-appointed, loathed, and detested task, first quietly dismissing Dinah to the next room, where Ernie was eating his supper, and I knew would soon be wanting to be put to bed. We changed places for a time, and it was not long before Mrs. Clayton pronounced the pain in her eyes "almost gone." The experiment was a desperate one, and I bore to it all the powers of my organization—mental and physical—and had the satisfaction in less than an hour to see her sleeping profoundly. She had been failing fast under her painful vigils, and I knew that a few hours of refreshing sleep would be worth to her more than all the drugs in the Pharmacopœia. Now came the test which was to make this slumber worth nothing or every thing to me. If she could be awakened from it without my coincidence, it would prove, perhaps, only a snare to my feet, but if her waking depended on my will, then might I indeed hope to baffle my Dragon, and, as far as she was concerned, make sure of my escape. I willed then earnestly that she should sleep until twelve o'clock; and at ten, when Dinah became impatient to retire, I gave her permission, in order to gain egress to try and arouse Mrs. Clayton.

In consequence of this immurement of our servant, I had remained supperless—beyond the crusts of bread left by Ernie and some cold tea in Mrs. Clayton's teapot, of which I partook with an appetite born of exhaustion. Those who have undertaken this "laying on of hands," for the purpose of soothing pain, will comprehend what the succeeding sensation of nerveless prostration is—those only—and give me their sympathy.

From her errand to arouse our sleeper in quest of the key, of course Dinah returned disconsolate. Greatly to my satisfaction, she stated that it was "out ob de question to try to git her eyes open. Why honey," she pursued, "ef I didn't know what a steady-goin' Christian creetur she was, I mout suppose she had bin 'bibin' of whisky or peach-brandy—dat's de sleepiest stuff goin', chile; but I does believe she has the fallin' fits, caze, even wen I pulled open one corner of her eyes, dey was rolled clean back in her head. Mebbe she's dyin', chile, an' ef she is—but no!"

she muttered, "dat ole creetur down-stairs nebber leaves dem back-doors open one minute, you had better believe, even ef he happens to turn his back a spell, an' it would be no use tryin' to git out ob de 'stablishment dat way, but I knows whar she keeps her key, an' I kin go to bed myself if you say so, an' you kin lock de do' inside, an' lay de key back undernefe her pillow: you see dar's a bolt outside, too, honey, an' I means to draw dat after me, as ole Caleb always does ob nights wen he goes to bed."

Chuckling low at the manifest disappointment in my face, she disappeared, to return almost instantly.

"I thought she must be possumin'," she said, "but I know she is as fas' asleep now as de bar' in de hollow ob a tree in cole wedder, for she made no 'sistance like wen I grabbed de key from undernefe her head, an' here it is, chile, an' ef you wants to try your 'speriment you kin, but I spec you'd better wait a spell," and she looked cunningly at me; "dere's traps everywhar in dese woods!"

It occurred to me as well that Mrs. Clayton might be feigning slumber, having penetrated my design of lulling and soothing her fitful spirit to rest; and feeling, as I did, an utter want of confidence in Sabra, not only as free agent but as watched attendant, I determined as far as in me lay to disarm suspicion by duplicity. So I lifted up my voice in testimony of deceit, and declared my weariness of bondage to be such that I had determined to embrace Mr. Bainrothe's conditions, and that in a few days I should be free again without assistance.

"So take the key, Dinah," I said, after observing it closely, and perceiving that it was several sizes larger than that I had made, as clumsy as that was, and, therefore, could be of no use to me. "Let yourself out, and bolt the door behind you, and Mrs. Clayton shall see that I will take no mean advantage of her slumbers."

This arragement having been carried with speedy effect, I returned to my own chamber after a close scrutiny of Mrs. Clayton's condition, and employed myself at once in running my penknife around the door concealed by my bed-head, and thus loosening the paper, pasted on cotton cloth, that covered it, from that of the wall, with which it was connected so intimately as to make the whole surface within the chamber seem to form one partition.

Long before this I had cut that which surrounded the lock, so that it lay like a flap over it, fastened down lightly, however, with gum-arabic (part of Ernie's draught for a catarrh), so as to baffle slight inspection. My heart beat wildly as, after having effected this preliminary step, I cautiously unlocked the door, which, for aught I knew, might be, like that of Mrs. Clayton's closet, bolted without, so as to frustrate all my efforts. It opened outwardly, and could have been readily so secured.

In the great providence of God, it was not bolted. I sank on my knees, weak and prayerful, I remember, as the door swung slightly back, revealing the platform beyond, and the short stair that led from it up to the second story. The hinges creaked a little, and these I hastened to oil; then closing and relocking the door softly, I crept (without pushing my bedstead back again the few inches I had wheeled it forward) to look once more upon the sleeping face of Mrs. Clayton.

It was still calm and unconscious. Ernie, too, slumbered peacefully. Every thing seemed propitious to my purpose. I threw on hastily the famous, flimsy black silk and mantle that had been prepared for me on shipboard, tied a dark veil over my head, and, with no other precaution, went forth, as I hoped, to freedom.

My heart seemed to suspend its action as, cautiously unlocking and opening the door, I stepped forth on the platform. It will be remembered that I knew the topography of the lower part of the house of old thoroughly.

I had been entertained there with my father more than once, when, as heiress of my mother's great estate, I had commanded the reverence of my hosts, and the situation of parlors, study, and dining-room, was perfectly familiar to me.

It was what in those days was called a single house, though a spacious-enough mansion; that is, all the rooms, with one exception, were placed either on the same side of the wide hall of entrance, or behind it in the ell. The study alone formed a small lateral projection on the other hand. The door of this apartment opened at the foot of that stair, on the upper platform of which I now stood trembling, weighing my fate by a hair. I had left the door ajar through which I had crept quietly, so that, in case of failure, I might have a chance of retreat before discovery should be made. It was well, perhaps, that I did so on this occasion, for otherwise I should scarcely have had nerve enough to avoid the sure and speedy detection which must have followed the slightest delay or noise made in returning.

I lingered to reconnoitre some minutes on the platform before I ventured to commence the wary descent of the broad, carpeted stairway. I had convinced myself that the second story was empty, though a lighted lamp swung in the upper entry, as well as in that below, throwing a flood of radiance on the scene with which I would fain have dispensed.

I heard the sound of voices from the closed parlors, and saw reposing on the rack before me several hats and canes, indicative of visitors. From the study, however, there fortunately came no murmur, and I found that it was dark. The front-door stood invitingly open; I could see the opposite lamp-post without, and I had made up my mind to dart on and downward, and reach at a bound the pavement, when the door of the first parlor was suddenly thrown back, and left so, by a servant coming out with a tray of wines and fruits which he had been evidently handing, and I had just time to shrink into shadow, favored in my wish for concealment by the black dress and veil I wore, when a once familiar form appeared in the door-way of the front hall, which I recognized at a glance as that of Gregory. Closing the door firmly after him, he prepared to divest himself of hat and cape in the hall, without a look in my direction. After the completion of which process he entered the parlor by the nearest door, setting that also wide open as he did so, with some exclamation about the heat of the apartment, which seemed to meet with acquiescence from the powers within.

I caught a panoramic view of that interior before I fled swiftly, noiselessly, hopelessly, back to my cage again, having lost my only chance of escape by that fatal delay of five minutes on the platform. I should have been out and away on the wings of the wind ere Gregory entered the inclosure before the house, had I not hesitated. Yet, after all, perhaps, I miscalculated. What if I had met him face to face—been seized and dragged back again to captivity! Perchance it was better as it was. Time would develop and determine this; but, in the interval, how woful was my disappointment!

I had time to get to bed again, and in some degree

recover my composure; indeed, I had been in bed an hour when the clock in the dining-room beneath me, which, since the evident occupancy of that long-deserted hall, had been wound and put in running order, struck twelve, with its deep-mouthed, melodramatic tones, and at the very moment I heard sounds indicative of the resurrection of the mesmeric sleeper.

She was evidently startled in some way on finding herself awake again, or perhaps from having fallen so soundly asleep in hands like mine, for she called aloud first for "Dinah," then, repeatedly, on "Miriam," both without effect. In a few moments after these appeals had died away she came in person, as I knew she would, to reconnoitre.

The bedstead had been pushed carefully and noiselessly back again on its grooved castors against the door, from the lock of which the wooden key had been removed, rewashed in oil, and hidden away in that hollow aperture in the bedstead, which formed a perfect box, by the skillful readjustment of one loosened compartment of the veneering of the massive post.

She shook me slightly, and I rose in my bed with a start and shudder, admirably simulated, I fancied, and which completely deceived her evidently. "I am sorry to have startled you so," she said, hurriedly, "but where is Dinah, Miss Monfort, and how did she get out?"

"I really cannot inform you where she is," I answered, petulantly. "I scarcely think it was worth while to disturb me for the sake of asking me a question you must have known my inability to answer."

"But how did she get out, Miss Harz?"

"By means of the key under your head, which you will find in the lock, no doubt, where it was left. She promised me, insolently enough, to bolt the door outside to prevent egress, and I, to prevent ingress, locked it within."

"So she assured you we were both prisoners by night, did she? Well, I am glad you have proof at last of what I told you."

"I have no proof; but, as I have made up my mind to come to terms of some kind very soon, I thought it useless to investigate. Do you feel better for my laying on of hands? You seem refreshed."

"Yes, greatly better; a good sleep was what I needed, and I fell into a doze while you were beside the bed, I believe. I have heard of magnetism before as a means of relief for pain; now I am convinced of its efficacy."

"Magnetism! You don't think it amounts to that, do you? You flatter me;" and I laughed.

"I do, indeed, and I am sure I am much obliged to you, Miss Monfort; though, for that matter, you can never say, even when you come to your own again—which you will now do shortly—that I have not been considerate and attentive to you while in confinement."

"You need not be afraid of any complaint as far as you are concerned. I think I comprehend you and your motives by this time. Let there be peace between us from this hour." And I extended my hand to her, which, very unexpectedly to me, she seized and kissed—a proceeding deprecated loathingly. "I assure you," I added, laughingly, "I would rather even marry Englehart than continue here."

"Then you will marry Mr. Gregory?"

"I do not know—either that or die, I suppose—whichever God pleases. I am weary of being a prisoner—weary of you, of every thing about me. All that I cared for is lost to me, and I might as well surrender, I suppose; not at discretion, however!"

She turned from me silently, and sought her couch again; but I felt instinctively that she slept no more; and so we lay, silently watching one another, until morning. I dared not renew my efforts to escape, at all events, in the night-time, when I knew the house was locked, and watched without, as well as within—for this was the old habit of the square.

One—two—three—four o'clock came, and passed, and were reported by the deep-tongued clock in the room beneath me, before I slept, and then I dreamed a vision so vivid, that I wakened from it excited—exhausted—as though its frightful figments had been stern realities.

I thought that the noble dog Ossian came to me again and laid the double-footed key upon my lap, as he had done at Beauseincourt—staining my white dress with blood, not mud, this time, and that Colonel La Vigne struck it furiously to the floor, and handed me instead the wooden one I had carved, with the words of the proverb:

"The opportunity lost is like the arrow sped: it comes no more. Your wooden key will fail you next time, as it has failed you this, and you will be baffled—baffled—as you tried to baffle me! Miriam, unseen I pursue you!"

Then he laughed horribly, and faded in the gray dawn, to which I awoke, covered with cold dew, and trembling in every limb. Had he been there, indeed, in spiritual presence? Was it his hand that had left that band about my brow—that surging in my brain—that weight upon my heart? O God! had I indeed become the sport of fiends? At last I wept, and in my tears found sullen comfort. The image so often caviled at as false in *Hamlet* came to me then as the readiest interpretation of what I suffered, and thus proved its own fidelity and truth. "A sea of sorrow" did indeed seem to roll above me, against which I felt the vanity of "taking arms."

My destruction was decreed, and I had nothing to do but suffer and submit!

All the persecution I had sustained since my father's death, at the hands of Evelyn and Basil Bainrothe—all my wrongs, beginning at the heart-betrayal of Claude, and ending with the immurement I was suffering now at the hands of his father—all my strange life at Beauseincourt, with its episode of horror, its one reality of perfect happiness too fair to last, its singular revelations, its warm and deep attachments, my fearful and nightmare-like experience on the burning ship, the level raft, with the green waves curling above it, the rescue, the snare into which I had inevitably fallen, the Inquisition-walls closing around me—all were there in one vivid and overwhelming mental summary!

I think if ever madness came near me in my life, it came that night, so crushing, so terrific was this weight which, Sysiphus-like, memory was rolling to the summit of the present moment, to fall back again by the power of its own weight to the valley below—the valley of despair—and destroy all that it encountered or found beneath it. Yet, by the time the sun was up, my eyes were sealed again in slumber.

Before I close this chapter, it will be as well to describe the tableau I had caught sight of through the open parlor-door when I tempted my fate and failed.

Standing close in the shadow, so that, even if directed toward me unconsciously, the glance of those within, I knew, could not penetrate the mystery of my presence, I scanned with a sad derision the scene before me. With a glance I received the impression that it required moments to convey in narrative.

On the hearth-rug, with his back to the fire, his legs apart, his coat-skirts parted behind him, stood Basil Bainrothe, monarch of all he surveyed, with extended hand, evidently demonstrating some axiom to the two visitors ensconced on the sofa near him, who, with the exception of their booted feet, and the straps of their pantaloons, were beyond my angle of vision. On the opposite side of the chimney from these inscrutable guests sat two ladies, elaborately dressed and rouged, in whom I recognized at a glance Evelyn Erle and Mrs. Raymond. Just before I vanished, Claude Bainrothe, courteous in manner and elegant in exterior, approached them from the other parlor, in time to witness the *entrée* of Gregory, to which I have referred, and to salute him cordially. That these were all confederates I could not doubt, and prepared to aid each other. How could I know that one pair of those evident feet belonged to the invisible body of a man who was one of the few whom I could have called to my defense from the ends of the earth, had choice of champions been afforded me? It was not until long afterward that I ascertained beyond a doubt that Major Favraud had formed one of that company on the occasion of my fatal failure. Had I dreamed of his presence, I should fearlessly have entered the parlor, and thrown myself on his brotherly protection, secure of his best efforts to rescue me, even though his own heart's blood had been the sacrifice.

Alas! should I ever find another dart like that, never to be recalled, to launch in the right direction, and fix quivering in the eye of the target?—God alone could know.

## CHAPTER X.

After the one hopeful excitement of my prison-life, my spirit drooped deplorably for a season, and all occupation became distasteful to me. My diary even was abandoned, the writing of which had so well assisted to fill my time, and, although destroyed daily, to impress upon my memory a faithful and sequent record of the monotonous hours, else remembered merely as a homogeneous whole. Had it not been for poor Ernie and his requirements, I should have sunk under this fresh phase of suffering, I am convinced. My health, too, was giving way. My strength, my energy were failing. I kept my bed, as I had never been willing to do before if able to arise from it, until noon sometimes, for want of nervous impulse, and my food was tasteless and innutritious, even when I forced myself to eat a portion of what was placed regularly before me. It seemed to me that, long ere this, Wardour Wentworth must have ascertained my fate, and the thought that he might be passive when my very soul was at stake, thrilled me with agony unspeakable.

This mood endured so long that even Mrs. Clayton grew alarmed. She insisted on Dr. Englehart again, and, when I shook my head drearily for all reply, begged that I would permit her to state my case to Mrs. Raymond, who might in turn see some able physician about me and procure remedies.

To this, at last, I consented.

The consequence was what I had hoped it might be: Mrs. Raymond came in person, and I had at last the opportunity I had long desired of seeing her alone. If thoughtless, if unrefined according to my views of good breeding, she was still young, and vivacious, and perhaps kind-hearted; besides this, sufficiently well pleased with herself to be generous to one who could no longer be her rival.

Her approach was heralded by a note from Mr. Bainrothe, full of his characteristic, guileful sophistry and cool impertinence. It ran as follows (I still possess this billet with others of his inditing—along with a snake's rattle):

"Miriam: I am glad to hear through Mrs. Clayton that reaction has occurred, and that you manifest repentance for your recent violence toward one who always means you well. A little jesting on the part of your guardian, my dear girl, should meet with a very different reception, and handsome women must submit to compliments with a good grace, or run the risk of being called prudes or viragos. Not that I mean to apply either term to you by any means. Your father's daughter could not be other than a lady, even if she tried, but I must confess your manners have deteriorated somewhat since you went into voluntary banishment among those outlandish people. I have heard no very good account of this old La Vigne who died in debt, it seems, and left his children beggars. I have some curiosity to know whether he paid your salary. 'Straws show,' you know, etc.

"It is now October; by the end of this month I hope

you will have made up that stubborn mind of yours (truly indomitable, as I often say to Evelyn) to leave seclusion, and enter your family once more in the only way you can do so respectably after what has occurred—as a married woman.

"You remember the French song which I was always fond of humming, 'Où est on si bien qu'au sein de sa famille?' How appropriate it seems to your condition!

"You will be surprised to hear that your step-mother's brother has appeared on the tapis, and that he has had the audacity to propose to adopt Mabel, whom he claims as his niece.

"He seems a gentlemanly person enough, but may be an impostor for aught I know. The young lady he was engaged to, Gregory tells me, perished in the Kosciusko, which proves a relief, after all, as it is rumored he has a wife in Europe. But such gossip can hardly interest you very vividly. The man has gone to California, and will probably return no more.

"Did you, or did you not, meet this person at Colonel La Vigne's? Favraud hinted something of the kind when he was here; but I can get no satisfaction from Gregory.

"They all believe you were drowned in Georgia, and I thought it best for the present not to undeceive Favraud, who laments your fate.

"The surprise will be all the more pleasant; and, of course, every thing will be explained to the satisfaction of friends when you appear publicly as the wife of Luke Gregory—'long secretly married!' You see, it will be necessary to go back a little to save appearances, on account of Ernie!"

The miscreant! I understood him now — oh, my God, for strength to tear his cowardly heart from his truculent body! But no; let there be no further unavailing anger. In God's good time all should recoil on his own head. For the present, I must bear, and make myself insensible, if possible; and yet, I would not willingly have had the living greenness of my spirit turned to stone, as we are told branches are in some strange, foreign rivers—crystal-cold!

Another extract, the closing one, and then forever away with Basil Bainrothe and his flimsy letters:

"Again, I must congratulate you on the subdued and humbled temper you manifest. Claude, and Evelyn, and I, had just been discussing a plan for removing you to another asylum, where stricter discipline and less luxurious externals are employed to conquer the otherwise unmanageable inmates. Dr. Englehart, you know, holds up the theory of indulgence to his patients, and I am rejoiced to find his measures have at last prevailed over your frenzy. Mabel, like your other friends, believes you dead, and is at home with Evelyn and Claude, and is growing in beauty and intelligence every day.

"She was quite shocked at her uncle's wild behavior, and positively refused to go with him, is fond of Mr. Gregory, and remembers you with affection.

"Owing to my knowledge of your condition for the last year, my dear child, I don't blame you for any thing that is past, not even for those delusions with regard to my own acts and intentions which formed your mania, nor for the misfortune and sense of shame which, no doubt, caused your hasty flight, and whose evidences you brought with you from the raft, in the shape of a nearly year-old child.

"I remain, faithfully yours,

"B. B."

The shameful accusations which brought the blood to my brow ought to have been easier to bear than all the rest, because so easily confuted, and because I knew not really believed; but they were not. The very idea of shame humiliated me more than positive ill-treatment could have done; and, spotless though I knew myself to be (as others knew me too—all I loved and cared for), still my purity was shocked by such injustice.

I felt like one who had gone out to walk in fresh attire, and been mud-pelted by rude urchins, so that the outward robes, at least, were soiled, and a sense of degradation and uncleanness became the consequence in spite of reason. But, after all, the dress could be easily changed when opportunity should occur, and all be made clean again, and the mud-pelting forgotten or overlooked, and the urchins punished or dismissed in scorn.

Surely, God would not much longer permit this fiend to subjugate me. Had I not suffered sufficiently? Alas! who but our Creator can judge of our deserts, or measure our power to bear?

In my adversity and lonely trouble I had drawn near to Him and his blessed Son—our Mediator, and example, and only strength. Dear as was still the memory of that earthly love, the only real passion I had ever known, could ever know, it came no longer to my spirit as a substitute for religion. I had learned to separate my worship of God from my fealty to man, yet was this last not weakened, but strengthened, by such discrimination.

If only for the gift of grace it brought to me, let me bless my sad captivity!

## CHAPTER XI.

The dreary days rolled on; the health of Mrs. Clayton declined so rapidly that a small stove was found necessary to the comfort of her contracted bedroom, which freed me from the unpleasant necessity of her actual presence. The stocking-basket was set aside, the gingerbread nuts were neglected, and the noise of constant crunching, as of bones, came no more from my dragon's den; nor yet the smell of Stilton cheese and porter, wherewith she had so frequently regaled herself and nauseated me between-meals, and in the night-season. I used to call her a chronic eater—a symptom, I believe, of the worst sort of dyspepsia, as well as too often its occasion.

I prefer, myself, the Indian notion of eating, seldom, and enough at a time. After all, is there any despot equal to the stomach and its requisitions? What an injustice it seems to all the rest of the organs, the royal brain especially, that this selfish, sensual sybarite should exact tribute, and even enforce concession, whenever denied its customary demands!

There are human beings, the poor of the earth, as we know, who pass their whole lives, merge their immortal souls in ministering to its absolute necessities, who go cold, ill-clad, and ignorant, to keep off the pangs of hunger; who sacrifice pride and affection at its miserable altar. There are others, fewer in number, it is true, but scarcely less to be pitied, who exceed this enforced servility in the most abject fashion of voluntary adulation; who flatter, persuade, and bring rich tribute to this smiling Moloch, only waiting his own time to turn upon and destroy his idolaters. For the pampered stomach, like all other spoiled potentates, is treacherous and ungrateful beyond belief.

Yet the philosophers tell us man's necessity for food lies at the root of civilization, and that the desire for a sufficiency and variety of aliment alone keeps up our energies! I cannot think so; I believe it is the stone about our necks that drags us down, and is intended to do so, and which keeps us truly from being "but a little lower than the angels."

"Revenons à nos moutons!"

The good-hearted vulgarian, who, whatever she was, and however detestable the part she was playing, was at least possessed of womanly sympathy, came frequently to see me during those weary days. Her engagement to Mr. Bainrothe was never by her acknowledged, or by me alluded to, and she seemed to have taken up the impression in some way that I was the victim of an unfortunate attachment to that subtle person, which had degenerated into a morbid and causeless hatred on my part, leading to mania.

Had she stated this conviction plainly, I might have been tempted to undeceive her; as it was, I suffered the error to continue, knowing that no condition of belief would influence her half so kindly toward me. Women as a class have a sincere friendship for those who have undergone slighting treatment at the hands of their lovers and husbands; and we all know what a common trick of trade it is with men who have been unsuccessful in their attempts to gain a woman's affections, or worse, in their evil designs on her honor, to give out such mendacious impressions!

Yet, to the end of time, the vanity and credulity of women will lead them to lend credence to such statements, rather than look matters firmly in the face, with the eyes of common-sense and experience. I, for one, am a very skeptic on this subject of manly dislike growing out of female susceptibility, and usually take the conservative view of the question.

During one of these condescending visits of the "Lady Anastasia," whose position toward Bainrothe I perfectly comprehended, through the inadvertence, it may be remembered, of Mrs. Clayton, I ventured to ask her whether she had met with her betrothed, as she had expected to do on landing at New York, and when her marriage was to take place.

"Whenever you come out of this retirement, dear; not before. You see I have set my heart on 'aving you for my bridesmaid, with your friends' permission."

"Then Mr. Bainrothe has concluded to annul the condition of my marriage before leaving the asylum."

"Oh, I had forgotten about that! Well, we will have the ceremony performed together, if you prefer; down in Dr. Englehart's drawing-rooms."

"You reside here, then?" I questioned; "you are at home in this house, whosesoever it may be?"

"Oh, no, you quite misunderstand me. I am staying with friends, and Mr. Bainrothe is over at home with his son and daughter-in-law"—with a jerk of her head in the right direction—"in the other city, I mean; I am such a stranger I forget names sometimes. This, you know, is solely Dr. Englehart's establishment."

"I suppose that gentleman is absent, as I have not seen him lately," I continued.

"He has been absent, but has just returned. He speaks of calling, I believe, very soon, to see you on the part of Mr. Gregory. How happy you are to inspire such a passion in the heart of that splendid man!"—and she rolled her eyes, and drew up her square, flat shoulders expressively. "Do tell me where you knew him, and all about it; I am sure he is much more suitable to you, in age and intellect, than—than—even Mr. Bainrothe."

"There is no question of him now," I responded, gravely, purposely misunderstanding her; "he has been married some time to my step-sister, Evelyn Erle, and, I suppose, with many of my other friends, believes me dead!"

"Oh, no, I assure you," she rejoined, with some confusion, "it is a mistake altogether. Both Mr. and Mrs. Claude Bainrothe are perfectly aware of your seclusion, and he, especially, recommended and contrived it."

"There *was* contrivance, then; you admit that!" I said, impressively.

At this juncture a feeble voice from the adjoining room was heard calling aloud, and I listened to it, uplifted as it was, evidently, in tones of remonstrance and reproof, for some moments afterward—the Lady Anastasia having hastened, with dutiful alacrity, to the bedside of her *soi-disant* servant.

I became aware, after this visit, that Mrs. Raymond had become my jailer as well as her mother's. She came regularly at supper-time thereafter to superintend Dinah's arrangements, to give Mrs. Clayton her night-draught, which did not assuage her direful vigilance one particle, but rather seemed to infuse new powers of wakefulness in those ever-watchful eyes, until sunrise, when, protected by the knowledge that others besides herself were on the watch, she permitted sleep to take possession of her senses.

I earnestly believe that no one ever so effectually controlled the predisposition to slumber as did this woman.

After locking us up regularly for the night, the "Lady Anastasia" withdrew, followed by Dinah; and I would hear, later, sounds of festivity, in which her well-known laugh was blended, in the dining-room below, where, with Bainrothe and his friends, she held wassail, frequently, until after midnight. The groans of Mrs. Clayton would then commence, and, with little intermission, last until morning's light.

Yet it was something to be rid of Mrs. Raymond's surveillance during those very hours I had selected for my second effort to escape. This must be hazarded, I knew, between eight and ten o'clock of the evening, during which time I had reason to suppose the house-door remained unlocked. The risk of encountering some one in the hall below—for there was constant passing and repassing of footsteps during those hours—constituted my chief danger; but, at all hazards, the experiment must then, if at all, be made.

October was fast drifting away, and I knew that at its close my course would be decided for me, should I not anticipate such despotism by setting it at naught, in the only possible way—that of flying from the scene of my oppression.

How to do this, and when, became the one problem of my existence; and it was well for me that Mrs. Clayton was too great a sufferer to notice beyond my external safety, or she might have seen clear indications of some strange change at work, stamped upon my features.

My unsettled intentions were suddenly brought to a crisis by the contents of a letter handed to me, as usual, in the shadows of the evening, by the long-absent Dr. Englehart, who came in person, in accordance with Mrs. Raymond's announcement (arriving, as it chanced, while Mrs. Clayton slumbered), to deliver it.

Gregory wrote a large, clear hand, not difficult to decipher, even by the dim light of a moonlight lamp; and, while Dr. Englehart stood regarding me in the shadow, anxiously enough, I perceived, to keep me entirely on my guard, I perused, with mingled derision and terror, this truly characteristic epistle. My running commentaries, as I read—entirely *sotto voce*, of course, for one does not care to rouse the wrath of a tiger on the crouch, by flinging pebbles in the jungle—may give some idea of the impression it made upon me, and the emotions it excited.

"Beloved Miriam" (insolent cur!)—"for by this tender title I am permitted to address you at last" (by whom?)—"I cannot flatter myself that, in concurring with the wishes of your friends, you return my fervent passion" (you are mistaken there; I do return it with the seal unbroken); "but will you not suffer me to hope that the deep, disinterested devotion of months may undo the past, and dissolve those bitter prejudices which I feel well aware were instilled into your heart by one of the coldest and most time-serving of men" (of course, hope is free to all; it is no longer kept in a box, as in the days of Pandora)? "When I assure you that Wentworth, with a perfect knowledge of your present situation, has repudiated the past, you will more perfectly understand my reference" (I will believe this when he tells me so, not before; your assertion simply reassures me). "It is not, however, to place my own devotion in contrast with his perfidy, that I now address you" (Nature drew the contrast, fortunately for him, without your assistance), "but to beseech you, for your own sake, to let nothing turn you from your recently-formed resolution" (I don't intend to let any thing turn me, if I can help it, this time!). "It remains with you to live a free and happy life, adored and indulged by one who would give his heart's blood to serve you" (a poor gift, I take it), "or pass your whole existence in the cell of a lunatic, cut off from every being who could care for or protect you." (Great Heavens! what can the wretch mean?) "Should you refuse to become my wife, and affix your signature to the papers in your possession, I have reason to know that Bainrothe designs to make, or rather continue, you dead, and imprison you in a lonely house on the sea-coast, which he owns, where others of his victims have before now lived and died unknown!" (Very melodramatic, truly; but I don't believe Cagliostro would dare to do it.) "To convince you of the truth of my allegations, Dr. Engelehart is instructed to place in your hands a note recently intercepted by me from that arch-conspirator to his son, which please return to him, my truest friend" (direst enemy, you mean), "along with this letter, as I send you both documents at my own peril, and dare not leave them in your hands" (how magnanimous!); and here I dropped the letter on the table, and extended my hand mutely to Dr. Englehart for the note, which was ready for me, in the hollow of his pudgy palm.

It did, indeed, most clearly confirm the statement,

true or false, of the ubiquitous Gregory. Returning it to the physician *pro tem.*, I then continued the perusal of this singular love-letter to the end, in which the lawyer and knave predominated in spite of Eros! Yet there was food for consideration here, and extremest terror.

"How long before this ultimatum is proposed to me, which Mr. Gregory seemed to anticipate, and with which you, no doubt, are acquainted?" I asked, coldly, after consideration.

"Ten days will close up de whole transaction, as I understand," was the no less cool reply, made in those husky, inimitable tones, peculiar to the man of petty pills.

"Ten days! It would seem a short time wherein to get up a reasonable trousseau, even!"

"True—true! but nosing of dat kind is necessaire under dese circumstances—only your mos' gracious and graceful consent!" He spoke eagerly, with bowed head and clasped hands, standing mutely before me when he had concluded.

"If Mr. Gregory loved me truly, he would not limit me thus," I hazarded. "He would give me time to learn to return his affection, as I must try to do, and to forget the past! He would not strike hands with my persecutors, but insist on my liberation—or obtain it, as he could readily do, without their coöperation, through you, Dr. Englehart, who seem to be his friend and ally, and who have already run such risks for his sake in bringing me these two dangerous letters," and as I spoke I pushed them across the table, to be gathered up and concealed with well-affected eagerness.

How perfectly he played his part, and how cunningly Bainrothe had contrived to convey to me his menace—real, or assumed for effect, I could not tell which, for my judgment spoke one language, my cowardice another! Yet, I confess, that the panic was complete, though I concealed it from the enemy.

"Women usually, at least romantic and incredulous women like me, demand some proof of a lover's devotion," I resumed, as coolly as I could, "before yielding him their faith and fealty; but Mr. Gregory has given me no evidence so far of the sincerity of his passion; I confess I find it difficult, under the circumstances, to believe in its existence."

He drew near to me, bent eagerly above me, then again concealed himself, as it was wise for him to do, in shadow; and I could hear his hissing breath, as it passed between his closed teeth—like that of a roused serpent. The impulse of the man came near betraying him, but he rallied and refrained from an exposure, as he would have supposed it, that must have been fatal to his success as a lover, even if it confirmed his power of possession.

His tones, low and deep, were unmistakably those of suppressed passion when he spoke again, and he had almost dropped his accent, so wonderfully assumed.

"When shall he come to you, and speak for himself? Let me take to him some word of encouragement from your lips—for de love of whom—he languishes—he dies! All other passions of his life have proved like cobwebs, compared to this—avarice, ambition, revenge, all yield before it! He is your slave! Do not trample on a fervent heart, thus laid at your feet! Have mercy on this unfortunate!"

"Strange language from a captor to a captive—mocking language, that I find unendurable! Let Mr. Gregory remain where he is until the extreme limit of the interval granted me by Basil Bainrothe—as breathing-space before execution; and before hope expires in thick darkness—then let him come and take what he will find of the victim of so much perfidy!"

"You do not—you cannot—meditate personal violence, self-murder?" He spoke in a voice of agony, that could scarcely be restrained from breaking into its natural tones.

"No—no—do not flatter yourselves that I could be driven by you—by *any* one to such God-offending," I hastened to say, for I felt the importance of keeping this barrier of disguise, of ice, between Gregory and myself as a means of safety for a season, and determined that he should not transcend it, if I could prevent an *exposé*, such as his excited feelings made imminent. "My hopes are dead—say this to Mr. Gregory—and I have reason to believe I should fare as well in his hands as in any other's, knowing him—as I know him to be—" and I hesitated here for a moment—"gentle, compassionate, faithful, where his feelings are fairly enlisted."

"He thanks you, through my lips, most lovely lady, for dis great proof of consideration; dis message, which I shall truthfully deliver, will fill his heart with joy, long a stranger to his breast, for he has feared your hatred."

"Now go, Dr. Englehart, and let no one come to me without previous warning, for I need all my strength to bear me up in this emergency. Nor would I meet Mr. Gregory without due preparation—even of apparel," and I glanced at my dress of spotted lawn, faded and unseasonable as it seemed in the autumn weather. "I know his fastidiousness on this subject, and from this time it ought to, it must be my study to try to please him."

Why was not the fate of Ananias or Sapphira mine after

that false utterance? Why did I triumph in the strength of guile that desperation gave me, rather than sink abashed and penitent beneath it? And this was the woman who had once lectured on duplicity and expediency, and deemed herself above them!

Bitter and nauseous as was this bowl to me, I drank it without a grimace; so much depended on the measure of deceit—hope, love, honor, life itself perhaps—for my terrors whispered that even such warnings as those Gregory had given were not to be disregarded where there was question of success or failure to Basil Bainrothe! But one alternative presented itself—escape! Delay, I scarce could hope for, and, even if granted, how could it avail me in the end? Those words—"He will make you dead!" rang in my ears, and seemed written on the wall. They confronted me everywhere. It was so easy to do this—so easy to repeat what the papers had already told the world—so easy to confine me in a maniac's cell under an assumed name, and by the aid of my own gold, and say, "She perished at sea!"

It would be to the interest of all who knew it, to preserve the secret, except the poor ship's captain, and he had been a dupe, and would scarcely recognize his folly, or, if he did, be the first to boast of and publish it. Besides that, should the matter be inquired into, how easy for Bainrothe to allege that my own family had sanctioned his course to save my reputation! For innuendo was over on this disgraceful subject. He had declared openly his base design.

Years might elapse before the final exposition, years of utter ruin to my prospects and my hopes. Wentworth might be married by that time, or indifferent, or dead; Ernie too old to make the matter of a year or two of consequence in the carrying out of the nefarious scheme to sustain which it would be so easy to summon and suborn witnesses.

All these possibilities represented themselves to me with frightful distinctness; my mind became imbued with them to the exclusion of all else—of reason even. I was literally panic-stricken, and nothing but flight could satisfy my instinct, my impulse of self-preservation. I must go, even if blown like a leaf before the gales of heaven; must fly, if even to certainty of destruction. I had felt this necessity once before, be it remembered, but never so stringently, so morbidly as now. I was yielding under the agony, the anxiety incident to my condition; my nervous system, too severely taxed, was breaking down, and it would succumb entirely, unless relief came to me (of this I felt convinced), before another weary month should roll away. Had I been imprisoned for a certain term of years as an expiation for crimes, I think I could have borne it better; but the injustice, the uncertainty of these proceedings were more than I could sustain.

I fell asleep, I remember, on the night of my interview with Gregory—*alias* Englehart—to dream confusedly of Baron Trenck and his iron collar, and the Princess Amelia and her unmitigated grief, and it seemed to me that I was given to drink from a cup the poor prisoner had carved (as memoirs tell us he carved and sold many such), filled with a sort of bitter wine, by the man in the iron mask—so vividly did Fancy, mixing her ingredients, typify the anguish of my waking moments, and reproduce its anxieties, in dreams of night that could not be controlled.

When I awoke in the morning it was to lie quietly, and listen to the doleful voice of Sabra, for such had been

Dinah's Congo name, uplifted in what she called a "sperritual" as she cleaned the brass mountings of the grate and kindled its tardy fires. With very slight alteration and adjustment, this picturesque and dramatic Obi hymn is given in this place, just as I jotted it down in my diary, thus imprinting it on my memory from her own dolphin-like lips and bellows-like lungs. Her forefathers, she informed me with considerable pride, had been snake-worshipers, and she certainly inherited their tendency to treat the worst enemy of mankind with respectful adoration.

It served to divert my mind from its one fixed idea for a little time to arrange this singular hymn, which, together with those she had given voice to on the raft, proved her poetic powers. For Sabra assured me that this gift of sacred song had come to her one day when she was washing her master's linen, and that she had felt it run cold streaks down her back and through her brain, and that from that time she was uplifted to sing "sperrituals" by spells and seasons. This, her longest and most successful inspiration, I now lay before the reader:

SABRA'S SPERITUAL.

We's on de road to Zion,
We's on de paf' to Zion,
But dar's a roarin' lion,
  For Satan stops de way.
Oh! lef' us pass, ole Masta,
Oh! lef' us pass, strong Masta,
Oh! lef' us pass, rich Masta—
  'T am near de break ob day!

We's on de road to Zion,
We's on de paf' to Zion,
But wid his red-hot iron
  He bars de hebbenly gate!

Oh! lef' us pass, ole Masta,
Oh! lef' us pass, kin' Masta,
Oh! lef' us pass, sweet Masta,
  For we is mighty late!

Does you hear de rain a-fallin'?
Does you hear de prophets callin'?
Does you hear de cherubs squallin'
  Wat's settin' on de gate?
Oh! lef' us pass, ole Masta,
Oh! step dis side, kin' Masta,
Unbar de do', dear Masta,
  We *dar'* no longer wait!

Does you hear de win' a blowin'?
Does you hear de chickens crowin'?
Does you see de niggars hoein'?
  It am de break ob day!
Oh! lef' us by, good Masta,
Oh! stan' aside, ole Masta,
Oh! light your lamp, sweet Sabiour,
  For we done los' our way!

We'll gib you all our money,
We'll fotch you yams and honey,
We'll fill your pipe wid 'baccer,
  An' twiss your tail wid hay!
We'll shod your hoofs wid copper,
We'll knob your horns wid silber,
We'll cook you rice and gopher,
  Ef you will clar de way!

He's gwine away, my bredderin,
He's stepped aside, my sisterin,
He's clared de track, my chillun,
  Now make de trumpets bray!
We tanks you kindly, Masta,
We gibs you tanks, ole Masta,
You is a buckra Masta,
  Whateber white folks say!

## CHAPTER XII.

During these last days of my captivity, Mrs. Clayton was truly a piteous sight to see—swathed in flannel and helpless as an infant, yet still perversely vigilant as she had been in her hours of health, and determined on the subject of opiates as before. I sometimes think she feared to place herself wholly in my hands, as she must have been under the influence of a powerful anodyne, and that, in spite of her professions of confidence, and even affection, she feared me as her foe. God knows that, had it been to save my own life, I would not have harmed one hair of her viperish head, as flat on top as if the stone of the Indian had been bound upon its crown from babyhood, yet full of brains to bursting around the base of the skull.

It was necessary for Dinah to be in constant attendance on my Argus, and even to feed her, so helpless were her hands, with the mucilages which now formed her principal diet, by the order of some celebrated physician who wrote his prescriptions without seeing his patient, after the form of the ancients, sending them daily through the hands of Mrs. Raymond. Still those vigilant green eyes never faltered in their task, and lying where —with the door opened between our chambers (as she tyrannically required it to be most of the time) she could command a view of almost every act of my life—I found her scrutiny more unendurable than when she had at least feigned to be absorbed with her stocking-basket. Ernie's noise, too, disturbed her, and I was obliged to keep him constantly amused, for fear that her wrath might culminate in eternal banishment.

The days slid on—November had passed through that exquisite phase of existence (which almost redeems it from the reproach cast upon it through all time, of being *par excellence the* gloomy month of the year), the sweet and balmy influences of which had reached us, even through the walls of our prison-house, in the shape of smoky sunshine, and balmy, odorous, and lingering blossoms, and was now asserting its traditional character with much angry bluster of sleet, and storm, and cutting wind. It was Herod lamenting his Mariamne slain by his own hand, and making others suffer the consequences of his regretted cruelty, his remorseful anguish. It was the fierce Viking making wild wail over his dead Oriana.

No more to come until another year had done its work of resurrection and decay, the lovely Indian Summer slumbered under her mound of withered flowers and heaps of gorgeous leaves, unheeding all, or unconscious of the grief of her stern bridegroom.

Cold and bitter and bleak howled the November blast, and ruthlessly drove the sleet against the shivering panes, exposed without, though shielded within by Venetian folding shutters, on that gray morning, when a passing whisper from most unlovely and altogether unfaithful lips nerved me paradoxically to sudden resolution.

False as I knew old Dinah to be—almost on principle —still, I could not disregard the possible truth of her passing warning, given in broken whisper first as she poured out my tea and afterward prepared my bath.

"Honey, don't you touch no tea nor coffee dis evening after Dinah goes out ob here an' de bolt am fetched home; jus' make 'tence to drene it down, like, but don't swaller one mortal drop, for dey is gwine to give you a dose of laudamy"—nodding sagaciously and peering into the teapot as she interpolated aloud; "sure enough, it is full ob grounds, honey! (I heerd 'um say dat wid my own two blessed yers), for de purpose of movin' you soun' asleep up to dat bell-tower (belfry, b'leves dey call it sometimes)—he! he! he! next door, in dat big house, war de res' on 'em libs, de little angel gal too. You see, honey, der was an ossifer to sarve a process writ about somebody here dis mornin', but dar was something wrong about it, so dey all said, an' he is comin' to sarch de house for you, I spec', to-morrow; for de hue an' cry is out somehow—or mebbe it's me—he! he! he! (very faintly) an' dey is gwine to move you, so dey says, to keep all dark, after you gets soun' asleep. But de ossifer is 'bleeged to wait till mornin' (court-time, as I heerd 'em say) comes roun' agin to git de *haby-corpy* fixed up right, an' dat's how he spounded hisself. Wat does dat mean, honey?"

"I can scarcely make you understand now, Dinah" (aside). "Don't ask me—just go on, low, very low; how did you hear all this?" (Aloud) "More cream, Dinah."

"Wid my ear to de key-hole, in de study, war dey axed de ossifer. My 'spicions was roused by de words he 'dressed to me wen I opened de front do', for, you see, dat ole nigger watch-dog ob dern, dat has nebber a good word for nobody, was gone to market, an' Madame Raymond she hel' de watch, an' she sont me from de kitchen to mine de front-do' bell.

"'Old dame,' says the ossifer (for so dey calls him),

as pleasant as a mornin' in May, 'has you a young gal locked up here as you knows ob? Now tell what you choose, and don't be afraid of dese folks. Dis is a free country for bofe black and white.'

"Den I answered him straightforward like de trufe: 'Dar's nobody in de house hèah but wat you kin see for axin' for 'em, as far as I knows on. Wat young gal do you 'lude to, masta?—Bridget Maloney, I spose, dat Irish heifer wat does de chambers ebery mornin' and goes home ob ebenin's. Ef you means her, she's off to church to-day, an' sleeps at her mammy's house.'

"'Does you feel willin' to swar to de trufe of your insertion, ole dame?' he disclaims. 'I shall resist on dat'—fierce as a buck-rabbit, holdin' up his right hand, an' blinkin' his little 'cute eyes.

"Sartin an' sure I does when de right time is come,' I sez. 'Jes' take me to de court-hous' ef you doubt Dinah's word compunctionable. I neber hab bin in dat place yit since I was sold in Georgy on de block befo' de high, wooden steps; but I knows it is more solemn to lie dar dan in Methody meetin'-house.'

"Den Mr. Bainrofe he cum out, hearin' de talk, in dat long-tailed, satin-flowered gownd ob his'n, wid a silk rope tied roun' his waist, an' gole tossels hangin' in front, jes' like a Catholic Roman or a king, an' he sez, 'Walk in here, my fren, an' don't tamper wid my servants—dat ain't gentlem'ly;' den he puts his han' on de ossifer's shoulder, an' dey walked in together, an' I listened at de do', in duty boun', an' I heerd him say, 'Plant a guard if you choose—do wateber you like—but, till dat writ am rectified, you can't sarch through my house, for a man's house is his castle here, as in de Great Britain, till de law reaches out a long arm an' a strong arm.' Dat was wat

Mr. Bainrofe spounded to de ossifer, an' he 'peared 'fused-like an' flusterfied, for I peeped fru de key-hole at 'em wen dey wus talkin'. 'An,' sez he, 'dis heah paper does want de secon' seal, sure enough, since I 'xamine it, wat you is so 'tickiler 'bout; but dat can easily be reconstructified, an' I'll be sartin sure to be here airly to-morrow morning. In de mean while, my man, McDermot, shall keep de house in his eye, an' mus' hab de liberty of lodgment.'

"Den Mr. Bainrofe he say, 'Oh, sartinly—your man, McDermot, am welcome to his bite an' sup, an' all he kin fine out'—an' he laughed, an' dey parted, mighty pleasant-like, and den he called Mrs. Raymun' and Mass' Gregory, an' I listened again. Dat's our colored way for reformation, child. An' I heerd 'em—"

"Dinah! Dinah! what are you muttering about—don't you hear Mrs. Raymond knocking? Miss Monfort must be tired out of your nonsense. What keeps you there so long?"

"I'se spounding another speritual to Miss Miramy, an', wen I gits 'gaged in dat way, I disregards airthly knockin'. I'se listenin' to de angels hammerin' overhead, an' Mrs. Raymun' will hab to wait a spell—he! he! he!"

"Oh, go at once, Dinah, and open the door for Mrs. Raymond. I can write your song down just as well another time," I remonstrated, taking up and laying down my note-book as I spoke, so as to display my ostensible occupation to the peering eyes of Mrs. Clayton (now sitting bolt upright in her bed, looking like a Chinese bonze), for the purpose of sweeping in my position definitively.

"That will do, Dinah. Now go and get Miss Monfort's bath ready," I heard my dragoness say, after a short whispered communication from her early visitor. It was the idea, probably, to remove me, as well as Dinah, while the plot was being unfolded, and my bathroom, with its closed door, promised security from quick ears and eyes to the brace of conspirators now plotting their final blow.

Once in that belfry, and truly might the sense of Dante's famous inscription become my motto for life: "Here hope is left behind."

I covered my eyes as I recalled that dreary, dreadful prison-house of clock and bell, into which I had clambered once by means of a movable step-ladder, rarely left there by the attendant, in order to rescue my famished cat, shut up there by accident. I recollected the maddened look of the creature, as it flew by me like a flash, frightened out of its wits, Mrs. Austin had said, by the clicking of the machinery of the huge clock, and the chiming of the responsive bell. Both were silent now, and there was room enough for a prisoner's cot in that lonely and dismantled turret as there once had been for a telescope and its rest, used for astronomical purposes at long intervals by my father and a few of his scientific friends, but finally dismantled and put aside forever.

I could imagine myself a denizen, at the will of Bainrothe, of that weird, gray belfry, shut up with that silent clock, in company with a bed, a chair, and table, denied, perchance, even the comfort of a stove, for fear the flue might utter smoke, and, with it, that kind of revelation, said proverbially to accompany such manifestations; denied books, even writing-materials, the sight of a human face, and furnished with food merely sufficing in quantity and quality to keep soul and body together!

Could I resist this state of things? Could I sustain it and retain my reason? No, I felt that the picture my fancy drew, if realized, would make me abject and submissive, change me to a cowardly, cringing slave. I was not made of the right stuff for martyrdom, only for battle, for resistance, and would put forth my last powers in the effort to save myself from the unendurable trials before me, even if destruction were the consequence. A pistol-ball in my brain would be preferable to what I saw awaiting me, should Bainrothe succeed in his stratagem, as I doubted not he would do, if determined on it. I should know freedom in its true sense never again, if that night were suffered to pass without its redemption, if that belfry once were entered.

As carelessly as I could I followed Dinah to the bath-room, ostensibly to direct the temperature of the water, but really to draw out from her all that was possible while the mood of communication possessed her, on the subject so vital to me and my welfare. Life and death almost were involved in her revelations, and I hastened to wind in the clew while it lingered in my hand; for I knew that she was an eccentric as well as a selfish creature, and might suddenly see fit to withdraw or snap its thread.

"Now, tell me about McDermot, Dinah, what sort of a look has he? Is he large or small, light or dark, and does he smoke a pipe?"

"He is a great big man, honey, wid red har an' sort ob chaney-blue eyes; mos while, sometimes he rolls em up in his head, an' he smells mighty strong of whisky. I tells you all; his bref mos knocked me down, but I didn't see no pipe?"

A discouraging account, truly; yet I persevered. It

seemed my only hope to enlist this man on my side, either through his sympathies or sense of duty. I had no power to command his services on the side of his avarice. The ring on my finger, the pledge of Wentworth's troth, a massive circlet of chased gold, was all that remained to me in the shape of valuables. I did not possess a stiver in that prison, nor own even the clothes on my back.

"Could you not take him a message from me, Dinah? It is his duty, you know, to assist me; it is on my account, doubtless, he is placed here; and hereafter I can reward him liberally, and you too. Just now, you know, I am penniless."

The woman stopped and looked at me, her small black irises mere points, set in extensive, muddy-looking whites, not unfrequently suffused and bloodshot.

"I dun told the ossifer dar wus no one here you knows, answerin' to your perscription."

"But that was only a measure of safety for yourself; you surely do not mean to take sides with my persecutors?"

"I has nuffin at all to do wid it, at all," hunching her back; "I has gib you far warnin' 'bout de laudamy an' der retentions, an' you mus' fight it out yourself, chile! I is afraid to go one step furder; but de debble sort o' tempted me dis mornin' to make a clean breast of der doins. Ef you mentions it, do; I is retermined to reny ebbery word of your ramification, and in dis here country a nigger's word, dey tells me, goes jus' as fur as a pore white gal's, if not furder; 'sides dat, I is gwine to swar favorable for my 'ployers, in course, at de court-house—unless"—hesitating and leering in my face—"you sees, honey, dey have not paid me yit—and mebbe dey won't, ef I displeases 'em, an' your gole watch is gone; an' den, Dinah would be lef' on de shelf."

"But I have other property, Dinah, other jewels, even. That watch was very little compared to what I possess outside of these prison-walls, and these possessions—"

"Whar is dey, honey? 'a bird in dis han' am worf two dozen in a bush,' as my ole masta used to say, wen de traders cum up to buy his corn an' cotton, an' I always sawed de dollars come down mighty quick after dat sayin' of his'n; for I used to watch round the dinin'-room pretty constant an' close in dem days, totin' in poplar-chips an' corn-cobs for kin'lin' an' litin' masta's long clay pipes—none ob de common sort, I tells you—an' brushin' up de harf an' keepin' off de flies, and so forf. You see I was a little shaver in dem days, an' masta liked my Congo straction, an' petted me a heap, an' I never seed the cotton-field till my ole masta died; den dey put me out ob de house, because Mass Jack Dillard's father—dat was my ole mistis's own step-brother's secon' son—he 'cused me ob stealin' his gole pencil-case wrongfully—like I had any use fur his writin' 'tensils!" (indignantly).

"Dinah," I adjured, cutting short the stream of her narrative, "for God's sake, see Mr. McDermot, and tell him of my situation! He shall have a thousand dollars to-morrow, and you also shall have money enough to buy your whole family, and bring them hither, if you will but assist me to escape *this* night. Don't stand and look at me, woman, but act at once, if you have a human heart. You must help me now, or never."

"You mus' tink I's one ob de born fools, Miss Mirimy, to bl'eve all dat stuff! Doesn't I know you loss all your trunks on de 'Scusco, an' wasn't you a pore gal, teachin' white folks's chilluns fur a livin' before? I has hearn all dat discounted since I come into dis 'stablishment. We all knows as how teachers is de meanest kine of white trash gwine; still, I specs you might'ly. You has been ob de quality; any nigger can see dat wid half an eye open; an' you has got more sense in de end ob yo little finger, ef you is crazy, dan all de res tied up in a bunch ob fedders! Wat I does for you, chile, I does for lub ob yo purliteness" (hesitating here). "You hasn't anoder ob dem gole-pieces anywhar, like dat you gib me befo', has you? I'se bery bad off fur 'baccer, I is, indeed, chile, an' de pay is mighty slow in dis house."

"I have not a five-penny bit, Dinah, not one copper cent, if it were to save my life or yours."

"Is dat ring of yours good guinea gole, honey?" asked the mercenary creature, leering at it. "It looks mighty bright and pretty, it does dat! But mebbe its nuffin but pinchbeck, after all."

"It looks what it is, Dinah"—and, after a moment's consideration, I drew it from my finger. "If I give you this, will you promise to deliver my message to McDermot faithfully?"

"Sartain sure, honey, but tell me again wat it is; I forgits de small patticklers."

"Get me my pencil and a scrap of paper, and let me write it down for him to read; or no, this might involve observation, detection. I must rely upon your memory, Dinah, which I have reason to know is good. Now, listen and understand me. I promise to Mr. McDermot one thousand dollars, to be paid down to-morrow morning, if he will help me to escape to-night. And I promise you liberty for all of your family, and security for yourself, if you will assist me, or even be silent, and let me go without a word, without informing. Do you understand this, Dinah? If so, repeat it to me low, yet distinctly."

She obeyed me, evincing wonderful shrewdness in her way of putting the affair, as she said she meant to do, in approaching McDermot.

"And do you believe me, Dinah, now that I have promised so solemnly to pay these rewards?"

"Dats neider here nor dar, Miss Mirim, so dat McDermot bleves you, dat's enough; wat dis chile bleves am her own business. Dem Irish am mighty stupid kine ob creeturs; dey swallows down mos' any thing you chooses to tell 'em."

A voice without, uplifted at this juncture, as if it had long been expending itself in ineffectual appeals, now summoned Dinah, harshly and emphatically.

The Lady Anastasia had departed, after a brief interview, and Mrs. Clayton, unable to leave her bed, felt naturally anxious to ascertain the cause of Dinah's prolonged ministry on her fellow-prisoner.

I heard only the words, "De pattikalerest lady I ebber come acrost about de feel of water, an' I is done tired out, I is—" The rest was lost, as Dinah vanished from the apartment of the invalid. In the next moment, I heard the key turned, and the outlet bolt drawn, and the growl of the surly sable watch-dog without, who, in Mrs. Raymond's absence, officiated as our jailer and Cerberus.

It was early evening when Dinah returned, for she brought to us but two meals at this season, the necessary food for Ernie being always ready in a closet. She came ushered in, as usual, by Mrs. Raymond, who bore with her on this occasion what she called savory broth, concocted, by her own fair hands, for the benefit of her suffering parent. While Clayton was employed in supping this mutton abomination, with a loud noise peculiar to the vulgar, and Mrs. Raymond whispering inaudible words above the bowl, I was ostensibly employed in tearing a croquet to pieces with my fork, while I interrogated Dinah, in a low, even voice, between each shred, unintelligible, I knew, in the next room, through its monotony, on the success of her mission, and caught her muttered rather than murmured replies eagerly in return.

"Did you speak with him, Dinah?"

"Dere was no use, honey; Bainrothe done bought him up. I peaked fru de key-hole, and seen de gole paid down wid my own two precious eyes. Dar's no mistake about dat," shaking her head dolefully. "All you has to do now, honey, is to keep wide awake, an' duly sober, as ole masta used to say, 'frain 'ligiously from de tea or coffee, one or de udder, dat she will offer you 'bout eight o'clock dis ebenin', or mebbe dey will send it up by me, I can't say yit. Howsomever, you needn't to drink dat stuff arter wat you knows; an' ef dey goes to take you forcefully off to de belfry in de night-time, you kin skreech ebbery step ob de way. Dat's de bes plan, chile, wat I kin project for your resistance; but I'se afeard dar is no hopin' you, any way we can fix it."

"Thank you, Dinah, you have done your best, no doubt; don't sell my ring, though; I shall want it back some day."

"La, chile, I done 'sposed ob it aready, an' dey give me a poun of backer an' a gole-piece fur it. It was good gole an' no mistake. I tells you all," adding aloud, "an' now, Miss Mirim, I has tole you ebbery syllable. I disremembered ob dat speritual ar. I is sorry you doesn't like dese crockets, fur de madame made un wid her own clean red hands."

"Say white hands, you old limb of Satan, or I shall be after you with a mop," cried the laughing voice of Mrs. Raymond from the side of the sick woman's bed, betraying at once how she had divided her attention. Then, advancing into my chamber, she added, as coolly as though she had been suggesting a visit to the theatre:

"Excuse me, Miss Monfort, for intruding, but I am about to ask you whether it would be agreeable to you to be married to-night at ten o'clock? This seems very sudden, but circumstances have forced the arrangement on us all, and I assure you, from the bottom of my heart, it is for both of us the preferable alternative of evils, as poor Sir Harry Raymond would have said. Alas, my dear! shall I ever again have such a helpmate as he was: so kind, so generous, so considerate"— and she clasped and wrung her large, rosy hands. "A second marriage is often a great sacrifice, and, in any case, a hazard, as I feel, as the time draws near, very sensibly. But you seem confounded, and yet you must have been somewhat prepared for this condition of things after your last interview with Dr. Englehart?"

The amazement of Dinah at this change in the programme, if possible, exceeded my own. She did not understand, as I did, that it was a measure prompted not only by humanity but self-interest, and that even the hard heart of Basil Bainrothe preferred a compromise to such violence and injustice as those he had otherwise meditated. Besides, what better or more sensible mode than this could there be, according to his views, of quashing the whole *esclandre*—quieting official inquiry as well as public indignation? As the wife of Gregory, I should be, of course, a *forçat* for life, walking abroad with the concealed brand and manacle, afraid and ashamed to complain and acknowledge my condition, and willing to condone every thing.

I saw, at a glance, that my true policy was to feign a reluctant consent to this proposition, and to determine later what recourse to take, as if indeed any remained to me in that den of serpents. I would consider, as soon as Mrs. Raymond was gone, what measures to pursue in order to elude the vigilance of McDermot, the detective; and then, if all proved vain, I could but perish! For I would have walked cheerfully over the burning ploughshares of old, lived again through the hideous nightmare of the burning ship and raft, nay, clasped hands with the spectre of La Vigne himself, had it offered to lead me to purgatory, rather than have married the knave, the liar, the half-breed Gregory!

My resolution was soon made.

"You will send me a suitable dress, I suppose," I said, calmly, "you know I am a pauper here."

"Yes, fortunately I have two almost alike. Which shall it be, a chally or barege?"

"It matters little, the color is all I care for. Let it be white; I have a superstition about being married in colors."

"So should I have, were this the first time, but, being a widow, I shall wear a lavender-satin, trimmed with blond, made up for a very different occasion."

"Yes, that will be quite suitable. Well, the long agony is over at last, and I am glad of it," and I drew a deep, free breath.

"You will have to sign the papers before you come down-stairs. Mr. Bainrothe told me to say this to you, and to ask you to have them ready; they will be witnessed below with the marriage, and at nine, *precisely*, expect me to appear with your gown, and make your toilet."

"Will not Bridget Maloney do as well?" I asked, desperately. She, at least, I thought, may be compassionate.

"It is strange you should know of her at all, or she of you. It is that girl, then, who has given us all this trouble," going to the bed, "when I did not suppose she knew of her existence. Explain this, Clayton, if you can."

"I suppose Ernie, who is fond of her, has mentioned her name to Miss Monfort; she thinks his mother is sick up-stairs, but knows no more, I am certain; besides, it's Dr. Englehart's establishment—such things are to be expected, and surprise no one of the attendants. Bridget is kept busy among them all." The farce was to be kept up, it seemed, to the end.

Old Dinah was evidently quaking in her shoes, and began to see her error, as she glanced reproachfully at me, but no further revelation seemed to be expected. It was, indeed, to divert, partly, immediate suspicion from one I still hoped to make my tool, that I mentioned the Irish girl at all, or craved her presence, but I soon found how futile in one instance was this trust. No sooner had Mrs. Raymond turned to depart, than Dinah followed her, protesting against being locked up the whole evening with the invalid, and begging leave to go out for an hour or two on business of her own, which she declared important.

"But Miss Monfort may need you in making her preparations," remonstrated Mrs. Raymond, "and Clayton and Ernie will want your attention; besides, fires will go down if not constantly mended, this cold evening."

"Dar's plenty of coal in de box, an' de tongs, wid claws, wat Ernie is so fond of handlin', ready and waitin' for dem wat's strong enough to use dem if dey choose, an' tea in de caddy, an' de kittle on de trivet, jes filled up, de brass toastin'-fork on de peg in de closet, 'sides bread an' butter, an' jam, an' new milk on de shelf, an' I is 'bliged to go anyway, case my ticklerest friend am dyin' ob de numony—I is jes got word; but at nine o'clock" (and she looked maliciously at me) "percisely Dinah 'll be in dis pickin' patch—he! he! he! can't possumbly cum no airlier."

In a flash I saw the advantage her prolonged absence would give me, unless, indeed, she had become my confederate, so I beheld her depart with a feeling of relief which reacted in the next moment to positive helplessness and terror as the bolt was drawn behind her. What could I do? What was there to be done? For a time I sat mute and crushed by consideration; then casting myself on my bed I slept for half an hour, the kind of slumber that confusion generates, and yet I woke refreshed, calmed, comforted, and with a clearly-formed resolution and plan of action. I rose and approached Mrs. Clayton, whose groans, perhaps, aroused me, and, as I stood beside her bed, the clock in the dining room-below struck six. I had still three hours for hope—for endeavor, before the circle of flame should close hopelessly around me forever! Three hours—were they not enough? Could I not compel them to concentration?

A cup of strong tea was hastily drawn and swallowed—another made for, and administered by my hand to, Mrs. Clayton, with toast *ad libitum*—a tedious process—and afterward Ernie's supper prepared and eaten—all in less than half an hour. By seven he was in bed and asleep, and I had taken my seat by Mrs. Clayton, for the purpose, apparently, of merciful ministry to her condition—a piece of self-abnegation, as it seemed, and as she felt it, scarcely to be expected on my blissful marriage-night.

"I feel very sorry for you; you suffer so, Mrs. Clayton," I had said, as I drew a chair beside her bed.

"And I for you, Miss Monfort; our fate seems equally hard, but we must bear it;" and she groaned heavily and closed her eyes, evidently in great pain.

"I have come to that conclusion, also, after a bitter struggle; physical pain is not so easily borne, however; the body has little philosophy."

"I thought all this was over," she rejoined, abstractedly, "when my hands were drawn as you see them by neuralgia ten years since. But I did not suffer as much then, I believe, as I do now; besides, I was younger, happier, better able to bear pain."

"Yes, that is true; the old should be at rest," at least my sense of justice whispered this; then, after a pause: "Does my rubbing ease your shoulder, Mrs. Clayton?"

"Somewhat—it is my head to-night, however, that troubles me chiefly. Be good enough to press my temples. Ah, that is great relief! You are very kind, Miss Monfort; yet, in reviewing the past, I hope you will not find that I have been wanting to you in my turn. I trust we shall part in peace and meet hereafter as friends. But you do not answer me."

"Pardon me, I was thinking. This is a crisis, you know—this night decides my fate for good or ill, all rests with merciful God!"

"Yes, all—of ourselves we are helpless, of course. It is a comfort to me, I confess, as I lie here, to feel that I have never willingly injured a fellow-being; to think that I—but, bless my soul, Miss Monfort, you must not hold me down in that way! you would not, I trust. But even if you did—no key this time, the door is fast without!"

"Oh, not for worlds! be still, the pain will pass. I have the gift, you know, of soothing physical suffering. There, rest, you must not stir; give yourself up to me, if you can—slumber will come."

"It must not come—see, we are all alone!"

Her glazing eye—her slower breathing began already to attest the influence of the electric fluid, so potent in my veins, so wanting in her own, both from temperament and disease, yet she resisted bravely and long, and, even when her limbs were powerless, her spirit rebelled against me in murmured words of defiant opposition; but this, too, yielded finally to silence and to stupor; and she slept the deep, calm, unmistakable slumber caused by magnetism.

Then, again, I went through the experiment of the preceding night, and strove to awaken her.

"Get up," I said, and yet without willing that she should do so. "Mrs. Raymond is here to show you her marriage-dress, and Mr. Bainrothe calls."

"Tell them to let me sleep; don't—don't—disturb me. I am so happy—so peaceful. It is sweet, too, to think that she will be married at last. Poor thing! it was no fault of hers, though—no fault. A young actress is exposed to so many temptations, and it was better so—Harry Raymond's mistress."

That secret would never have escaped her devoted lips had she been able to retain it.

As carefully as the eyes of the dead are closed, I drew down her gaping lids, and turned away. As I did so, the clock struck eight. Fatima never listened more anxiously to the toll of parting time than I did that night; but, alas for me! no sister Anne kept watch on the tower; no brother hastened to arrest the sword. I was deserted by all save God and desperation. One hour comprised my fate! Very quietly I closed the door between Mrs. Clayton's room and my own. The bolt was on the other side, so I could not secure my privacy, even for a moment, should she chance to wake, or should Mrs. Raymond or Dinah return unexpectedly. As rapidly as I could, I altered my dress—this time above my clothes—threw on the black silk frock and mantilla prepared for me on shipboard, tied a dark veil over my head, an old woolen scarf about my throat, provided for Ernie's sore-throat and croup, and stood equipped for my enterprise.

Neither bonnet, nor gloves, nor boots, did I possess—Mrs. Raymond's loan having long since been condoned on behalf of some one else, and my clothing, in my captivity, had been contrived to suit my circumstances.

Wheeling the bedstead very gently on its noiseless castors a few inches from the wall, I insinuated myself between them, and, sheltered by the head-board, loosened again the slightly-adhering covering of paper that concealed the door, and fitted into the key-hole the well-oiled wooden key, which once before had proved its efficiency. It did not fail me now, in my hour of extremity, for a moment later I had turned and removed it from its socket, stepped forth upon the landing, and relocked without the door of my prison; but, perhaps, with too much of nervous haste, too little caution, for, to my inexpressible confusion, the handle of the instrument of my emancipation remained in my hand, broken off at the lock, and useless forever more.

In delaying probable pursuit from within, I had cut off all possibility of my own retreat in case of failure.

My bridges were literally burned behind me, and I had no alternative left between flight and detection. And yet there was something in the situation that, inconsistently enough, made me smile, albeit with a trembling heart.

I shook my head drearily, as a couplet from Collins's "Camel-Driver," with its strange appropriateness, irresistibly crossed my brain.

Why is it that, in times like these, such conceits beset us, such comparisons arise? Does the quality called presence of mind find root in the same source that impels us to apt quotation?—

> "What if the lion in his rage I meet?
> Oft in the dust I see his printed feet."

I gained fresh heart from that trivial diversion of thought, and stood quietly contemplating alternately the hall below and that above (both of which were visible from my place on the intermediate platform; all was still in both of these wide corridors), to make sure of the safety of my enterprise; and now, once more my foot was on the brink of those mysterious stairs which led, I felt, to doom or to liberty. I commenced, very cautiously, to descend them. The study-door at their foot was closed, and all seemed silent within. The murmur of voices, and the remote rattling of china proceeding from the ell behind the hall, encouraged me to believe that on this bitter night the family was concentrated, for greater comfort, in the supper-room.

With my hand on the baluster, pausing at every step, I crept quietly down the stairway; then, as if my feet were suddenly winged with terror, I darted by the study-door, flew lightly over the carpeted hall, and found myself, in another moment, secure within the small enclosed vestibule into which the door of entrance gave. My worst misgivings had never compassed the terrific truth. At this early hour of the evening, not only was the front door locked, but the key had been withdrawn. This was despair.

My knees gave way beneath me, and I sank like a flaccid heap in the corner, against one of the leaves of the small folding-door that divided the arched vestibule from the long entry, and which was secured to the floor by a bolt, while the other one was thrown back. Crouched in the shadow, powerless to move or think, I heard, with inexpressible terror, the door of the study open, and the voice and step of Bainrothe in the hall, approaching me.

Had he heard me? Would he come? Was I betrayed?

I felt my hair rise on my head as these questions rang like a tocsin through my brain, and I think, at that moment, I had a foretaste of the chief agony of death.

They were answered by Bainrothe himself, as he paused midway between the study-door and my place of refuge; and again I breathed—I lived.

"I was mistaken, 'Stasia, it is not he! the wind, probably; and that marble looks so cold—so uninviting—I shall not explore it. He has a key, you know, and can come when he likes; for my part, I shall go in to supper while the oysters are hot. Do as you like, though."

"Had we not better wait? You know he is sure to come to-night, bad as the weather is, on account of that affair. It was late when Wentworth notified him."

This was the rejoinder made from within the study,

in which I recognized the voice of Mrs. Raymond, clear and shrill.

"Well, have it as you please. If you prefer courtesy to comfort, you shall be gratified; but what's the use of ceremony with Gregory? He will be here in twenty minutes, Mr. Bainrothe; but don't wait. I shall have time to sup with him before I go up-stairs, you know. I believe I will stay where I am until he comes, and finish taking in the poor thing's wedding-gown. Well, any thing is better than removal to the belfry"—and I thought I heard a sigh.

"A matter of mere temporary necessity, you know, only she might have frozen in the interval," said Bainrothe, jauntily, as he walked up the hall to the door of the dining-room, which I heard him open and let fall against its sill again. It closed with a spring, and in the next moment the study-door was also softly shut, and all was still.

My resolution was promptly taken. The folding leaves of the inner door—that which divided the marble-paved vestibule from the carpeted entry—against one of which I had been leaning, I well knew worked to and fro on pulleys which obeyed the drawing of a cord and tassel hanging at one side, and thus they could readily be closed with a touch by any one standing in the vestibule as they opened out into the hall on which side was the latch and bolt. I recalled this quaint arrangement with a quickness born of emergency, as one that might serve me now, and speadily possessed myself of the tassel at the extremity of the controlling cord. Thus armed, and praying inwardly for strength and courage, and wherewith to carry out my scheme successfully, I took my stand in one of the two niches (just large enough for the purpose) in the door-frame, preferring, of course, that next to the lock, prepared to darken the vestibule at the first approach of the expected guest (I was afraid to do it before, lest attention might be called to it from within the house), and make my escape by rushing past him ere he could recover himself as he entered in the gloom.

The hazard was extreme, the result uncertain, the effort almost foolhardy, it may be thought; but the storm and darkness were in my favor, and I was fleet of foot, as were not all of my pursuers, as far as I could foresee who these might be.

Momently I grew cooler, more determined, more calm, more desperate, more regardless of consequences; and now the culmination of endeavor approached in the shape of the sound of stamping feet upon the icy platform of the steps which they had softly ascended, and the uncertain fitting of a dead-latch key in its dark socket, the feeling for the knob with half-frozen fingers, and finally the sudden and violent throwing forward and open of the door into the darkened vestibule, for I had drawn the cord at the first symptoms of Gregory's advent, which yet took me by surprise. I had closed the inner doors, it is true, but paralyzed with sudden terror I had taken no advantage of the darkness thus evoked, and, as the tall form of the expected and expectant bridegroom staggered in, literally blown forward by the tempest, with introverted umbrella, and wet and streaming garments (dimly discerned in the gloom) that brushed against me as he passed, I continued to stand transfixed to stone in the niche I still occupied.

The dream in which La Vigne had prophesied my failure flashed over me like lightning, and my knees trembled beneath me, yet I still clung spasmodically to the cord I held, and with such desperate force that, when Gregory pushed against the door, he believed it latched within, and so desisted from further effort.

"Dark as Erebus," he muttered, "and on such a night! Confound such hospitality! I suppose I must go back and ring;" and in pursuance of this idea he again suddenly opened the front-door, which, swinging violently back as he turned his face within, once more afforded me the golden opportunity so lately lost. Quick as thought I dropped the cord I held, and in the sudden gust the leaves of the inner door, thus released, flew open and impelled my foe irresistibly forward. With his flapping coat and hat he drifted into the lighted hall before the driving blast, and, roused to instantaneous action, I slid from the niche I filled to the icy platform without, and swift and silent as a spectre sped down the sleety steps to the outward darkness. I was free!

A moment after, I heard the door slammed heavily after me, while I crouched by the gate-post for concealment.

Rising up, I mutely blessed the friendly portal that made me an outcast in the storm-swept streets from which the very dogs shrank terrified.

One moment, one only, I paused as I passed by my father's gate-way, crowned with stone lions that glimmered in the gloom. The force of association and of contrast shook me with emotion—I could not enter there. My own roof afforded me no shelter from the biting blast; but squares away, with a comparative stranger, I must seek (if I ever gained it on that dreadful night) a refuge from the storms and sure protection from my foes.

I moved rapidly along toward the tall street-lamp that diffused a dim and murky light from its frost-crusted lantern at the corner of the square, and before I reached it I encountered the first danger of my undertaking.

Protected, fortunately, by the shadow of the high stone-wall near which I walked rapidly, I met Dinah, so nearly face to face that the whiff of the pipe she was smoking was warm upon my cheek. Wrapped in her old cloth shawl and quilted hood, she muttered as she went, and staggered too, I thought, though here the northeast wind, that swept her along before it, might have been at fault, while, blowing in my face, it retarded my progress.

I passed her unchallenged, but, glancing back just as I turned the corner, I became aware that she was retracing her steps. I fled rapidly on until I reached the shelter of a friendly nook between two houses (well remembered of old), when, turning again to gaze, I saw her standing immovable as a statue beneath the lamp-post, evidently looking in the direction I had taken. There seemed no way of escape now save in persistent flight. My place of concealment might be too readily detected by a cautious observer, a savage on the war-trail. Should Dinah herself pursue me, I knew my speed would distance her; but, that prompt pursuit of some kind was imminent, I knew from that moment.

My aim was to reach the house of Dr. Pemberton, no intermediate one presenting itself as that of an acquaintance of whom I could ask shelter, and belief in the truth of my assertions. Of this house I remembered the position with tolerable accuracy. It formed one, I knew, of a long block of buildings extending from one street to another, and was near the centre.

I had been there only on rare occasions, when his niece abode with him, for he dwelt ordinarily in widowed solitude, although our intimacy was that of relatives rather than of patient and physician.

For this desired goal I strained every nerve, every muscle, every faculty, on that never-to-be-forgotten night of bitter, freezing cold, and driving sleet and blast, which seemed to proclaim itself, in every howling gust, "The wind Euroclydon!"

## CHAPTER XIII.

At first, excitement and terror winged my feet; but even these refused, after I had gone a few squares, to do their friendly office.

Bareheaded, but for a filmy veil, soon thoroughly drenched through; barehanded and almost barefooted, for my thin silk slippers and stockings formed not, after my first few steps, the slightest impediment to wet or cold, I felt that I must perish by the wayside. The sleety storm drove sharply in my face, rendered doubly sensitive to its rigor by long absence from outward air. My insufficient clothing clung closely about me, freezing in every fold, and I glided rather than walked along the icy pavement, scarcely lifting my stiffened feet, or having power to do so.

One stern hope—it almost seemed a forlorn one—now possessed me to the exclusion of all else; one prayer trembled on my quivering lips—that I might reach my destination, if only to tell my story and drop dead a moment after.

Yet I think, in spite of this resolve—this prayer—that, had a friendly door been opened on the way, an area even emitting light and warmth, I should have instinctively turned aside and, at any risk, pleaded for shelter, both from storm and foeman.

In those days that seem far back in the march of luxury, because of the vast impetus of human momentum, stores were closed early, and the primitive family tea-table still existed which marked the assemblage of the household around the evening comet and hearth.

I remember the closed, inhospitable look of the houses past which I sped—the solid wooden shutters, then universal, which closed from the wayfarer every evidence of internal life, and the cold sheen of the icy-white marble steps, made visible by dim lamp-light.

I gained a street-corner not very far, as it seemed to me, from my place of destination. Yet, until I glanced across the way, I was uncertain, and, but for the friendly refuge this opportunity presented, I think I must have faltered and perhaps fallen and frozen to death on the road-side.

To my bewildered and disordered brain, Aladdin's palace seemed suddenly to rise before me in that wilderness of sealed houses and uninhabited streets; for, as I have said before, the very dogs had crept away that night into secure corners, and not even a pariah chimney-sweep, with his dingy blanket drawn close around him, nodded and dozed by a watch-box or slept on a door-step.

I crept across the space that divided me from this cynosure of warmth and luxury, as a poor, draggled moth might do, to bask in the revivifying light of an astral lamp, attracted beyond my power to resist, to pause before the resplendent window, rich in green and purple and amber rotund vases, whose transparent contents were set forth and revealed by fiery jets of gas, toward which I feebly stretched my half-frozen fingers.

There was a splendid vision, also, of goldfish, in glass globes, jars of leaden rock-work, baskets of waxen fruits and flowers, crystal bottles containing rose and amber essences; but, above all, there was light — there was heat.

With one greedy, insatiate gaze my eyes swept in the details of this mimic Eden, and, in another moment, my hand turned the knob of the ground-glass door near the window, and I found myself in paradise!

Rest, shelter, heat—these must I have or perish, and, but for the timely refuge of this thrice-blessed apothecary's shop, I might have left this retrospect unwritten!

I staggered to a chair, and seated myself, unbidden, by the almost red-hot stove, and cowered above it for a time, oblivious of all else.

Then I looked timidly around me.

The master of this Eden was standing, at the moment when he first caught my eyes, holding up a bottle, scrutinizingly, between his face and the light, one of many of the same sort that a lad, in a long, white apron, was engaged in washing.

The odor of the various drugs and essences over which he presided formed an aromatic atmosphere singularly suggestive of incense, as did his costume, that of a high-priest of the temple; but, very soon discarding a gray-linen cape or talma, worn for the protection of his speckless coat, and tossing a bundle of corks rather disdainfully to his assistant, the head of the establishment came politely forward, standing on the other side of the stove, with clasped hands, expectantly.

"You will tell me your errand here when you are quite ready," he said, kindly. "Do rest and warm yourself first. The stove has a narcotic tendency when one has just come out of cold like this! The thermometer has fallen twenty degrees since noonday; but that is only half the trouble. Hem! This sleet and wind are beyond any former experience of mine at this season."

I heard the words of the speaker as if bound in a dreadful dream, but they were clearly understood, and now I made an effort at utterance, but failed, until after repeated endeavors, to enunciate one word. Yet I noted distinctly, and even with a nice discrimination of scrutiny, the red-haired and bright-eyed man, portly and somewhat pompous-looking, with his plump hands folded over his vest, who stood before me, looking pityingly down on my suffering face.

After a time I gathered up my forces sufficiently to inquire, being quite thawed and comforted by the reviving heat of the apartment, how far it might be to the house of Dr. Pemberton, who resided in the block of houses known as Kendrick's Row, on Maple Street.

"It is nearly a square and a half, miss, by street measurement just now, as, on account of changes, this is impassable," was the prompt reply. "Scarcely half a square by the alley that runs from my back-door, after a short turn, straight through to Maple Street; and, if it is only question of a message, I can send Caleb, so that you may await the coming of the doctor in comfort, in this emporium. He always uses his gig for night-visits, and will, no doubt, be happy to carry you home in his wolf-skin."

"Thanks—there is no question of a medical visit. I have very important business with him. I must see him in his own house. I will go without further delay. But, perhaps"—lingering a moment—"you would be so good as to suffer Mr. Caleb to show me the short way you spoke of? I shall not mind going through the alley at all."

I rose prepared to depart, and glanced beseechingly at Caleb, who laid down his bottle uncorked, and folded his arms with an approving knightly bow, unperceived by his employer.

"We have just had a similar inquiry as to Dr. Pemberton's locality; I mean," said the master of the emporium, without replying to my request, "on the part of a very distinguished-looking personage—I might say, well got up in the fur and overcoat line—and, had you come in a few moments earlier, you might have had his escort; or perhaps you are on his track now—probably one of his party?" hesitatingly. "No! Well, it is a strange coincidence, to say the least—very strange—as the doctor is so well known hereabouts. As to going out in the storm again, I have my misgivings, miss, for you, when I look at the flimsiness of your attire and its drenched condition. I can't see, indeed, how a delicate-looking lady like yourself ever held her own against this terrific wind. Eolus seems to have lost his bags! But, perhaps you had an escort to the corner?"

"No—no—no—I came quite alone! Oh, for pity's sake, put me on my way and let me go! My business is most urgent!" I hesitated—my heart sank. Had Bainrothe been before me to spirit the doctor away by some feigned message of need, of distress, to which no inclemency of weather could close that benevolent medical ear? And did he lie in wait for me on the way?"

"Perhaps I had, after all, better go alone," I continued; "it might be too great an inconvenience"—and I moved toward the ground-glass door.

"Not if you will accept my services, miss," said Caleb, timidly, pushing away the remaining corks as he spoke, and glancing furtively at his master.

"How often must I remind you, Caleb Fink," said the owner of the emporium, "that your sphere is circumscribed to your duties? Attend to those phials, and drain them well before you bottle the citrate of magnesia. The last was spoiled by your unpardonable carelessness. I have not forgotten this!"

And again, with a deprecatory look at me, Caleb Fink subsided into a nonentity.

"Truly has the great and wise Dr. Perkins remarked that 'the women of America are suicidal from the cradle to the grave!' I will give you one of his pamphlets, miss, to take away with you, and you will be convinced that slippers are serpents in disguise in winter weather! The wooden shoes of Germany rather! Ay, or even the *sabot* of France! You must not stir another step in those. Be seated, pray, and I will not detain you long, while I procure a substitute or protection for such shams, worth nothing in such Siberian weather.—Caleb, a word with you;" and he whispered to his apprentice, who glided away, to return in a trice with a pair of India-rubber overshoes, into which benign boats he proceeded to thrust my unresisting feet, as I stood leaning on the counter; after which a muffler was tied about my ears, and a heavy honey-comb shawl thrown over my shoulders by the same expeditious hands.

"Could you be always as spry, Caleb! Your gloves now—I shall need my own"—and a pair of stalwart knitted mits were forthwith drawn over my passive hands, in which my fingers nestled undivided and warm.

"Now you look something like going for the doctor! My overcoat, Caleb—gloves—fur-cape—cane! All hanging near the bed. There, we are ready now for old Borealis himself, if he chooses to blow! But I forget—God bless me, you are as pale as the ghost of Pompey, at Philippi !—Caleb, the Perkins elixir—a glass !—Now, young lady, just take it down at a gulp. It is the only alcoholic preparation that Napoleon Bonaparte Burress ever suffered to pass his temperate lips. Father Matthew does not object to it at all, I am told, on emergencies. It may be had at this repository very low, either by the gross or dozen "—speaking the last words mechanically, and he tendered me a small glass of some nauseous, bitter-sweet, and potent beverage, that coursed through my veins like liquid fire.

"Thank you ; it is very comforting," I gasped, and, setting the glass down on the counter, I covered my face with my hands and burst into tears.

The whole forlornness of my outcast and eleemosynary condition rushed over me simultaneously with the flood of warmth caused by the Perkins elixir, which nerved me the next moment for the encounter with the elements.

I saw the kindly master of the emporium turn away, either to conceal his own emotion or his observation of mine, and Caleb stood trembling and crying like a girl before me.

I had shrunk, it may be remembered, from the description Sabra gave me of McDermot, when I heard of his red hair and "chaney-blue eyes ;" but to this red-haired, hazel-eyed man I yearned instinctively, for there are moral differences discernible in the temperament greater than any other, and, when a red-haired man is tender-hearted, he usually usurps the womanly prerogative, and gushes.

But Caleb's sympathy touched me even more.

"We will go now, if you please," I said, recovering myself by a strong effort, and Napoleon B. Burress mutely tendered me his stout, overcoated arm. "The short way you mentioned—let us go that way, if not disagreeable to you," I pleaded.

"Oh, no; it will be an absolute saving of time to me; but, I warn you, the alley is narrow and dark!"

"Never mind; I prefer the short cut, be it what it may. Time is every thing to me."

We passed through the shop, threaded a narrow entry, opened a back-door, which gave upon a strip of paved yard, leading in turn to a back-gate, through which we emerged into a dark and dirty-looking alley.

But first the work of unlocking a padlock, which confined a chain, had to be effected, and, while Mr. N. B. Burress was thus unfastening his back-gate preparatory to egress, I stood gazing back, Eurydice-like, in the place I had left, for the doors of the long entry stood open, revealing the shop beyond and its illuminated window.

Standing thus, I saw, as through a vista and in a perfect ecstasy of terror, the ground-glass shop-door open, and two well-known forms in succession block its portals —those of Gregory and Bainrothe! Would Caleb send them on our track, or would the better part of valor come to his aid and save me from their clutches?

A thought occurred to me. "Mr. Burress," I said (I had retained his name with its remarkable prefix), "will you not lock the gate outside? I can wait patiently until you secure your premises—and—and bring away the key."

"I had meant to leave it here until my return, but you are right," speaking indulgently. "I suppose burglars are abroad on nights like this," and he quietly relocked the alley-gate. "You are very considerate," he said, dryly, after we had gone a few yards in profound silence, "but had I not better return for a lantern?"

"Oh, not for worlds! Faster—faster, Mr. Burress, and Heaven will reward you! Never mind the stones—the snow—the mud—so that we get there first! Yes, I see where the lane turns; I see very well in the dark—never fear—only do not delay—I am so glad you locked the alley-gate. They cannot come that way."

"Of whom are you afraid, poor young lady? Nobody would harm you, I am sure; such a gentle, tender thing as you seem to be!"

"Oh, yes! Fiends are on my track! Don't let them get possession of me again, Mr. Burress. I am pursued—yes—faster—faster!"

"But what has startled you, poor thing, since we left the Repository? You seemed quite calm after the Perkins elixir—and those tears. Ah! I understand!" and he coughed several times significantly. "The doctor will set all right, I suppose, when I give you into his hands. I am glad I came with you myself—courage, we shall soon be there!"

"Yes—yes—he is my only hope! I will explain all when we are safe with him. It is not as you think! I have no strength now. Don't question me further, it exhausts me to talk. Just drag me along."

And silently and valiantly did he betake himself to his task. The noisome alley was threaded, and again we emerged into the sleety, lamp-lit street, a few doors from the corner of that block, in the centre of which Dr. Pemberton resided.

As we approached the friendly threshold, the exact situation of which was familiar to my companion, he pointed it out triumphantly with his stick.

"We shall soon be there," he reiterated, "no need for hurry now." But as he spoke I saw a carriage turn the corner we were facing, and again I urged on my lagging escort to his utmost speed. I ran up the sleety steps in advance of him, and rang the bell with convulsive energy. Its summons was answered promptly, but not a second too soon, for, as the door opened to admit me, the carriage paused before the door, and two men leaped from it, one of whom, the taller, thrusting Burress aside, rushed up the steps after me with outstretched arms.

I had found refuge in the vestibule, and slammed the door in his face—closing, as it did, with a spring-lock—before he reached the platform. Then turning to his companion, he fled down to the street again, with the cry that reached my ear distinctly, of "Baffled, by God!" on his profane lips, and the twain drove off as rapidly as they had come.

A moment later a feeble ring at the door, and a voice from without, assuring the inmates that it was only N. B. Burress, and conjuring them not to be alarmed, caused him to be admitted at once by the house-maid, and shown into the same small front study into which she had conducted me to await the doctor's appearance.

"What name shall I give? The doctor is engaged," said the house-maid, lingering.

"None at all, merely let me know when he is ready to see me. I am tired and cold, and can wait patiently by this good fire."

"It may be some time, miss; would you like a cup of hot coffee, you and this gentleman? The doctor has just had his supper, and there is a pint or more left in the urn."

"Thanks—nothing could be more welcome," and the house-maid disappeared.

"That is the way of this house—patients are always entertained, if in need of refreshment," said Mr. Burress, advancing to the chimney, while he rubbed his hands in a self-gratulatory manner, then expanded them before the bright glare that filled every pore with warmth.

I was tremulous, and silent, and half exhausted, and he seemed to take this in at a friendly glance, for he made none of those inquiries that I knew were burning on his inquisitive lips; but after a few moments of further enjoyment before the grate, and having duly turned himself as on a spit, so as to absorb every ray of heat possible, he betook himself to an arm-chair and a book, near the drop-light on a corner table, the soft rustling of the turning leaves of which had a most soothing effect on my nerves.

"I shall only stay a few minutes," he said, apologetically. "I wish, however, to see you safe in Dr. Pemberton's hands before I leave you, as a sort of duty, you know, you being a charge of mine, and should you need further escort—"

"Oh, thank you, kindly; you have surely had enough trouble on my account already."

"Not a particle—only a pleasure, miss; but the push I got from your pursuer upset me on the pavement and made sparks fly out of my eyes, and, before I could gather myself up, they were back again in the carriage and off. You will have to give me the man's name, miss—you will, indeed, on my own account, when all your fatigue and fright are over. Such favors are generally returned by me with compound interest."

"Oh, be thankful you have not a compound fracture, Mr. Burress, and let the fellow go. He is beneath contempt. But I shall not be satisfied until Dr. Pemberton tells me himself that you are uninjured."

"A lump as big as a potato—that's all, miss; not worth minding, I assure you;" and he raised his hand to his occipital region. "An application, before retiring to bed, of 'Prang's Blood and Life Regenerator,' will make all right again. An astonishing remedy, miss, which no family should be without, and which may be obtained cheaply by the gross or dozen at my emporium. You have heard of Hercules Prang?"

These were the last words I heard distinctly from the lips of Napoleon B. Burress; nor were they answered, even by the brief "Never" which might have proclaimed my ignorance of the very existence of that demi-god of charlatanry, who, for the benefit of suffering mankind, had condescended to compel his genius into the shape of a "revivifying balsam."

I had, with the aid of the house-maid, divested myself of my wet overshoes and wrappings before the advent of my companion, and had already ensconced myself in a deep Spanish chair, that stood invitingly and with extended arms in one corner of the fireplace, when he advanced to place himself on the rug for a general roasting.

It was precisely twenty minutes past ten, Mr. Burress told me later, when he detected, by stealing on tiptoe to my chair, and bending above me, that I was sound asleep, and the mantel clock was on the stroke of eleven when I awoke.

In one corner of the room sat a stern statue of Silence, in the shape of N. B. Burress, watching my repose, and from the adjoining office came the murmur of voices that proved that the long interview between Dr. Pemberton and his patient was still in progress.

At this moment, one of the walnut-leaves of the

small folding-door, that formed a communication between the study and office of the good physician, swung itself gently on its noiseless hinges, into the position distinguished in description as "slightly ajar," and thus remained fixed, after a fashion that spiritual mediums might have been able to account for, on supernatural principles.

The low murmur of voices then readily resolved itself into shaped words and sentences, and, but for my deep languor, and the delightful sense of security that possessed me, I should have risen and closed the obliging door, to shut out unintentional communications.

As it was, I lingered and listened, as one might do to the dash of waves, or the rustling of branches, until suddenly the tones and meaning of the principal interlocutor caused me to rise to my loftiest sitting posture, and clasp the arms of the chair I occupied, while the strained ear of attention drank in every syllable of the remainder of the narrative, evidently drawing near its close.

The low monotony of a continued discourse pervaded the voice, the manner of the speaker, the thread of whose story was no longer interrupted, as before, by the comments or questions of his companion, intent upon the vital interest of the tale.

"So I turned back at Panama," said the *raconteur*, probably, of a series of adventures, "and abandoned my project altogether. The man spoke with an air and tone of truth; the sketch was unmistakably hers. The whole thing was full of *vraisemblance*, so to speak, and bore me completely off my feet. The initials beneath the sketch of Christian Garth were identical with her own.

"He referred me to Captain Van Dorne for confirmation of the saving of the few remaining passengers on the raft, and her presence in the ship Latona, together with that of the child and negress.

"I have seen Captain Van Dorne, and he admits the part he played, on the representation of Bainrothe; and, through the evidence of a newspaper advertisement, of the previous autumn, which had met his eye, to satisfy the puerile scruples of this really good but ignorant man—going no deeper than the surface in his code of morals—they were obliged to tear out the record of their names, and take refuge temporarily in the long-boat, before he would swear to Miriam, in her state-room, that Bainrothe was not on board.

"As to the *habeas corpus* which would have gone into effect to-day, and which the wretch managed to defeat by requiring an error to be corrected in the writ, that no guiltless man would have observed, I fear sometimes it will prove ineffectual if we wait for the morrow. My plan was to go at midnight with a party of my friends to the house of this miscreant, and take the law in my own hands; but, in this I could not stir, for the reasons I have given you. Besides that, it was risking too much—her safety and reputation.

"She cannot be secretly removed, of course, for we have a detective in the house able and strong, besides the old well-paid negress, both of whom—"

"Have played you false," I interrupted, rising impetuously, and throwing back the loose leaf of the door, "and I am here to tell you this. O friends, have you forgotten me?"

And, rushing forward, I threw an arm around each of those dear necks, weeping alternately on the shoulder of one and the other of the two men I loved best in the world, and who, for some moments, sat silent and amazed!

Then Wentworth rose mutely, and clasped me to his breast, and silence prevailed between us. It comprehended all.

I think, when we meet again in heaven, after that severance which is inevitable to those who wear a mortal shape, we may feel as we did then, but never before! The rapture—the relief—the spiritual ecstasy—surmounting, as on wings of fire, pain, fatigue, suspense, anguish of mind and body—were in themselves lessons of immortality beyond any that book or sage has issued from midnight vigil or earthly tabernacle.

Not until a new order of things is established, and we have done with tribulation, tears, and death, shall we again know such sensations; nor is it indeed quite certain that human heart and brain could twice sustain them here below!

## CHAPTER XIV.

Reaction came at last! Life is full of bathos as well as pathos. An hour later, we four companions in the rejoicing over this redemption, if chiefly strangers before, were partaking cheerfully together of hot coffee and oysters. The services of Mrs. Jessup had been called in—the doctor's excellent old Quaker house-keeper—and, amid many "thous" and "thees," she had served us a capital and expeditious supper.

No one enjoyed the festive occasion more than Mr. Burress, who, on the point of stealing lightly away after witnessing from the front study the scene of recognition and meeting, had been arrested on the threshold by Dr. Pemberton himself.

Either to allow a full explanation between two long-parted lovers, or to conceal his own emotion and get back his customary calm, our dear doctor had seen fit to step into the front-study for a few minutes, and he checked Mr. Burress, with his hand on the door-knob, with some very natural questions as to the mode and time of our meeting, and ended by requiring his presence at the slight collation he ordered at once.

The part the worthy apothecary had played in my closing adventure; the certainty that to his zeal and promptness I owed my immunity from further captivity

—for, had I walked around the square in the usual way, the men at watch from the carriage-windows must have espied and seized me—or, had we loitered in the alley, and arrived a moment later at the central house of Kendrick Row, there is no doubt that they would have been there to await my arrival, nor could Mr. Burress have saved me from their clutches—the whole thing seemed especially providential; but, as the efficient medium of such mercy, Napoleon B. Burress did, indeed, seem to all present crowned with a perfect nimbus of glory. Dr. Pemberton led him back to my presence with his arm encircling his shoulder; Captain Wentworth shook his hand mutely but long, with his eyes dimmed with tears, and words that found imperfect utterance, at last compelling him to strange silence.

"I thank you, I bless you," he said, at last. "I do not hope to be able to return such services, but, what I *can do*, command."

"And I to think that she was crazy all the time; escaped from the great asylum a mile away. Sweetest creature, too, I ever saw in my life; and Caleb thought so, too."

The speaker brushed a briny drop or two from his eyes with the back of his hand as he spoke; then, smiling archly, asked:

"Can you forgive me, miss, for belying you so, even in thought? You see, I have made a clean breast of it now; but such a pity!"

"Forgive you?" And I advanced toward him, and put both my hands in one of his large white extremities, and, before I knew what I was doing, I had stooped over and kissed it, and was bathing it with my tears.

"O miss! this is too much; it is, indeed!" said Napoleon B., blushing to the roots of his hair, and withdrawing his hand with a slightly-mortified air; "you nonplus me completely."

"You see she was too much overcome, Mr. Burress, to speak otherwise than this," said Wentworth, drawing me to his bosom. "You must honor this expression of feeling as I do."

"O sir! it is the greatest honor I ever received in my life; and she, poor thing, like Penelope, tangled up in a web so long, and free at last! Well, it is a great joy to me to think I helped a little to cut the ropes."

"Helped! Why, I owe every thing to you. Listen," and then as briefly as I could I recounted the trials in store for me that very night—the compulsory marriage, or the removal to the belfry-tower—one or the other inevitable, and either of which must have made the proposed rescue of the following day, on the part of Captain Wentworth and his friends, in one sense or the other unavailing. As the wife of Gregory, or as the prisoner of the turret, I should in one case have been morally, and in the other physically, dead or lost forever!

Mutely, and tearfully even, was my skill in setting forth the magnitude of the wrong, from which Mr. Burress had been instrumental in saving me, acknowledged by my audience, not excepting Jenny the house-maid, who, arrested on the threshold, stood wiping her eyes with her neat cotton apron in token of sympathy.

"Caleb will be wondering what has become of me, and tired out of watching if I don't go home at once," said Mr. Burress, after his emotion had subsided, and accepting gracefully the civic crown with which he had been metaphorically rewarded. Mine was in store, but how could he dream of this?

A statue of the Greek Slave, a copy made by a master-hand, soon adorned his window, and his bride wore pearls of price, the joint gift of Miriam and Wardour Wentworth, a twelvemonth later, when a mistress of the emporium was brought home, much to the solace of Caleb, who was remembered by us also, let me not forget to add.

Truly kind and benevolent as he was, Napoleon Burress had a despotic manner, which relaxed beneath the genial smile of Marian March.

"I must go, indeed, my dear sir" (to Dr. Pemberton), "but this night will be memorable in my annals. God bless you all! Farewell. Afraid of an encounter? Not I. Like Horatio Cockleshell of old, I learned to carry pistols constantly about me when I had to pass the bridge every night as a youngster. My parents lived in Hamilton village. I still keep up the custom, and therefore pay my fine yearly to the council."

When at last we separated, the clock was on the stroke of one, and I went to a clean and quiet chamber above the little study, where a bright fire was burning, but whence the smell of lavender, which always accompanies the fresh sheets of Quakerhood, still prevailed with a summer-like fragrance. The attentive house-maid disrobed me, and bathed my chilled and frosted feet and swollen hands in water tempered with alcohol. Then arraying me in a mob-cap and snowy cotton gown, the property of good Mrs. Jessup, placed me in the soft nest prepared for sojourners beneath that homely but hospitable roof.

"I hope thee is comfortable, Miriam Monfort," said Mrs. Jessup, after I was ensconced in bed. "Why, thy face is the same, after all, that I remember when thou wert a very little girl, and used to walk out with Mrs. Austin. She is well, I hope?" settling the bed-cover.

"I cannot tell you, Mrs. Jessup. I must rather ask such questions of you. When did you see her last? and Mabel—do you know my little sister?"

"Oh, yes, I know her perfectly well by sight. Let me see, it was Sabbath before last that, just as I was coming out of Friends' meeting-house, I saw Mabel Monfort, a pretty maiden, truly, walking with her step-sister, I think, and a tall and stately gentleman. But Mrs. Austin I have not seen since last rose-time, and then only in passing. She seemed well, but wore a troubled face."

"Yes, yes; she was troubled, no doubt, things were so altered; and, if her heart had not turned to stone, she must have thought of me sometimes regretfully. But all bids fair now, Mrs. Jessup, both for me and her, and for Mabel. For the rest, let them go—they are fiends!"

"Thee has a very flushed and hot cheek, Miriam, now that I see thee closely and touch thy face"—doing so lightly with the back of her hand as she spoke. "A bowl of sage-tea would, no doubt, be of service to thee; shall I—"

"Oh, no, Mrs. Jessup; I never could drink that wise stuff in the world. I have just had a good supper, and am excited, that is all. Jenny will tell you what she overheard concerning my escape of to-night, and that will account for all."

"Good-night, then, Miriam; may the Lord have thee in his care this night"—and she withdrew, followed by Jenny, eager, no doubt, to commence the recital of my adventure, or to hear what more Captain Wentworth and Dr. Pemberton had to say on the subject.

It was nearly daylight when they parted, one to snatch a few hours of needful slumber before setting out on his professional tour, the other to go at once to the officers of justice, and, at the very earliest hour possible, obtain the authority to arrest the brace of arch-conspirators, still protected by the shadows of the dawn.

For Justice has its time of sleeping and waking in large cities, and will not be denied its meals, its hours of rest, and even recreation. So it was seven o'clock in the cold November morning before the proper ceremonials could be accomplished which placed it in the power of Wentworth to arraign Basil Bainrothe and Luke Gregory.

He occupied one seat in the hackney-coach, which was otherwise filled by the officers of the law; but, when he rang a sonorous peal on the portal bell of Bainrothe's residence, it was unanswered, and, though the house had been watched since daylight by an armed police force, who had no connection with McDermot, it was found, when an entrance had been effected, that the only inhabitants of the mansion were a sick woman, an old negress, and a child, apparently, from its puny size, about a twelvemonth old. The woman could not be aroused from the coma in which she seemed to have fallen, either as a crisis of her disease or a precursor of death (medical opinion was divided), until suddenly, about noon, she waked, perfectly clear in mind and comfortable in body, and called loudly for nourishment!

I had slept profoundly until that hour, and my first thought in waking was of Mrs. Clayton and her probable condition; then came the concentrated effort necessary for her release; and she, too, awoke, as I have shown, to consciousness and physical ease.

Her surprise, her indignation, at being thus deserted,

surpassed even her disappointment at my escape, and her involuntary somnolency was a theme of self-reproach and marvel both. But all yielded in turn to terror when she found herself under arrest in her own chamber, in company with her fellow-conspirator Sabra.

The child was brought to me, at my earnest request, and, during the few days of my sojourn under Dr. Pemberton's roof, managed to make friends of all around him. His deformity soon became a matter of interest and medical examination, and it was decided that it was not beyond the reach of surgical skill.

The process would be very gradual, Dr. Pemberton thought, of straightening the spinal curvature; but, should the health of the child prove good after his tardy and difficult dentition, much might be hoped from the aid of Nature herself. This was joyous intelligence to me.

The noble soul of Ernie should still wear a fitting frame, and the stature of his kind be accorded to him! The "picaninny" wicked old Sabra had gloated on as a dainty morsel, on the raft, might live to put Fate itself to shame; for had I not marveled that his mother even should care to preserve a thing so frail and wretched, when we sat hand-in-hand together on the burning ship? And, later, had I not pondered over the wisdom of his preservation? Who, then, shall penetrate the mysteries of divine intention?

Claude Bainrothe had been arrested, but, after close and thorough examination, was dismissed as irresponsible for and ignorant of his father's acts and designs, a sentence afterward revoked, as far as public opinion was concerned.

Evelyn, Mabel, and Mrs. Austin, were, of course, beyond suspicion—the last two deservedly so; and if, indeed, Evelyn had been guilty of coöperation, I knew it had been through the force of circumstances alone, too potent for her egotism and vanity. She never wished to destroy, only to govern me, and make my being and interests subordinate to her own. Mrs. Austin and Mabel received me with earnest joy, and Evelyn even manifested a decent sense of sisterly gratulation.

I never saw Claude Bainrothe nor entered my father's house until after he had left it and forever—accompanied not by his wife, who lingered behind in distress and wretched dependence, most bitter to a spirit like hers, neither loving to give or receive favors—for, gathering up all of his own and his father's valuables, and drawing from the bank every dollar he could command, this worthy son of an unprincipled sire fled to join his parent, with his minion, Ada Greene. Evelyn had been for some time sensible of his infatuation, and striven vainly to combat it by every means in her power, forbearance having been her first alternative, vivid reproach her last. But experiments had failed. The first only fostered guilt beneath her own roof—the last urged it to its consummation.

Still young and beautiful, she was deserted by the only man she had ever loved—the being for whom she had ruthlessly sacrificed the welfare of her sisters and every sentiment of honor; to whom she had given up her liberty to pander to his and his father's ignominy, and her home to their desecration.

In her great grief she retired to the solitude of her own chamber, and refused to see any face save that of Mrs. Austin, who from this period became her sole attendant, even after time had somewhat ameliorated the first agony incident to her condition.

For there came to her another phase of being which

made this attendance no less a necessity than her present form of bitter and helpless grief. Hope revived, but in a form that promised no fruition, and which later will be made plainer to the reader. Just now I must continue my *résumé*.

Old Martin was dead of paralysis, after praying vainly to be spared to see his master's child return and take possession of her own, for he had never believed in my suicide, an idea that Bainrothe had taken pains to propagate. Nor did he lend any faith to my demise; knowing what he did, he believed that I had gone to England to get assistance from my mother's relatives—and Mrs. Austin had shared his opinion; she had nursed him to the last, faithfully, and Evelyn had been tolerant of his presence. This, at least, was a consolation.

Sabra and Mrs. Clayton were not prosecuted, and I did, perhaps, the most inexorable act of my life when I refused to see either of them again, or assist them to more than a mere subsistence until health could be restored to the one and her "owners" written to in order that the other might be reclaimed to bondage, in which condition alone she, and such as she, can be restrained from wrong-doing. "For there are devils on the earth," says Swedenborg, "as well as angels, and they both wear human guise—but by this may we know them, that no mortal ties bind them, no sphere confines them. They walk abroad, the one solely to evil for its own sake, the other to universal good for the Father. Such as these die not, but are translated, the one to hell, the other to heaven."

Do we not right, then, to confine and enslave devils while they abide with us, or, if we can, to destroy them utterly? And if we discern them, shall we not adore God's angels?

These dwell not long among us, and their eyes are fixed always with a far, pure yearning for some sphere in which we have no part. We feel this in our daily intercourse with them, for angels like these dwell often in the lowliest form about us, and our common contact with them thrills and awes us, though we scarcely realize that it is from them we have these sensations, or what renders them so far, though near at hand!

Little children, submissive slaves, sad women, unresisting men, patient physicians, great patriots, persistent preachers, martyr poets—all these forms and phases in turn do our associate angels enter into and inform.

But ever the sign is there! They are not ours! Among us, but not of us—set apart, here for a season be it, longer or shorter, ready at any time to spread their wings! My sister was of these—I did not recognize this truth in the time of my great sorrow, when the parting plumes had not revealed themselves to my undiscerning eyes.

A mighty touchstone has been applied to these earthly orbs since then, and the power to discriminate has been given to my soul. As Gregory and Sabra were devils, I verily believe, so was Mabel one of Swedenborg's angels. Who shall gainsay me? Who knows more than I on this subtle subject? Not the wisest theologian that lives and breathes this earthly air! Only those who never speak to enlighten us, and who have passed into infinite light and knowledge through the portals of the grave.

When I knelt beside Wardour Wentworth in the old church of chimes a fortnight after my emancipation from the thraldom of demons, I acquired with this new allegiance of mine a more Christian and forbearing spirit than had ever before possessed me; but the pearl of great price came not yet. Into the deeps of sorrow was my soul first compelled to enter, a diver in the great ocean, whence alone all such precious pearls are borne.

Notice had been given to Claude Bainrothe to evacuate my father's premises before my return from the brief wedding-trip which comprised business as well as recreation. Captain Wentworth took me with him to Richmond and to Washington, to both of which places his affairs led him. In the last I had the pleasure of grasping Old Hickory by his honest hand. He was my husband's patron and benefactor, and as such alone entitled to my regard; but there was more. As patriot, soldier, gentleman in the truest sense of the word, I have not seen his peer.

It was a great delight to me, in spite of the shadow Evelyn's grief threw over our threshold, to stand once more as mistress in my father's house, even in the wreck of fortune, and control the education and destiny of my young sister. Little Ernie, too, had his place in the household as son by adoption, and grew daily stronger and more vigorous in our sight, the thoughtful, loving, and reticent child, heralding the man of power, affection, and principle, that he has become.

The employment of my husband lay near the city of my nativity. He was occupied in making the great railroad through Jersey that was the pioneer of engineering progress, and a mighty link between two kindred States. He was in this way, though often absent, never for any length of time, and his return was always a fresh source of joy to his household. Mabel worshiped him; Ernie silently revered; Evelyn with all of her growing peculiarities acknowledged he had merit; and Mrs. Austin regarded him with mingled awe and affection, for to her he was singularly kind and affectionate.

"To grow old in servitude," he would say, "what sadder fate can befall any being, or more entitle him or her to forbearance and respect? What life-long hardships does this condition not impose? And this is a field for universal charity, which costs not much, only a little patience and a few kind words and smiles."

Ours was a happy household; no cloud rested upon it, save for a few brief days of illness or discomfort, until the great blow fell. In her seventeenth year and on the eve of her marriage with Norman Stansbury (again our neighbor, at intervals, when he came to visit his relatives, a man of noble qualities and singularly devoted to my sister), Mabel died suddenly of some secret disease of the heart which had simulated radiant health and bloom.

I had sometimes observed with anxiety a slight shortness of breath, a gasping after unusual exercise, and called the attention of physicians to this state of things in my sister, who regarded it merely as a nervous symptom, and this was all to indicate that the fell destroyer was silently at work. She had just laid a bunch of white roses on her toilet, and crossed the chamber for water to place them in, when she called my name in a strange, excited way, that brought me speedily to her side from the adjoining room. She was lying white and speechless on her bed, beside which the crystal goblet lay in fragments.

The waters of her own existence had flowed forth with those prepared for her flowers, and before assistance could be summoned she expired peacefully in my arms, without a struggle. She had inherited her mother's malady.

The anguish and disappointment of the lover, and my own despair, may be better imagined than portrayed. My baby died a few weeks later—partly, I think, from the effect of my own condition on her frail organization, and the hope of years was blighted in this fragile blossom—the first that had blessed our union.

The little Constance slumbered by Mabel's side, and a slip from that bunch of white roses, the last my sister had gathered, shadows the marbles that guard both of those now-distant, yet not neglected graves. Thus death at last entered our happy household!

A great shadow fell over me, which I vainly strove to dispel with all the effort of my reason and my will. Physicians, remembering my mother's inscrutable melancholy—a part of that mysterious malady that consumed her life—whispered their warnings in my husband's ears, and he resolved, with that energy which belongs to men of his nature, to lay the axe at once to the root of this evil in the only way that presented itself to his mind—as possible of accomplishment.

At first I resisted faintly the coincidence of his will, which he knew was sure to come sooner or later; and to the very last it was agony unspeakable to me, to think that my father's house should pass into the hands of strangers, and that the place that knew me should know me no more!

Very resolutely and calmly did Wardour endure and stem my opposition. Swift and strong as the current of my will flowed naturally, he was ever its master, as the stone dam can stay and lull the fiercest rivers. He persisted, knowing well what was at stake, and to my surprise Dr. Pemberton and Mr. Gerald Stansbury co-operated with his decision. Nor did Mr. Lodore oppose it, though losing thereby one of his most liberal parishioners.

A great struggle was going on in my heart just then

—that I think would have perished in darkness, had I not found myself free and emancipated from all fetters of custom and observance by our change of residence.

From the shallow streams of conventional Christianity, moving with tardy current, and full of shoals and sand-banks, I was drifting down, slowly but surely, with that great ocean of deep and unsounded religion, to which all profound natures, that have suffered, do, I believe—if left to themselves—inevitably tend.

In this new land of promise—the golden California—lying like a bride by the side of her bridegroom—the great Pacific Ocean—and shut away by deserts and mountains, from all old conventional cliques and prejudices of our Eastern cities, my soul took wing. What poetry was in me found its outlet; what religious capacity God had endued me with, went forth from the clash of cymbals and the sound of the sackbut, that ever had reminded me, in all seasons of sorrow, or even of joyous excitement, that I was one of an ancient people, astray in foreign pastures—went forth (even as the compromise was made at first by Christ and his apostles with the magnificent but soulless worship of the Jews) to merge these sounds of ancient rite and form in the deep roll of the organ, that fills the churches where the Host is present.

I needed this abiding miracle to stay my faith—to give it a new rapture, never experienced before—to sustain me in my sorrow. In the presence of the holy Eucharist—in the sweet belief that saints communed with me, and that the Mother of God, who, like me, had wept and suffered, interceded for me at the throne of Christ, I regained the vitality that seemed gone forever.

There is no cup like this for the lips of the parched and weary wayfarer—none!

## CHAPTER XV.

Let me go back a little in this retrospect, into which I am compelling into a small space much that would take time in the telling, as a necessary retrenchment for too much affluence of description in the beginning.

The mind of the narrator, like the stone descending the shaft, gathers accelerated velocity with its momentum toward the last, and so expends itself in a more brief and sententious manner than in the commencement. It should be also, but rarely is, more powerful, and more condensed as it nears its *finale.*

Why these things do *not* go more uniformly together, as according to popular opinion they invariably must, is better understood by the artist than his readers.

Details are requisite to fill up a mental picture, and impress it on the memory, and, though brevity is certainly the soul of wit, it cannot be said to be infallible in enforcing description to do its duty—that of painting a panoramic picture on the brain.

Life is full of pre-Raphaelitism, and so is fiction, if indeed it resembles life—such as we know it, or such as it might be. The art of verisimilitude is found alone in detail.

Let me go back, then, for a brief summary of some of the principal events and personages of Monfort Hall and

Beauseincourt, the earlier portions of this retrospect. I will begin with the La Vignes.

George Gaston, in one of the brief pauses of his stormy political career, wooed and married Margaret La Vigne, the year before her mother espoused in second nuptials her early lover (the brother of that saintly minister who came to her rescue in the first days of her widowhood), and in this marriage she has been happy and prosperous.

They continue to reside under the same roof, and Bellevue awaits its master. It will be empty, I think, if I understand George Gaston's character, so long as Major Favraud is a wanderer on the face of the Continent of Europe, and held, for his especial benefit and return, in readiness.

Vernon and his sweet wife Marion spent the first season of their happy married life under my lintel-tree, and are now our nearest neighbors in our new land of sojourn. A slender iron fence divides our grounds from theirs. A golden cord of affection binds our lives together. Our interests, too, are the same.

Vernon is leagued with my husband in the great engineering projects which have enriched them both—the capital to enlist in which sphere of enterprise was furnished by the sale to a company of our "gold-gashed" lands in Georgia—revealed to my knowledge, as it may be remembered, by the inadvertence of Gregory.

The career of Bertie La Vigne had been a varied one, as might have been foreseen perhaps from her early manifestations and proclivities.

She came to me, while still we dwelt in the city of my birth, when she was approaching her seventeenth year, and remained a twelvemonth under my roof, engaged in the study of Shakespeare with that accomplished *artiste* Mr.

Mortimer. She intended to pursue what gift she had of voice and histrionic talent as a means of livelihood, she told me from the first, and to get rid of the ineffable weariness and monotony of her life at Beauseincourt as well.

The two motives seemed to me to be worthy of all praise. There are, indeed, abodes that kill the soul as well as the body, and this was one of them in my estimation, yet I remembered as a seeming inconsistency that, when, in her sixteenth year, it was proposed that Bertie should come to me for the purpose of attending schools for the accomplishments, she steadily refused to do so.

Her sense of duty might have been at the root of this firm and persistent refusal to accept from my hand a gift richer far than "jewels of the mine"—the power of varied occupation—but something had secretly whispered to me that this was not all on which her apparent self-abnegation was based, and I think that I was right in my conjecture.

Have you seen a plant, scathed by frost, that has made a strong and successful effort to live, and still in its struggling existence bears the mark of the early blight on leaf and blossom?

Such was the impression made on my mind by Bertie La Vigne after three years of separation, and yet she had grown into majestic stature and into comparative beauty since we parted at Beauseincourt.

Tall, slender, straight as a young palm-tree, with exquisite extremities, and a face of aristocratic if not Grecian proportions, there still was wanting in her step, her eye, her smile, that wonderful *abandon* that had formed her chief charm in her earlier years.

She had been crystallized, so to speak, by some strange

process of suffering, into a cold and dull propriety, never infringed on save at times when she found herself alone with me, and when the old frolic-spirit would for a little time possess her. It was not dead, but sleeping.

"And what, my dear Bertie," I said, one day, when Mr. Mortimer had departed, and she came to throw herself down on the sofa in my chamber and *rest*, "what has reconciled you to the old Parrot, as you used to call our sublime Shakespeare?"

"Sublime! I shall think you affected, Miriam, if you apply that word again to that old commonplace. If he were sublime, do you suppose all the world would read him or go to see his plays? Do reserve that epithet for Milton, Dante, Tasso, Schiller, and the like inaccessibilities. Yes, I do revere 'Wallenstein' more than any thing Shakespeare ever spouted"—in answer to my gently-shaking head—"I should break down over *Thekla*, I should, indeed."

"Do you think his bed was soft under the war-horses?"—and she waved her hand—"O God! what a tragedy; what a love!" and she covered her face with her quivering palm.

"Bertie, you are still too excitable. I am sorry to see it."

"Philosopher, cure thyself."

"Yes, I know that was always a fault of mine."

"That is why you married the man in the iron mask, you know. I could never have loved that person."

"Describe the man you think you could have loved, Bertie La Vigne."

"Could have loved? That time is past forever, child. 'Frozen, and dead forever,' as Shelley says. *He* was my affinity, I believe, only he died before I was born. What a pity! I would rather be his widow than the wife of any man living."

"*She* would like to hear that, no doubt, Bertie."

"Well, she may hear it if she chooses when I go to England to read the old Parrot in the right way, under their very noses, Kembles and all. I'll let Mrs. Shelley know I'm there," and she laughed merrily.

"And what is your idea of the way to read Shakespeare, Bertie dear?" I asked, playfully.

"As one having authority, a head and shoulders above him and all his prating, just as you would talk to your every-day next neighbor, read him without any fear of his old deer-stealing ghost? Why, Miriam, he knew himself better than we knew him. He had no more idea of being a genius than you have! He was a sort of artesian well of a man, and could not help spouting platitudes, that was all. Besides, he had eyes to see and ears to hear, and a very Yankee spirit of investigation. It is the fashion to crack him up like the Bible, both encyclopædias, that's all! Every man can see himself in these books, and every man likes a looking-glass, and that's the whole secret of their success."

"Bertie, you are incorrigible."

"No, I am not; only genuine. I do think there is a good deal in both of the works in question, but their sublimity I dispute. They are homely, coarse, commonplace, as birth and death."

There was something that almost froze my blood in the way she said those last words, lying back upon the sofa with far-off-looking eyes and hands clasped beneath her head.

"Miriam," she said, after a while, "life is a humbug. I have thought so for some time."

"Poor child, poor child!"

"Ay, poorer than the poorest, Miriam Harz," and, laying aside my work, I went to and knelt beside her, and kissed her brow.

"I have no soul to open! I am as empty as a chrysalis-case, that the butterfly has gone out of to dwell amid sunshine and flowers. Yet I believe I had one once"—in ineffably mournful accents—"but two men killed it; and yet, neither intended the blow! O Miriam! I understand at last what Coleridge meant by his "life in death." There is such a thing—and that great necromancer found it out! I am the breathing impersonation of that loathly thing, I believe. Listen"—and she sat up with one raised finger and gave the poet's words with rare expression:

"'The nightmare—life in death was she,
That chilled men's blood with cold.'

Doesn't that describe me as I am, Miriam?"

"You are, indeed, much changed, Bertie; perhaps it would be well could you confide in me."

"No, it would not be well! I never could keep any thing wholly to myself, neither can I tell it wholly, even to such as you—reticent! merciful! But this believe, I have done nothing wrong, nothing to be ashamed of, to wear sackcloth and ashes for, and I am preparing to put my foot on it all. Ay, from the snake's head of first discovery to the snake's tail of the last disappointment, ranging over half a dozen years! A long serpent, truly!" laughing. "But I mean to be galvanized and get back my life. I am determined to be famous, rich, beautiful!" and she nodded to me with the old sweet sparkle in her eye, the glad smile on her lip.

"You laugh at the last threat!—laugh on! 'He who

laughs best, laughs last!' says the old proverb. There is such a thing as training one's features, isn't there, as well as one's setters? Miriam, I shall develop slowly; I am still in my very downiest adolescence as to looks. You will see me when I have filled out and ripened, and when I put on my grand Marie Antoinette *tenu*, some day! Hair drawn back, *à la Pompadour*, powdered with gold-dust; a touch of rouge, perhaps, on either cheek; ruffles of rich lace at shoulders and elbows; pink brocade and emeralds, picked out with diamonds! Mr. Mortimer's teachings in every graceful movement! It will be all humbug, for I have no real beauty, not much grace; but people will think me beautiful and graceful for all that, while I wear my costumes. They are several—this is only one—all highly becoming! I have a vision of a sea-green dress and moss-roses; of a violet-satin robe, trimmed and twisted everywhere with flowers of yellow jasmine; of pale-gold and tipped marabouts in my hair; also of an azure silk with blond and pearls and a tiara on my forehead" (she laughed archly). "You don't know my capabilities, my dear, for appearing to look well—they are wonderful!"

"The very prospect transfigures you, Bertie. I am glad you are so courageous."

"Were you courageous when you clung to your ropes on the sea-tossed raft! No, Miriam! that was instinct—nothing more; and I, too, have very strong intuitions of self-preservation. Heaven grant that they may be successful! Let us pray."

And, with moving lips and down-drawn lids, from beneath which the large tears stole one by one, like crystal globes, this suffering spirit communed with its God, silently.

So best, I felt! Bertie was only a lip-deep scoffer. Her heart was open to conviction yet, and, when the time came, I believed that the seed sown in old days would germinate and bear good harvest. All was chaos now!

Shall I keep on with Bertie, now that the theme has possession of me, and go back to the others when she is finally dismissed? I think this will be wisest, especially as my space is small, and mood concentrative rather than erratic.

Let us pass over, then, five eventful years, during which the sorrows and changes I have spoken of had taken place, and Wentworth had fixed his home in the vicinity of San Francisco.

I had heard of Bertie in the interval as a successful *débutante* as a reader of Shakespeare, and had received her sparse and sparkling letters confirming report, truly "angel visits, few and far between."

At last one came announcing her intention of visiting California professionally, and sojourning beneath my roof while in San Francisco. It was to be a stay of several weeks.

She was accompanied and sometimes assisted by Mr. and Mrs. Mortimer, professional readers both—the last distinguished more for grace and beauty, even though now on the wane of life, than she ever had been for talent, but eminently fitted, both by education and character, for a guide and companion.

An English maid, as perfect as an automaton in her training and regularity, accompanied Bertie, to whom were confided all details of dress, all keys and jewels, with entire confidence and safety. An elaborate doll seemed the red-and-white and stupidly-staring Euphemia. Yet was she adroit, obedient, and expert, just to move in the groove of her requirements.

I have spoken only of her accessories; but now for Bertie herself.

"Is she not magnificent?" was my exclamation when alone with my husband on the night of her arrival, after our guest, with her sparkling face and conversation, her superb toilet and bearing, her graceful, nymph-like walk, had retired to her chamber, attended by the mechanical "Miss Euphemia."

The Mortimers, with their children and servants, remained at the principal hotel.

"The very word for her," he replied; "only that and nothing more."

"Wardour!"

"Well, love!"

"How little enthusiasm you possess about the beautiful! Now, if there were question of a new railroad-bridge, the vocabulary would have been exhausted."

"What would you have me say, dear? Is not that word a very comprehensive one? The lady above-stairs is indeed magnificent; but, Miriam, where is Bertie?" and he laughed.

"Ah! I understand; you find her artificial."

"She is too fine an actress for that, Miriam; only transfigured."

"Yes, I see what you mean" (sadly). "Bertie *is* wholly changed. Whom does she resemble, Wardour? What queen, bethink you, whose likeness you have seen? Not Mary Queen of Scots—not Elizabeth—"

"No, surely not; but she is, now that you draw my attention to it, strikingly like Marie Antoinette."

"She said she would be, and she has succeeded!" and I mused on the wonderful transition.

Four years more, and we heard of Bertie in England,

as the rarely-gifted and beautiful American reader, "Lavinia La Vigne." Out of the *répertoire* of her family names she had fished up this alliteration, and "Bertie" was reserved for those behind the scenes.

It was declared also in the public sheets, what great and distinguished men were in her train; how wits bowed to her wit, and authors to her criticisms! But, when she wrote to me, she said nothing of all this, only telling of her visit to Mrs. Shelley, who had received her kindly, and to the tomb of Shakespeare, whose painted effigy she especially derided. "It looks indeed like a man who would cut his wife off with an old feather-bed and a tea-kettle," was one of her characteristic remarks, I remember; but there was a little postscript, that told the whole story of her life, on a separate scrap of paper meant only for my eye I clearly saw, and committed instantly to the flames after perusal:

"Ah, Miriam, this is all a magic lantern! The people are phantoms, the realities are shadows, and I a wretched humbug, duller than all! Two men have lived and breathed for me on the face of this earth—two only. One was my much-offending and deeply-suffering father. The other—O, Miriam, to think of him is crime; but in his life, and that alone, I live. I send you Praed's last beautiful little song—'Tell him I love him yet.' It will tell you every thing. An answer I have scribbled to it as if written by a man. Keep both, and when I am dead, should you survive me, dear, lay them if you can in my coffin, close, close to my heart!"

Three years more, and Bertie is in Rome, independent, at last, through her own exertions, and able to gratify her tastes. I receive thence statues, and pictures, and cameos, all exquisite of their kind, her princely gifts, her legacies. Then comes a long silence. She knew what faith was mine when she last abode beneath my roof and made herself a little impertinently merry at my expense in consequence of this new order of things.

Now comes a letter (a paper envelope accompanying it)—Bertie La Vigne has entered the Catholic Church, through baptism and confirmation, so briefly states the letter written in her own hand and of date some months back, retained, no doubt, through forgetfulness, until reminded. The paper, of recent issue, tells of the ceremony at St. Peter's, which admitted to the novitiate several noble ladies, native and foreign, and among the rest an *artist* of merit, Miss Lavinia La Vigne, of Georgia, United States of America.

On the margin of the paper were a few penciled words in her own handwriting: "I have found the reality." This was all.

I shall never see her again unless I go to Rome, and then only through a grating, or in the presence of others like herself, for she has taken the black veil, and retired behind a shadow deep as that cast from the cypress-shaded tomb. Yet, under existing circumstances, and in consideration of her early experiences which no success nor later future could obliterate, or render less unendurable, I believe she has chosen the wiser part.

Peace be with thee, Bertie, whether in earth or in heaven!

EDITOR'S NOTE.— . . . Some years after the closing of Miriam Monfort's Retrospect, the civil war broke out in the United States, and Pope Pius IX. was pleased to grant permission to several American nuns, Southern ladies, whose vocation was religious, to visit their own States, and lend what succor, spiritual and physical, they could to the wounded and dying, on the battle-fields and in the Confederate camps. Among these came the Sister Ursula, from the convent of the Carthusians, known once as Lavinia, or

Our home overlooks the calm bay of San Francisco, standing, as it does, on an eminence, surrounded with stately forest-trees, and dark from a distance with evergreens which trail their majestic branches over roods of lawn.

These trees have ever been a passion with me. I love their aromatic odors, reminding one of balm and frankincense, and the great Temple of Solomon itself, built of fine cedar-wood. I admire their stately symmetry, and the majesty of their unchanging presence, and stand well pleased and invigorated in their shadow.

Our house is built of stone, and faced with white marble brought from beyond the seas. Its architectural details are composite, and yet of dream-like beauty and perfection.

There are statues and blooming plants in the great lower corridors and porticos, and vast hall of entrance, oval and open to the roof, with its marble gallery surrounding it and suspended midway, secured by its exquisite and lace-like screen of iron balustrading. Pictures of the great modern masters adorn the walls.

The skylight above floods the whole house with sunshine at the touching of a cord, which controls the venetians that in summer-time shade the halls below; and the parlors, and saloon, and library, and dining-room, and the quiet, spacious chambers above-stairs, are all admirably proportioned and finished, and furnished as well, for the comfort of those that abide in them—hosts and guests.

Bertie La Vigne. She was particularly fearless and efficient, and was killed by a cannon-ball at Shiloh while kneeling beside a dying officer, ascertained to be her sister's husband, the gallant George Gaston of the Seventh Georgia. By order of Colonel Favraud, they were buried in one grave. He best knew wherefore this was done. . . . . . . . . . . .

In one of the most private and luxurious of these apartments abode, for some years, a pale and shadowy being, refusing all intercourse with society, and vowed to gloom and hypochondria. It was her strange and mournful mania to look upon all human creatures with suspicion, nay, with loathing.

The fairest linen, the whitest raiment, the most exquisite repast, whether prepared by human hands, or furnished by divine Providence itself, in the shape of tempting fruits, if touched by another, became at once revolting and unpalatable. Thus, with servants to relieve her of all cares, and Mrs. Austin as her devoted attendant, she preferred, by the aid of her own small culinary contrivance, to prepare her fastidious meals, to spread her own snowy couch, so often a bed of thorns to her, to put on her own attire, regularly fumigated and purified by some process she affected, as it came from the laundry, and touched only with gloved hands by herself, as were the books into which she occasionally glanced for solace.

Most of her time was spent in gazing from her window, that overlooked the bay, and dreaming of the return of one who had long since heartlessly deserted her, leaving her dependent on those she had injured, and from whom she bitterly and even derisively received shelter, tender ministry, and all possible manifestations of compassion and interest.

Her mind had been partially overthrown at the time of her husband's desertion and her dead baby's birth—events that occurred almost conjointly; and it was the wreck of Evelyn Erle we cherished until her slow consumption, long delayed by the balmy air of California, culminated mercifully to herself and all around her, and removed her from this sphere of suffering.

Whither? Alas! the impotence of that question! Are there not beings who seem, indeed, to lack the great essential for salvation—a soul to be saved? How far are such responsible?

Claude Bainrothe is married again, and not to Ada Greene, who, outcast and poor, came some years since as an adventuress to California, and signalized herself later, in the *demi-monde*, as a leader of great audacity, beauty, and reckless extravagance. The lady of his choice (or heart?) was a fat baroness, about twenty years his senior, who lets apartments, and maintains the externes of her rank in a saloon fifteen feet square, furnished with red velveteen, and accessible by means of an antechamber paved with tiles!

He has grown stout, drinks beer, and smokes a meerschaum, but is still known on the principal promenade, and in the casino of the German town in which he resides, as "the handsome American." He is said, however, to have spells of melancholy.

The "Chevalier Bainrothan," and the "Lady Charlotte Fremont," his step-daughter, for as such she passes, for some quaint or wicked reason unrevealed to society, with their respectable and hideous house-keeper, Madame Clayton, dwell under the same roof, and enjoy the privilege of access to the *salon* of the baroness, and a weekly game of *écarté* at her *soirées*, usually profitable to the chevalier in a small way.

All this did Major Favraud, in his own merry mood, communicate to us on the occasion of his memorable visit to San Francisco, when he remained our delighted guest during one long delicious summer season. Of Gregory, we never heard.

"I had hoped to hear of your marriage long before

this," I said to him one day. "Tell me why you have not wedded some fair lady before this time. Now tell me frankly as you can."

"Simply because you did not wait for me."

"Nonsense! the truth. I want no *badinage*."

"Because, then—because I never could forget Celia—never love any one else."

"She was one of Swedenborg's angels, Major Favraud—no real wife of yours. She never was married"—and I shook my head—"only united to a being of the earth with whom she had no real affinity. Choose yours elsewhere."

"I believe you are half right," he said, sadly. "She never seemed to belong to me by right—only a bird I had caught and caged, that loved me well, yet was eager to escape."

"Such was the state of the case, I cannot doubt; a more out and out flesh-and-blood organization would suit you better. Your life is not half spent; the dreary time is to come. Go back to Bellevue, and get you a kind companion, and let children climb your knees, and surround your hearth. You would be so much happier."

"Suggest one, then. Come, help me to a wife."

"No, no, I can make no matches; but you know Madame de St. Aube is a widow now. You were always congenial."

"Yes, but"—with a shrug of his shoulders, worthy of a Frenchman—"*que voulez vous?* That woman has five children already, and a plantation mortgaged to Maginnis!"

"Maginnis again! The very name sends a chill through my bones! No, that will never do. Some maiden lady, then—some sage person of thirty-four or five."

"I do not fancy such. I'll tell you what! I believe I will go back and court Bertie on some of her play-acting rounds, and make a decent woman of that little vagabond. Because she was disappointed once, is that a reason? Great Heavens! this tongue of mine! Cut it out, Mrs. Wentworth, and cast it to the seals in the bay. I came very near—"

"Betraying what I have long suspected, Major Favraud. Who *was* that man?"

"Don't ask me, my dear woman; I must not say another word, in honor. It was a most unfortunate affair—a sheer misunderstanding. He loved her all the time; I knew this, but you know her manner! He did not understand her flippant way; her keen, unsparing, and bitter wit; her devoted, passionate, proud, and breaking heart; and so there was a coolness, and they parted; and what happened afterward nearly killed her! So she left her home."[1]

"I must not ask you, I feel, for you say you cannot tell me more in honor, but I think I know. The man, of all the earth, I would have chosen for her. Oh, hard is woman's fate!"

To the very last I have reserved what lay nearest my heart of hearts.

Three children have been born to us in California, and have made our home a paradise. The two elder are sons, named severally for my father and theirs, Reginald and Wardour.

The last is a daughter, a second Mabel, beautiful as the first, and strangely resembling her, though of a stronger frame and more vital nature. She is the sunshine of the house, the idol of her father and brothers, who *all* are

[1] This was previous to Bertie's visit.

mine, as well as the fair child of seven summers herself.

Mrs. Austin presides, in imagination, over our nursery, but, in reality, is only its most honored occasional visitor, her chamber being distinct, and my own rule being absolute therein, with the aid of a docile adjunct.

Ernest Wentworth, our adopted son—so-called for want of any other name—is the standard of perfection in mind and morals, for the imitation of the rest of the band of children.

He has gained the usual stature of young men of his age, with a slight defect of curvature of the shoulders that does but confirm his scholarly appearance.

His face, with its magnificent brow, piercing dark eyes, pale complexion, and clustering hair, is striking, if not handsome.

He has graduated as a student of law, and, should his health permit, will, I cannot doubt, distinguish himself as a forensic orator.

George Gaston and Madge have promised a visit to the Vernons; but I cannot help hoping, rather without than *for* any good reason, that they will not come! I love them both, yet I feel they are mismated, even if happy.

My husband is noted among his peers for his liberal and noble-minded use of a princely income, and his great public spirit. He unites agricultural pursuits with his profession, and has placed, among other managers, my old ally, Christian Garth and his family, on the ranch he holds nearest to San Francisco.

Thence, at due seasons, seated on a wain loaded with the fruits of their labor, the worthy pair come up to the city to trade, and never fail in their tribute to our house.

The immigrant possessed of worth and industry, however poor; the adventurous man, who seeks by the aid of his profession alone to establish himself in California; the artist, the man of letters, all meet a helping hand from Wardour Wentworth, who in his charities observes but one principle of action, one hope of recompense, both to be found in the teachings of philanthropy:

"As I do unto you, go you and do unto others." This is his maxim.

Our lives have been strangely happy and successful up to this hour, so that sometimes my emotional nature, too often in extremes, trembles beneath its burden of prosperity, and conjures up strange phantoms of dark possibilities, that send me, tearful and depressed, to my husband's arms, to find strength and courage in his rare and calm philosophy and equipoise.

Never on his sweet serene brow have I seen a frown of discontent, or a cloud of sourceless sorrow, such as too often come—the last especially to mine—born of that melancholy which has its root far back in the bosoms of my ancestors.

Such as his life is, he accepts it manfully; and in his shadow I find protection and grow strong.

Reader, farewell!

THE END.

**APPLETONS' (so-called) PLUM-PUDDING EDITION**

OF THE

# WORKS OF CHARLES DICKENS.

Now Complete,

***IN 18 VOLS. PAPER COVERS. PRICE, $5.00.***

---

LIST OF THE WORKS.

|  |  |  |
|---|---|---|
| **Oliver Twist** | 172 pp. | 25 cts. |
| **American Notes** | 104 " | 15 " |
| **Dombey and Son** | 356 " | 35 " |
| **Martin Chuzzlewit** | 341 " | 35 " |
| **Our Mutual Friend** | 340 " | 35 " |
| **Christmas Stories** | 168 " | 25 " |
| **Tale of Two Cities** | 144 " | 20 " |
| **Hard Times, and Additional Christmas Stories** | 202 " | 25 " |
| **Nicholas Nickleby** | 338 " | 35 " |
| **Bleak House** | 352 pp. | 35 cts. |
| **Little Dorrit** | 348 " | 35 " |
| **Pickwick Papers** | 326 " | 35 " |
| **David Copperfield** | 351 " | 35 " |
| **Barnaby Rudge** | 257 " | 30 " |
| **Old Curiosity Shop** | 221 " | 30 " |
| **Great Expectations** | 188 " | 25 " |
| **Sketches** | 194 " | 25 " |
| **Uncommercial Traveller, Pictures of Italy, etc.** | 300 " | 35 " |

Any person ordering the entire set, and remitting $5, will receive a Portrait of Dickens, suitable for framing. The entire set will be sent by mail or express, at our option, postage or freight prepaid, to any part of the United States.

*Single copies of any of the above sent to any address in the United States on the receipt of the price affixed.*

---

**LIBRARY EDITION**

OF

# CHARLES DICKENS'S WORKS.

***Complete in Six Volumes,***

With Thirty-two Illustrations.

**Price, $1.75 per Vol., or $10.50 the Set; Half calf, $3.50 per Vol**

# APPLETONS' JOURNAL

## OF POPULAR LITERATURE.

APPLETONS' JOURNAL, now enlarged to the extent of four more pages of reading, gives, in a weekly form, all the features of a monthly magazine. Its weekly issue brings it a more frequent visitor to the family than is the case with a monthly periodical, while, in course of the year, a much greater aggregate and a larger variety of papers are furnished than are given in any of the regular monthlies. But, for those who prefer it, the JOURNAL is put up in *Monthly Parts*, and in this form its scope and variety, as compared with other magazines, become conspicuously apparent.

APPLETONS' JOURNAL continues to present healthful, sound, instructive, and entertaining literature. It contains the best serial novels and short stories attainable; it gives picturesque descriptions of places, and stirring narratives of travel and adventure; entertaining papers upon various subjects that pertain to the pursuits and recreations of the people; portraits and sketches of persons distinguished in various walks of life; social sketches, having in special view those things the knowledge of which will contribute to the welfare and happiness of the household; describes phases of life in all quarters of the globe, and discusses the important events of the time, and the advances made in art, literature, and science. Illustrations are used sufficiently to give variety and animation to its pages; but the aim is to make it rather a journal of popular high-class literature than merely a vehicle for pictures.

---

*Price,* 10 *cents per Number; or,* $4.00 *per Annum, in advance. Subscriptions received for Twelve or Six Months. Subscription Price of Monthly Parts,* $4.50.

Any person procuring FIVE Yearly Subscriptions, for weekly numbers, and remitting $20, will be entitled to a copy for one year *gratis;* FIFTEEN Yearly Subscribers, for weekly numbers, and remitting $50, will entitle sender to a copy for one year *gratis.*

The postage within the United States is 20 cents a year, payable quarterly, in advance, at the office where received. Subscriptions from Canada must be accompanied with 20 cents additional, to prepay the United States postage. New York City subscribers will be charged 20 cents per annum additional, which will prepay for postage and delivery of their numbers.

In remitting by mail, a post-office order or draft, payable to the order of D. APPLETON & Co., is preferable to bank-notes, as, if lost, the order or draft can be recovered without loss to the sender.

Volumes begin with January and July of each year.

APPLETONS' JOURNAL and either *Harper's Weekly, Harper's Bazar, Harper's Magazine, Lippincott's Magazine,* the *Atlantic Monthly, Scribner's Monthly,* or the *Galaxy,* for one year, on receipt of $7; APPLETONS' JOURNAL and *Littell's Living Age,* for $10; APPLETONS' JOURNAL and *Oliver Optic's Magazine,* for $5; the JOURNAL and POPULAR SCIENCE MONTHLY, for $8.

D. APPLETON & CO., Publishers,
549 & 551 BROADWAY, NEW YORK.

www.ingramcontent.com/pod-product-compliance
Lightning Source LLC
LaVergne TN
LVHW021233110826
845150LV00002B/317

* 9 7 8 1 4 2 5 5 6 2 4 4 1 *